BABY-SITTERS
LITTLE SISTER

DON'T MISS THE OTHER BABY-SITTERS LITTLE SISTER GRAPHIC NOVELS!

KAREN'S WITCH

KAREN'S ROLLER SKATES

KAREN'S WORST DAY

KAREN'S KITTYCAT CLUB

KAREN'S SCHOOL PICTURE

ANN M. MARTIN

BABY-SITTERS LITTLE SISTER®

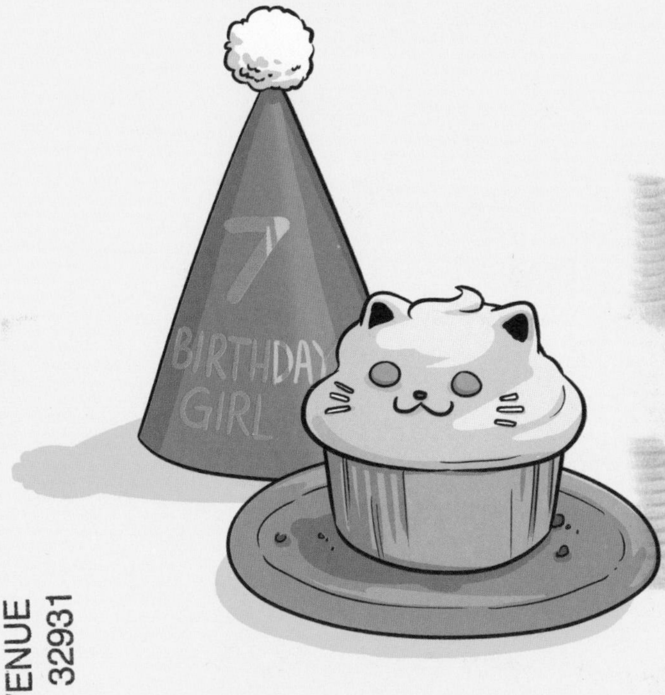
7
BIRTHDAY
GIRL

KAREN'S BIRTHDAY

A GRAPHIC NOVEL BY
KATY FARINA
WITH COLOR BY BRADEN LAMB

graphix
An Imprint of
SCHOLASTIC

This book is for the Fultons —
Pam and Jim, Andrew and Patrick
A. M. M.

For my grandma, who gives the
best hugs and makes the best pasta
K. F.

Text copyright © 2023 by Ann M. Martin
Art copyright © 2023 by Katy Farina

All rights reserved. Published by Graphix, an imprint of
Scholastic Inc., *Publishers since 1920.* SCHOLASTIC, GRAPHIX,
BABY-SITTERS LITTLE SISTER, and associated logos are trademarks
and/or registered trademarks of Scholastic Inc.

Library of Congress Control Number: 2022930700

ISBN 978-1-338-76259-4 (hardcover)
ISBN 978-1-338-76258-7 (paperback)

10 9 8 7 6 5 4 3 2 1   23 24 25 26 27

Printed in China   62
First edition, January 2023

Edited by Cassandra Pelham Fulton and David Levithan
Book design by Shivana Sookdeo
Creative Director: Phil Falco
Publisher: David Saylor

CHAPTER 1

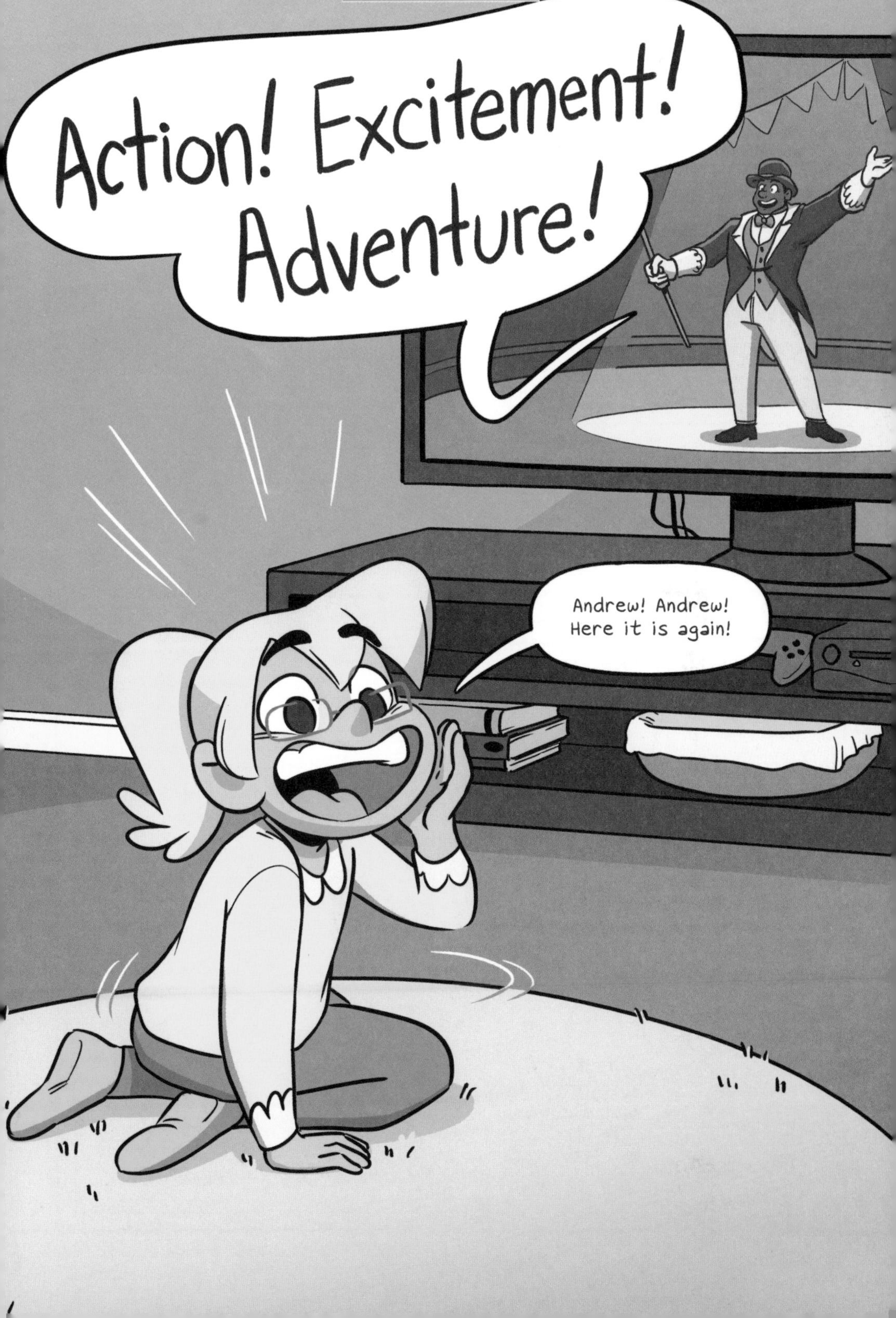
Action! Excitement! Adventure!
Andrew! Andrew! Here it is again!

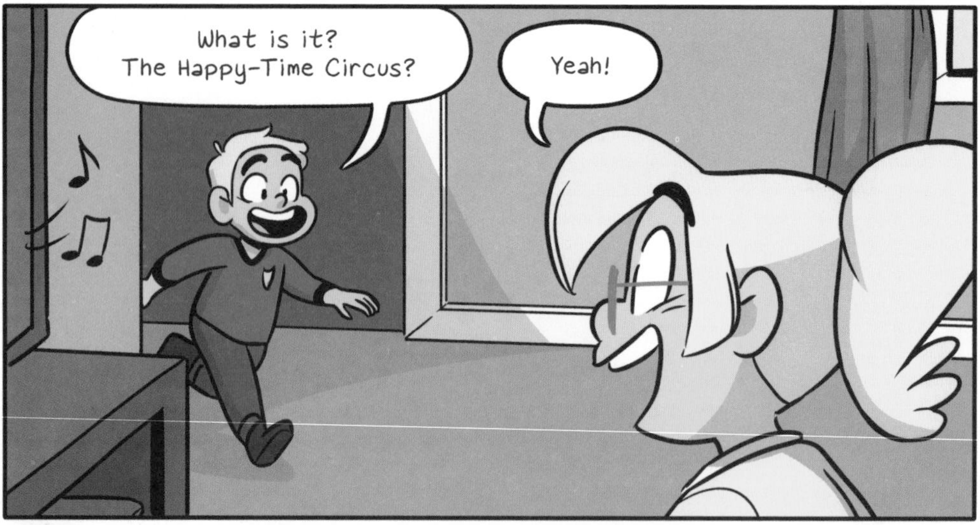
What is it?
The Happy-Time Circus?
Yeah!

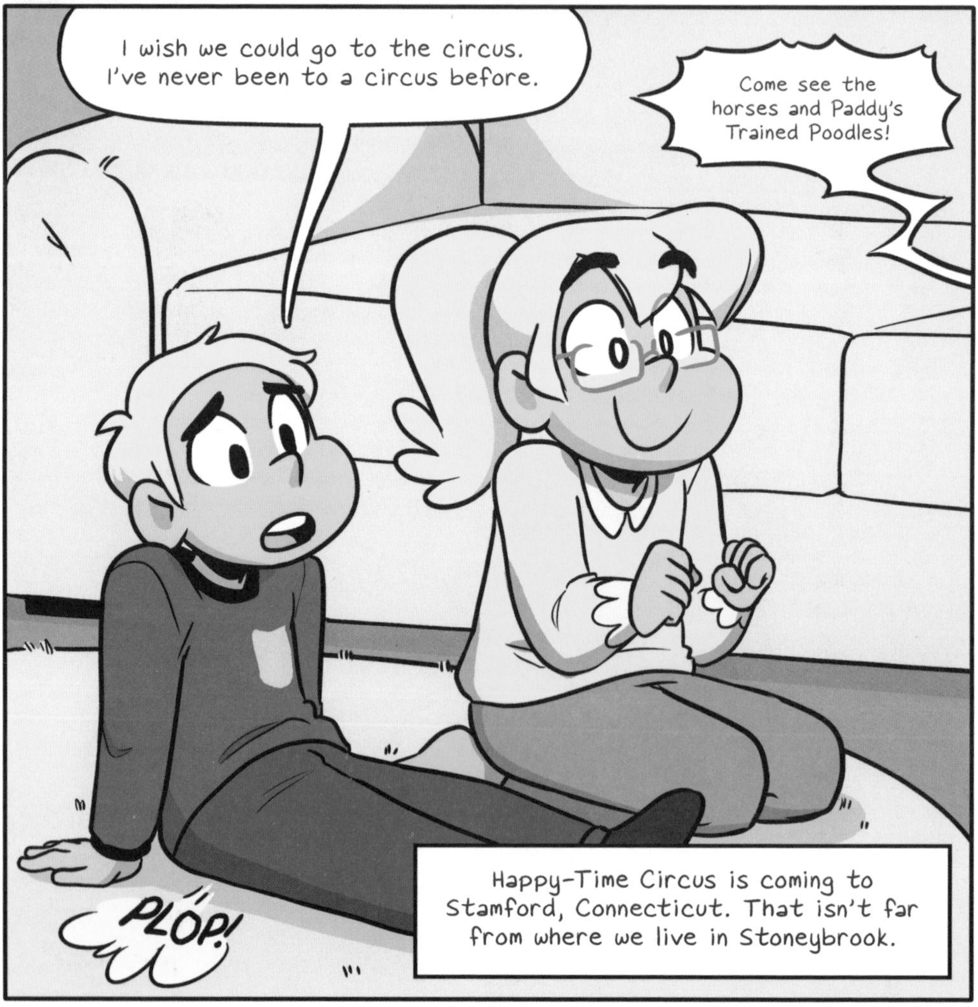
I wish we could go to the circus.
I've never been to a circus before.
Come see the horses and Paddy's Trained Poodles!
PLOP!
Happy-Time Circus is coming to Stamford, Connecticut. That isn't far from where we live in Stoneybrook.

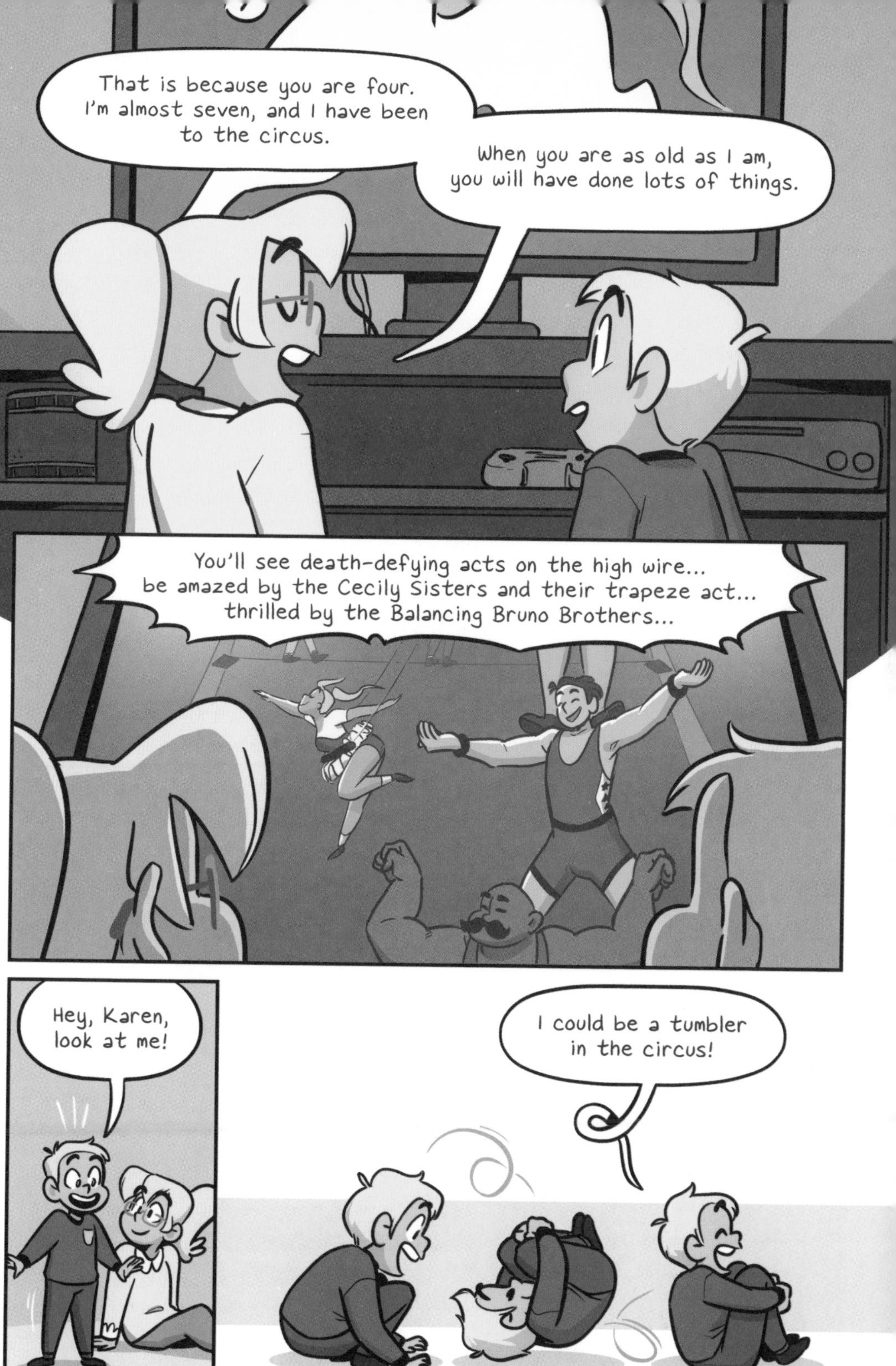

That is because you are four. I'm almost seven, and I have been to the circus.
When you are as old as I am, you will have done lots of things.
You'll see death-defying acts on the high wire... be amazed by the Cecily Sisters and their trapeze act... thrilled by the Balancing Bruno Brothers...
Hey, Karen, look at me!
I could be a tumbler in the circus!

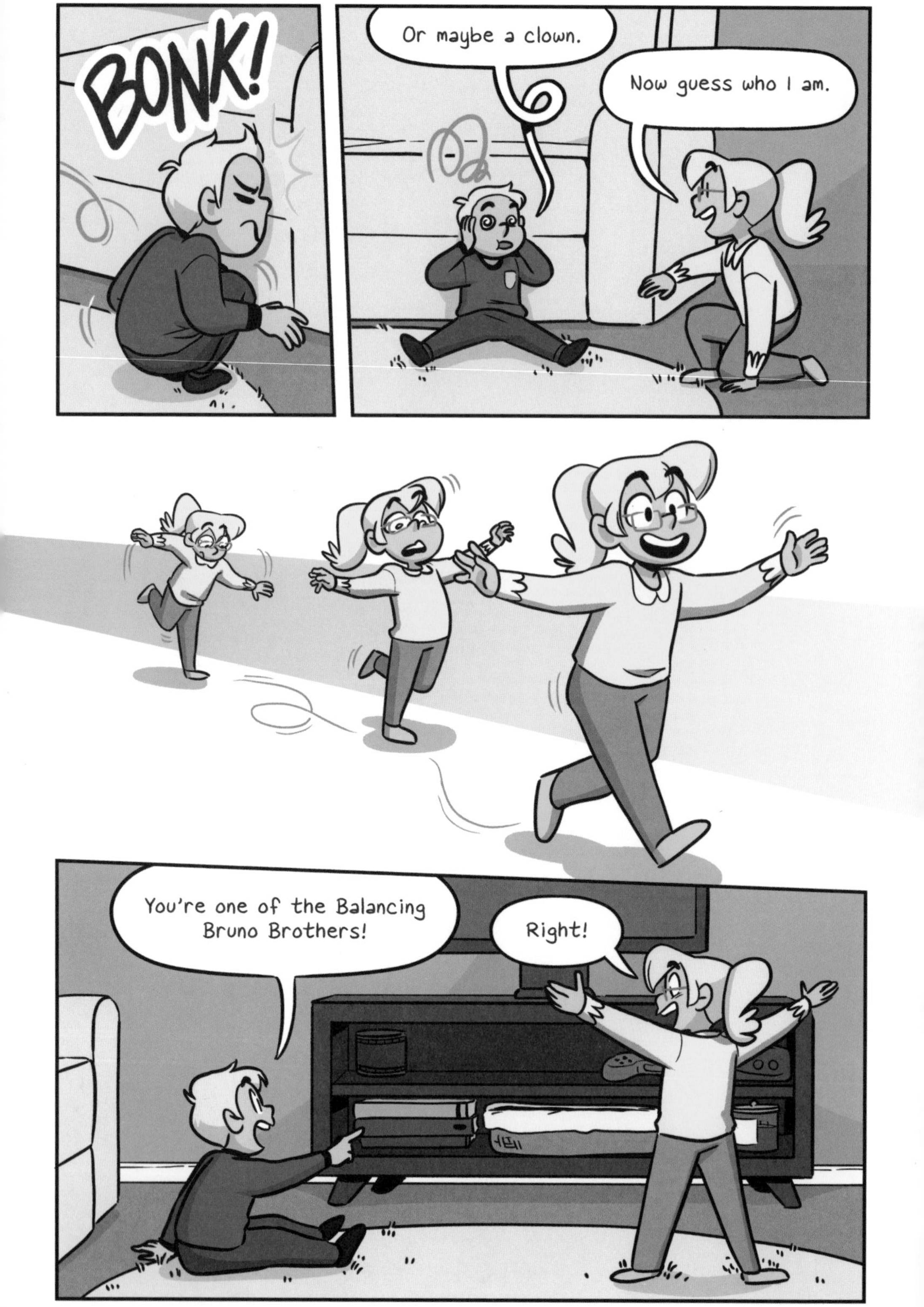
BONK!
Or maybe a clown.
Now guess who I am.
You're one of the Balancing Bruno Brothers!
Right!

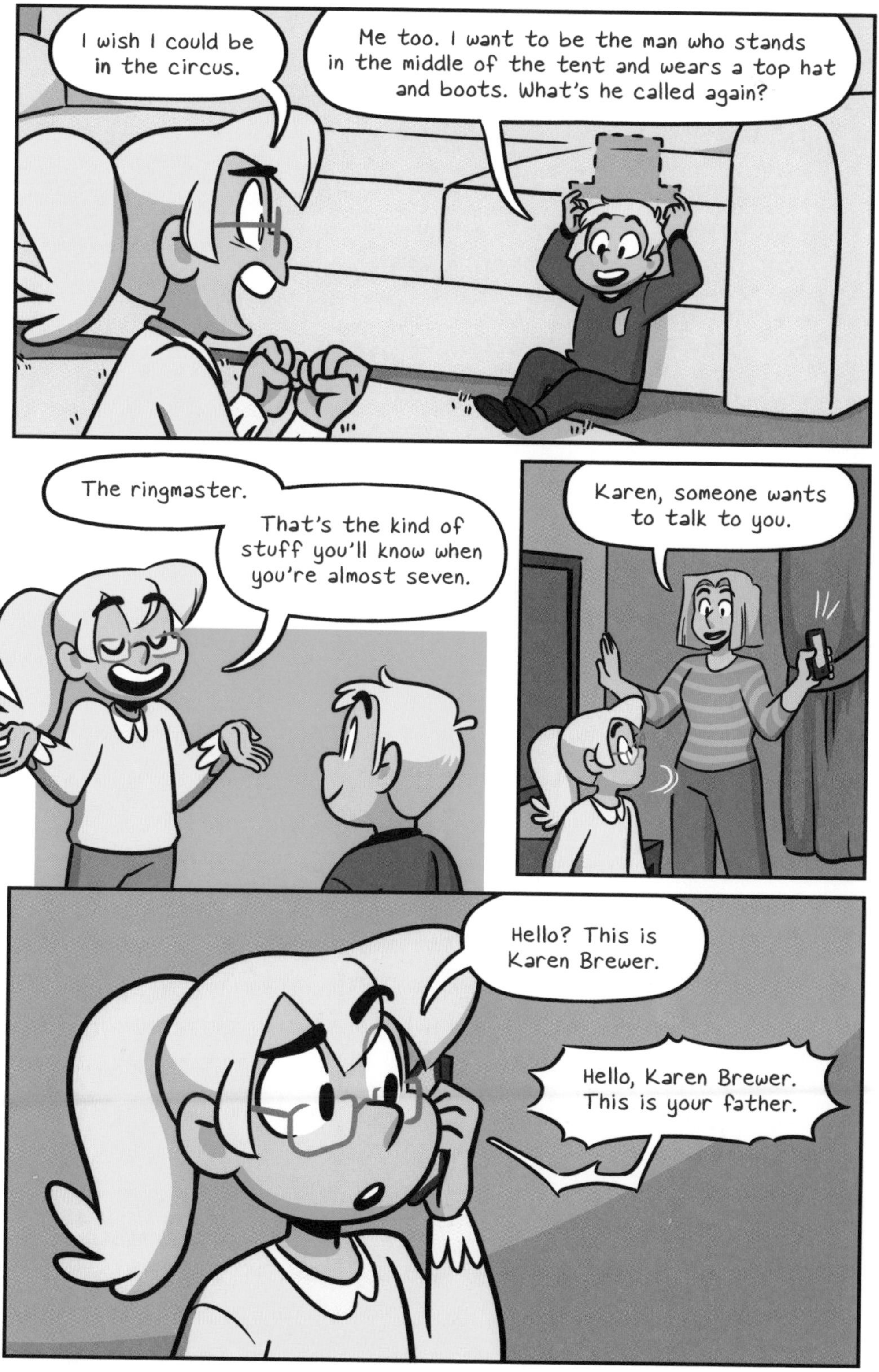
I wish I could be in the circus.
Me too. I want to be the man who stands in the middle of the tent and wears a top hat and boots. What's he called again?
The ringmaster.
That's the kind of stuff you'll know when you're almost seven.
Karen, someone wants to talk to you.
Hello? This is Karen Brewer.
Hello, Karen Brewer. This is your father.

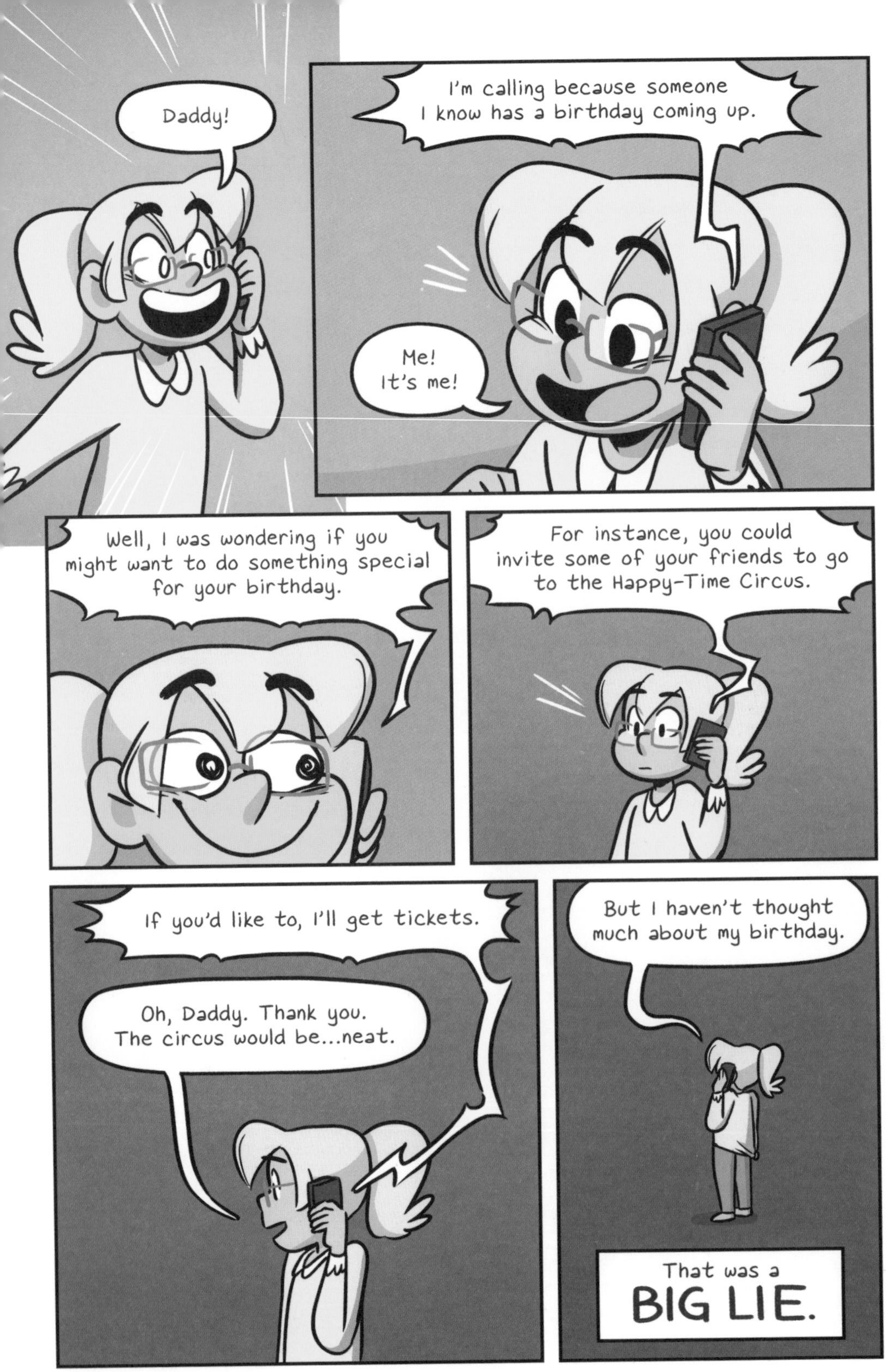
Daddy!
I'm calling because someone I know has a birthday coming up.
Me! It's me!
Well, I was wondering if you might want to do something special for your birthday.
For instance, you could invite some of your friends to go to the Happy-Time Circus.
If you'd like to, I'll get tickets.
Oh, Daddy. Thank you. The circus would be...neat.
But I haven't thought much about my birthday.
That was a BIG LIE.

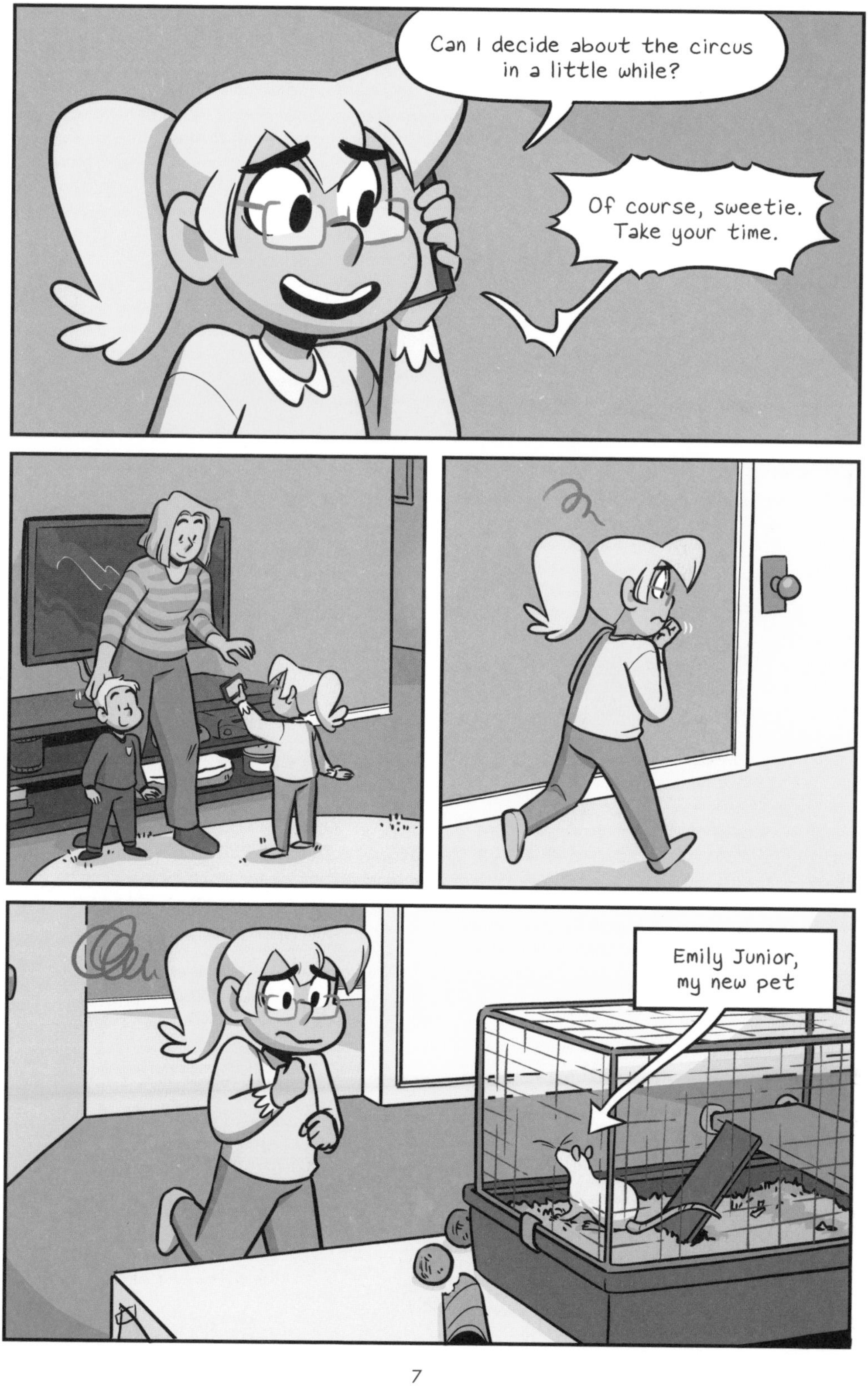
Can I decide about the circus in a little while?
Of course, sweetie. Take your time.
Emily Junior, my new pet

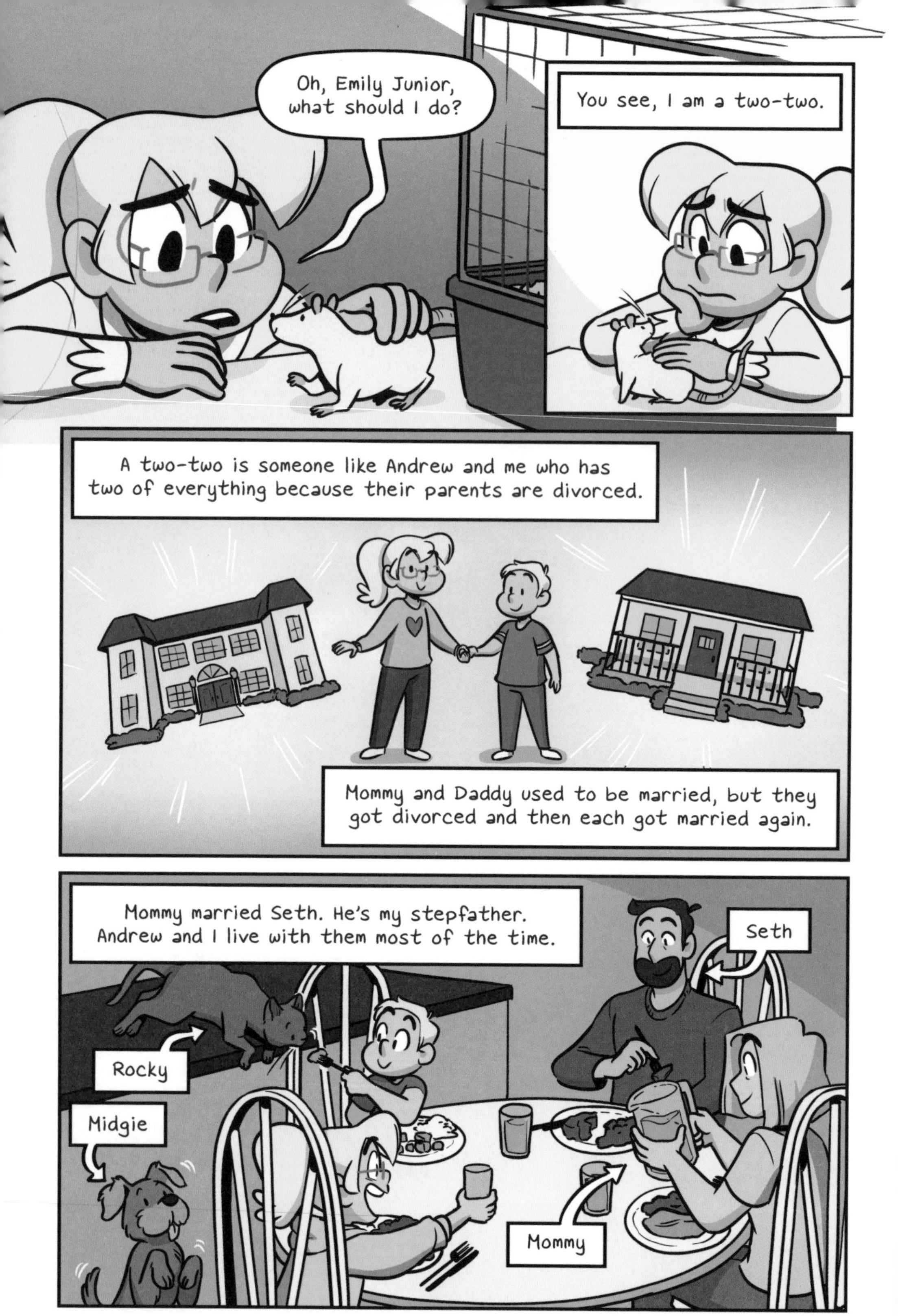
Oh, Emily Junior, what should I do?
You see, I am a two-two.
A two-two is someone like Andrew and me who has two of everything because their parents are divorced.
Mommy and Daddy used to be married, but they got divorced and then each got married again.
Mommy married Seth. He's my stepfather. Andrew and I live with them most of the time.
Seth
Rocky
Midgie
Mommy

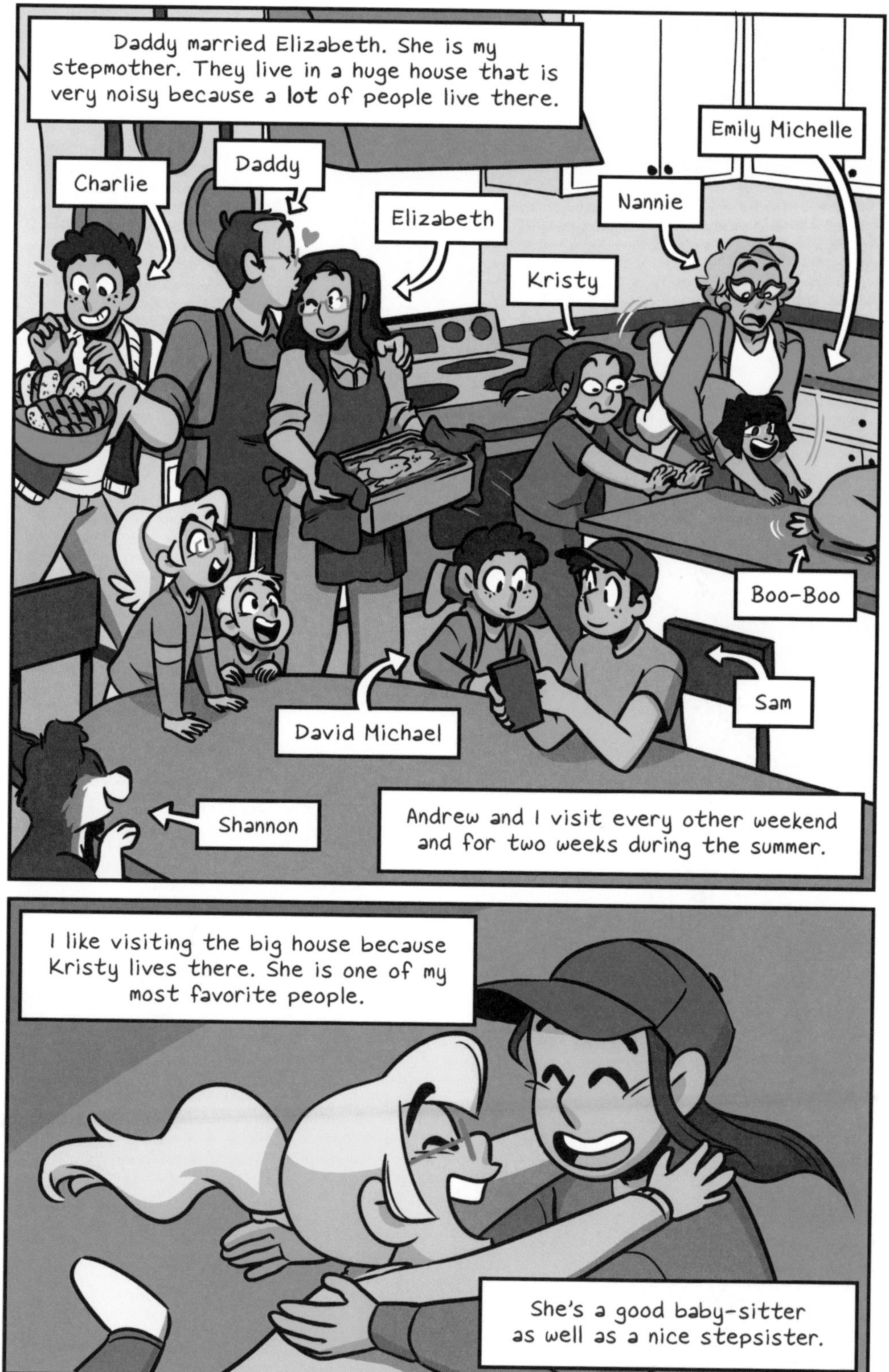
Daddy married Elizabeth. She is my stepmother. They live in a huge house that is very noisy because a **lot** of people live there.
Charlie
Daddy
Elizabeth
Kristy
Nannie
Emily Michelle
Boo-Boo
David Michael
Sam
Shannon
Andrew and I visit every other weekend and for two weeks during the summer.
I like visiting the big house because Kristy lives there. She is one of my most favorite people.
She's a good baby-sitter as well as a nice stepsister.

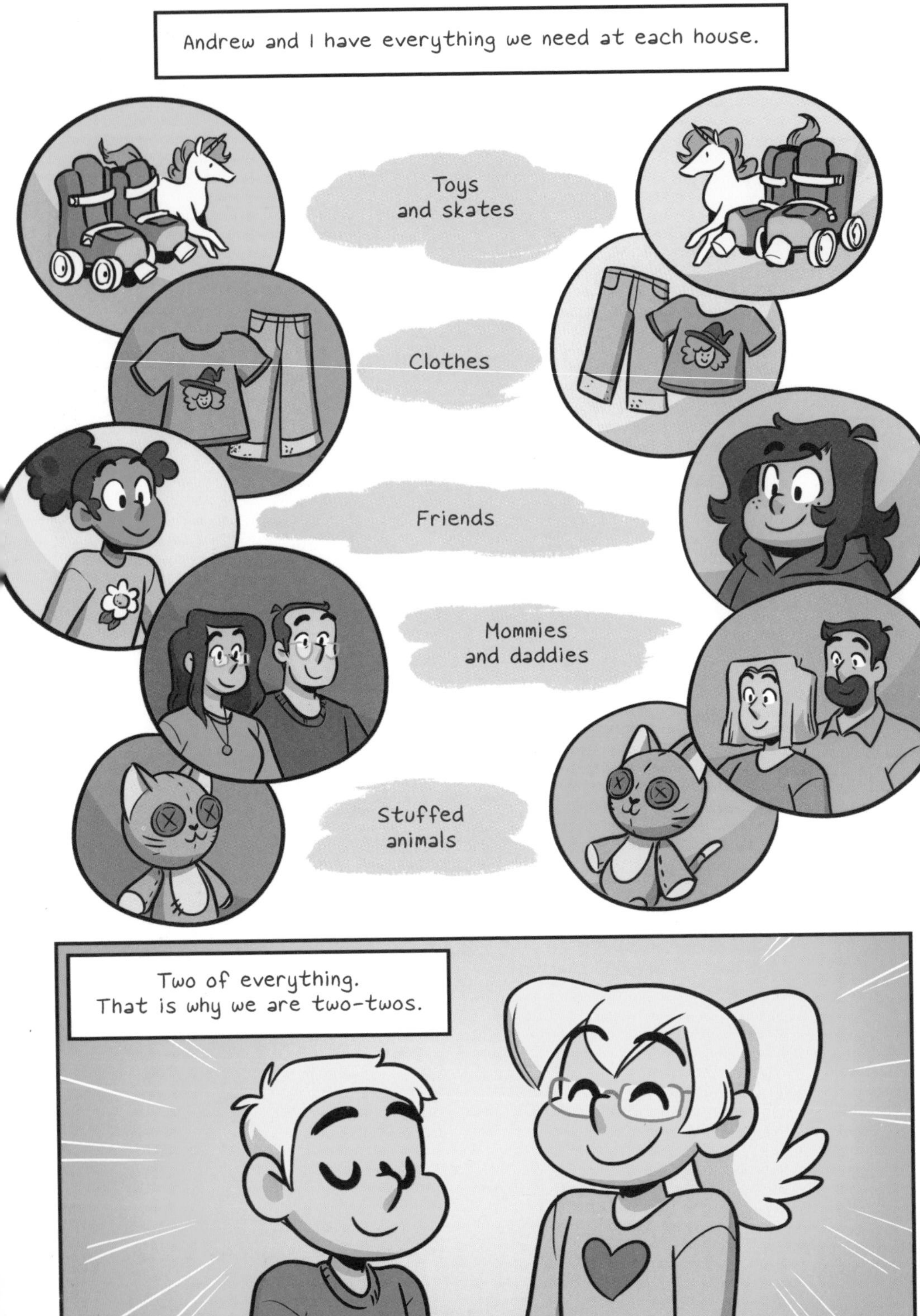
Andrew and I have everything we need at each house.
Toys and skates
Clothes
Friends
Mommies and daddies
Stuffed animals
Two of everything. That is why we are two-twos.

Being a two-two might sound like fun, and it can be.

But here is one thing that I do not like about being a two-two:

I never get to see everybody in my whole family all at once.

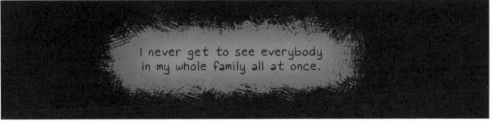

I either see the little-house family...

Or the big-house family.

Seeing everyone together would be a very, **very** big treat.

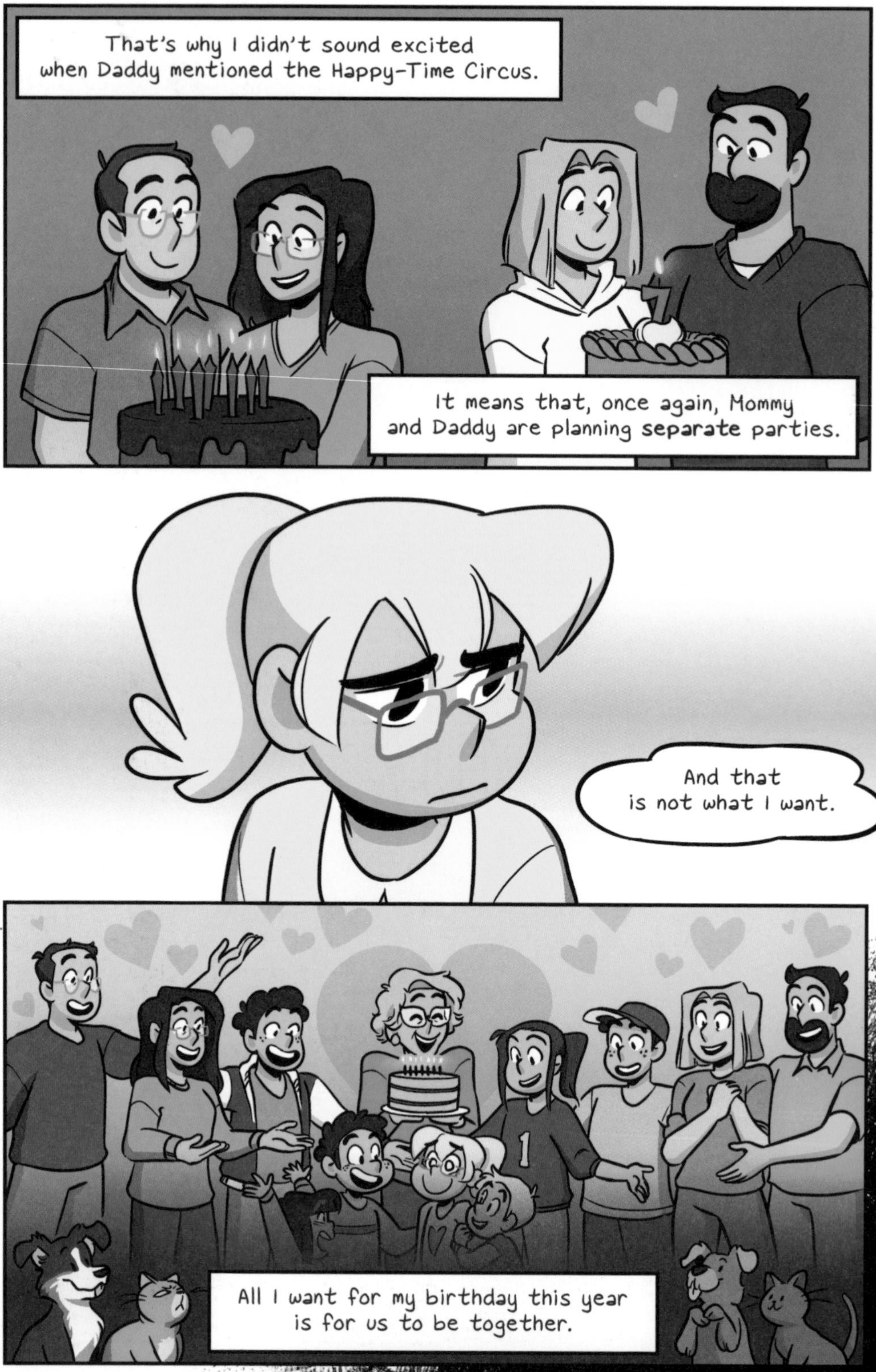
That's why I didn't sound excited when Daddy mentioned the Happy-Time Circus.
It means that, once again, Mommy and Daddy are planning **separate** parties.
And that is not what I want.
All I want for my birthday this year is for us to be together.

CHAPTER 2

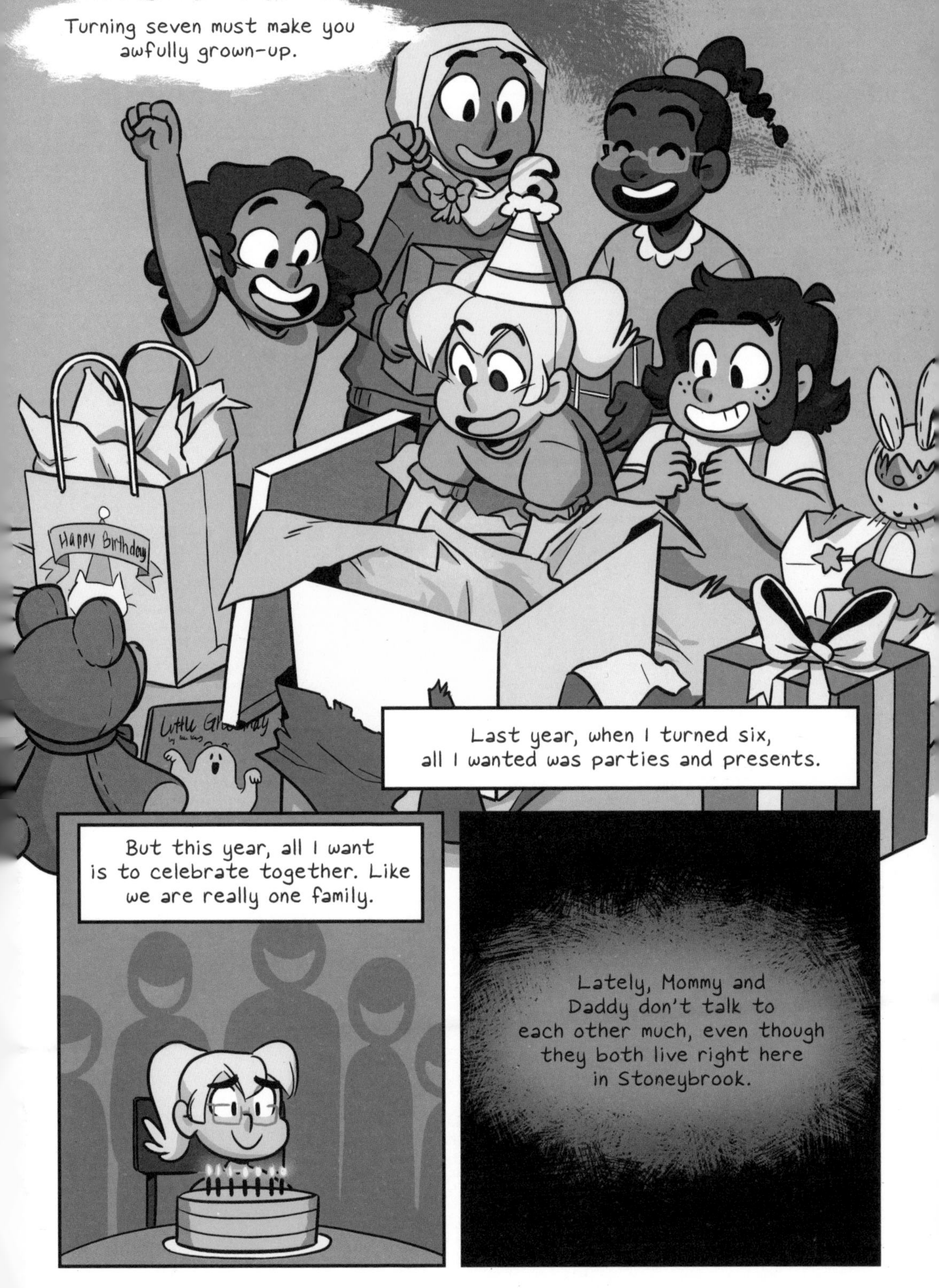

Turning seven must make you awfully grown-up.
Happy Birthday
Last year, when I turned six, all I wanted was parties and presents.
But this year, all I want is to celebrate together. Like we are really one family.
Lately, Mommy and Daddy don't talk to each other much, even though they both live right here in Stoneybrook.

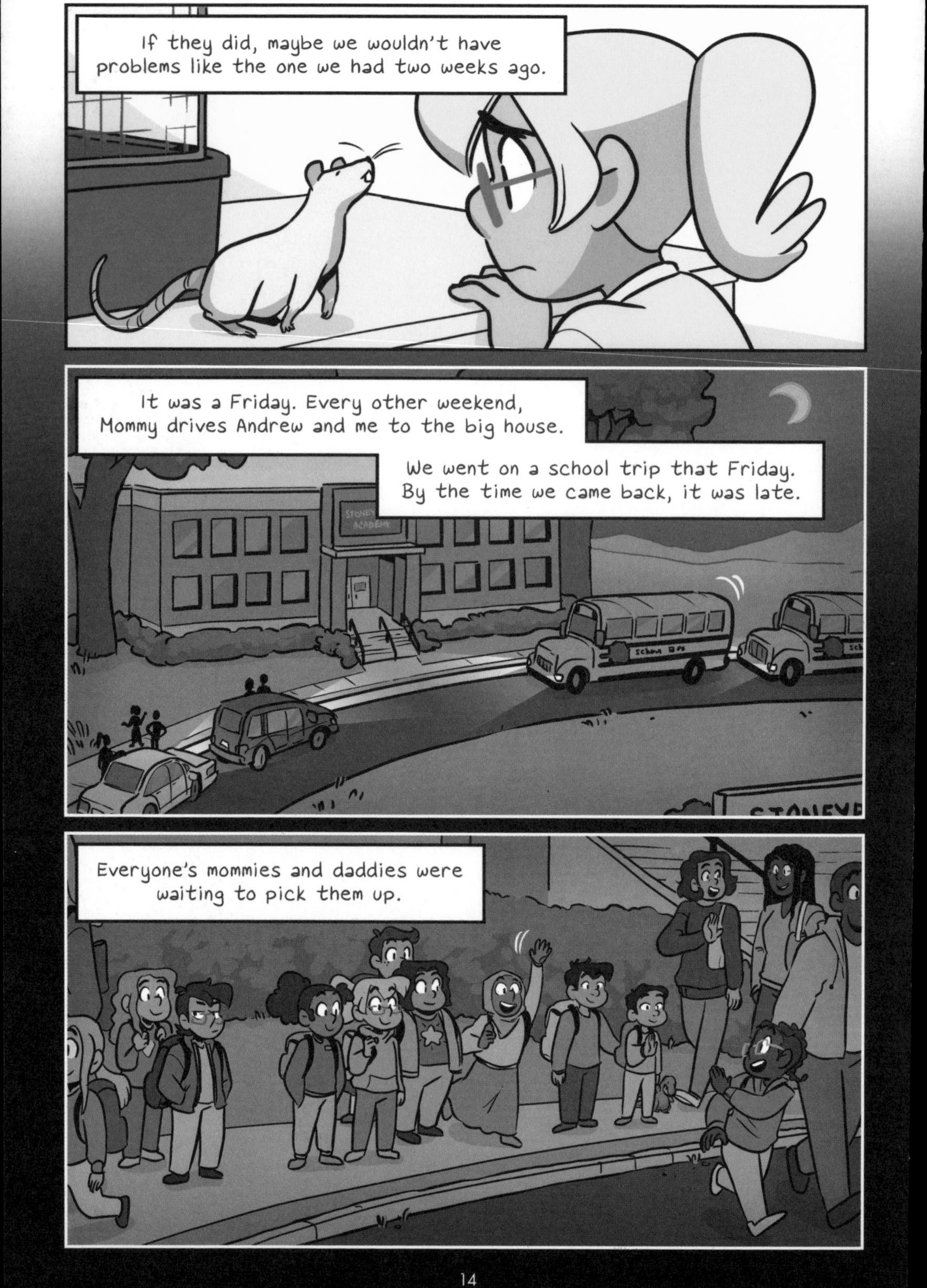
If they did, maybe we wouldn't have problems like the one we had two weeks ago.
It was a Friday. Every other weekend, Mommy drives Andrew and me to the big house.
We went on a school trip that Friday. By the time we came back, it was late.
Everyone's mommies and daddies were waiting to pick them up.

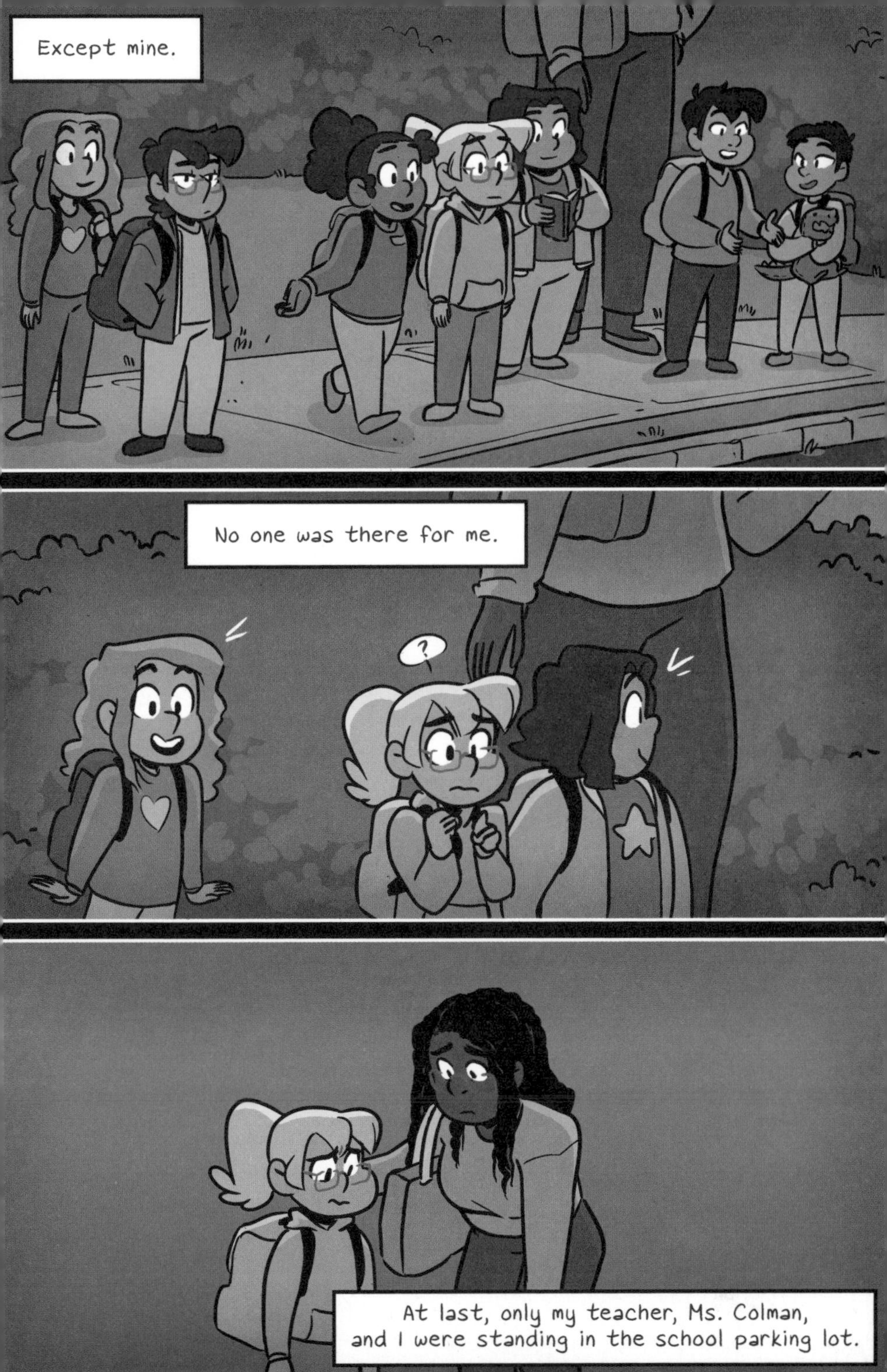
Except mine.
No one was there for me.
?
At last, only my teacher, Ms. Colman,
and I were standing in the school parking lot.

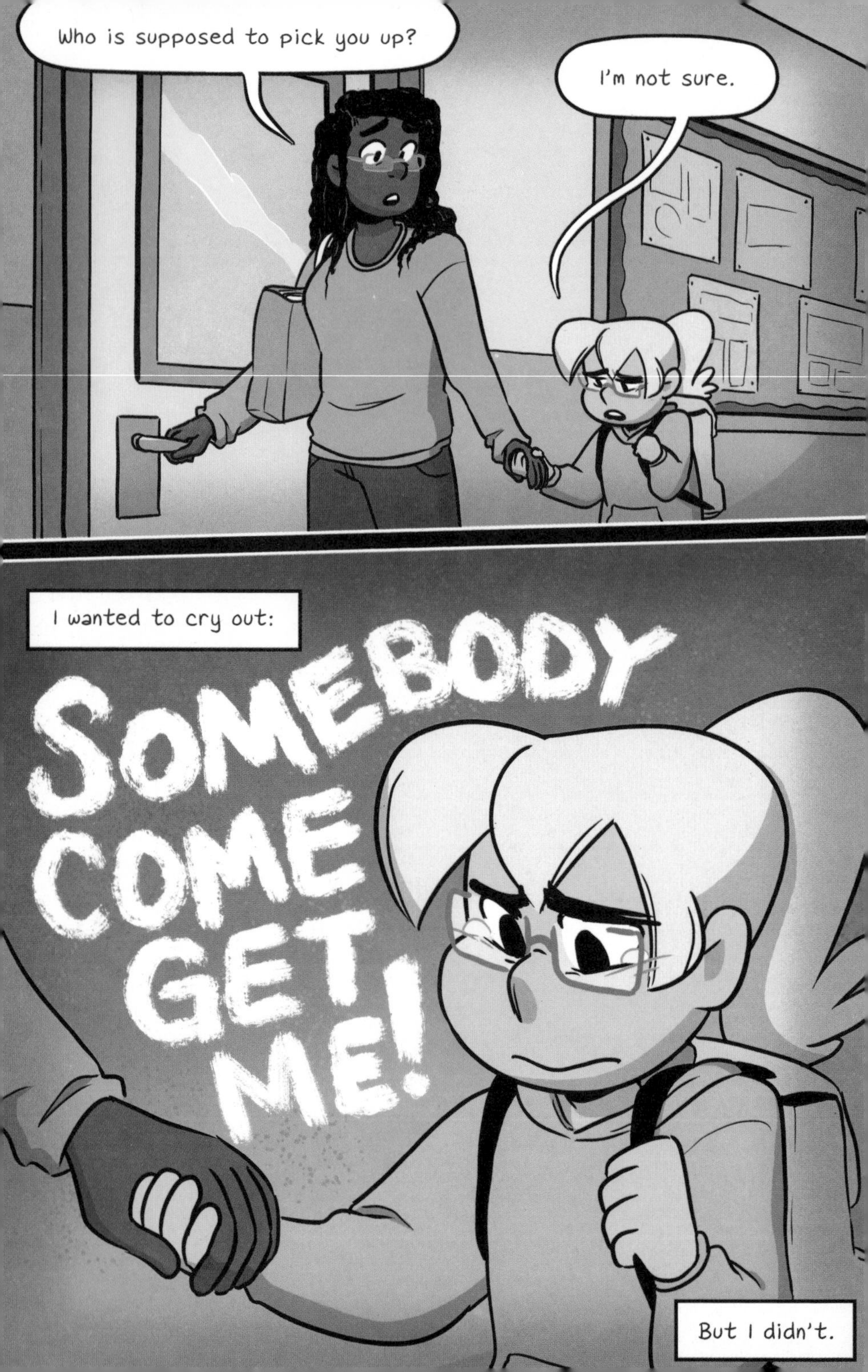

Who is supposed to pick you up?
I'm not sure.
I wanted to cry out:
SOMEBODY COME GET ME!
But I didn't.

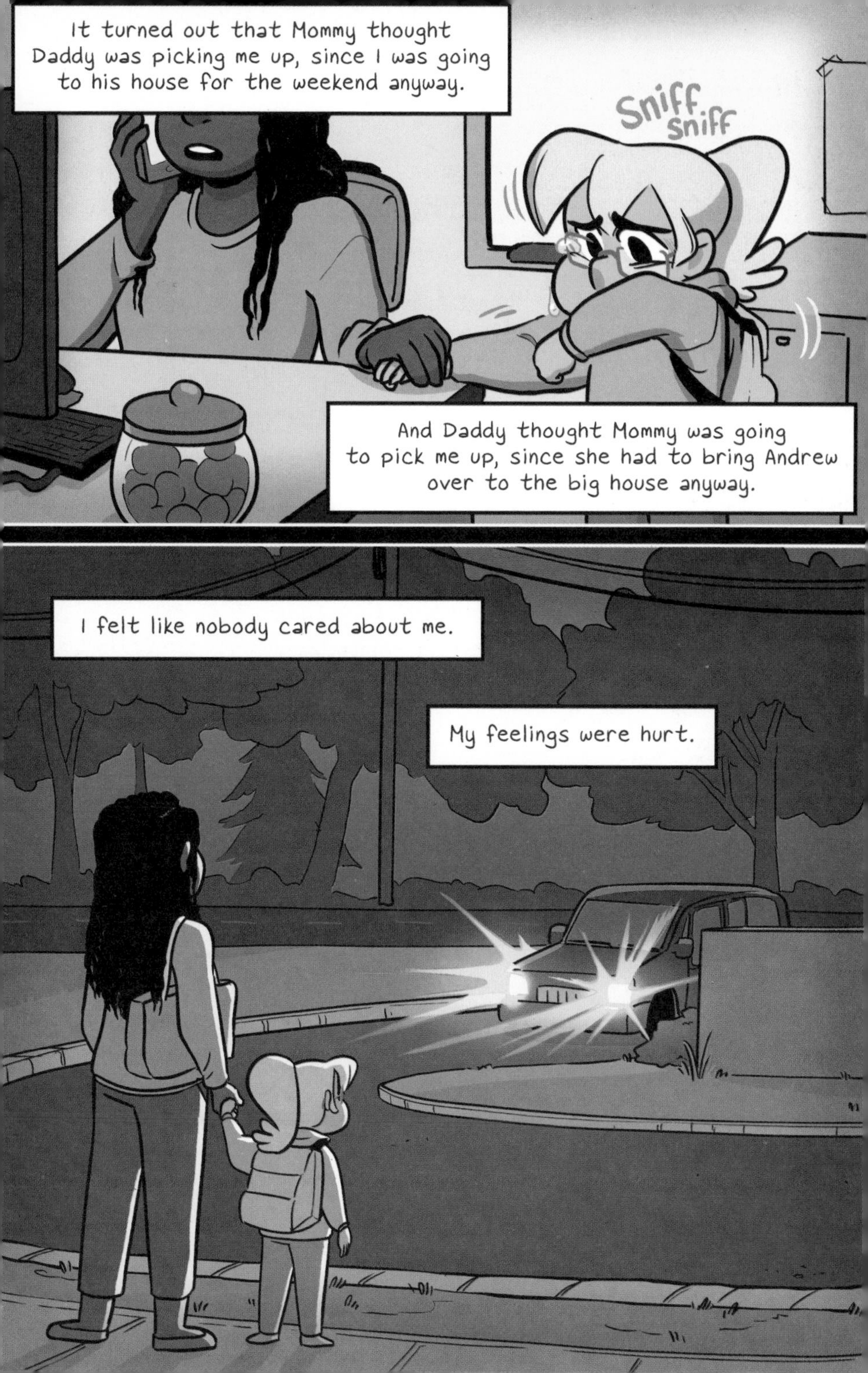
It turned out that Mommy thought Daddy was picking me up, since I was going to his house for the weekend anyway.
Sniff sniff
And Daddy thought Mommy was going to pick me up, since she had to bring Andrew over to the big house anyway.
I felt like nobody cared about me.
My feelings were hurt.

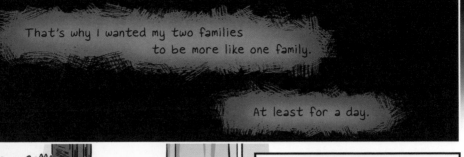

That's why I wanted my two families to be more like one family.

At least for a day.

KNOCK KNOCK!

Honey, I've been thinking.

Your birthday is coming up, and seven is a pretty grown-up age.

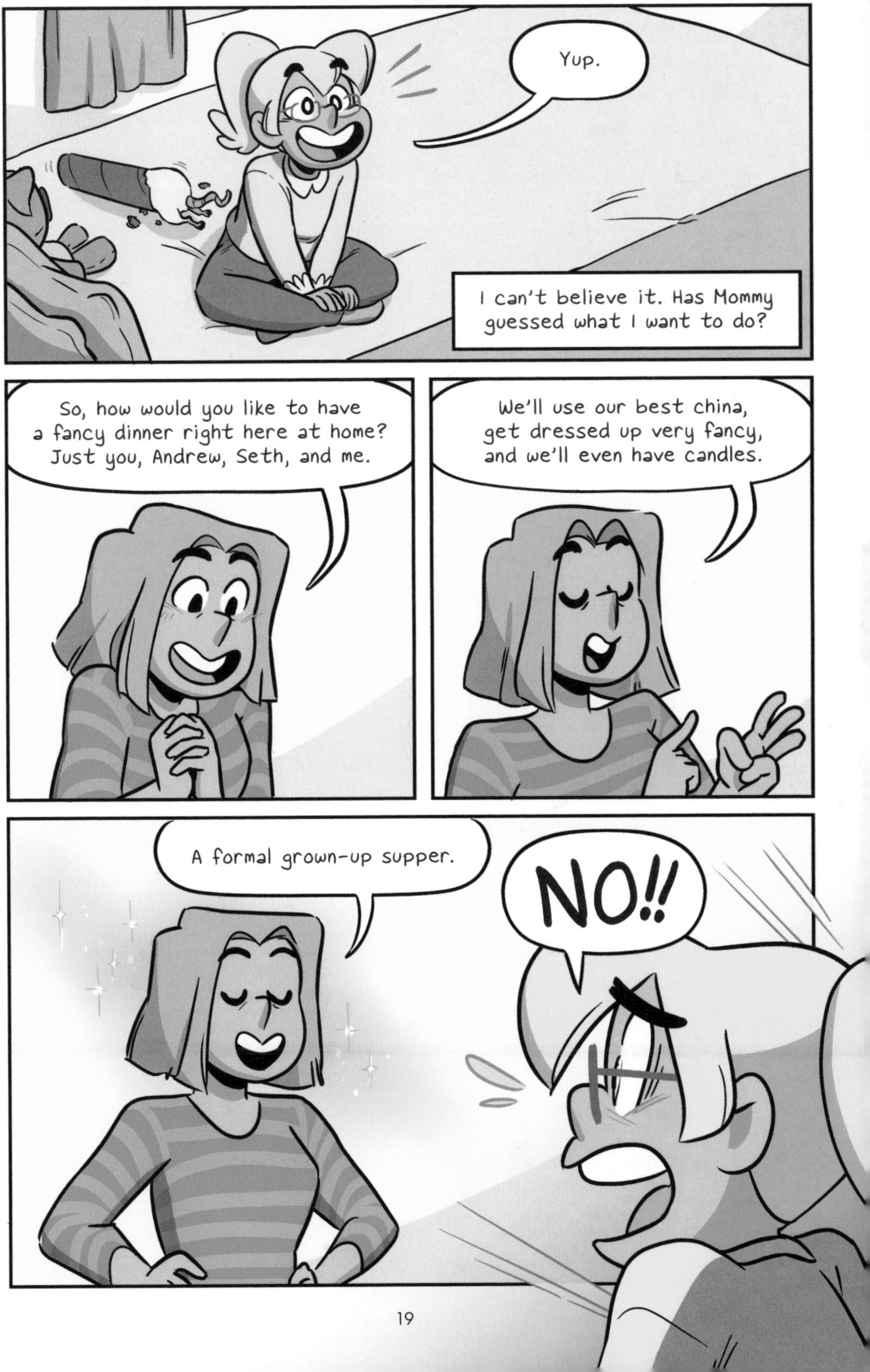
Yup.
I can't believe it. Has Mommy guessed what I want to do?
So, how would you like to have a fancy dinner right here at home? Just you, Andrew, Seth, and me.
We'll use our best china, get dressed up very fancy, and we'll even have candles.
A formal grown-up supper.
NO!!

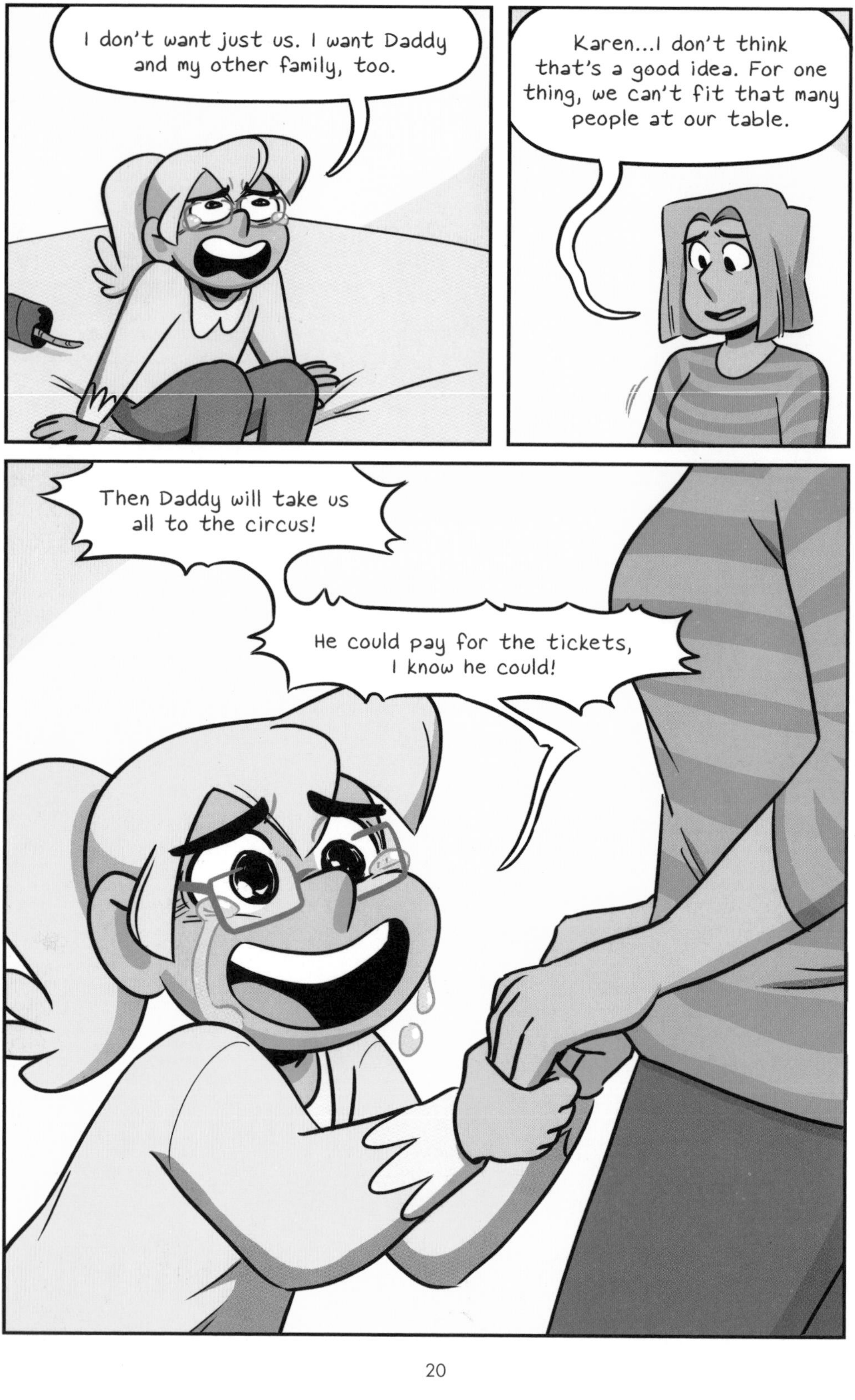
I don't want just us. I want Daddy and my other family, too.
Karen...I don't think that's a good idea. For one thing, we can't fit that many people at our table.
Then Daddy will take us all to the circus!
He could pay for the tickets, I know he could!

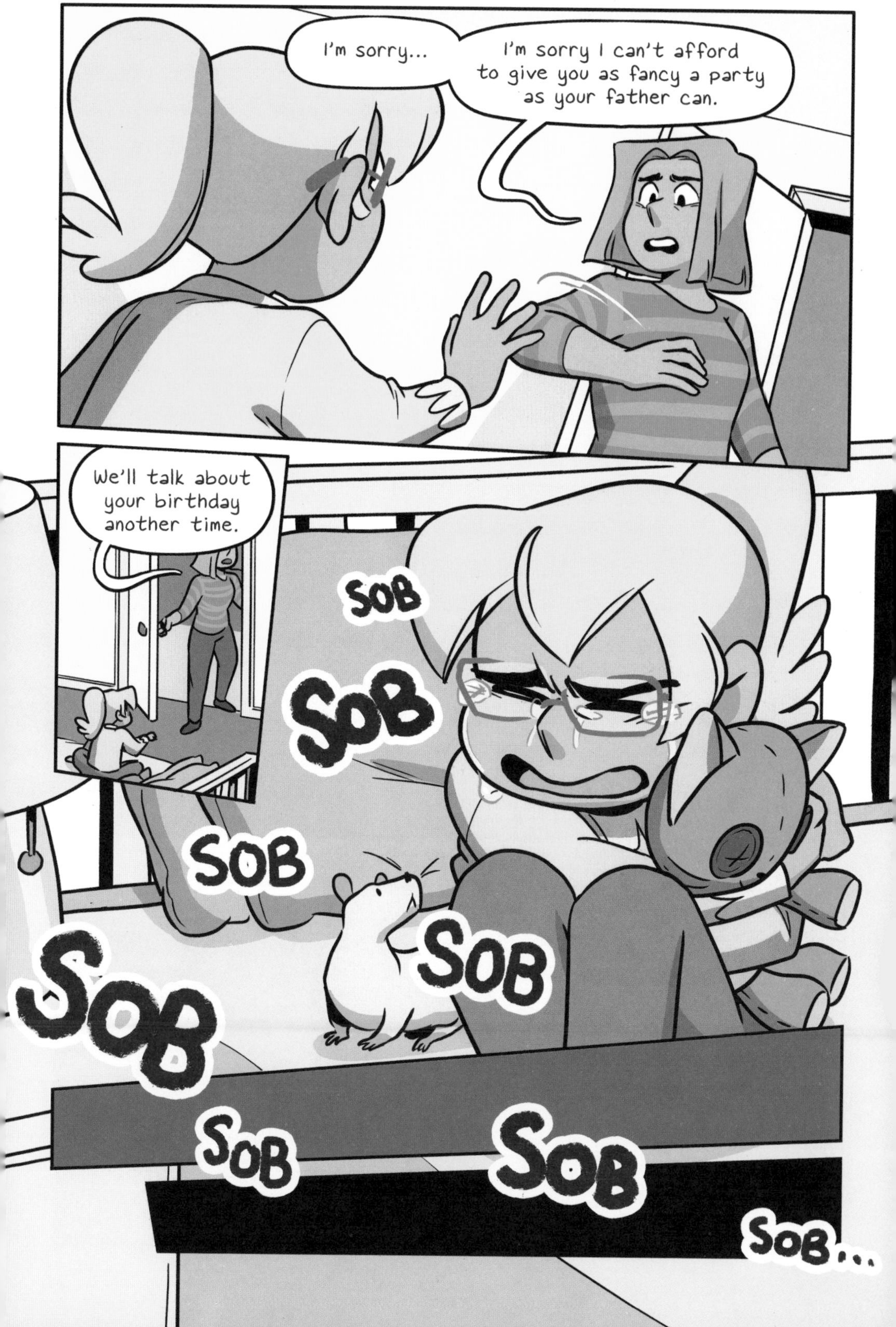
I'm sorry...
I'm sorry I can't afford to give you as fancy a party as your father can.
We'll talk about your birthday another time.
SOB
SOB
SOB
SOB
SOB
SOB
SOB
SOB...

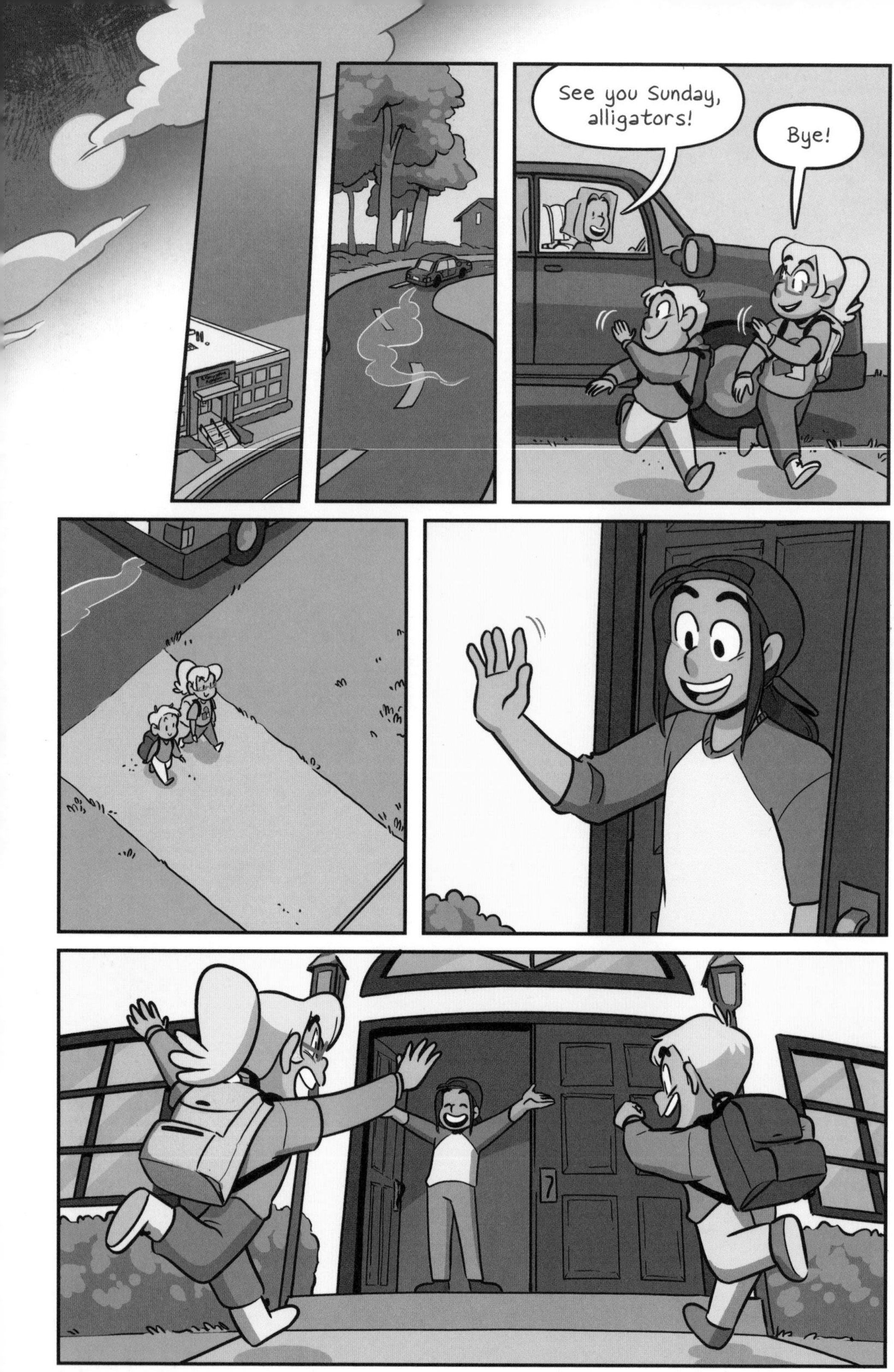
See you Sunday, alligators!
Bye!

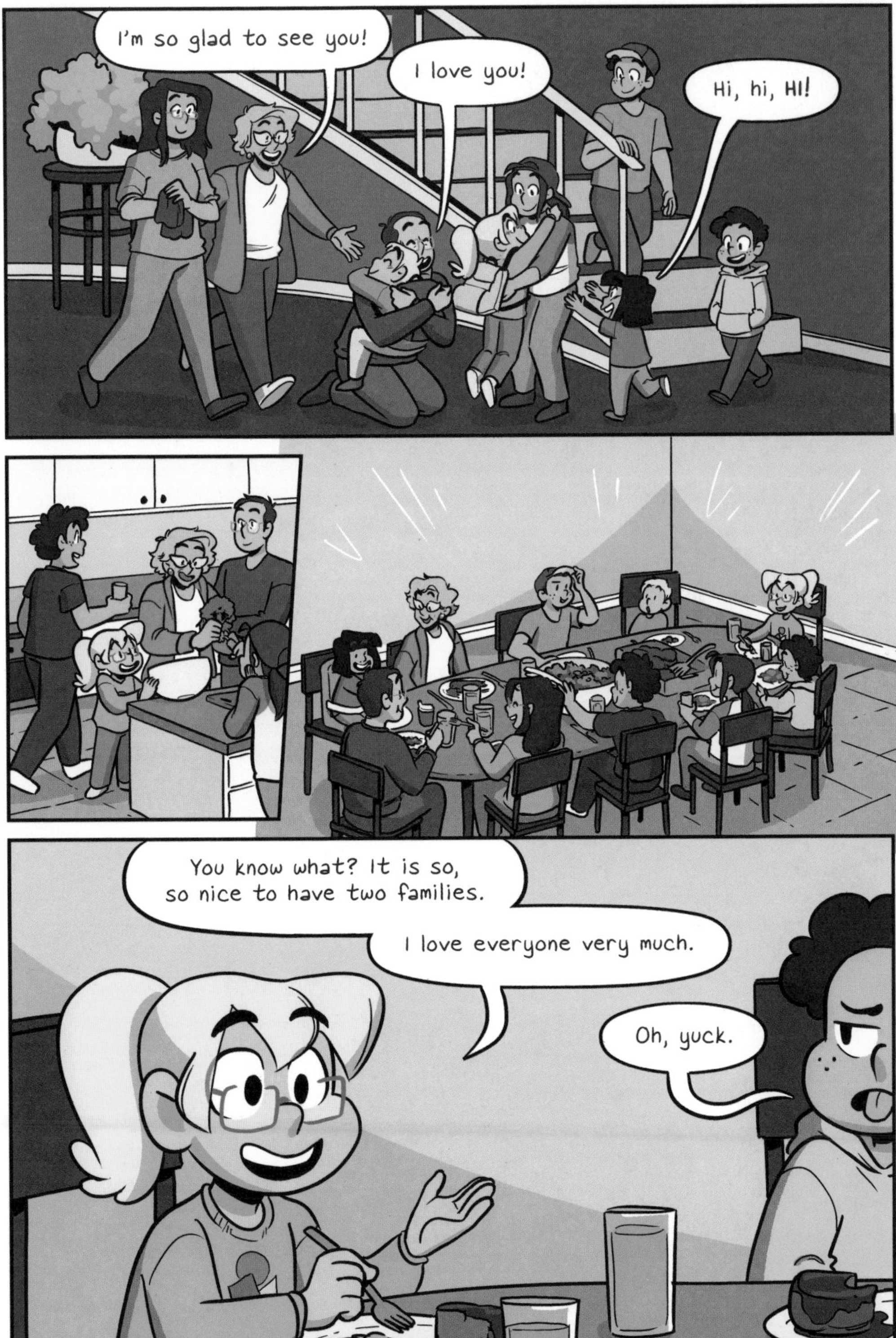
I'm so glad to see you!
I love you!
Hi, hi, HI!
You know what? It is so, so nice to have two families.
I love everyone very much.
Oh, yuck.

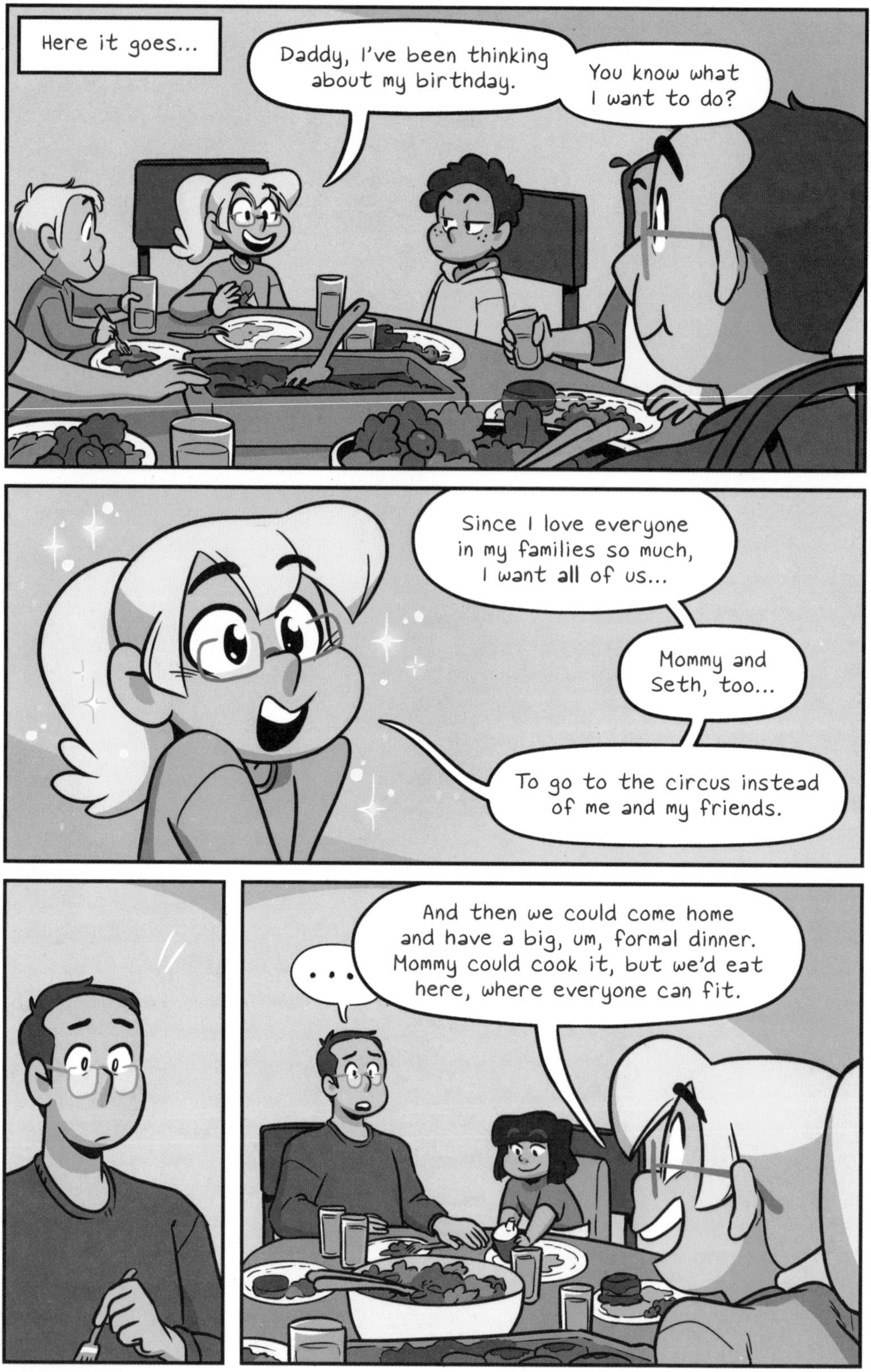
Here it goes...
Daddy, I've been thinking about my birthday.
You know what I want to do?
Since I love everyone in my families so much, I want all of us...
Mommy and Seth, too...
To go to the circus instead of me and my friends.
...
And then we could come home and have a big, um, formal dinner. Mommy could cook it, but we'd eat here, where everyone can fit.

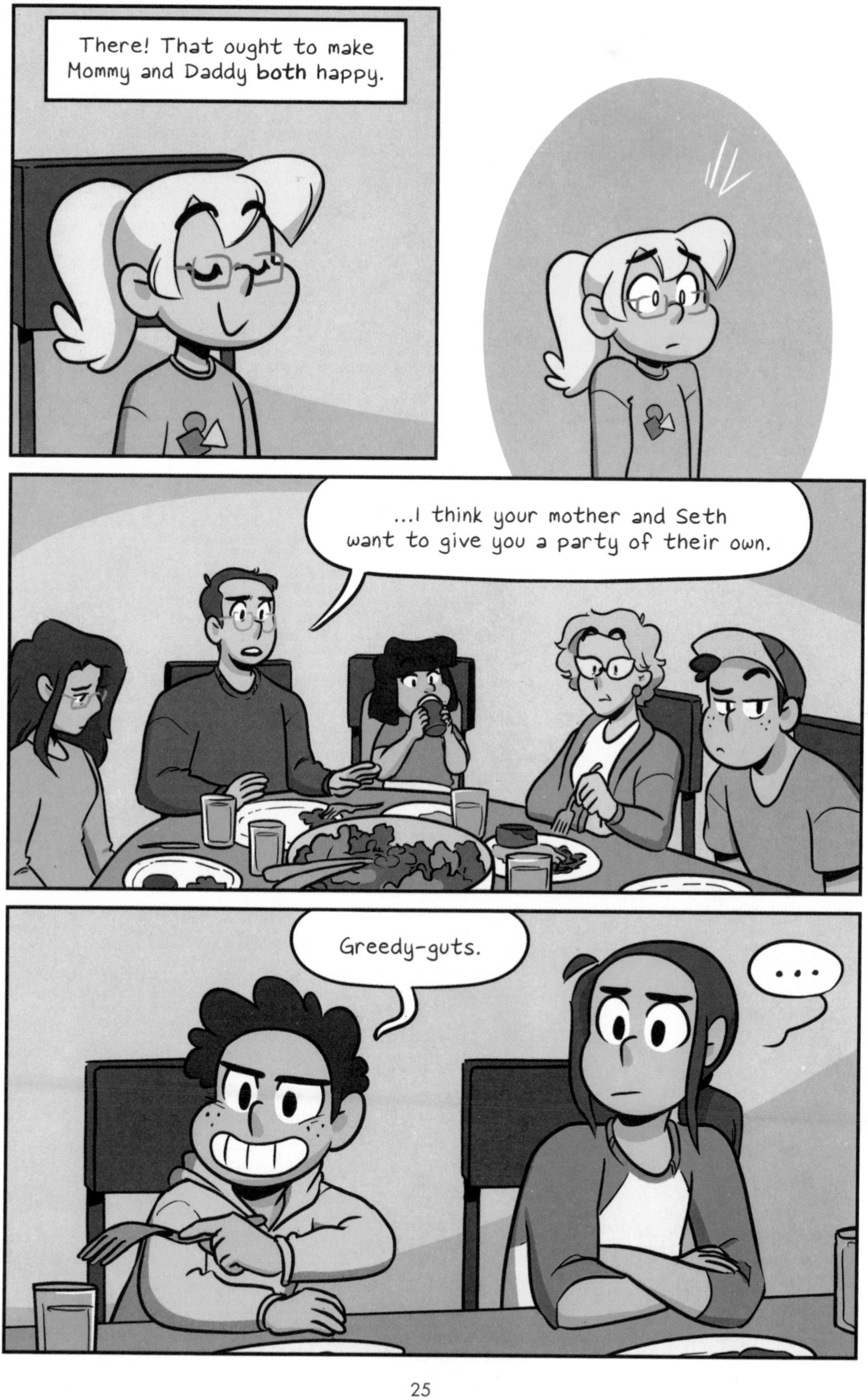
There! That ought to make Mommy and Daddy **both** happy.
...I think your mother and Seth want to give you a party of their own.
Greedy-guts.
...

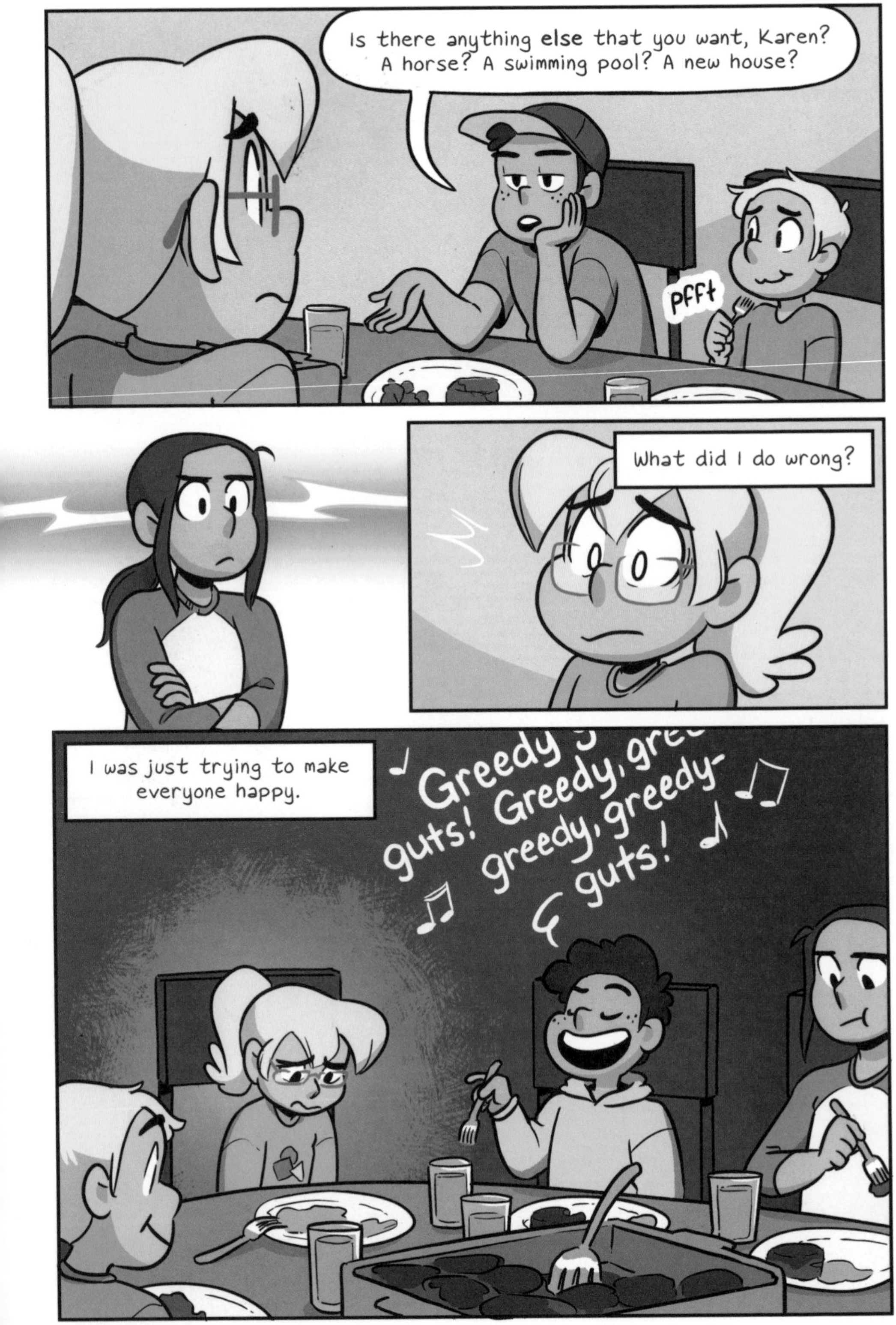
Is there anything **else** that you want, Karen? A horse? A swimming pool? A new house?
pfft
What did I do wrong?
I was just trying to make everyone happy.
Greedy guts! Greedy, greedy-greedy, greedy guts!

CHAPTER 3

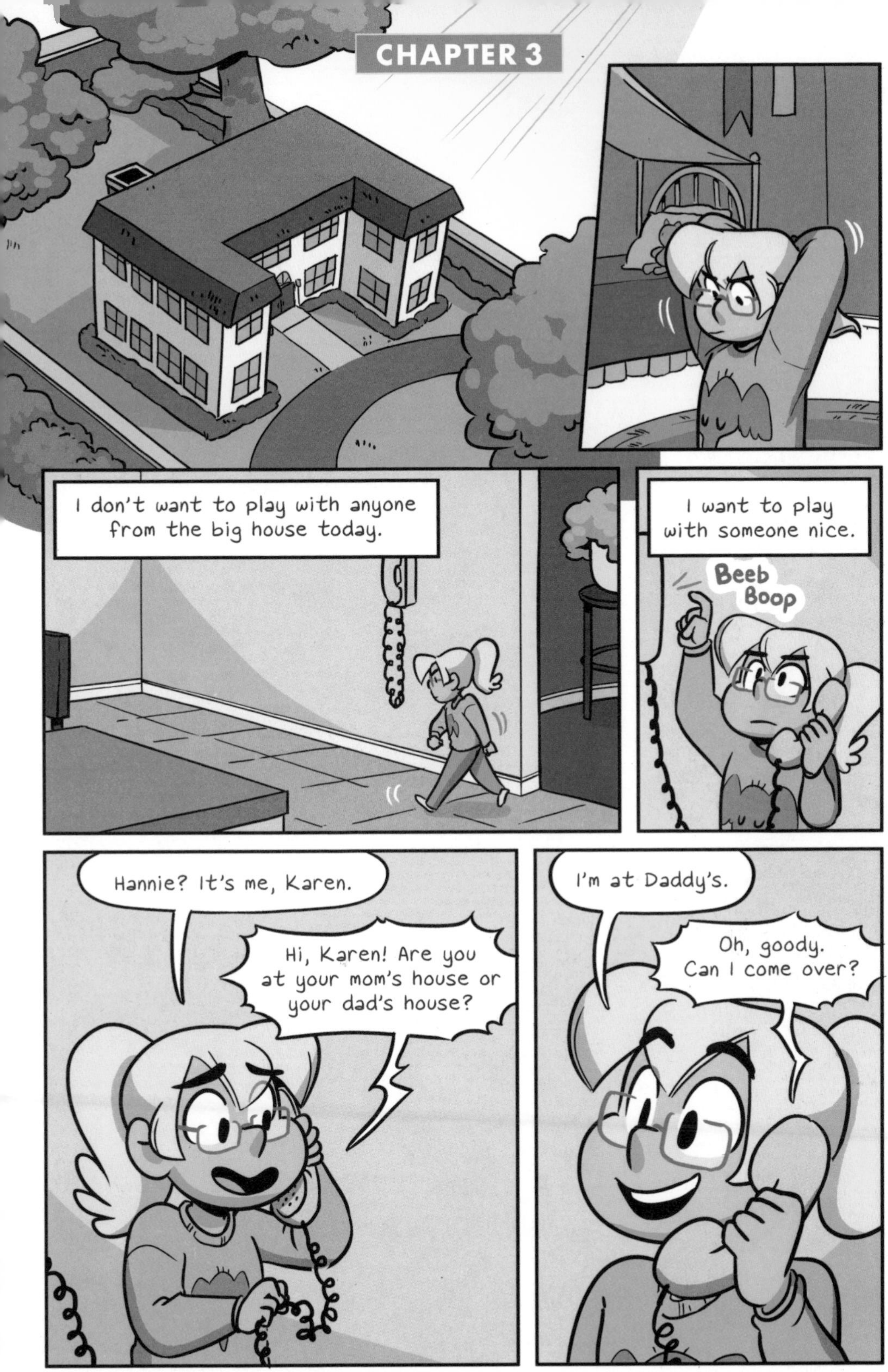
I don't want to play with anyone from the big house today.
I want to play with someone nice.
Beeb Boop
Hannie? It's me, Karen.
Hi, Karen! Are you at your mom's house or your dad's house?
I'm at Daddy's.
Oh, goody. Can I come over?

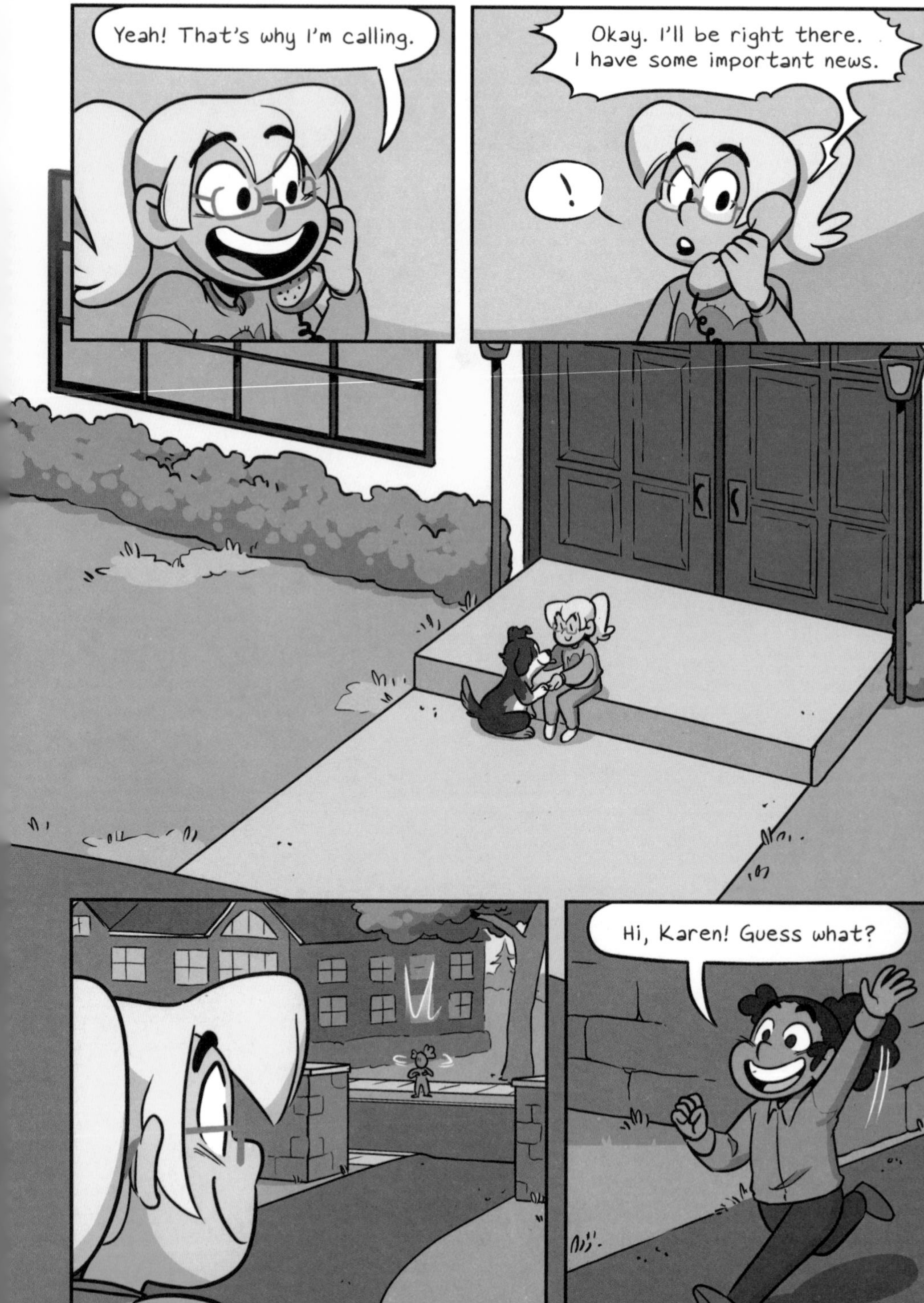
Yeah! That's why I'm calling.
Okay. I'll be right there. I have some important news.
!
Hi, Karen! Guess what?

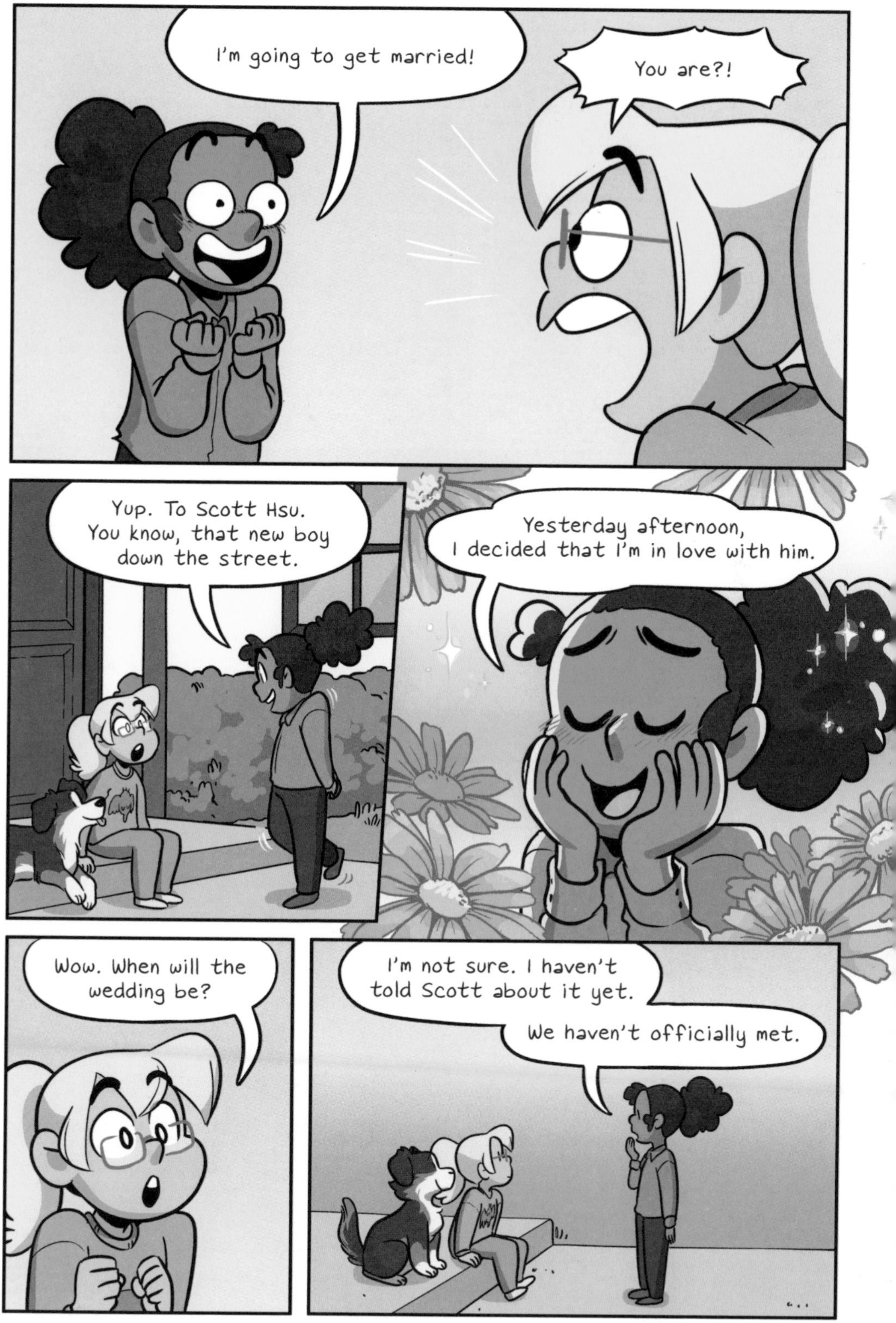
I'm going to get married!
You are?!
Yup. To Scott Hsu. You know, that new boy down the street.
Yesterday afternoon, I decided that I'm in love with him.
Wow. When will the wedding be?
I'm not sure. I haven't told Scott about it yet.
We haven't officially met.

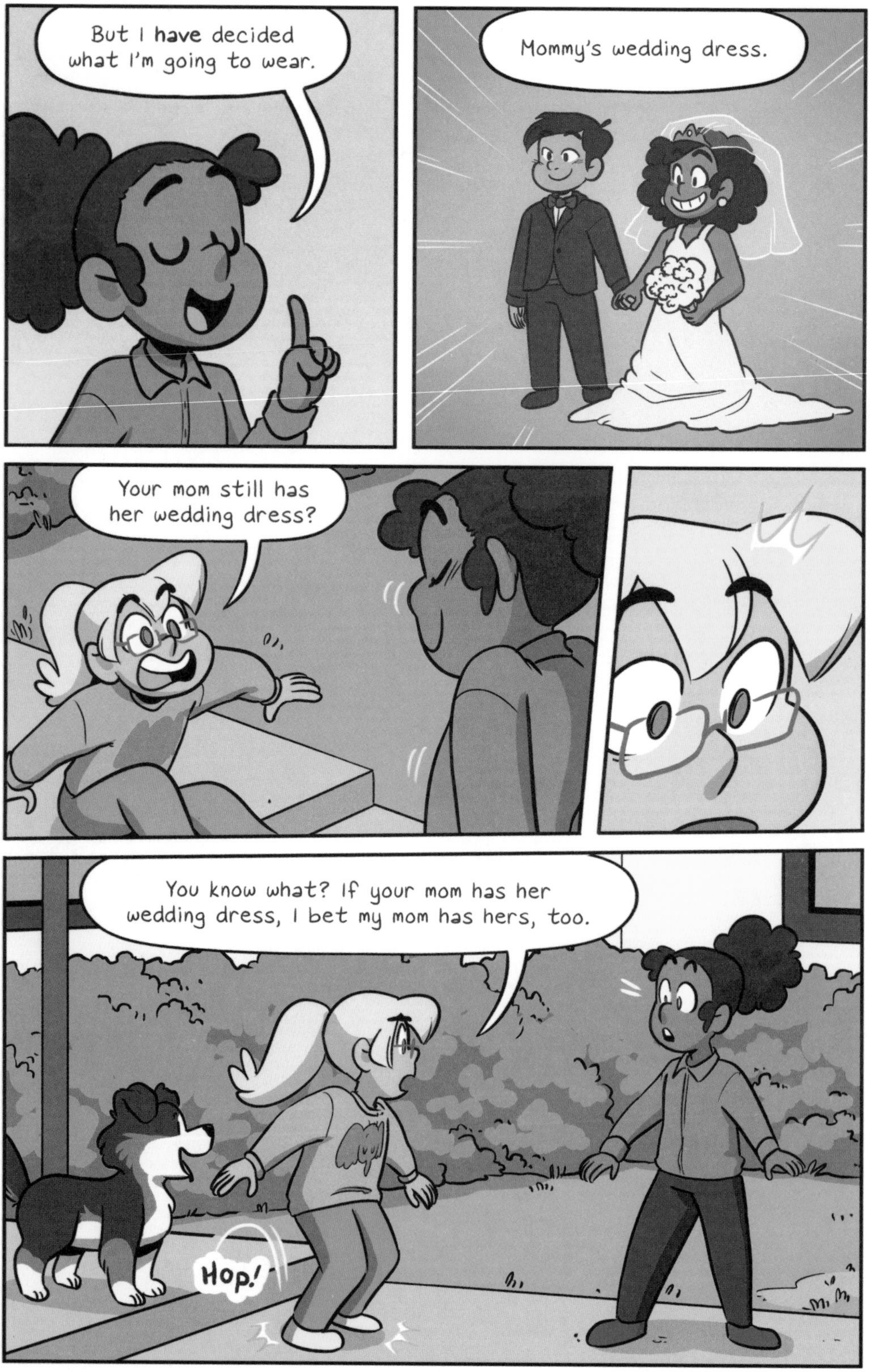
But I **have** decided what I'm going to wear.
Mommy's wedding dress.
Your mom still has her wedding dress?
You know what? If your mom has her wedding dress, I bet my mom has hers, too.
Hop!

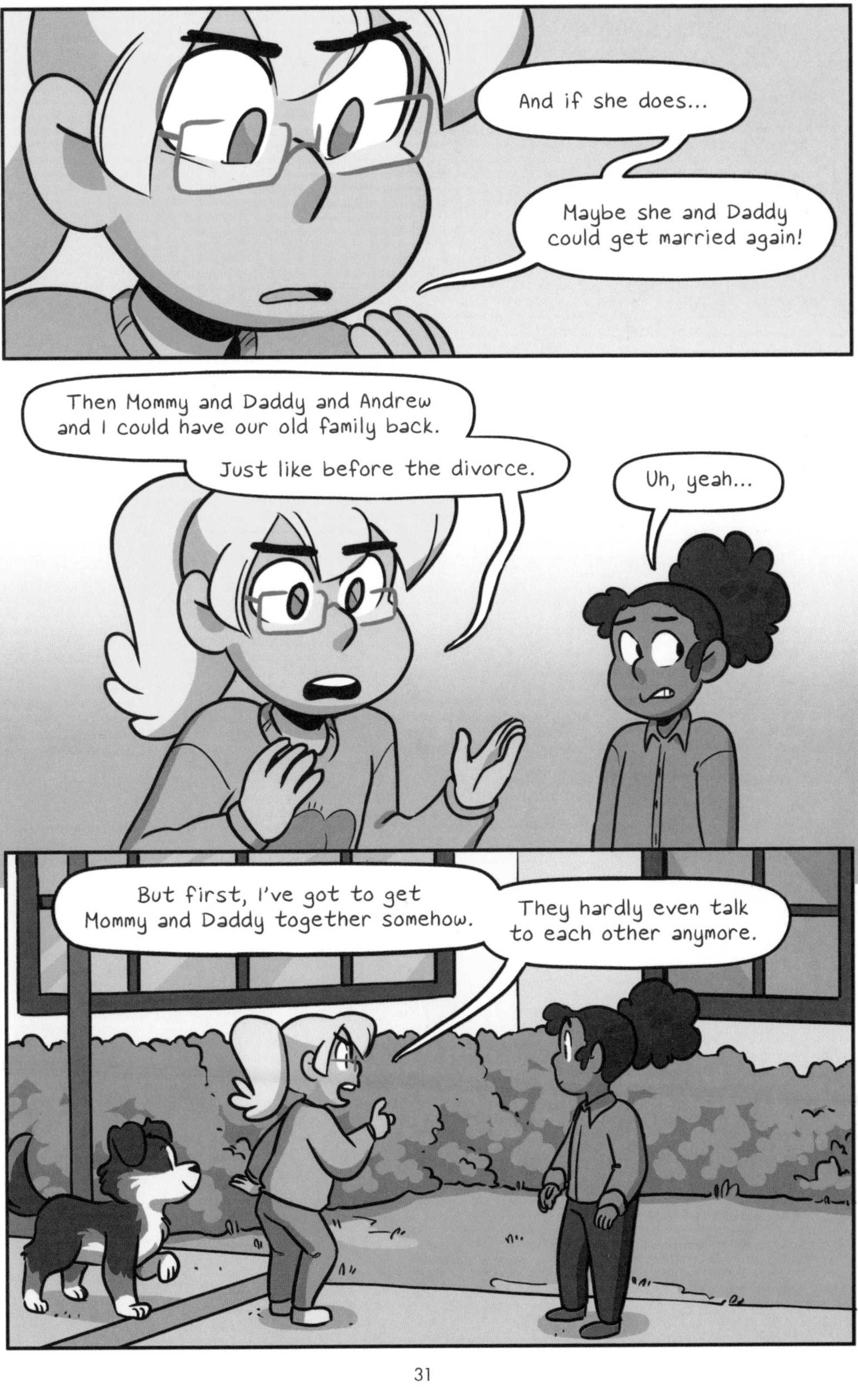
And if she does...
Maybe she and Daddy could get married again!
Then Mommy and Daddy and Andrew and I could have our old family back.
Just like before the divorce.
Uh, yeah...
But first, I've got to get Mommy and Daddy together somehow.
They hardly even talk to each other anymore.

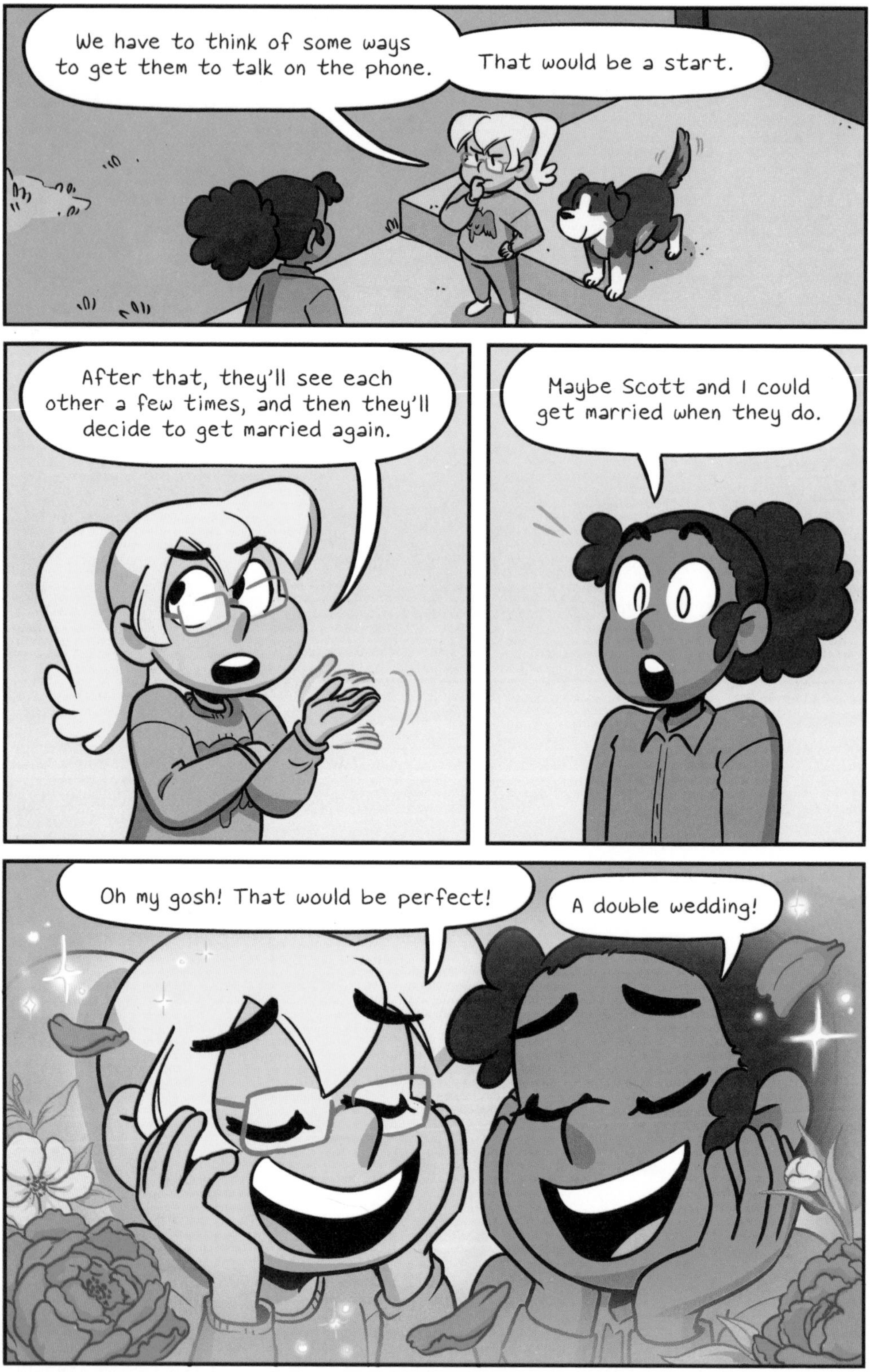
We have to think of some ways to get them to talk on the phone.
That would be a start.
After that, they'll see each other a few times, and then they'll decide to get married again.
Maybe Scott and I could get married when they do.
Oh my gosh! That would be perfect!
A double wedding!

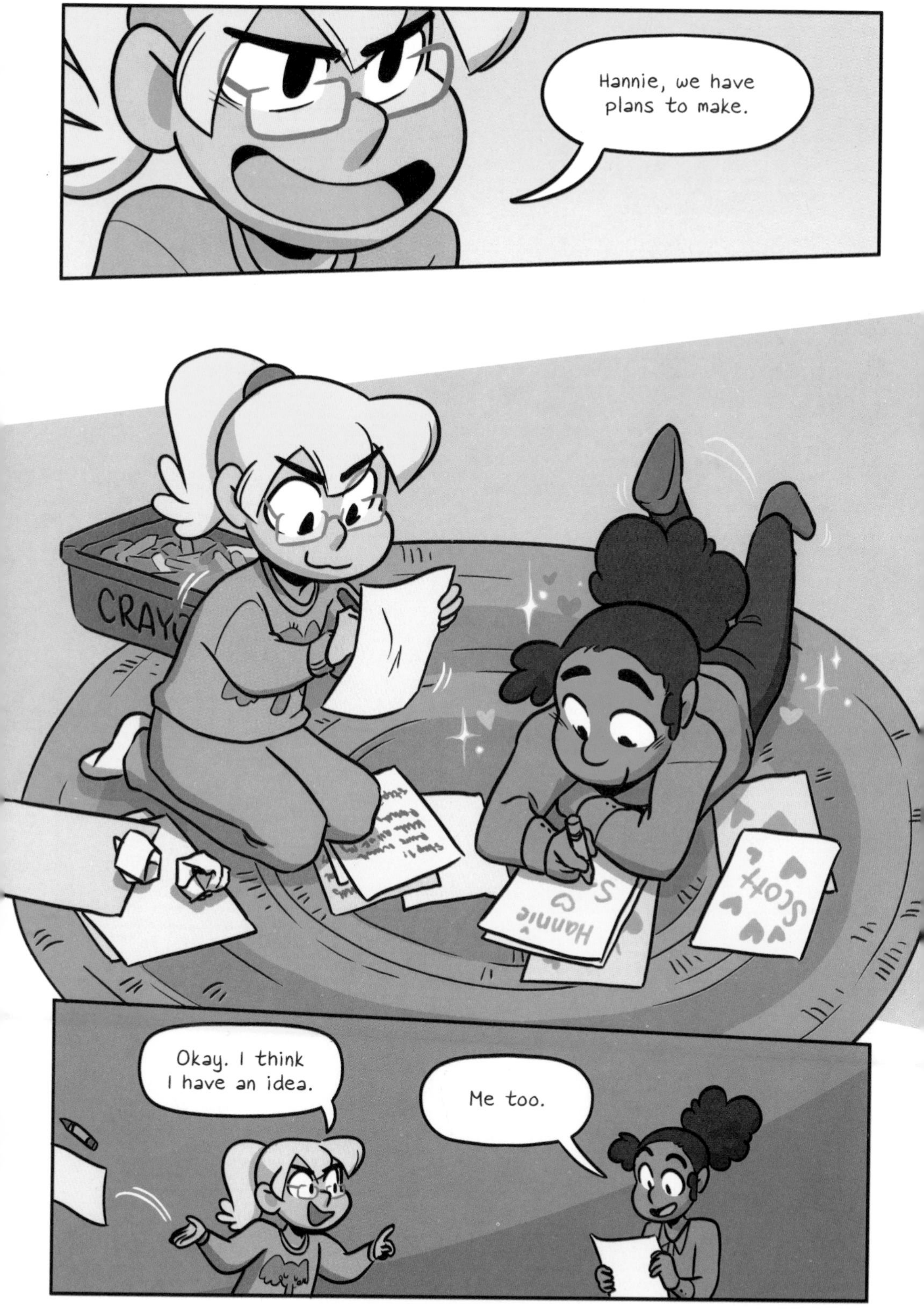
Hannie, we have plans to make.
Hannie
Scott
Okay. I think I have an idea.
Me too.

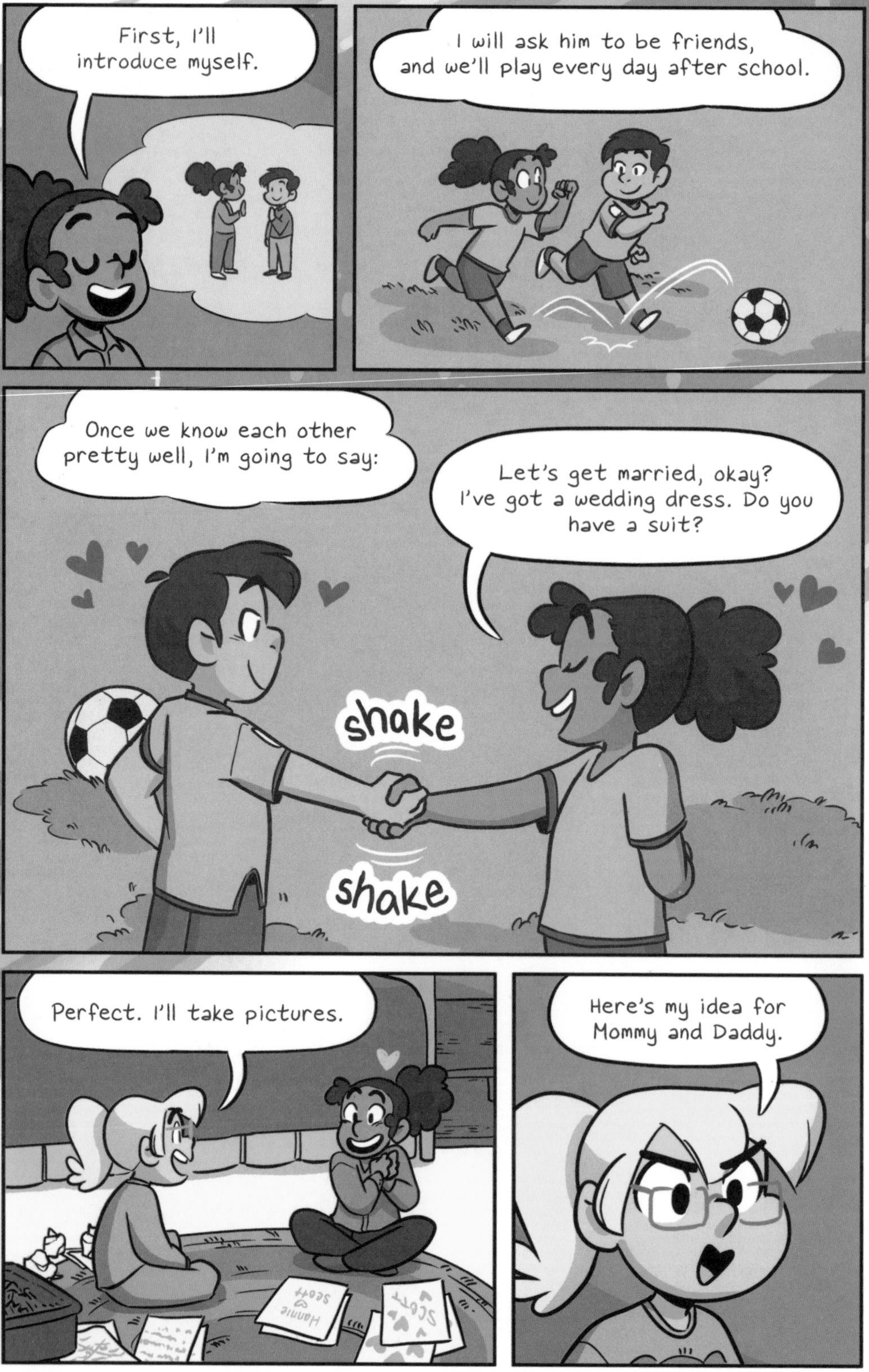
First, I'll introduce myself.
I will ask him to be friends, and we'll play every day after school.
Once we know each other pretty well, I'm going to say:
Let's get married, okay? I've got a wedding dress. Do you have a suit?
shake
shake
Perfect. I'll take pictures.
Here's my idea for Mommy and Daddy.

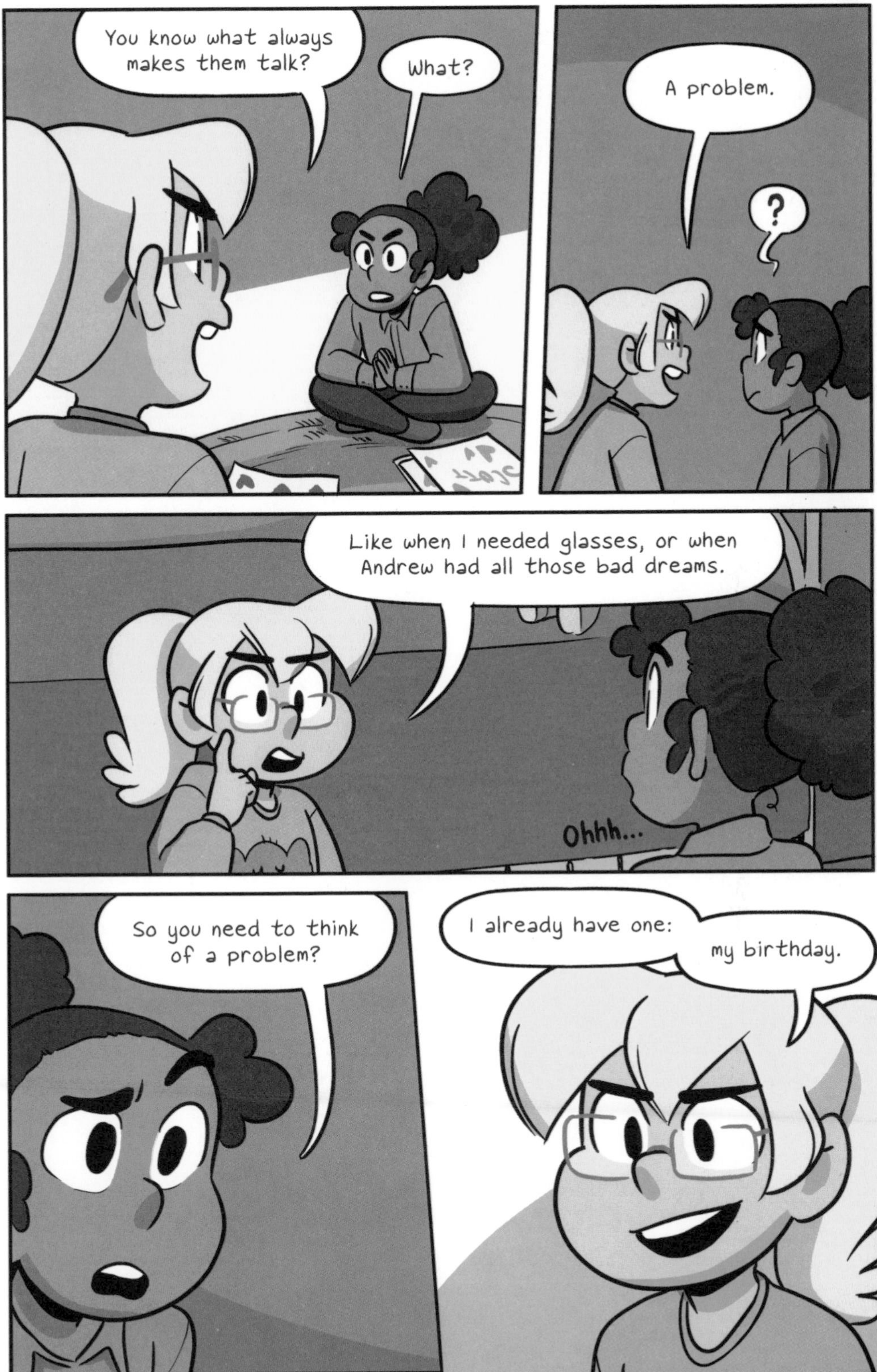
You know what always makes them talk?
What?
A problem.
?
Like when I needed glasses, or when Andrew had all those bad dreams.
Ohhh...
So you need to think of a problem?
I already have one:
my birthday.

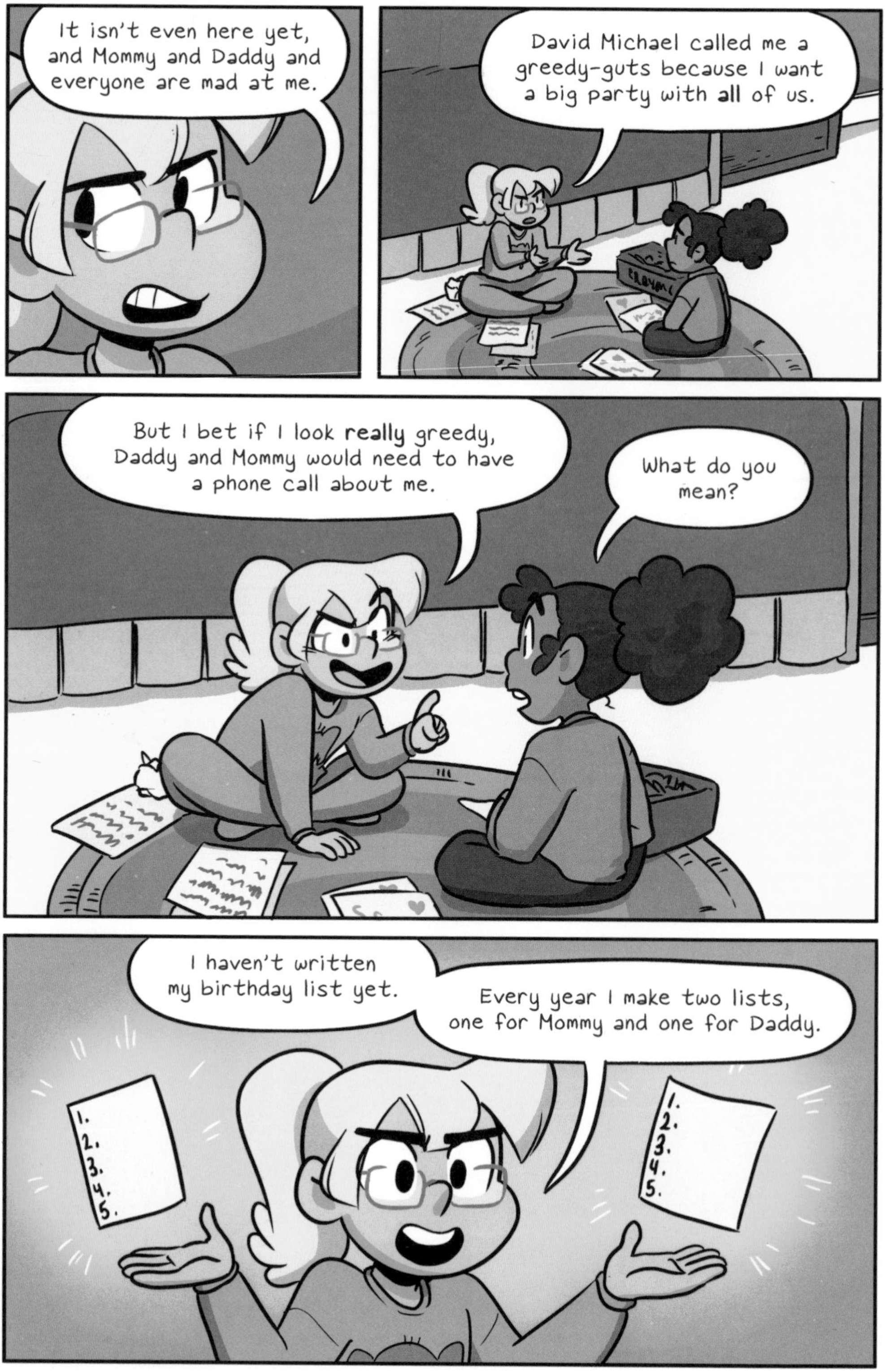
It isn't even here yet, and Mommy and Daddy and everyone are mad at me.
David Michael called me a greedy-guts because I want a big party with all of us.
But I bet if I look really greedy, Daddy and Mommy would need to have a phone call about me.
What do you mean?
I haven't written my birthday list yet.
Every year I make two lists, one for Mommy and one for Daddy.
1.
2.
3.
4.
5.
1.
2.
3.
4.
5.

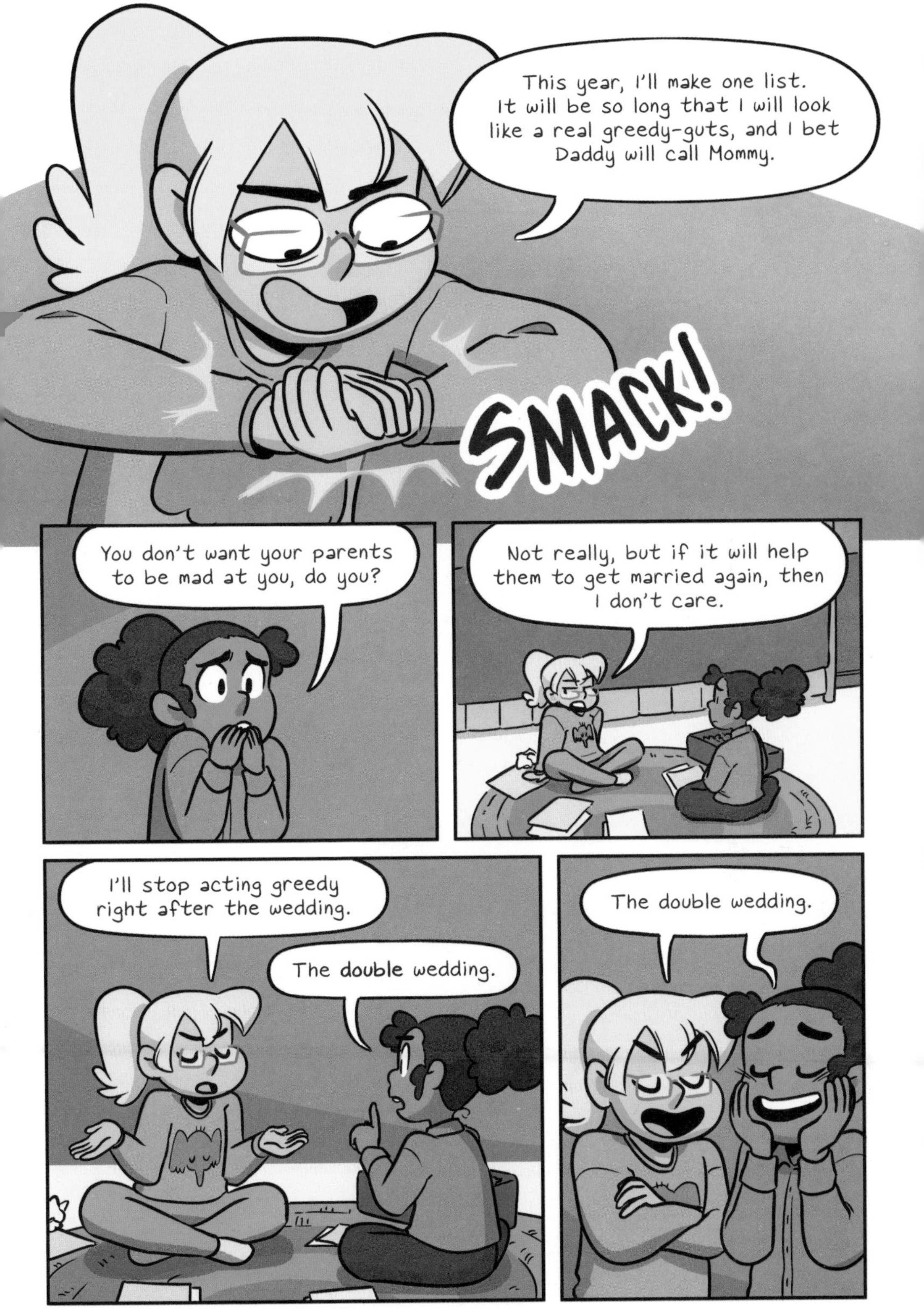
This year, I'll make one list. It will be so long that I will look like a real greedy-guts, and I bet Daddy will call Mommy.
SMACK!
You don't want your parents to be mad at you, do you?
Not really, but if it will help them to get married again, then I don't care.
I'll stop acting greedy right after the wedding.
The **double** wedding.
The double wedding.

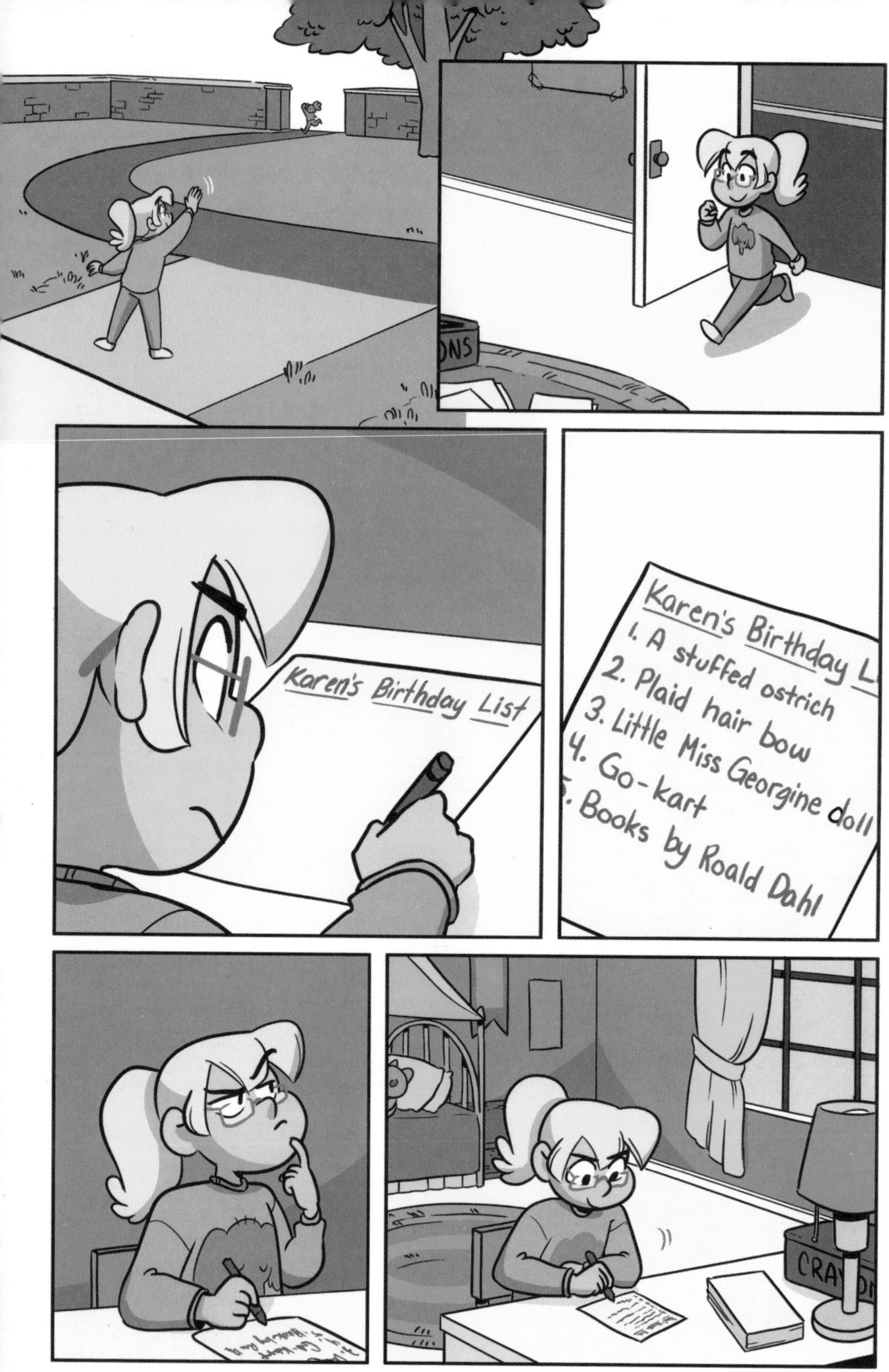
Karen's Birthday List
Karen's Birthday List
1. A stuffed ostrich
2. Plaid hair bow
3. Little Miss Georgine doll
4. Go-kart
5. Books by Roald Dahl
CRAY

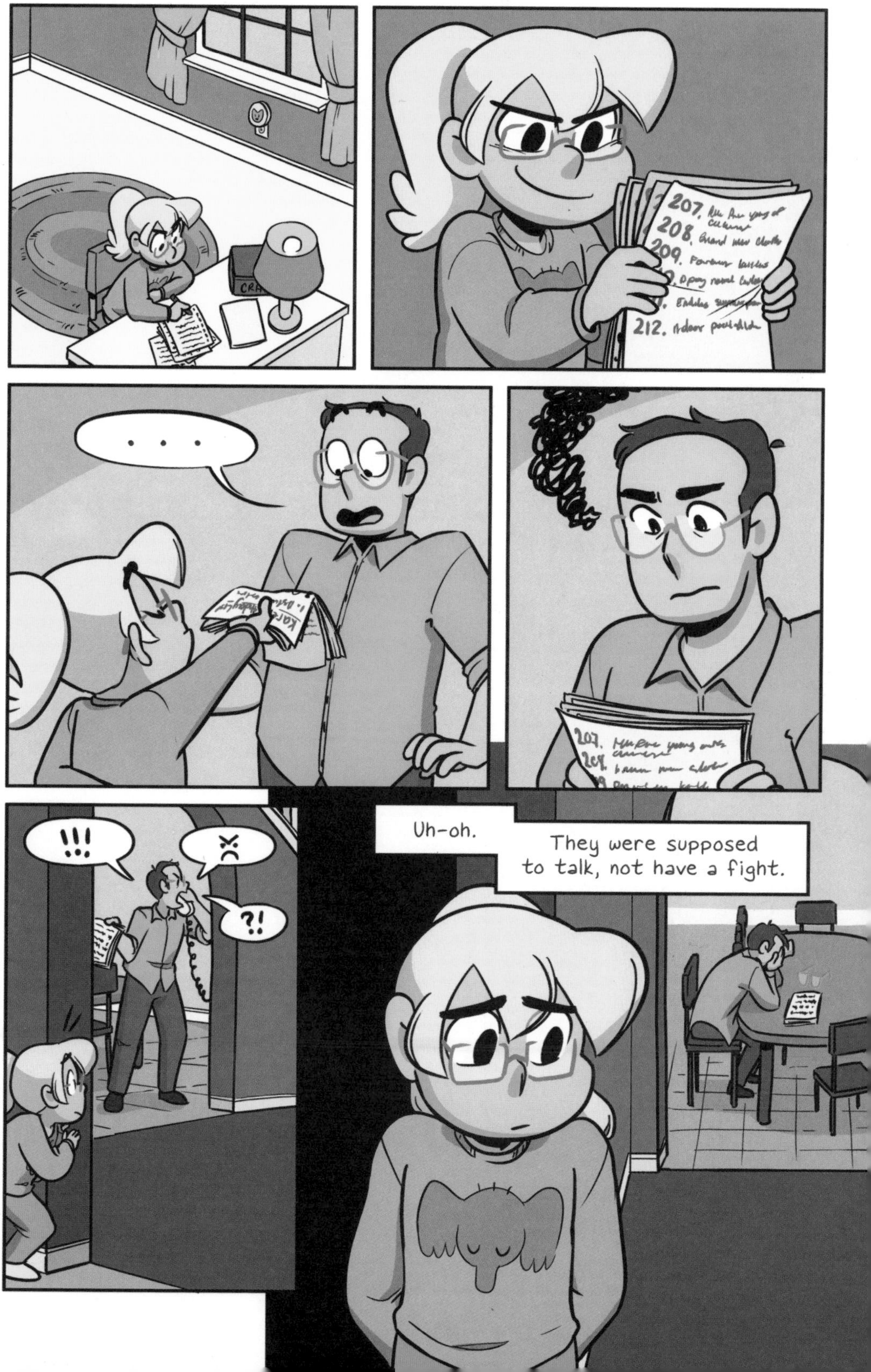
. . .
!!!
?!
Uh-oh.
They were supposed to talk, not have a fight.

CHAPTER 4

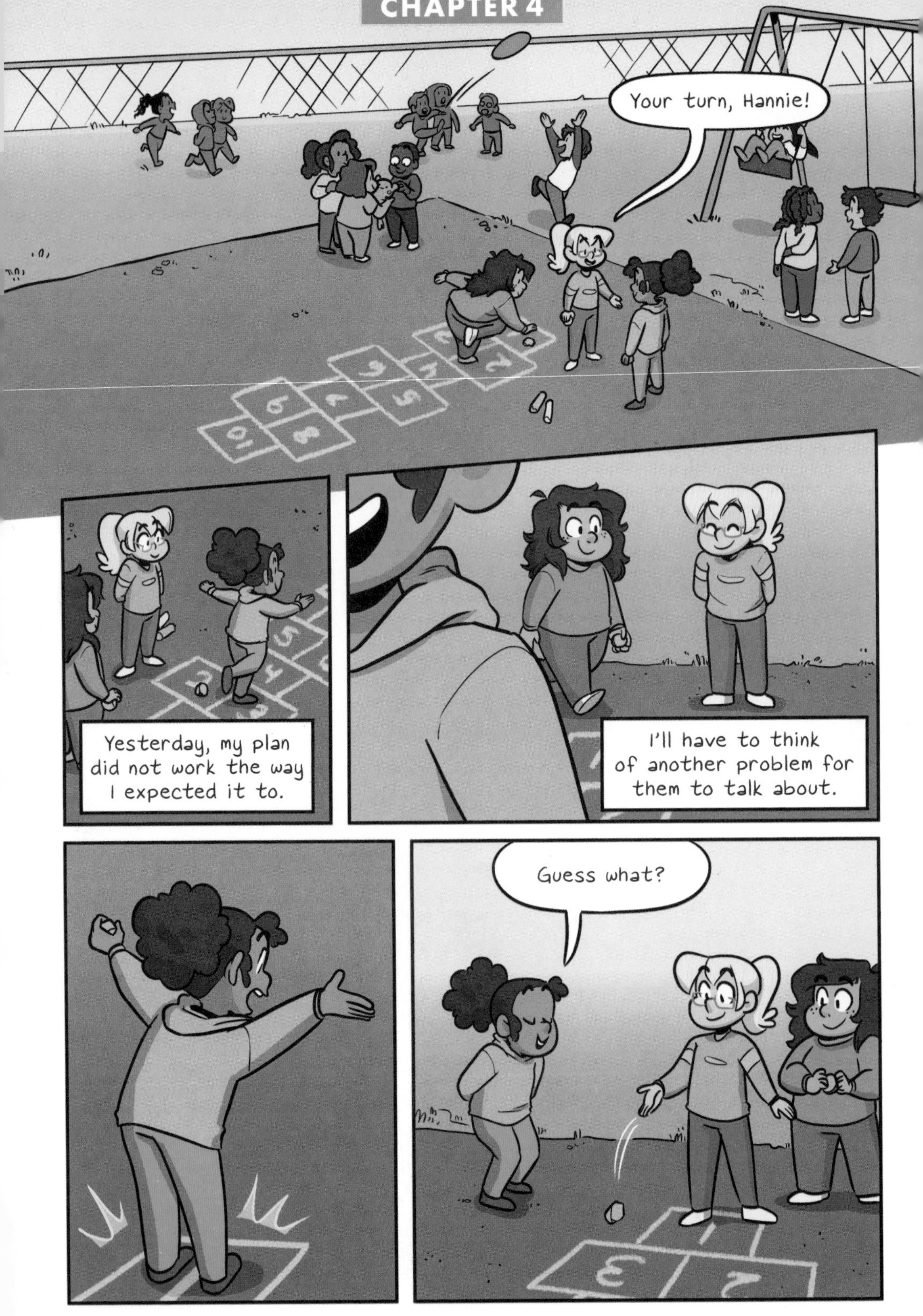
Your turn, Hannie!
Yesterday, my plan did not work the way I expected it to.
I'll have to think of another problem for them to talk about.
Guess what?

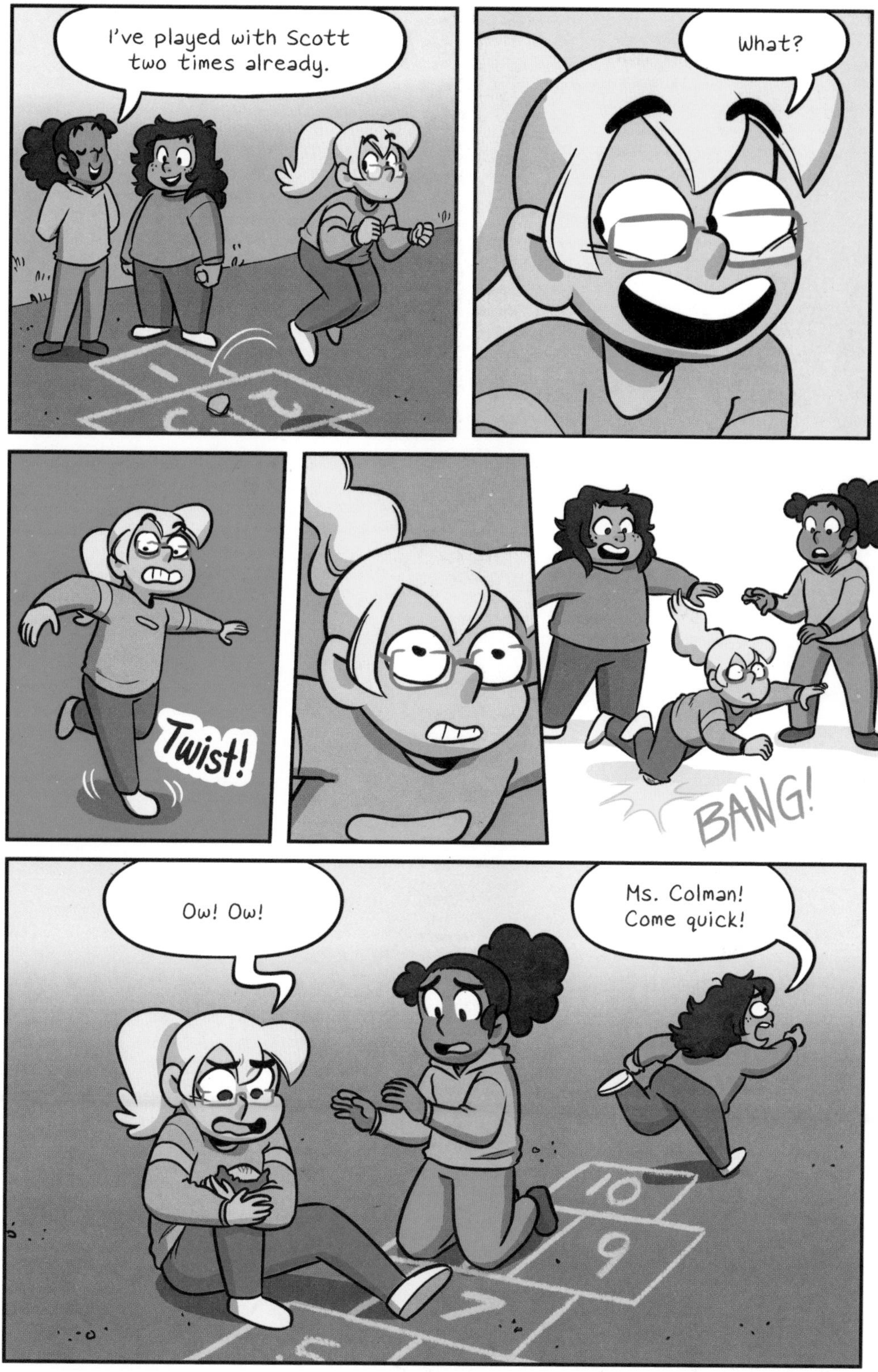
I've played with Scott two times already.
What?
Twist!
BANG!
Ow! Ow!
Ms. Colman! Come quick!

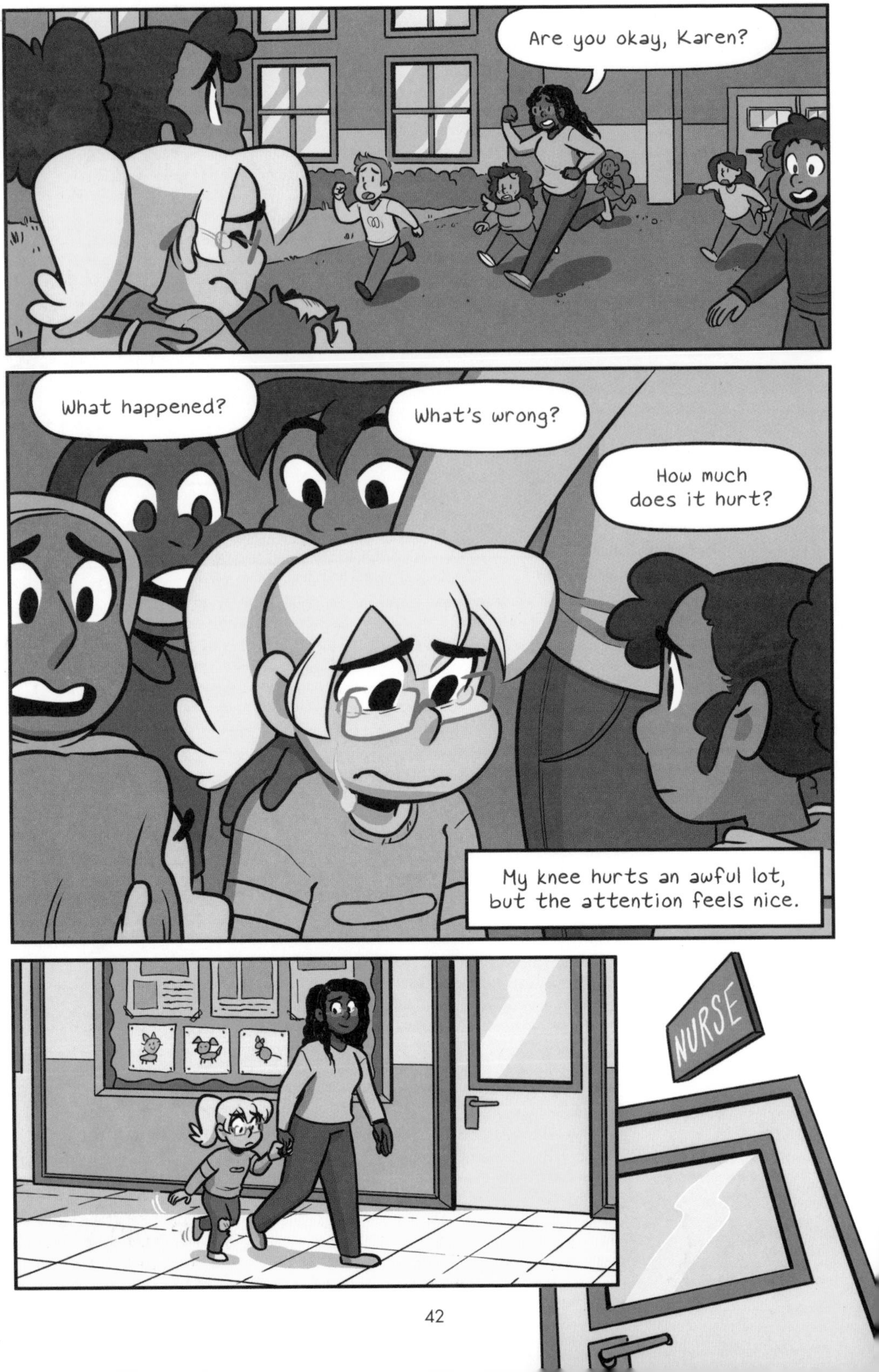
Are you okay, Karen?
What happened?
What's wrong?
How much does it hurt?
My knee hurts an awful lot, but the attention feels nice.
NURSE

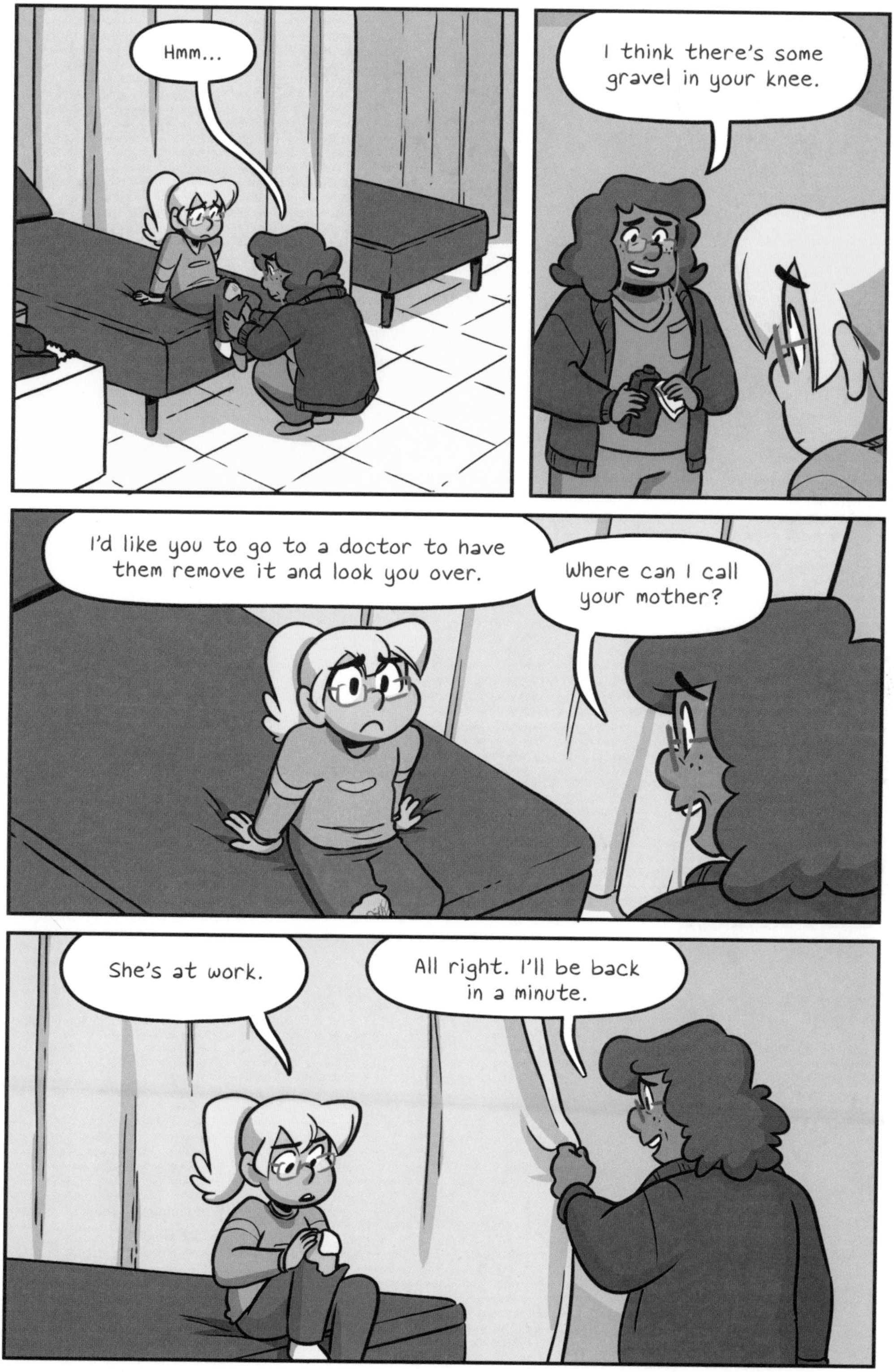
Hmm...
I think there's some gravel in your knee.
I'd like you to go to a doctor to have them remove it and look you over.
Where can I call your mother?
She's at work.
All right. I'll be back in a minute.

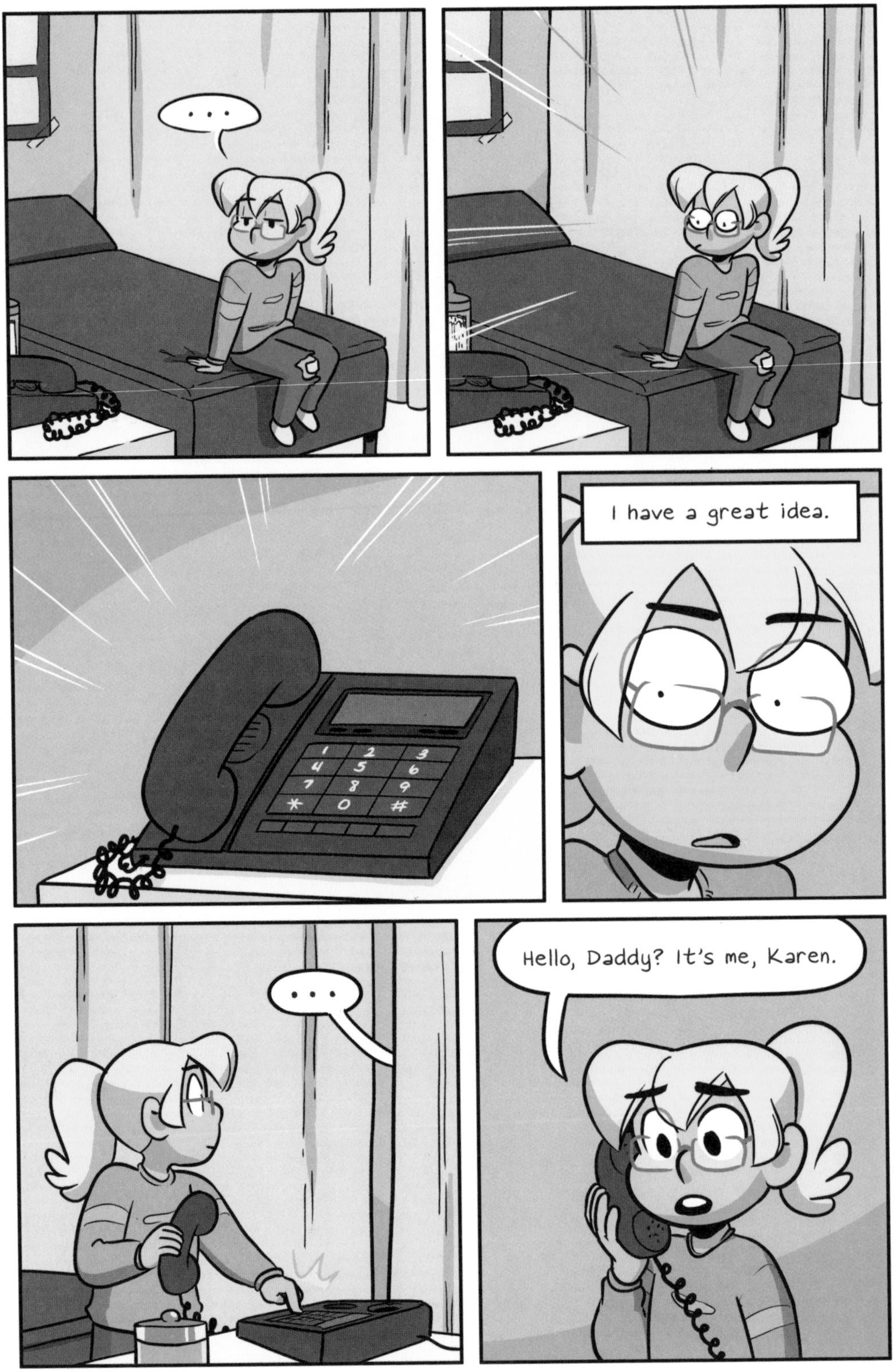
...
I have a great idea.
...
Hello, Daddy? It's me, Karen.

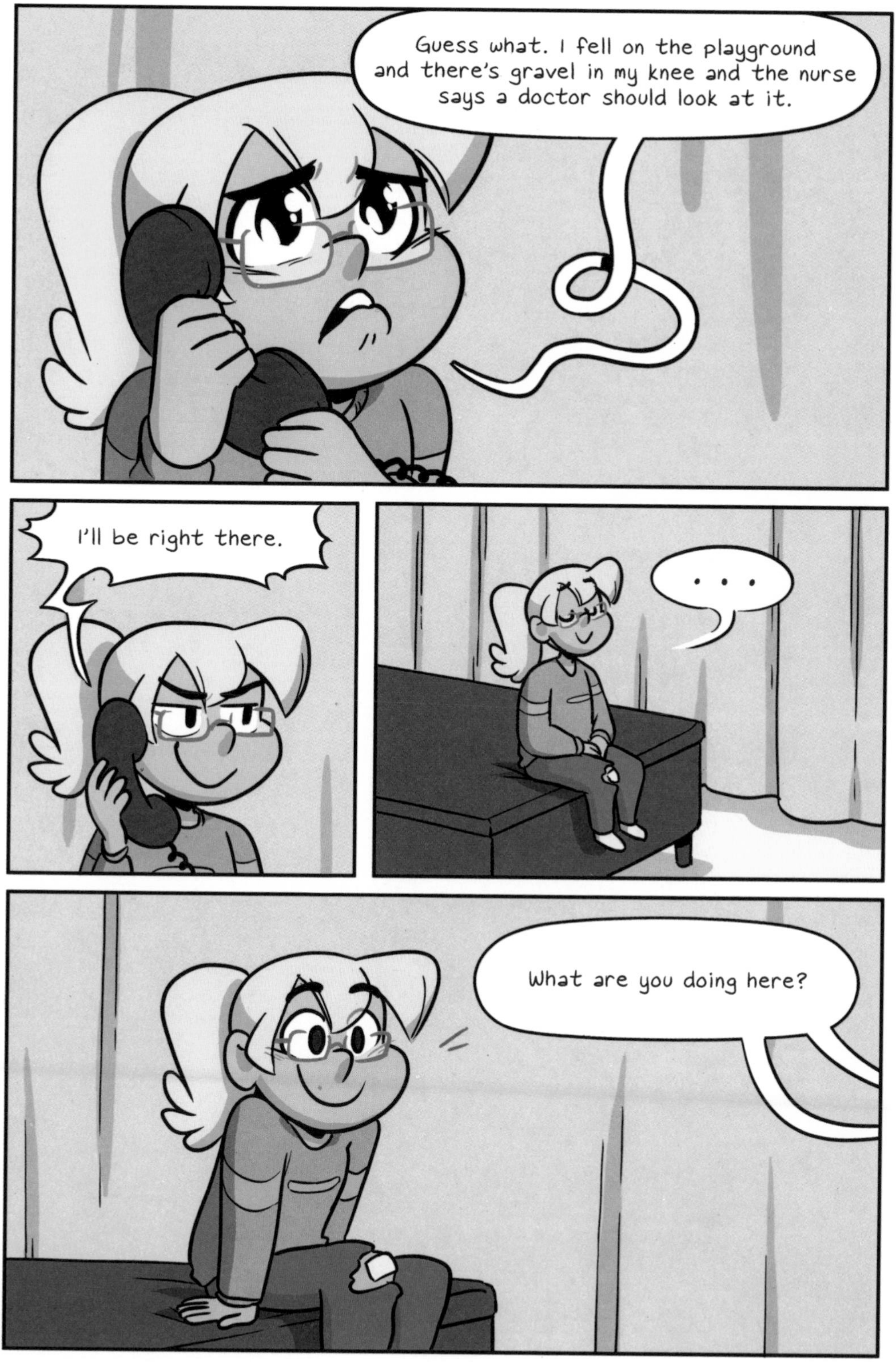
Guess what. I fell on the playground and there's gravel in my knee and the nurse says a doctor should look at it.
I'll be right there.
. . .
What are you doing here?

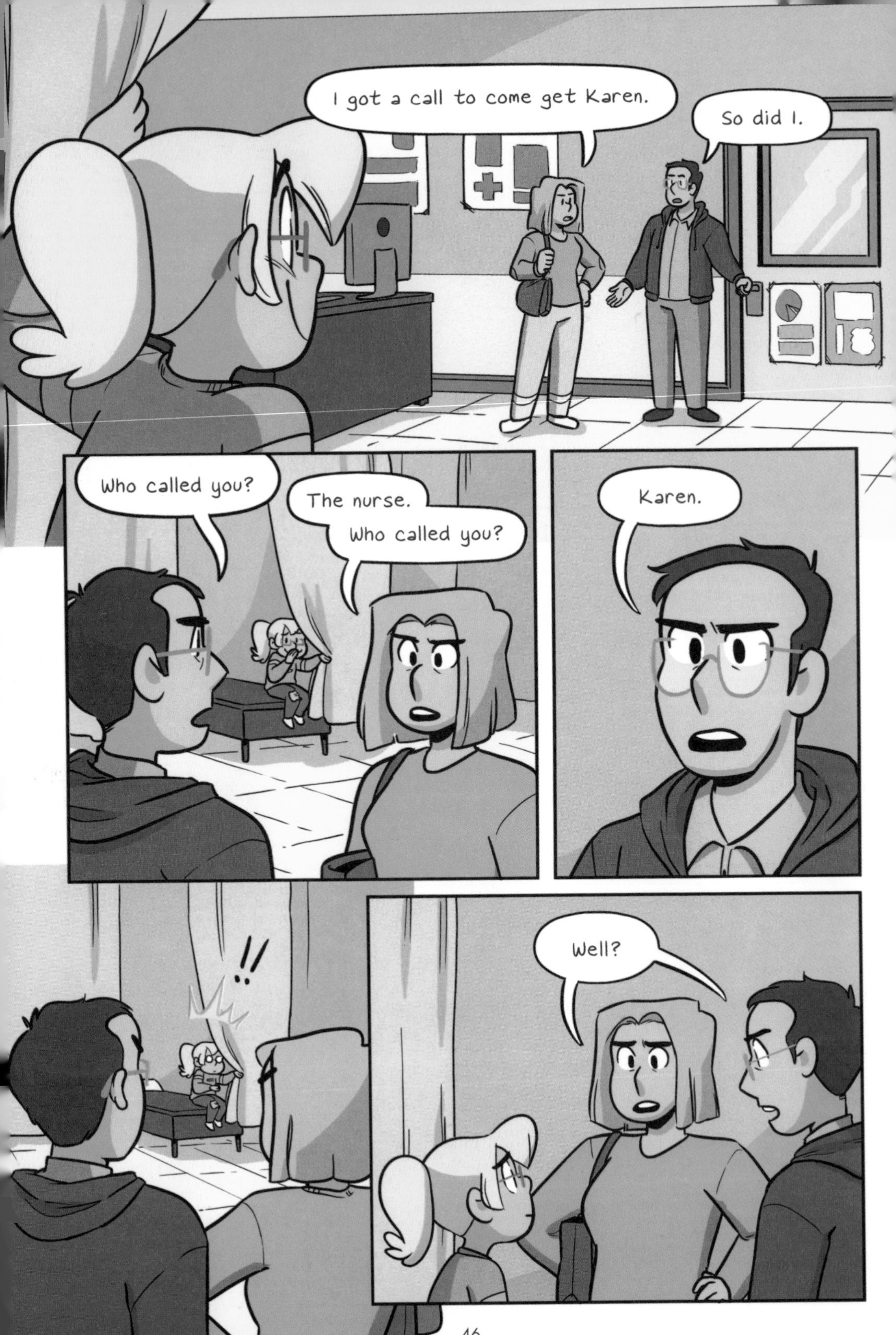
I got a call to come get Karen.
So did I.
Who called you?
The nurse.
Who called you?
Karen.
!!
Well?

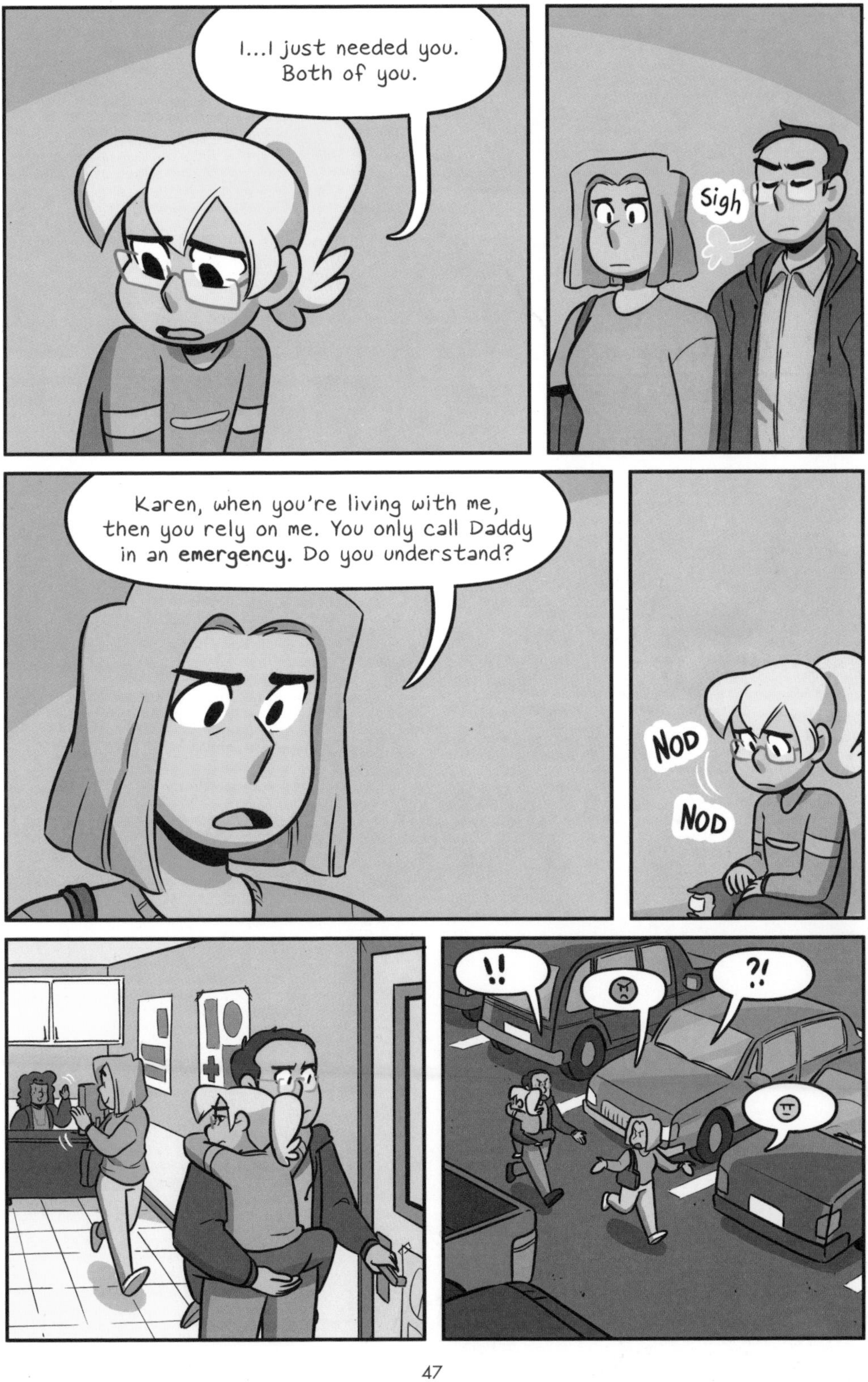
I...I just needed you. Both of you.
Sigh
Karen, when you're living with me, then you rely on me. You only call Daddy in an **emergency**. Do you understand?
NOD
NOD
!!
?!

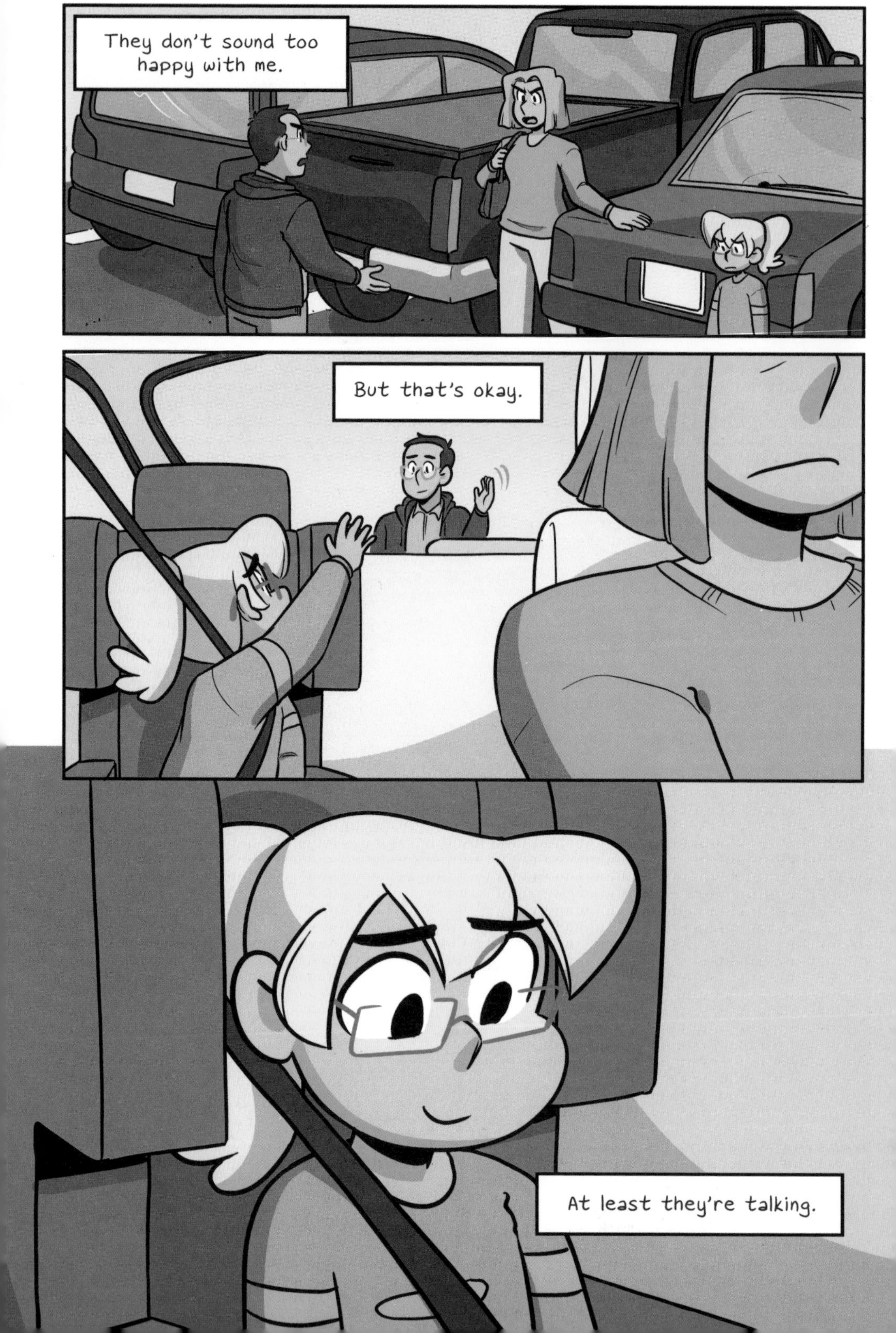
They don't sound too happy with me.
But that's okay.
At least they're talking.

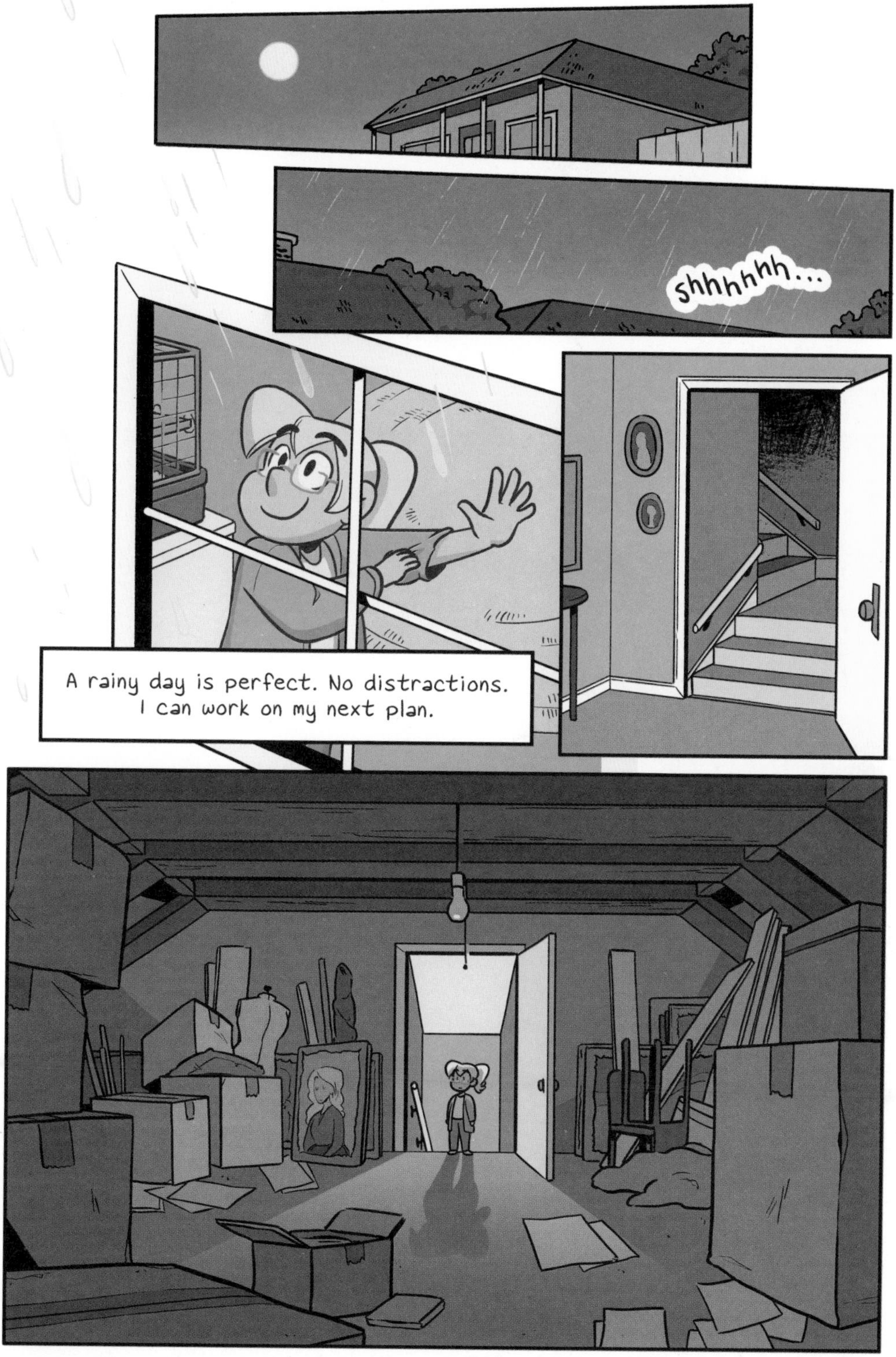
shhhhhh...
A rainy day is perfect. No distractions. I can work on my next plan.

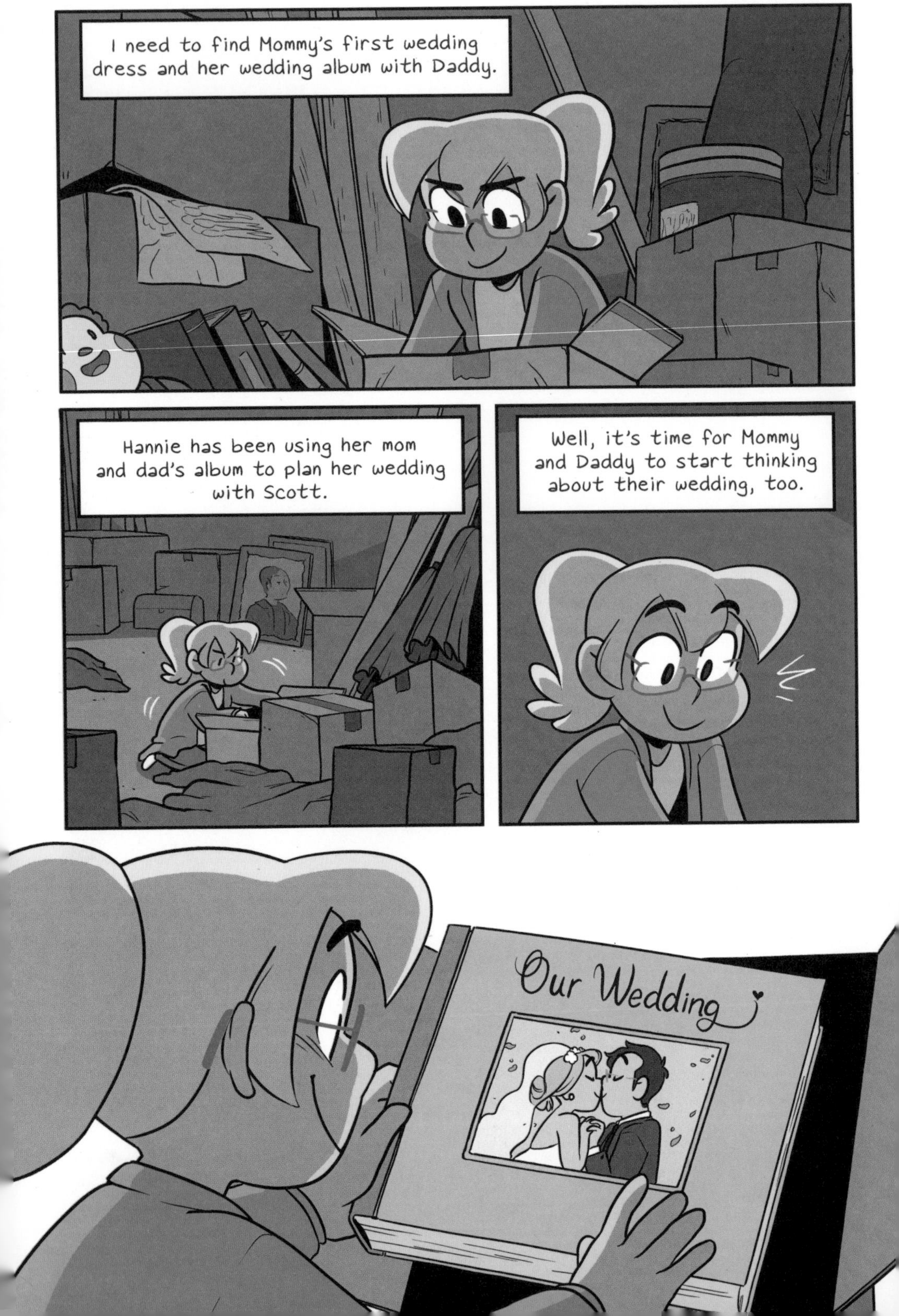
I need to find Mommy's first wedding dress and her wedding album with Daddy.
Hannie has been using her mom and dad's album to plan her wedding with Scott.
Well, it's time for Mommy and Daddy to start thinking about their wedding, too.
Our Wedding

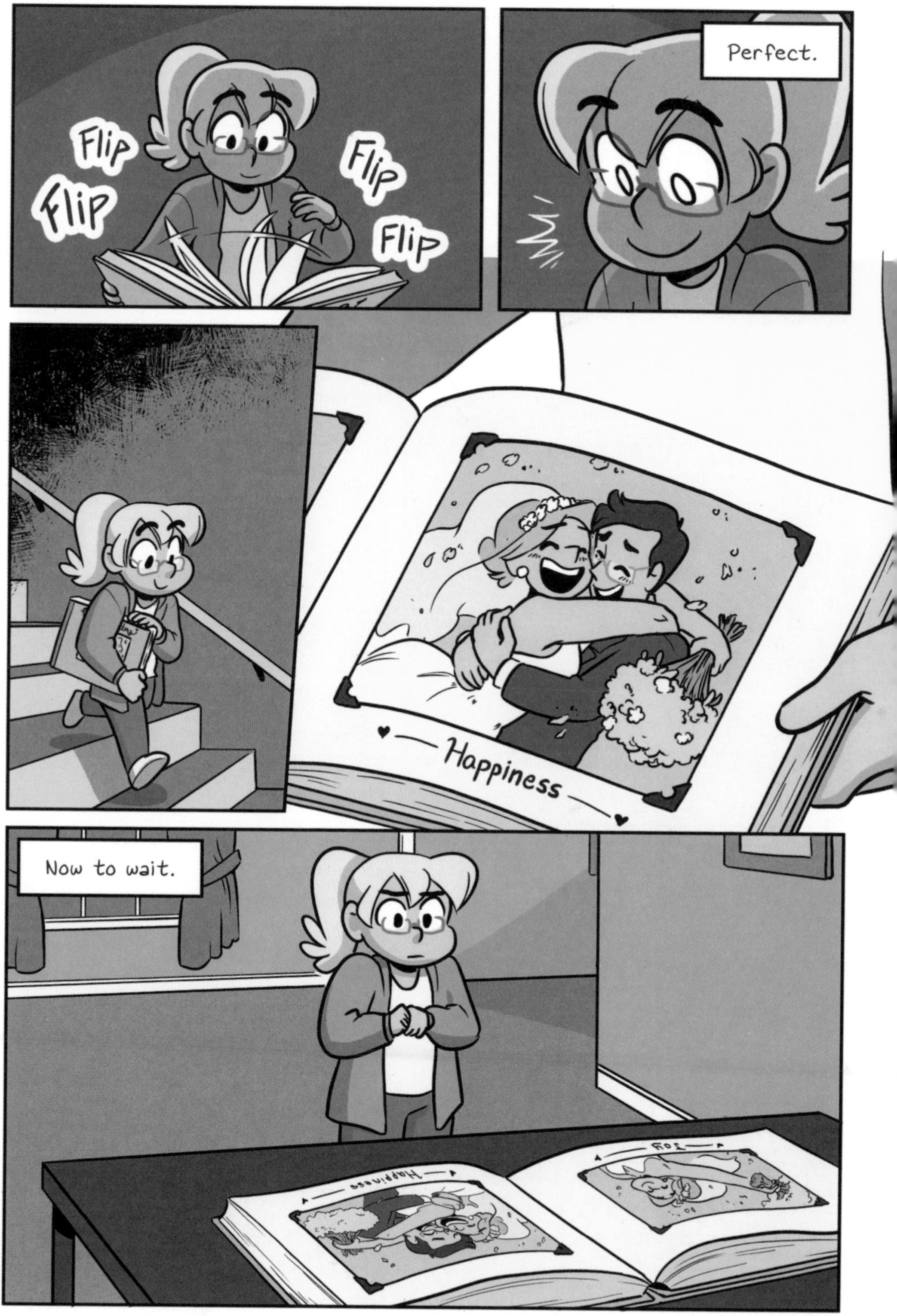
Flip
Flip
Flip
Flip
Perfect.
Happiness
Now to wait.

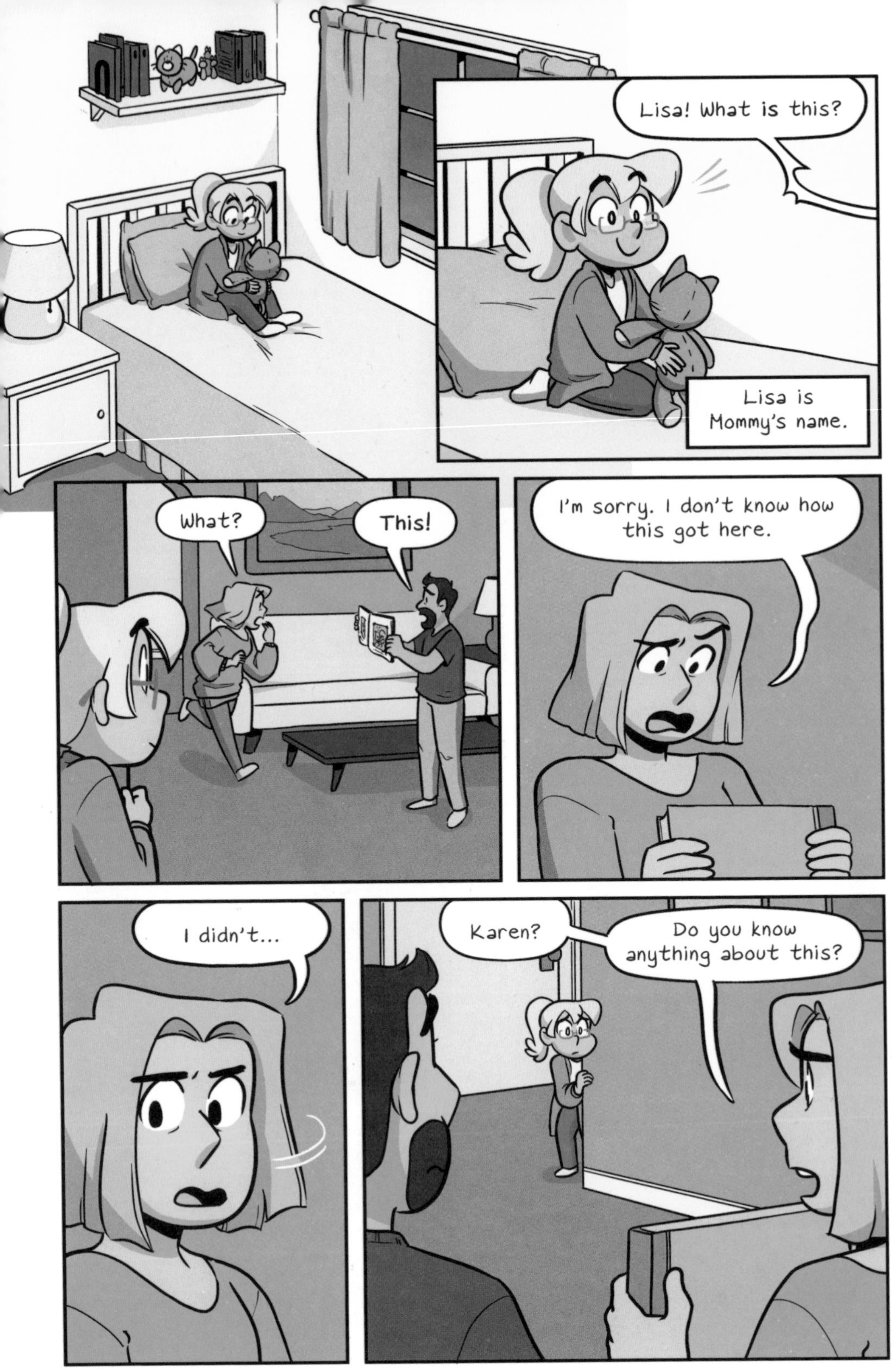
Lisa! What is this?
Lisa is Mommy's name.
What?
This!
I'm sorry. I don't know how this got here.
I didn't...
Karen?
Do you know anything about this?

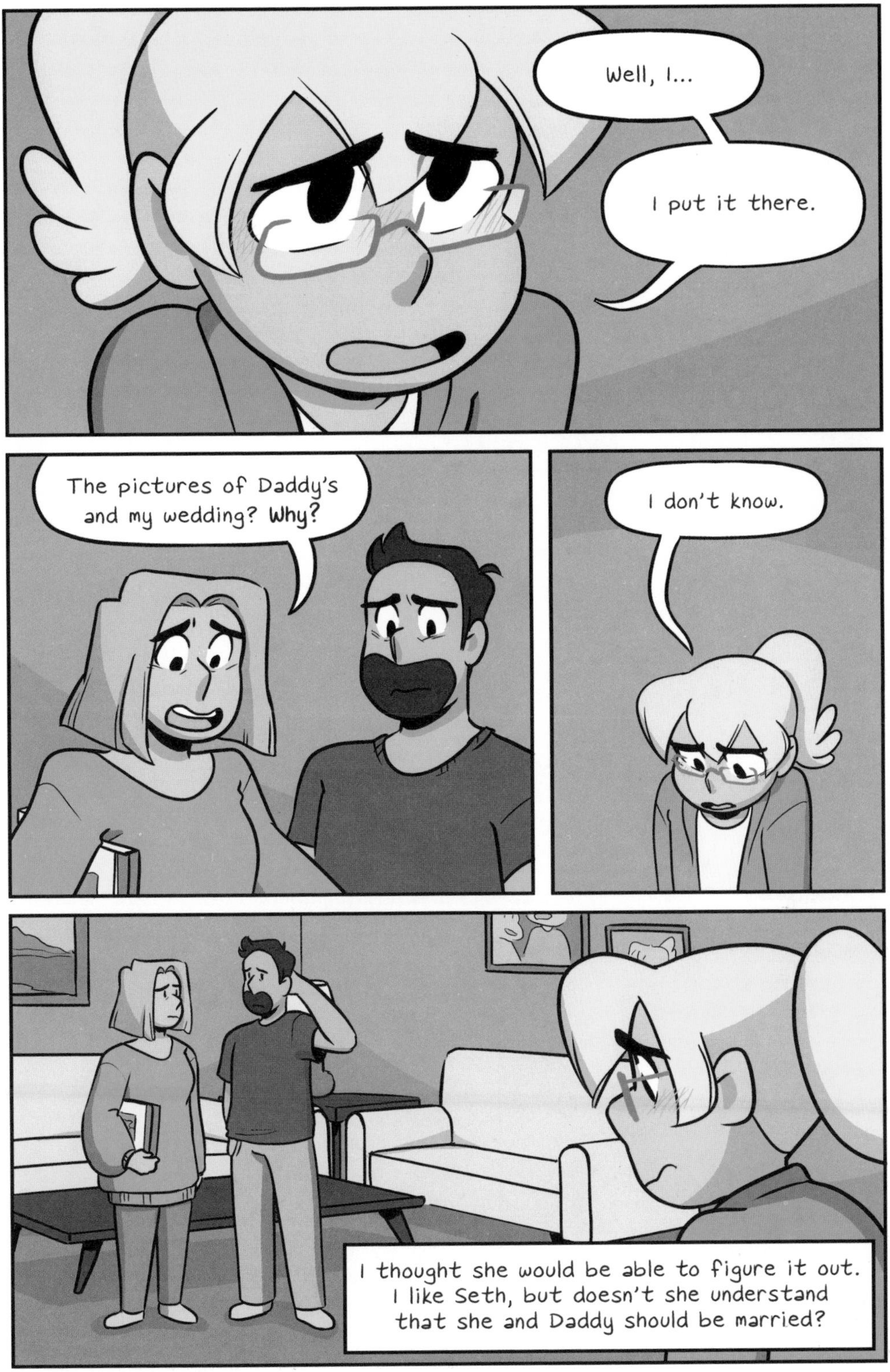
Well, I...
I put it there.
The pictures of Daddy's and my wedding? Why?
I don't know.
I thought she would be able to figure it out. I like Seth, but doesn't she understand that she and Daddy should be married?

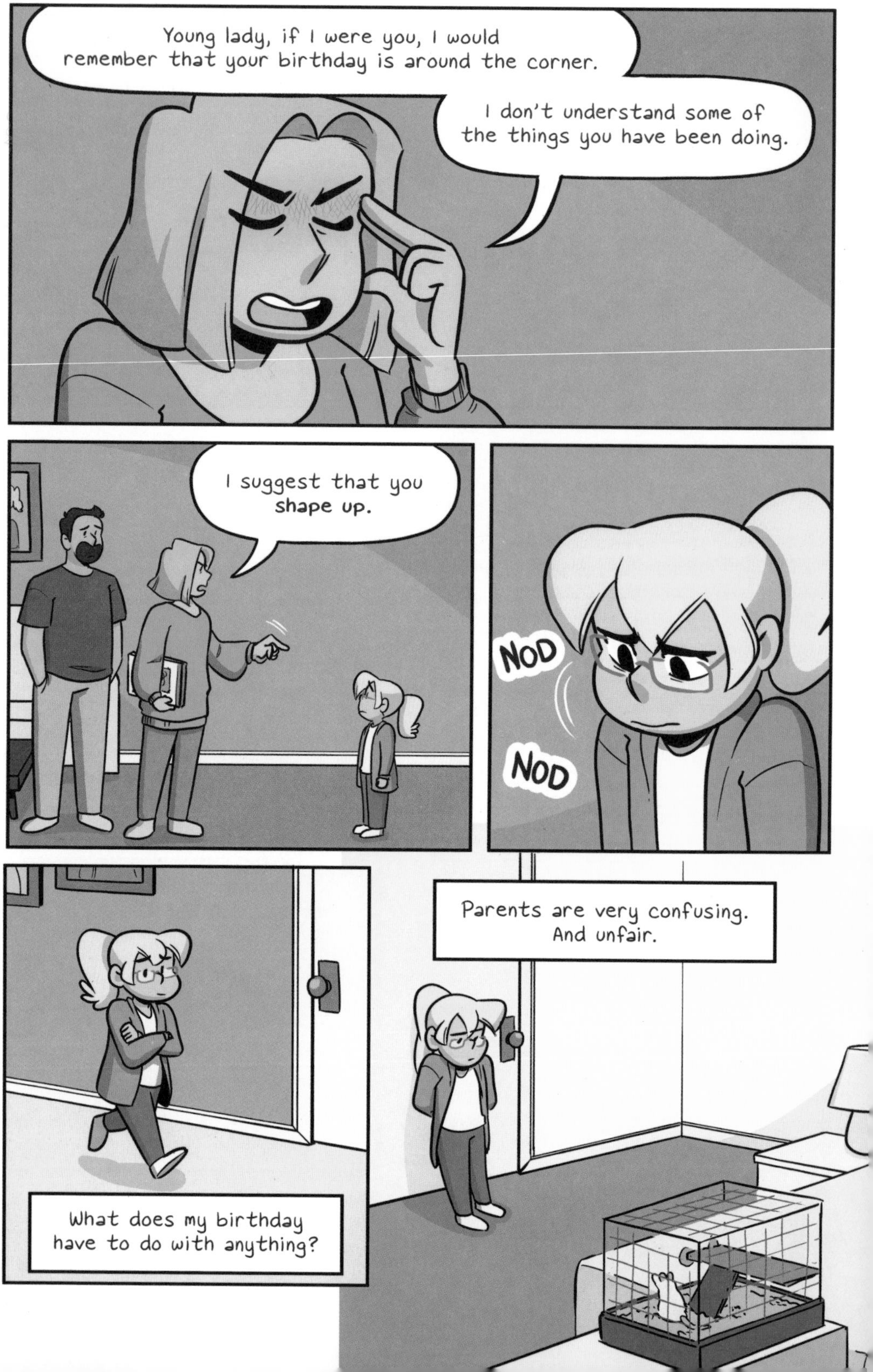
Young lady, if I were you, I would remember that your birthday is around the corner.
I don't understand some of the things you have been doing.
I suggest that you **shape up.**
NOD
NOD
Parents are very confusing. And unfair.
What does my birthday have to do with anything?

CHAPTER 5

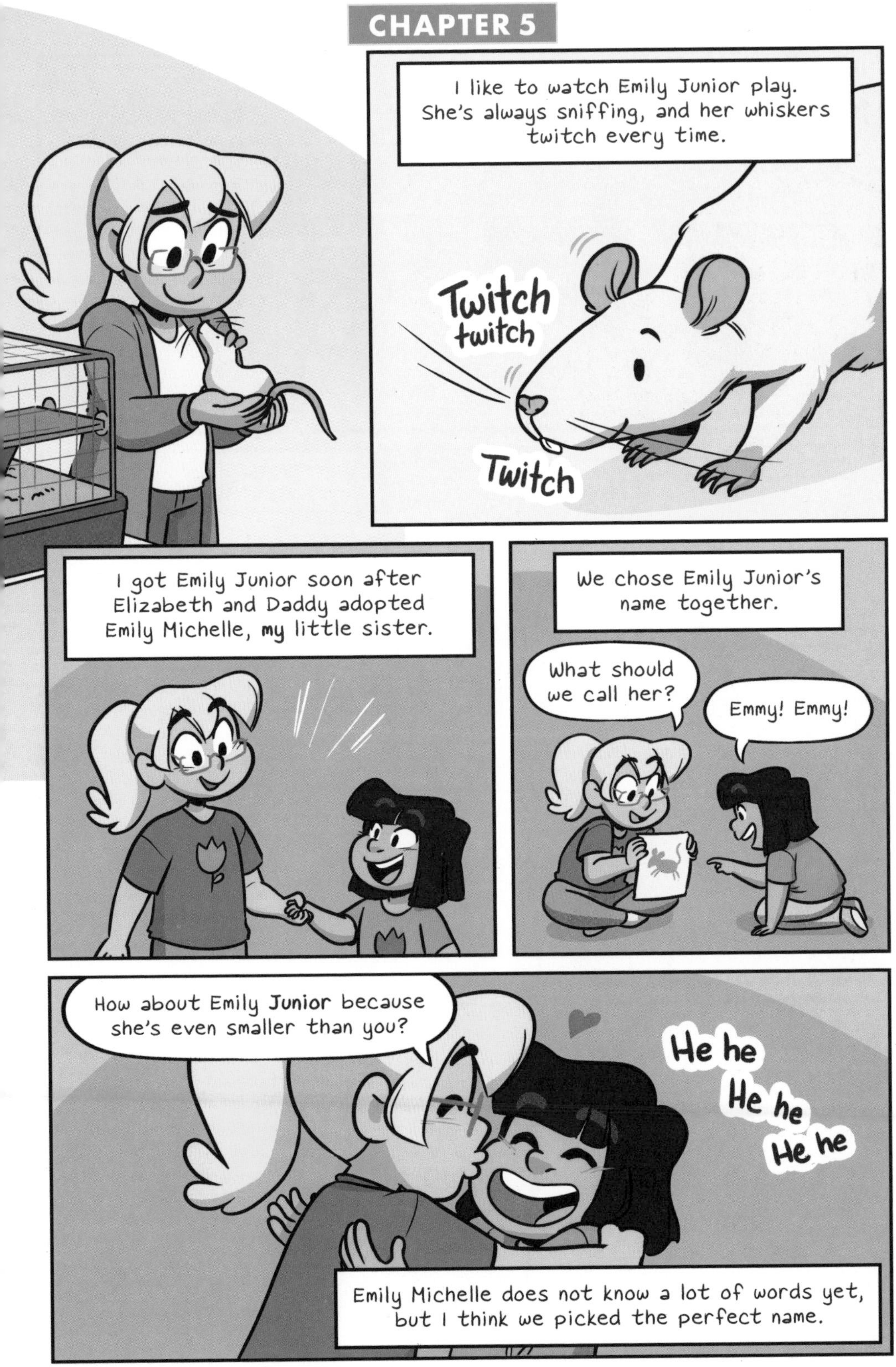

I like to watch Emily Junior play. She's always sniffing, and her whiskers twitch every time.
Twitch twitch
Twitch
I got Emily Junior soon after Elizabeth and Daddy adopted Emily Michelle, my little sister.
We chose Emily Junior's name together.
What should we call her?
Emmy! Emmy!
How about Emily **Junior** because she's even smaller than you?
He he
He he
He he
Emily Michelle does not know a lot of words yet, but I think we picked the perfect name.

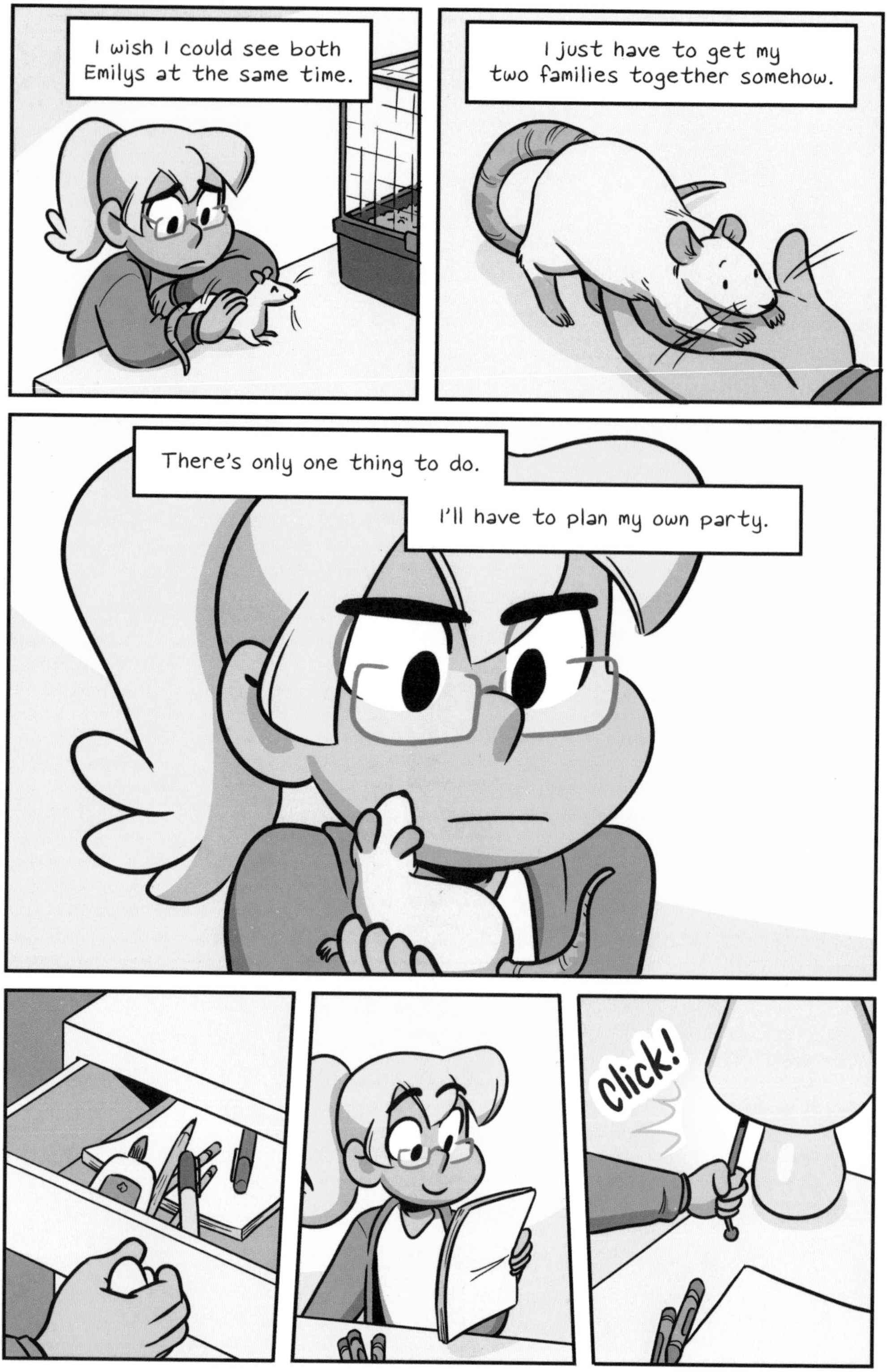
I wish I could see both Emilys at the same time.
I just have to get my two families together somehow.
There's only one thing to do.
I'll have to plan my own party.
Click!

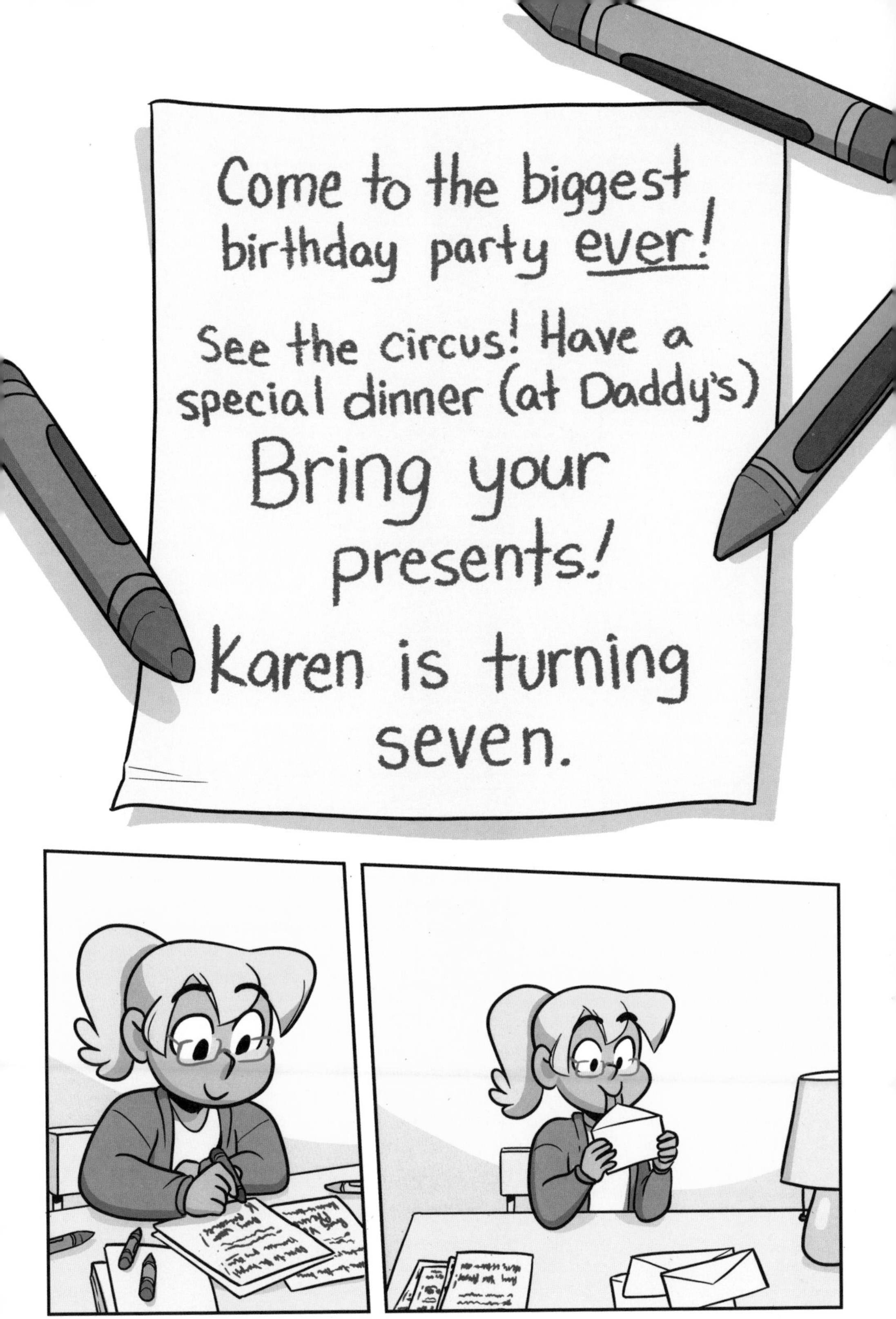

Come to the biggest birthday party ever!
See the circus! Have a special dinner (at Daddy's)
Bring your presents!
Karen is turning seven.

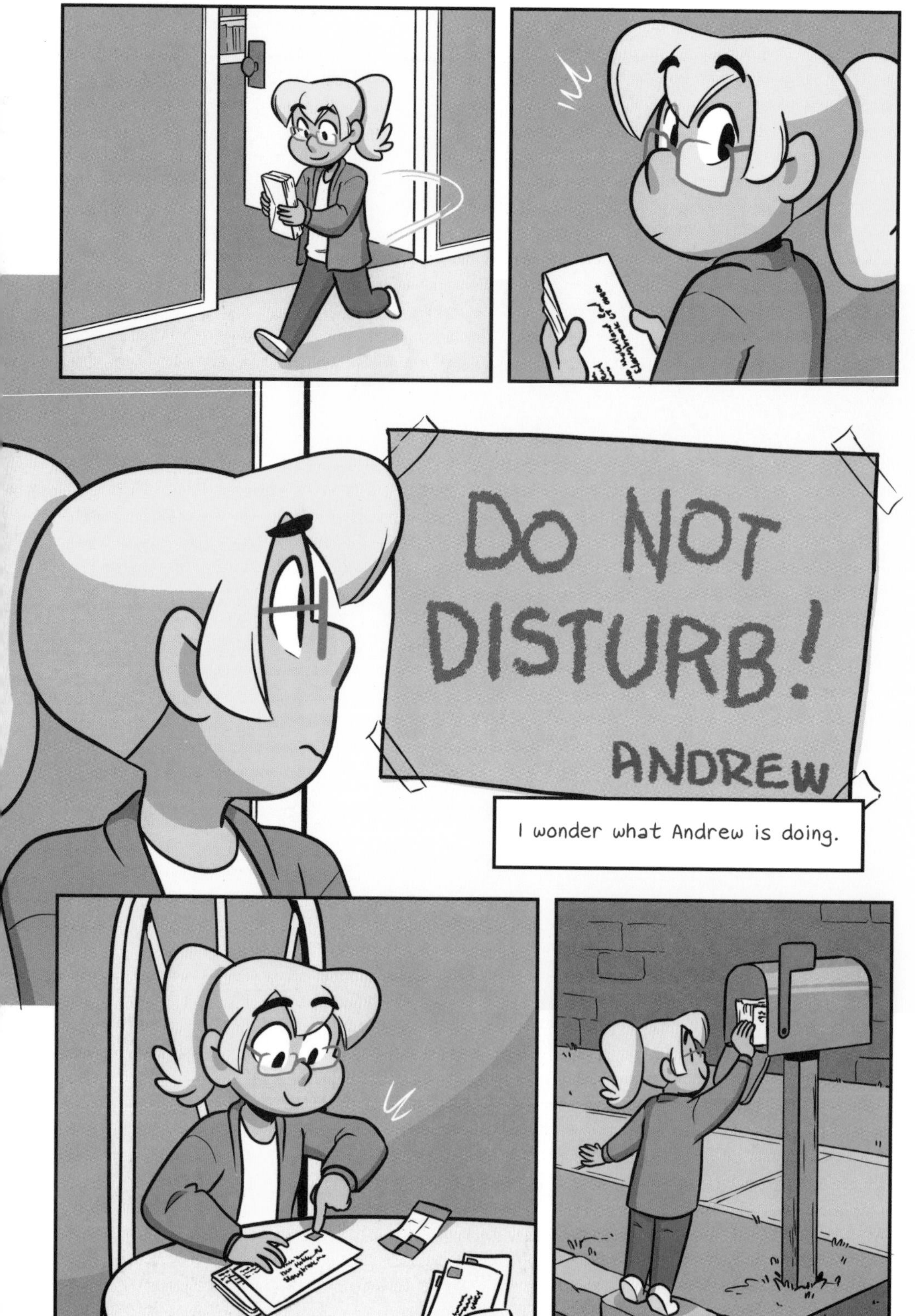
DO NOT DISTURB!
ANDREW
I wonder what Andrew is doing.

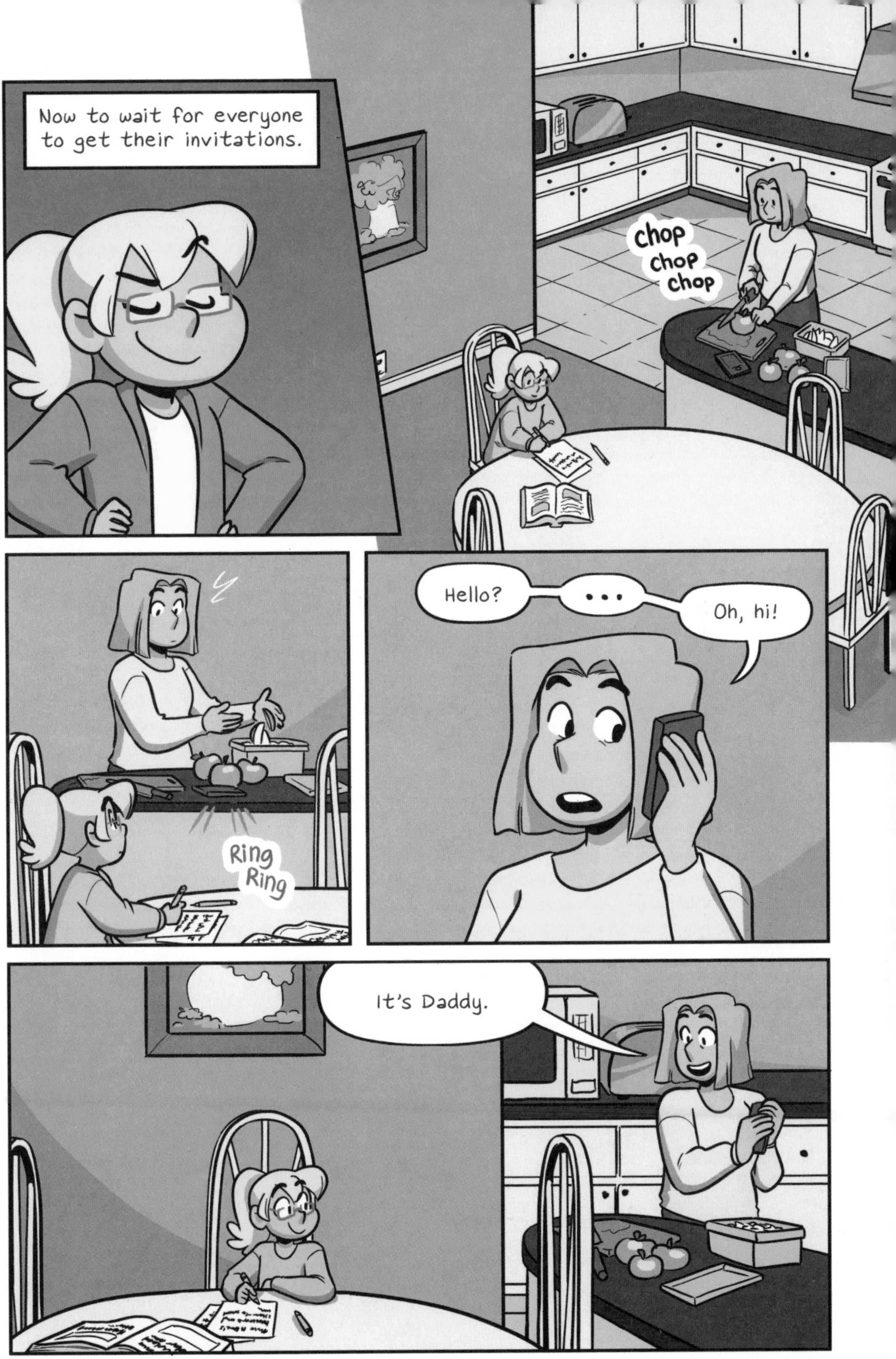
Now to wait for everyone to get their invitations.
chop
chop
chop
Ring
Ring
Hello?
...
Oh, hi!
It's Daddy.

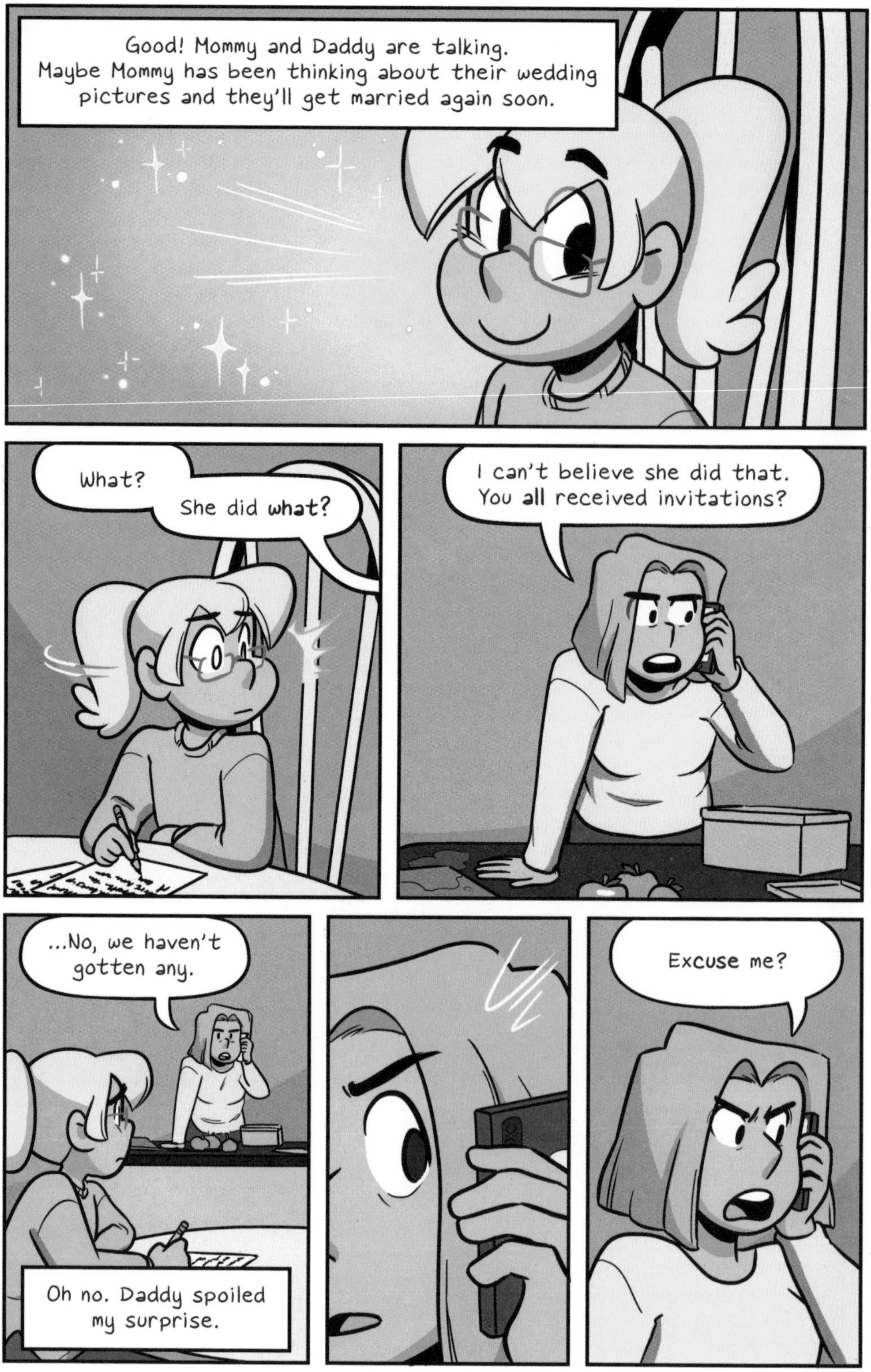
Good! Mommy and Daddy are talking. Maybe Mommy has been thinking about their wedding pictures and they'll get married again soon.
What?
She did **what**?
I can't believe she did that. You **all** received invitations?
...No, we haven't gotten any.
Oh no. Daddy spoiled my surprise.
Excuse me?

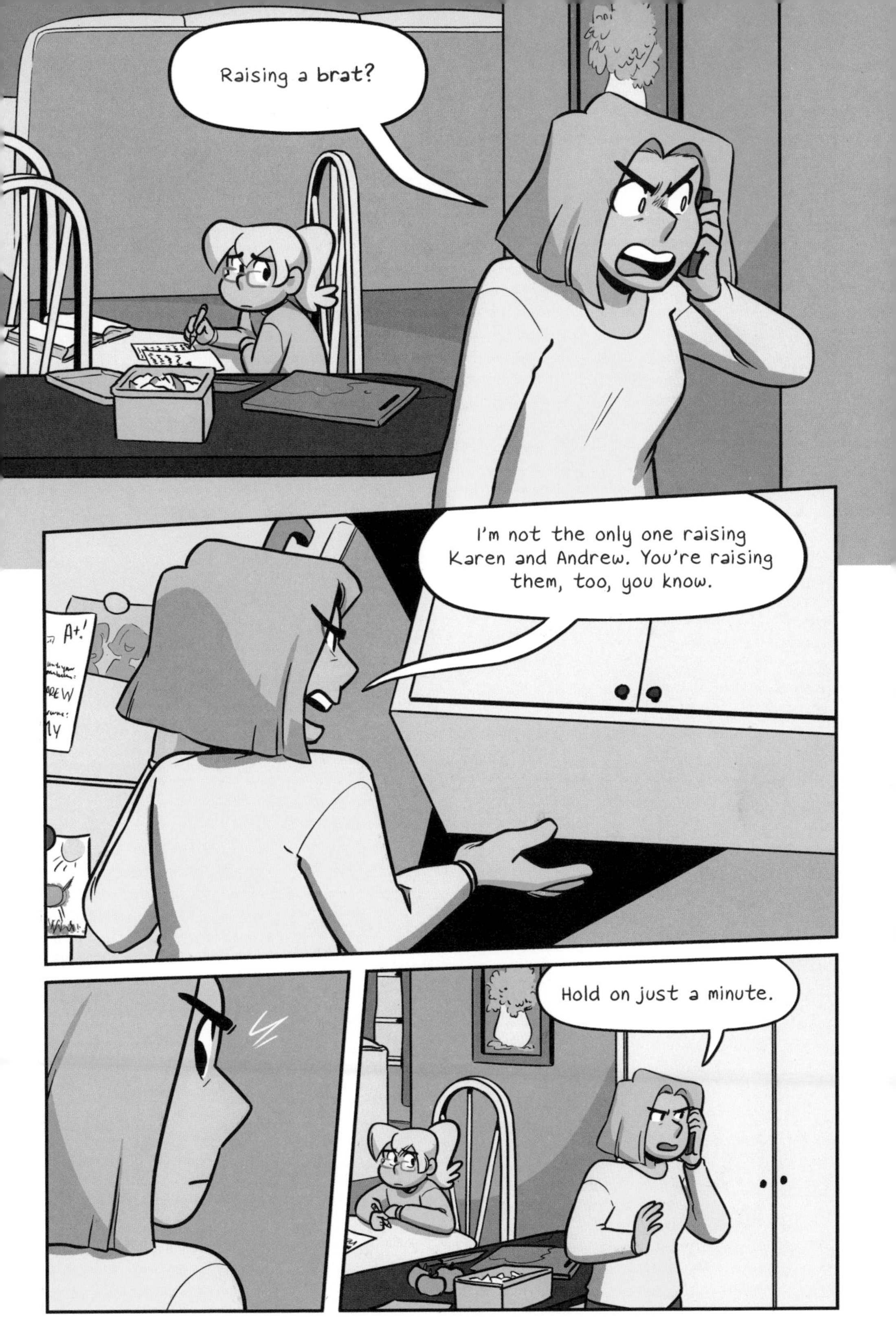
Raising a brat?
I'm not the only one raising Karen and Andrew. You're raising them, too, you know.
Hold on just a minute.

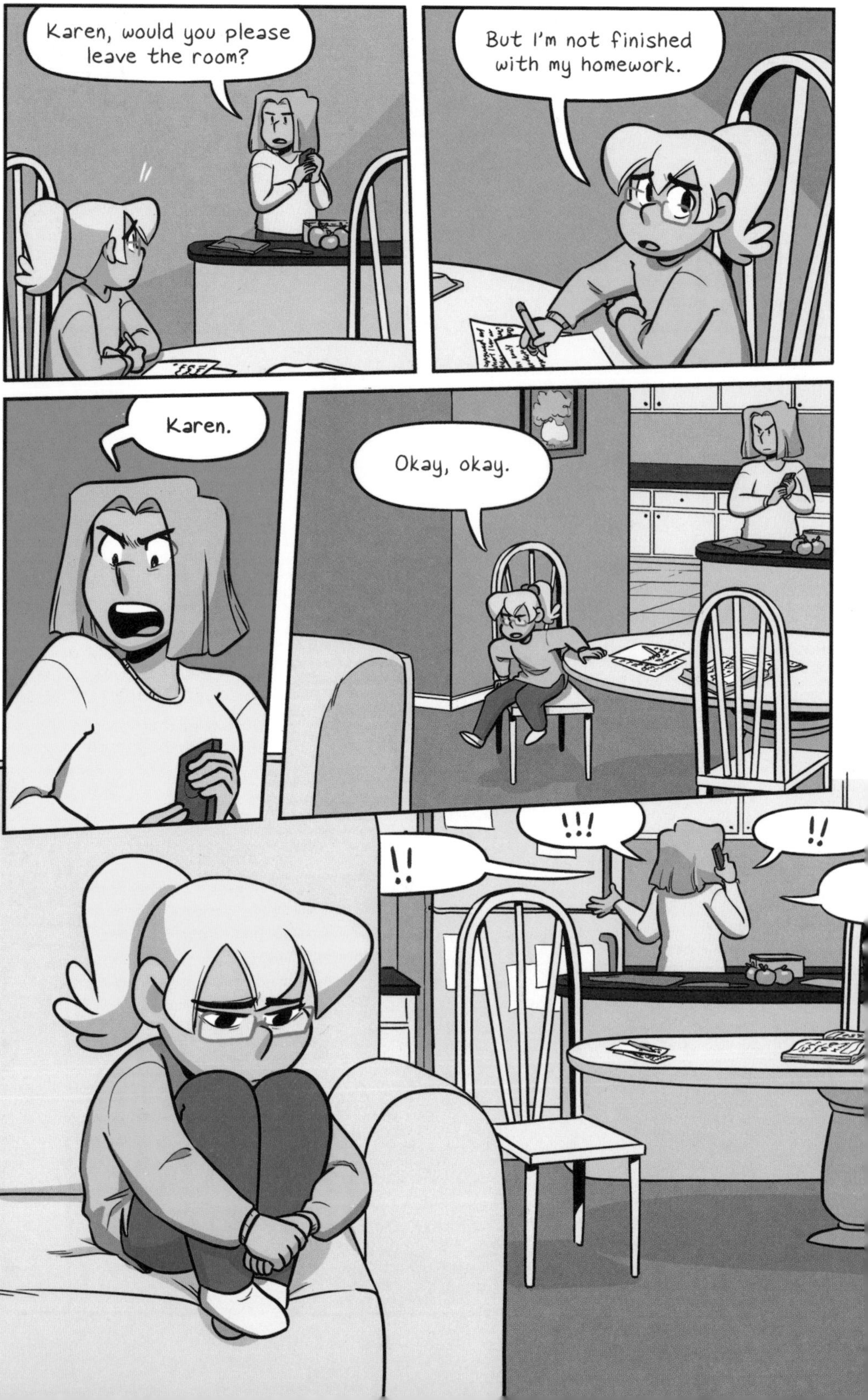
Karen, would you please leave the room?
But I'm not finished with my homework.
Karen.
Okay, okay.
!!
!!!
!!

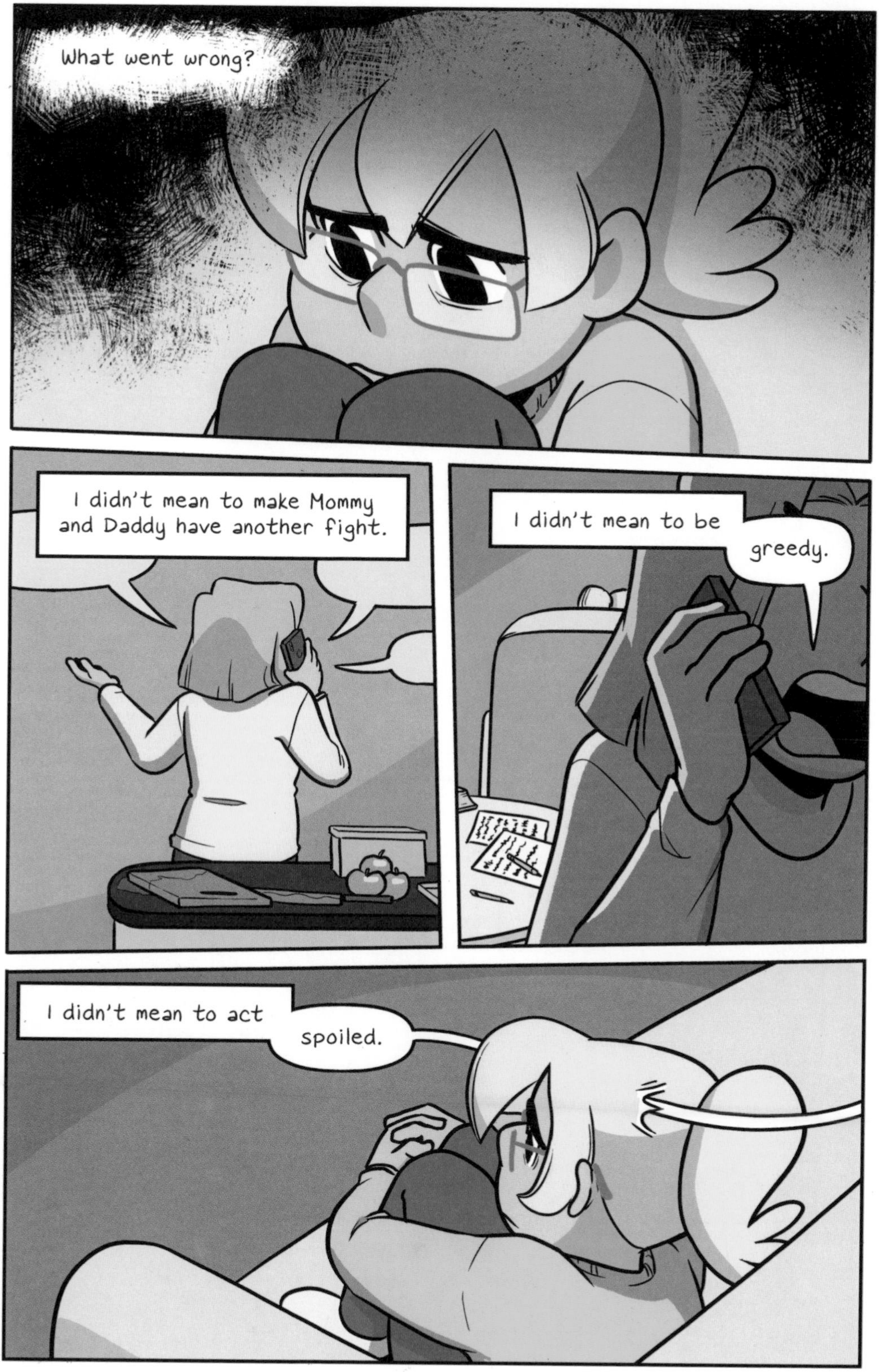
What went wrong?
I didn't mean to make Mommy and Daddy have another fight.
I didn't mean to be
greedy.
I didn't mean to act
spoiled.

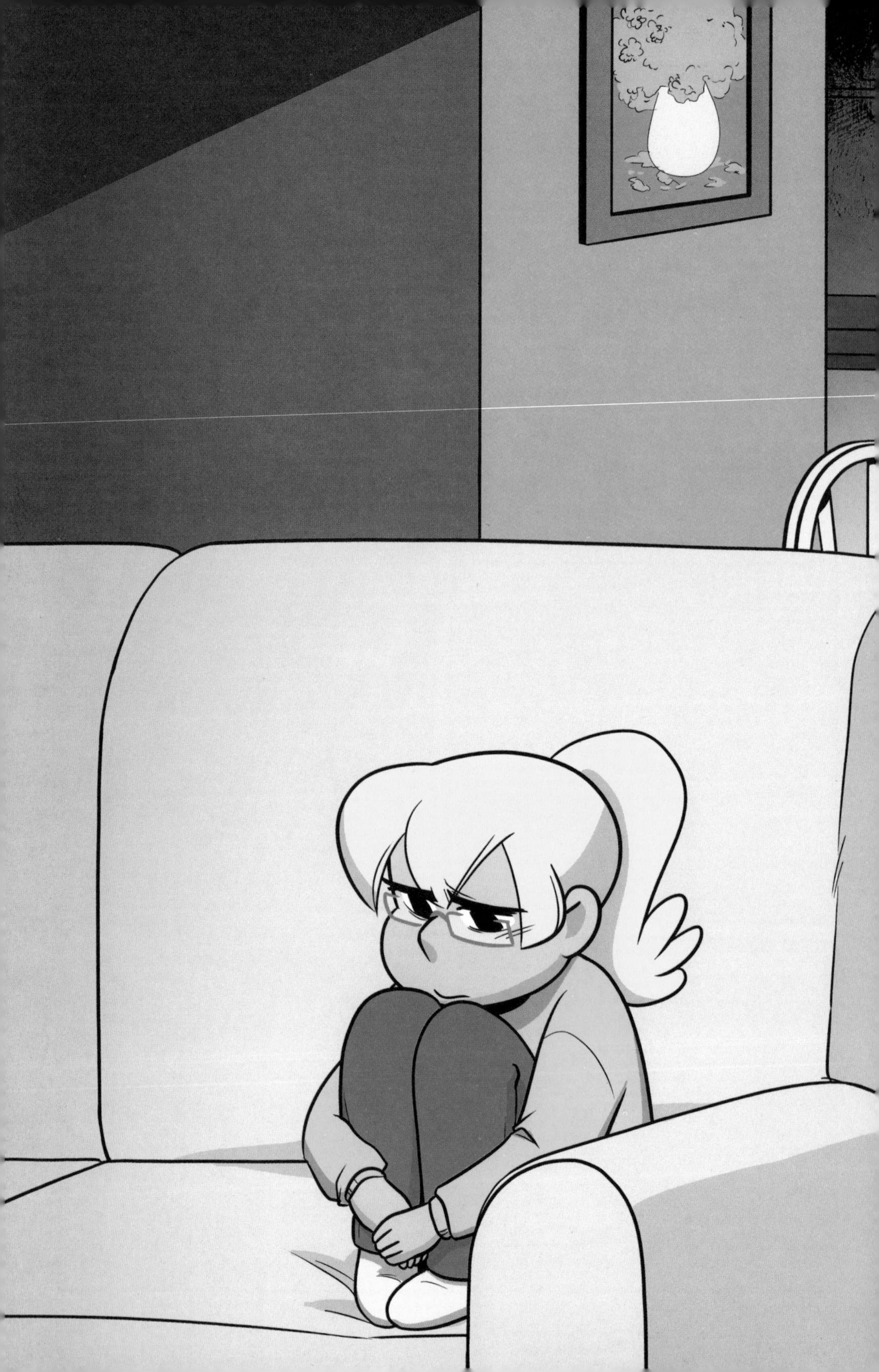

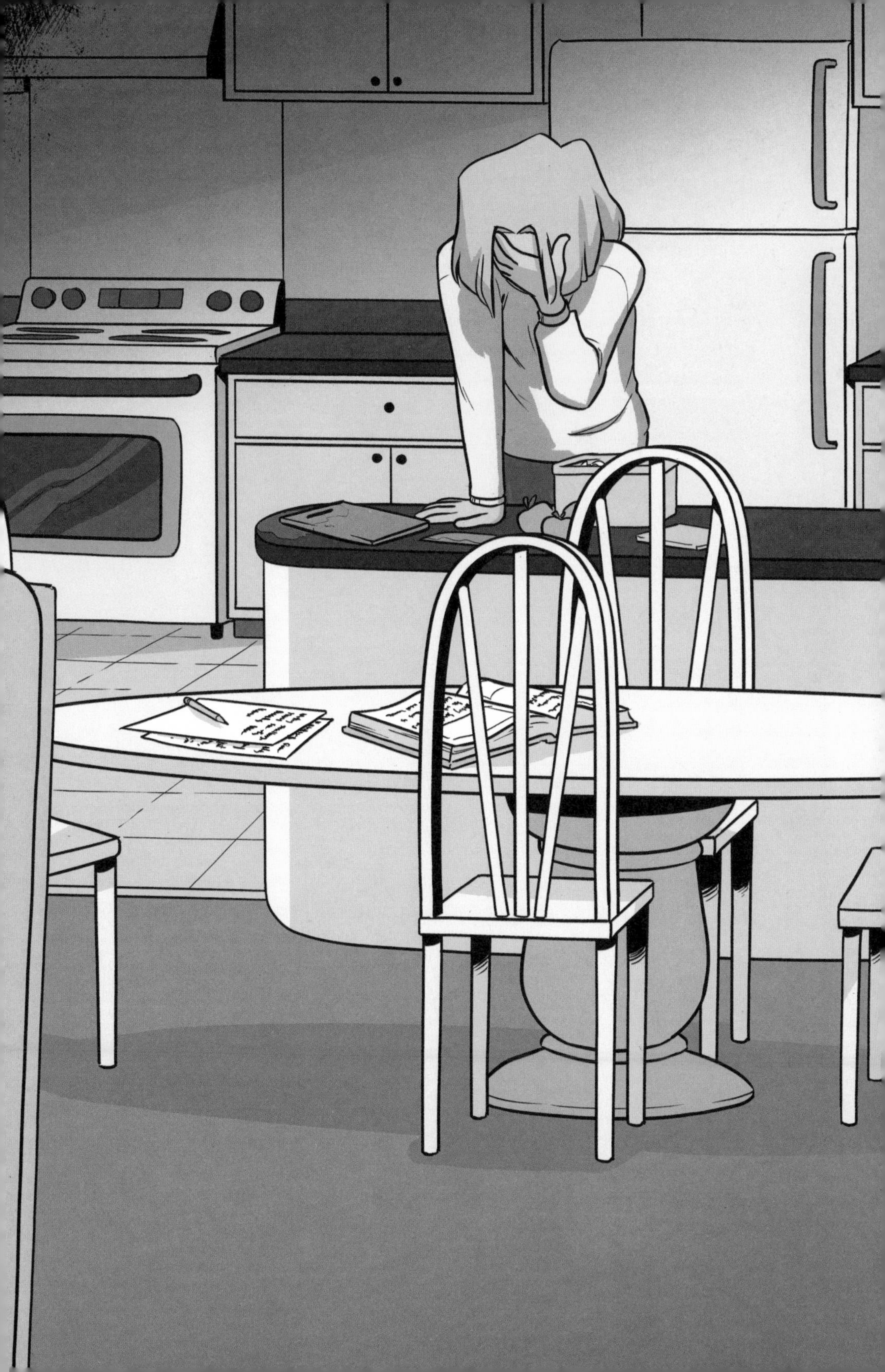

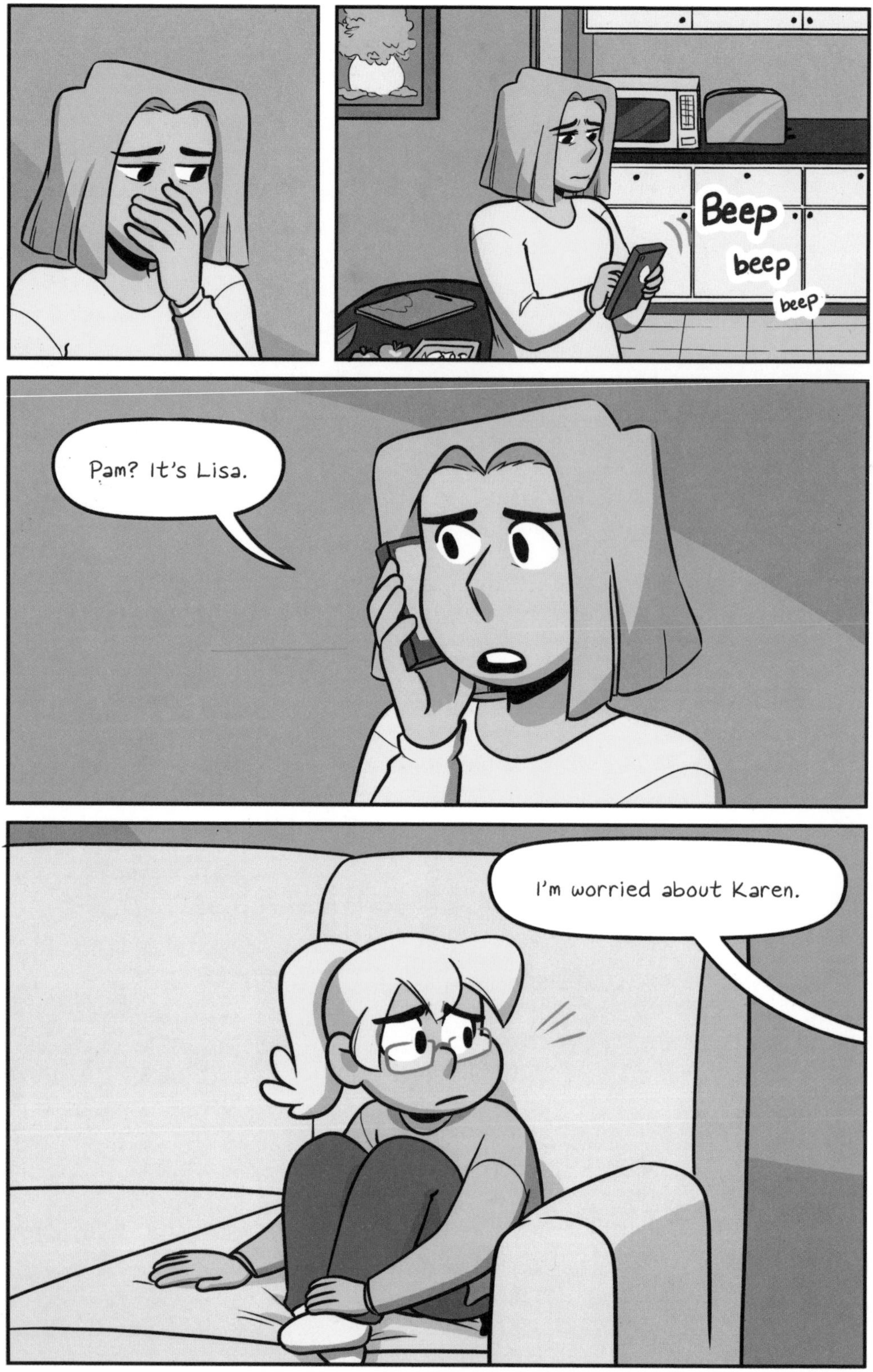
Beep
beep
beep
Pam? It's Lisa.
I'm worried about Karen.

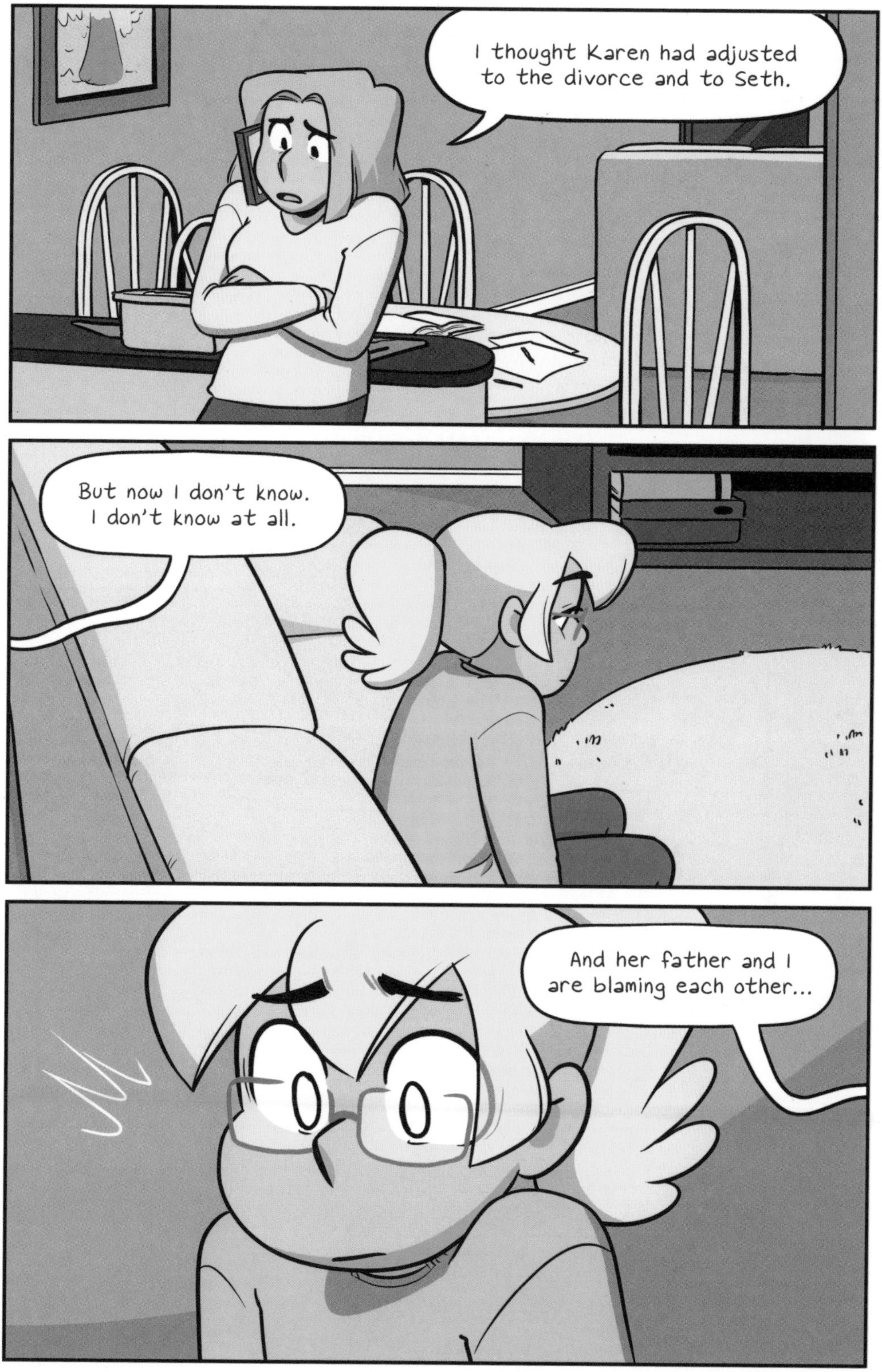
I thought Karen had adjusted to the divorce and to Seth.
But now I don't know. I don't know at all.
And her father and I are blaming each other...

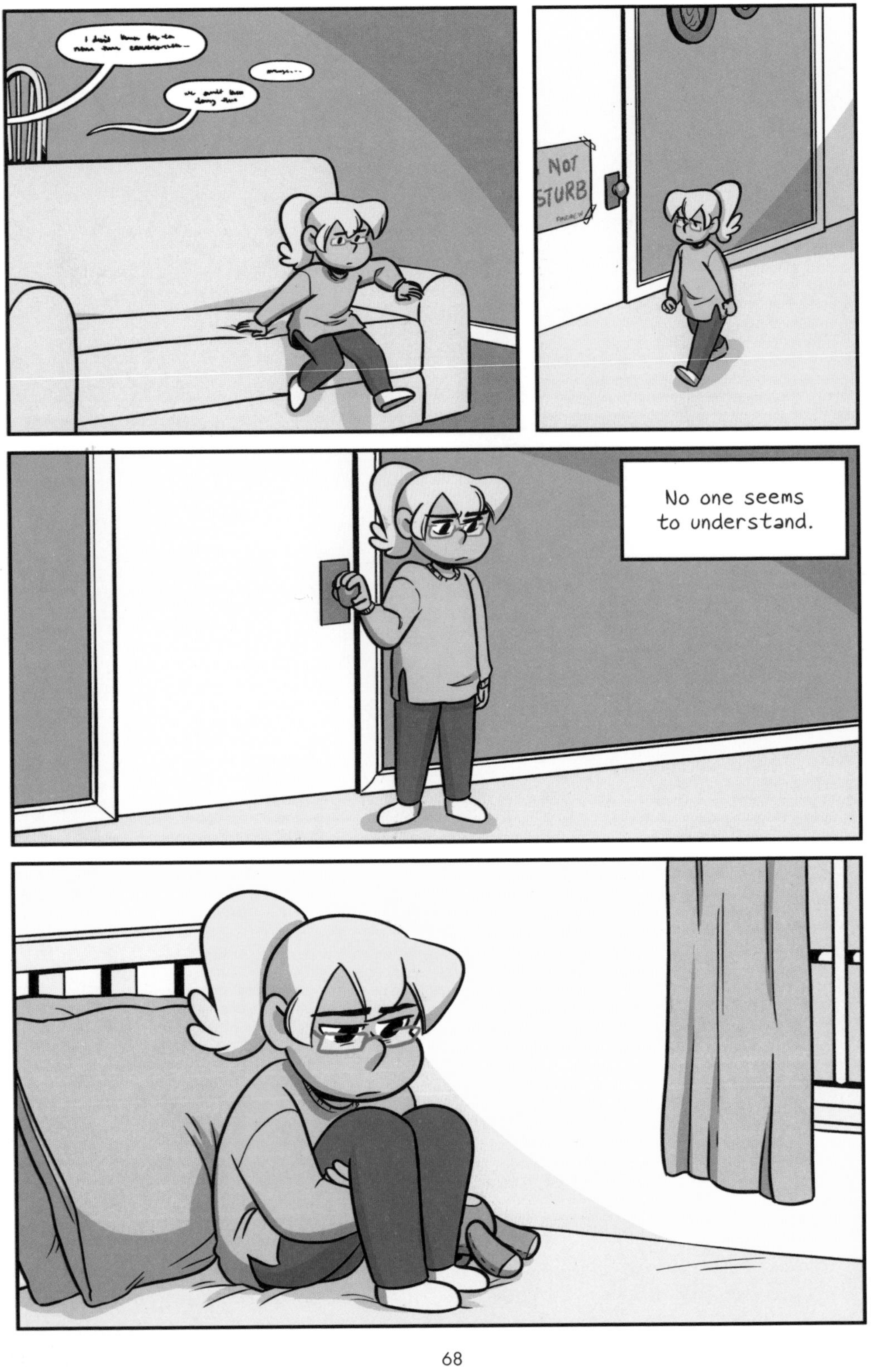
NOT
STURB
No one seems to understand.

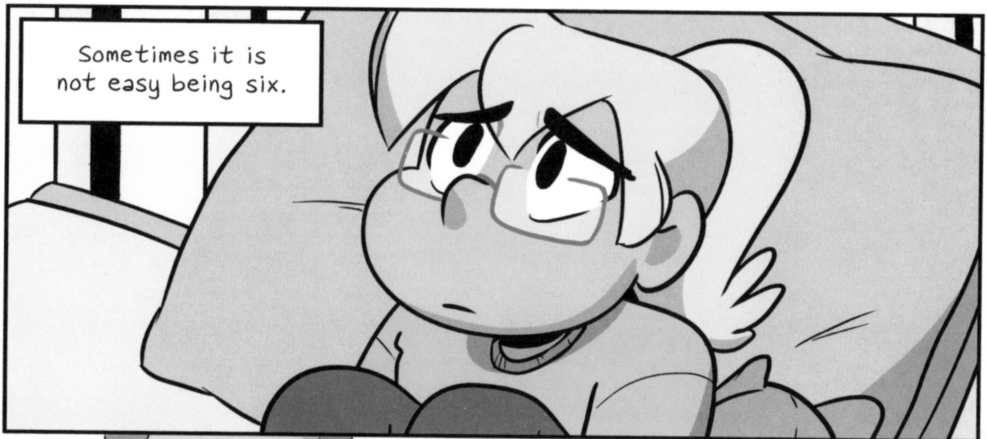
Sometimes it is
not easy being six.

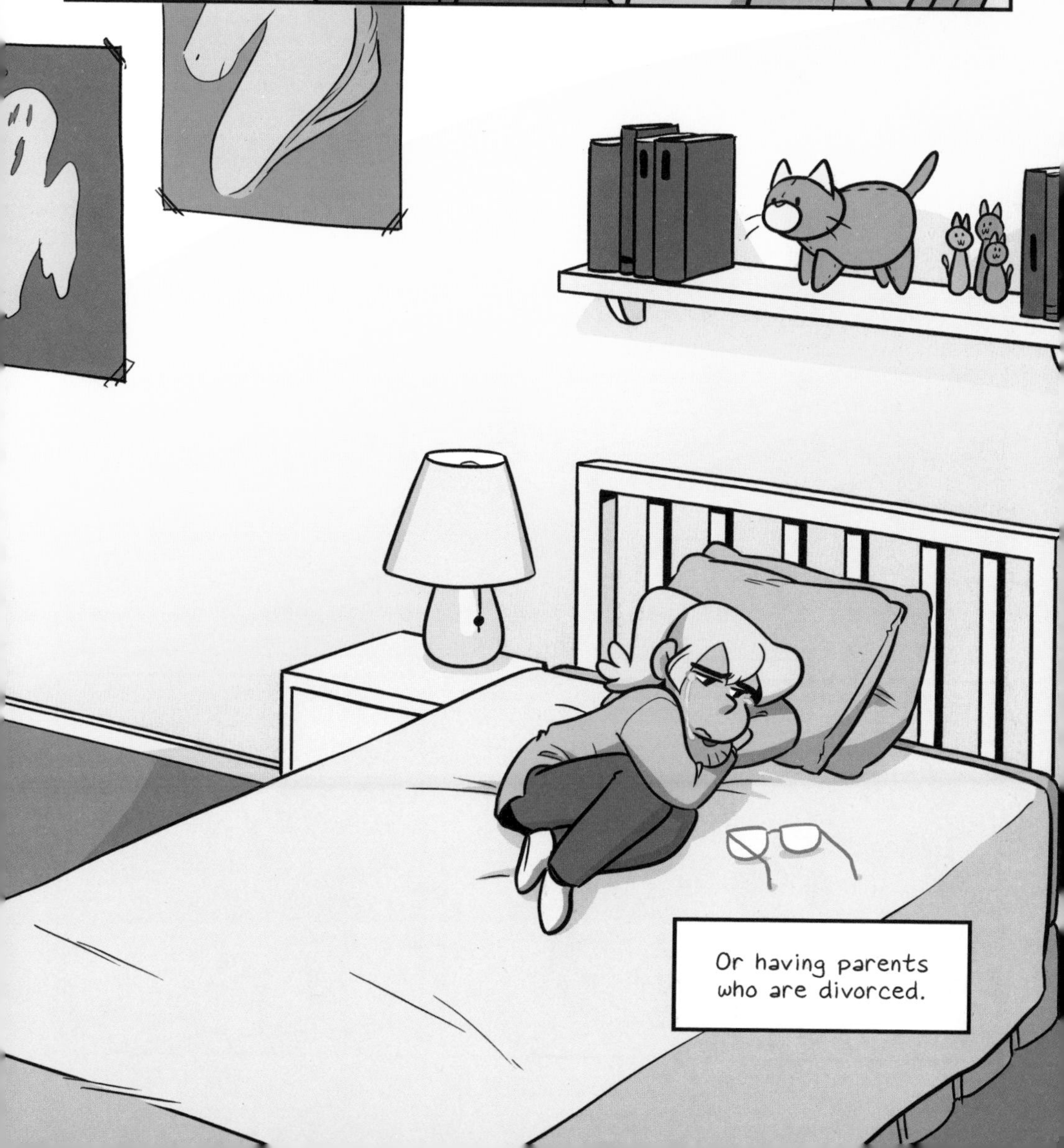
Or having parents
who are divorced.

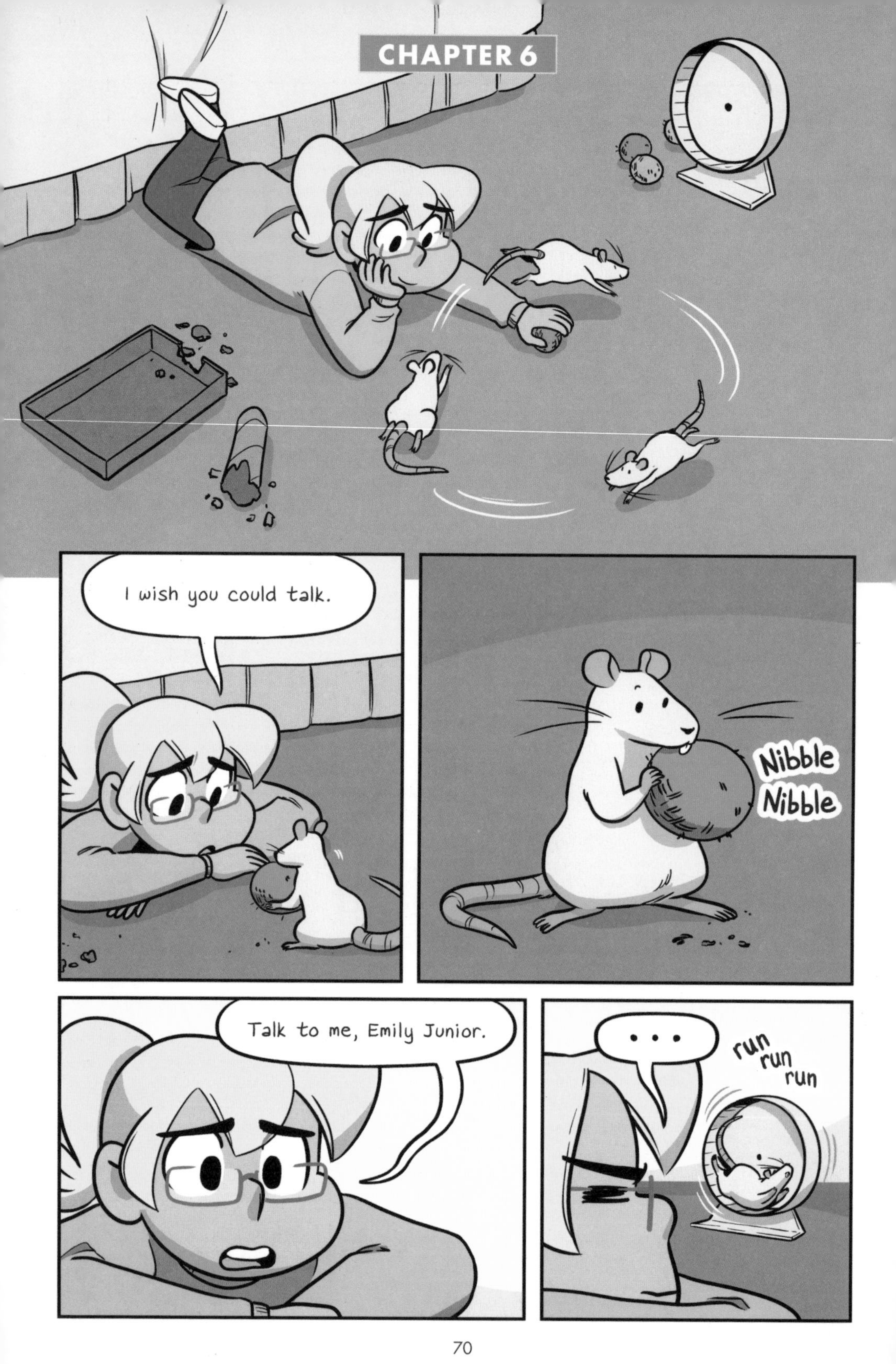
CHAPTER 6
I wish you could talk.
Nibble
Nibble
Talk to me, Emily Junior.
. . .
run
run
run

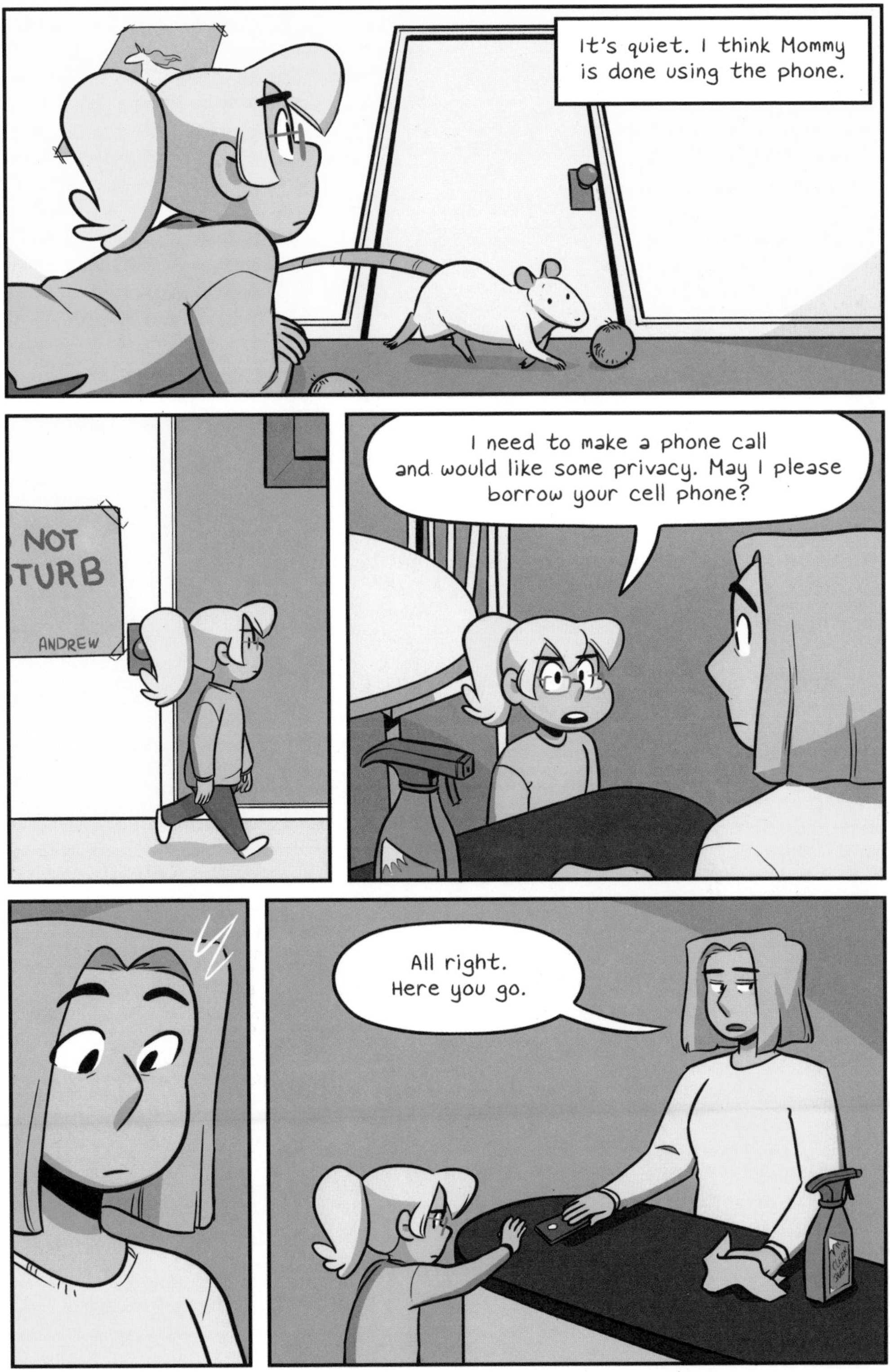
It's quiet. I think Mommy is done using the phone.
NOT
STURB
ANDREW
I need to make a phone call and would like some privacy. May I please borrow your cell phone?
All right. Here you go.

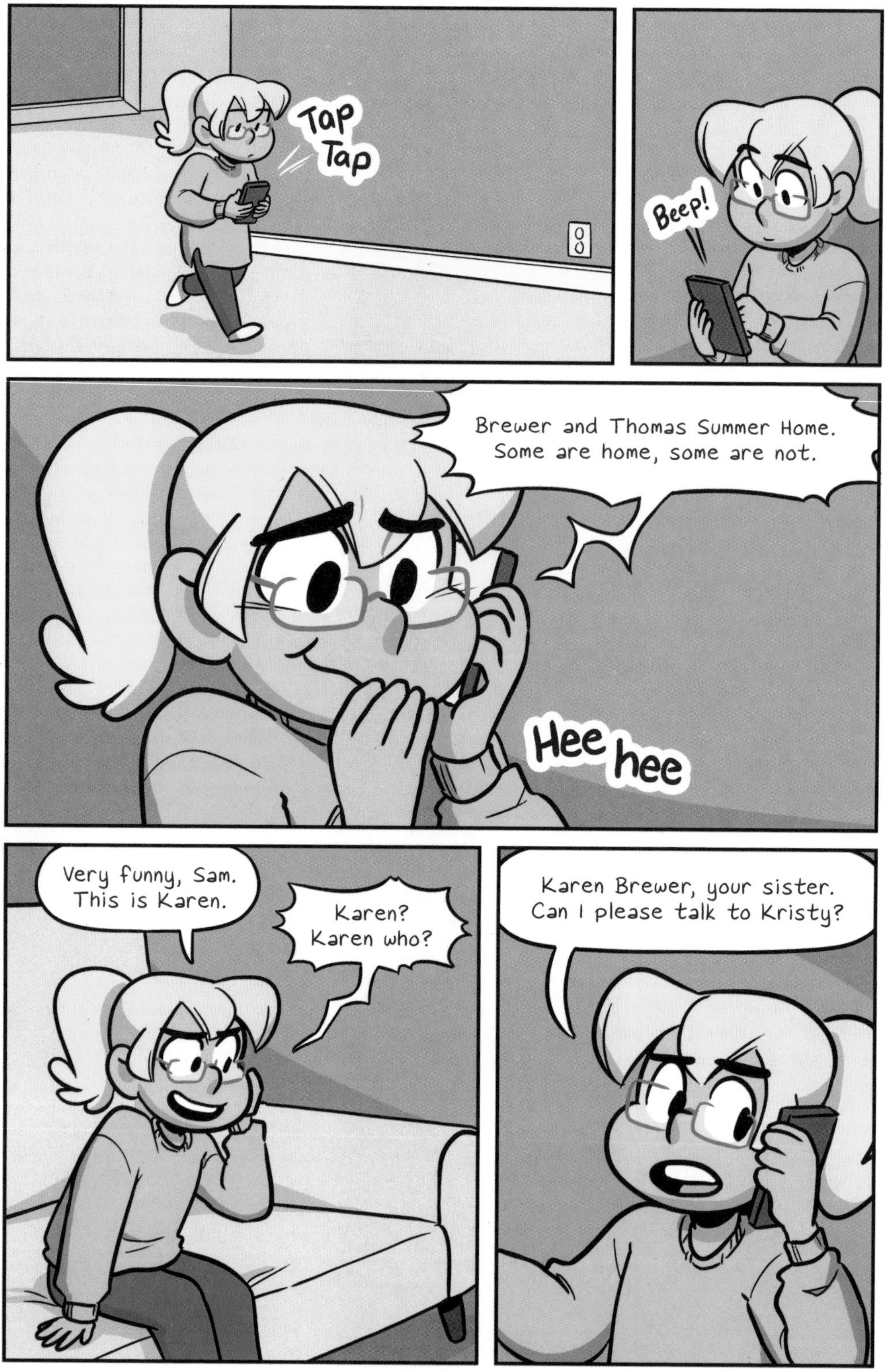

Tap
Tap
Beep!
Brewer and Thomas Summer Home. Some are home, some are not.
Hee hee
Very funny, Sam. This is Karen.
Karen? Karen who?
Karen Brewer, your sister. Can I please talk to Kristy?

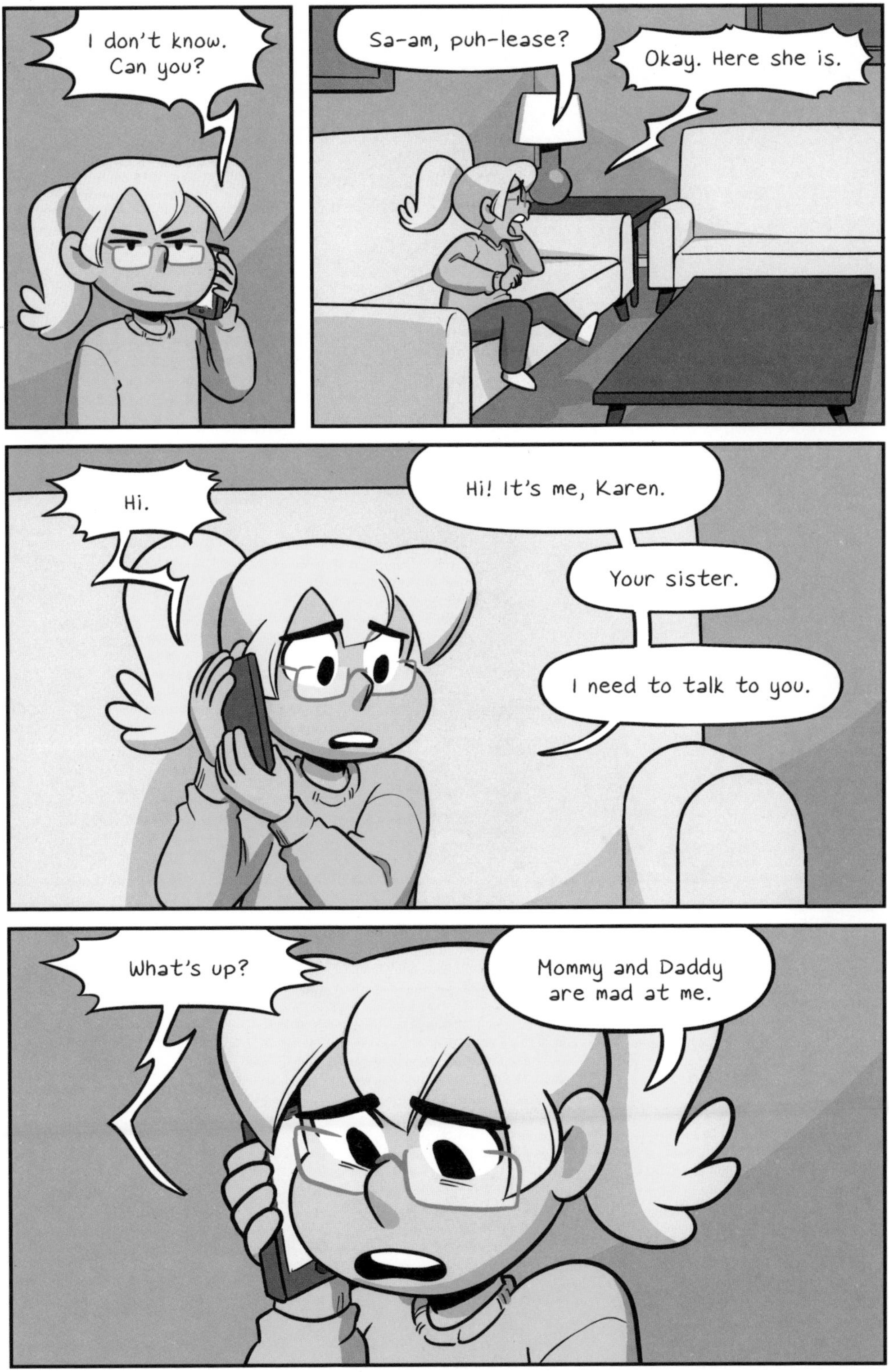
I don't know.
Can you?
Sa-am, puh-lease?
Okay. Here she is.
Hi.
Hi! It's me, Karen.
Your sister.
I need to talk to you.
What's up?
Mommy and Daddy
are mad at me.

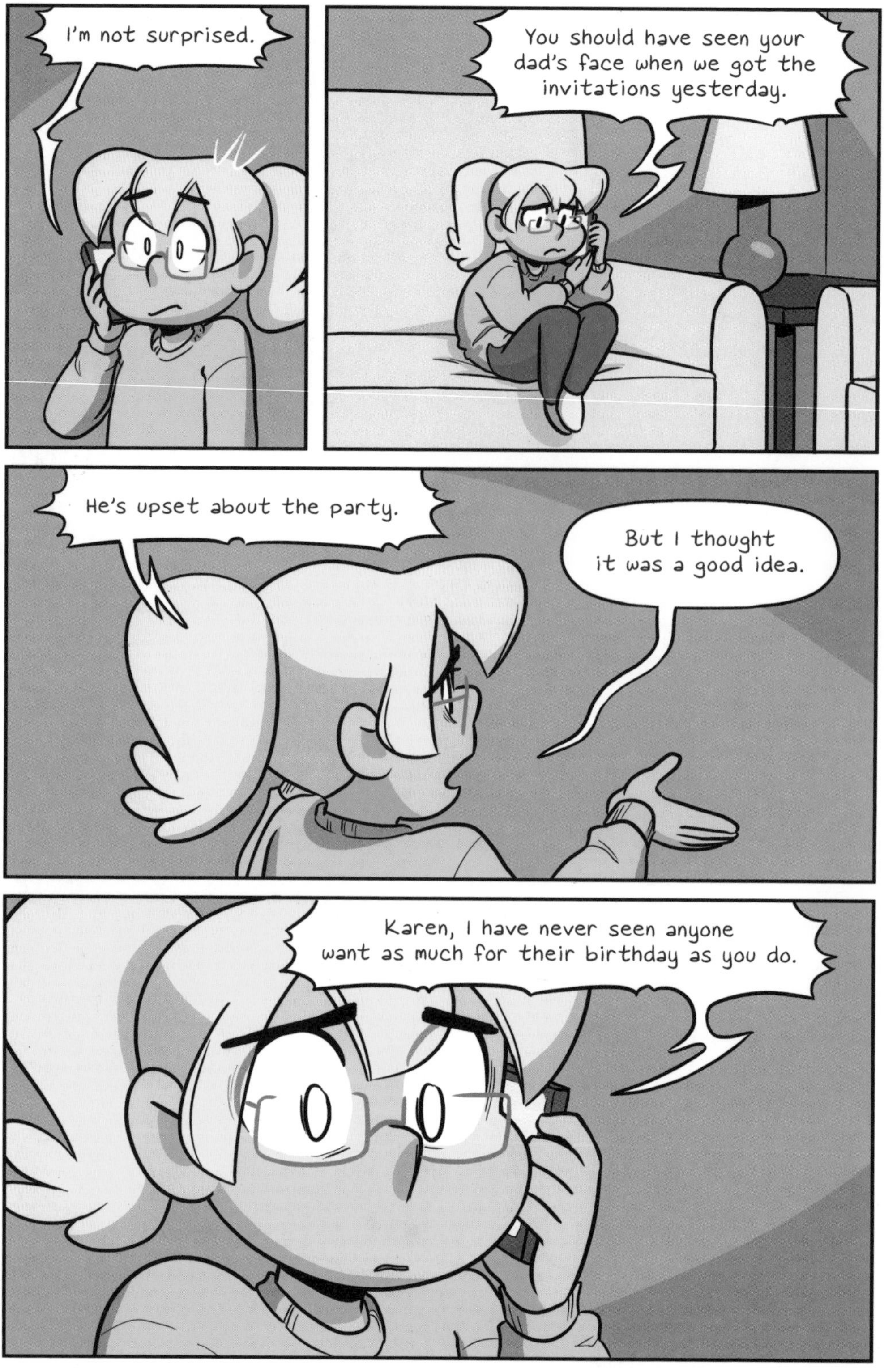
I'm not surprised.
You should have seen your dad's face when we got the invitations yesterday.
He's upset about the party.
But I thought it was a good idea.
Karen, I have never seen anyone want as much for their birthday as you do.

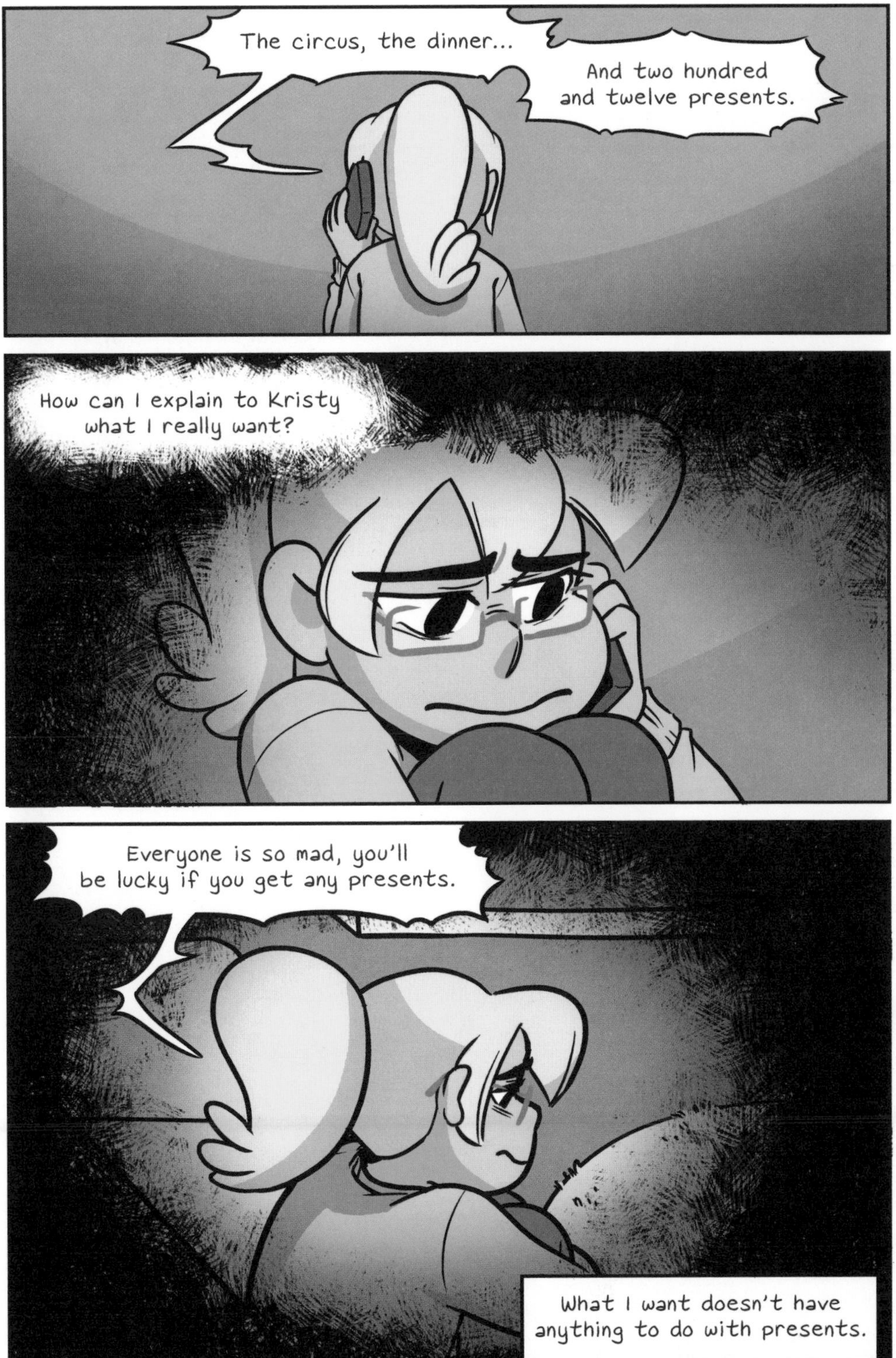
The circus, the dinner...
And two hundred and twelve presents.
How can I explain to Kristy what I really want?
Everyone is so mad, you'll be lucky if you get any presents.
What I want doesn't have anything to do with presents.

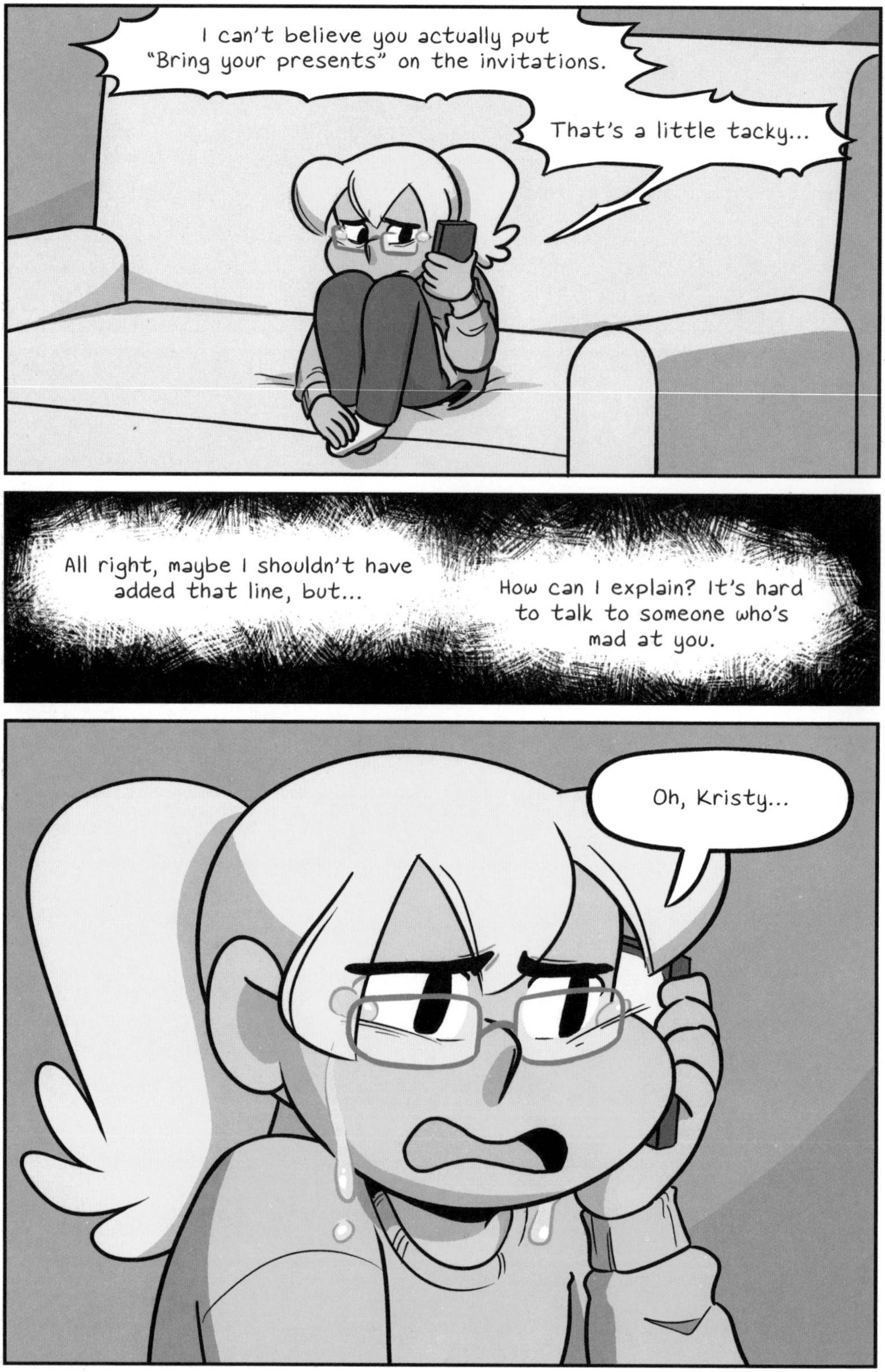
I can't believe you actually put "Bring your presents" on the invitations.
That's a little tacky...
All right, maybe I shouldn't have added that line, but...
How can I explain? It's hard to talk to someone who's mad at you.
Oh, Kristy...

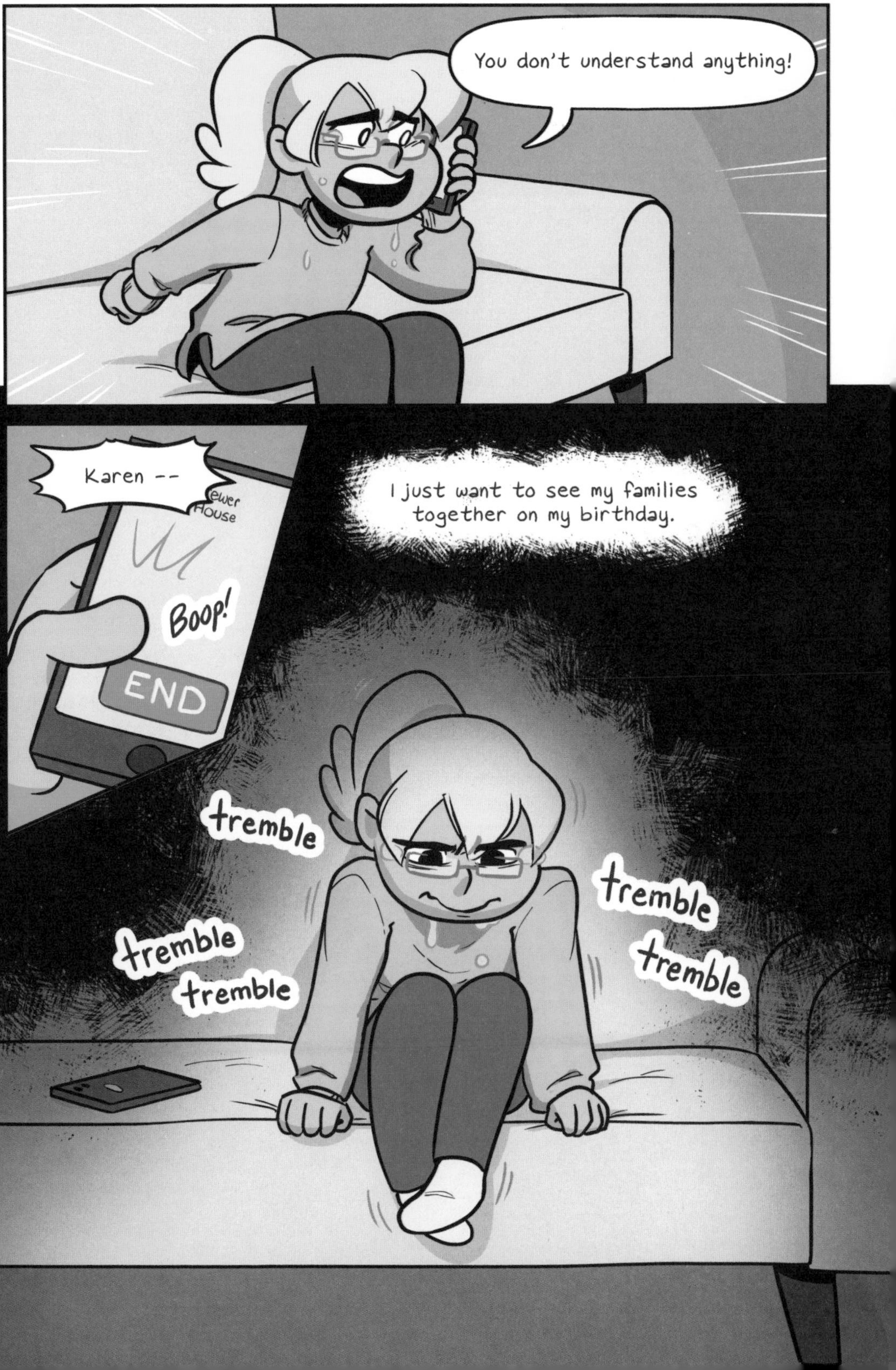
You don't understand anything!
Karen --
Boop!
END
I just want to see my families together on my birthday.
tremble
tremble
tremble
tremble
tremble
tremble

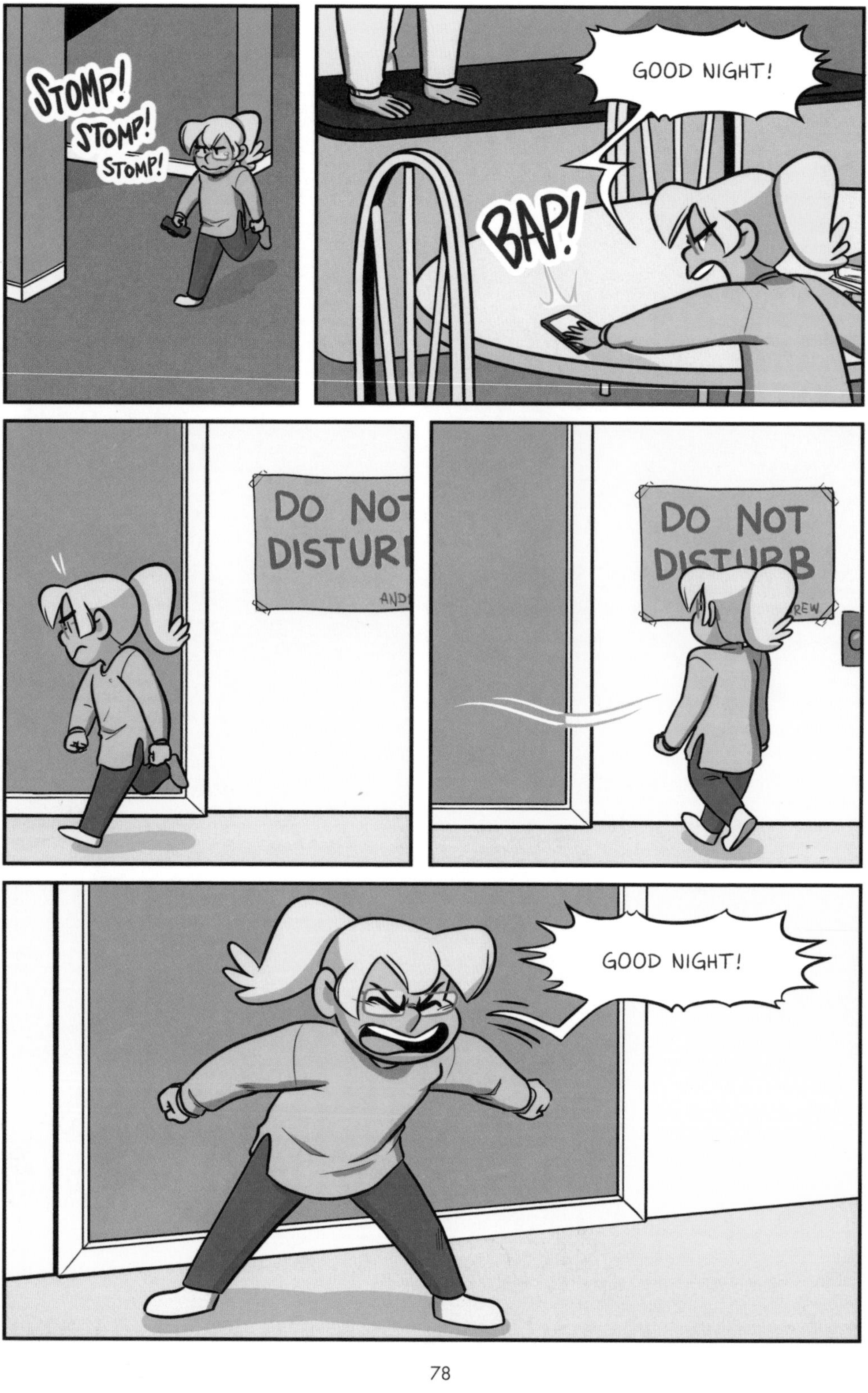
STOMP!
STOMP!
STOMP!
GOOD NIGHT!
BAP!
DO NOT
DO NOT
GOOD NIGHT!

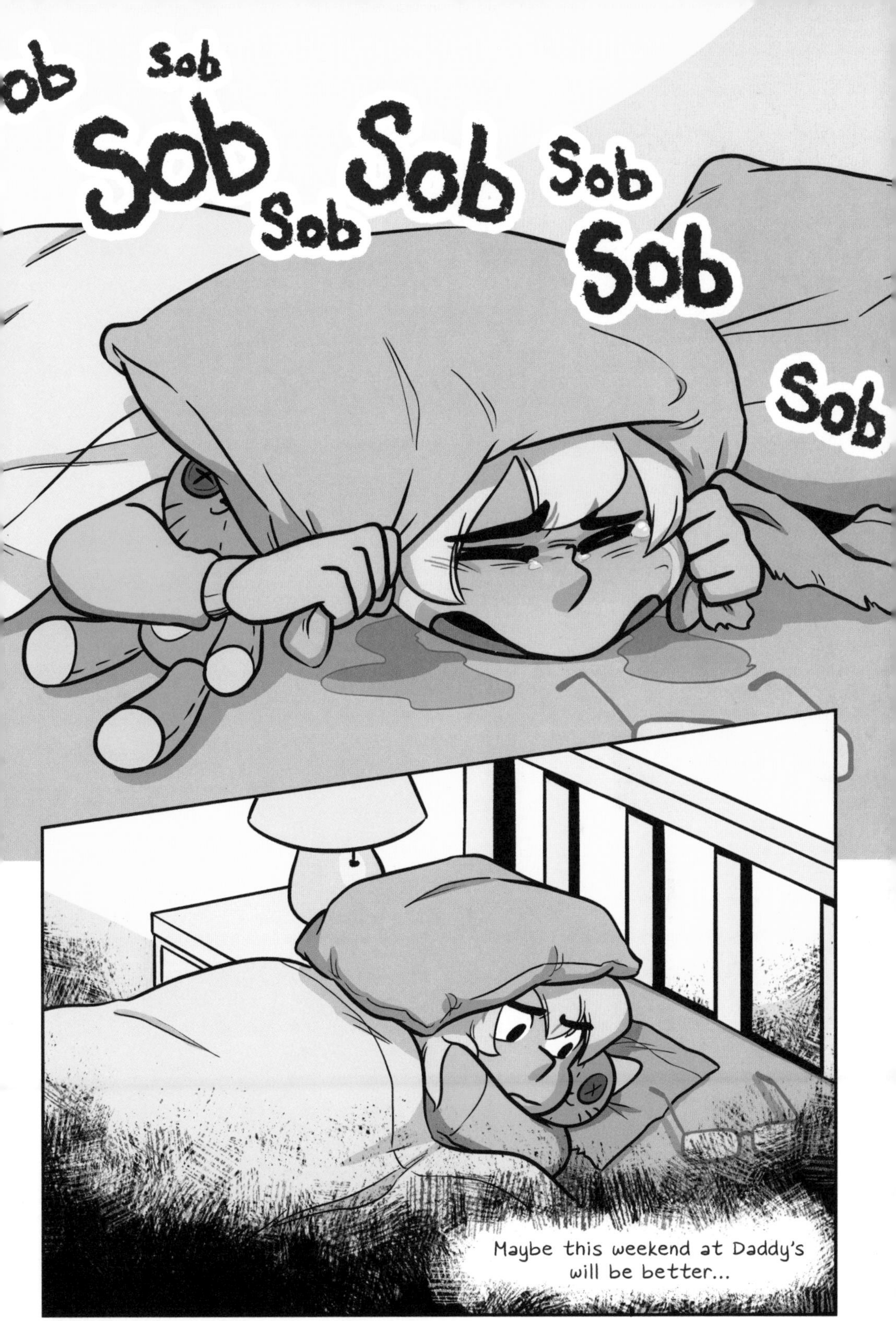

Sob
Sob
Sob
Sob
Sob
Sob
Sob
Sob
Maybe this weekend at Daddy's will be better...

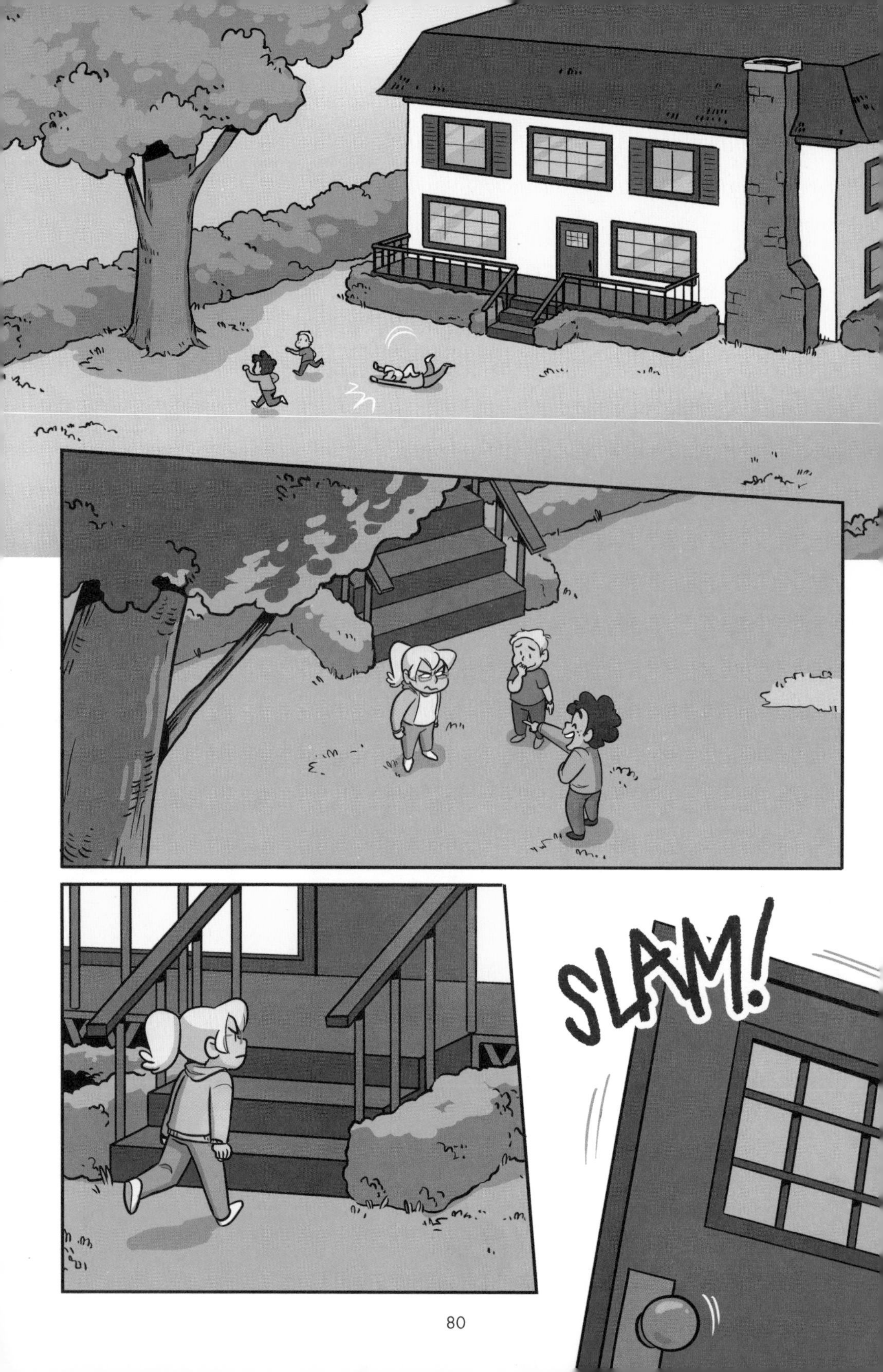
SLAM!

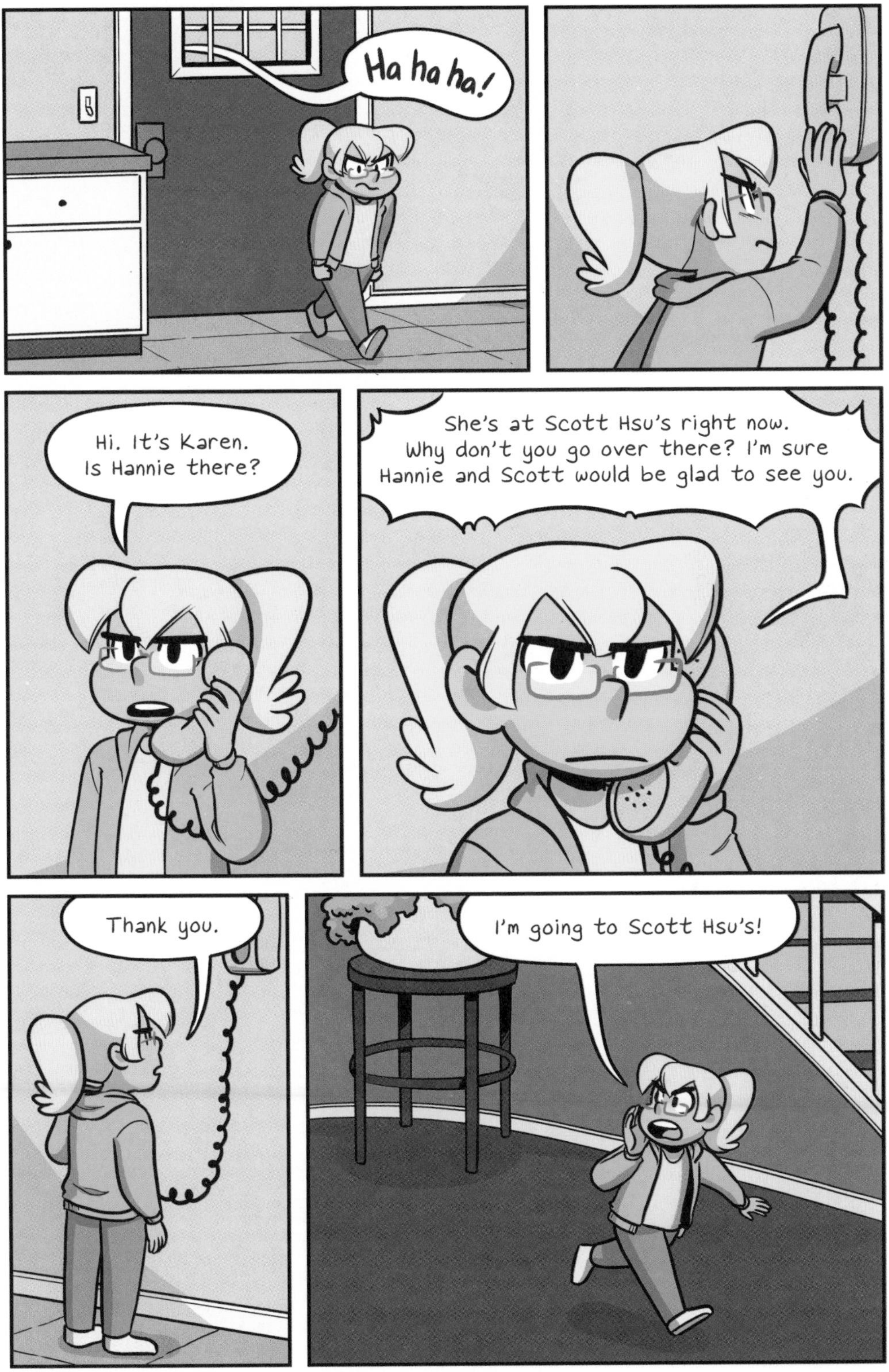
Ha ha ha!
Hi. It's Karen. Is Hannie there?
She's at Scott Hsu's right now. Why don't you go over there? I'm sure Hannie and Scott would be glad to see you.
Thank you.
I'm going to Scott Hsu's!

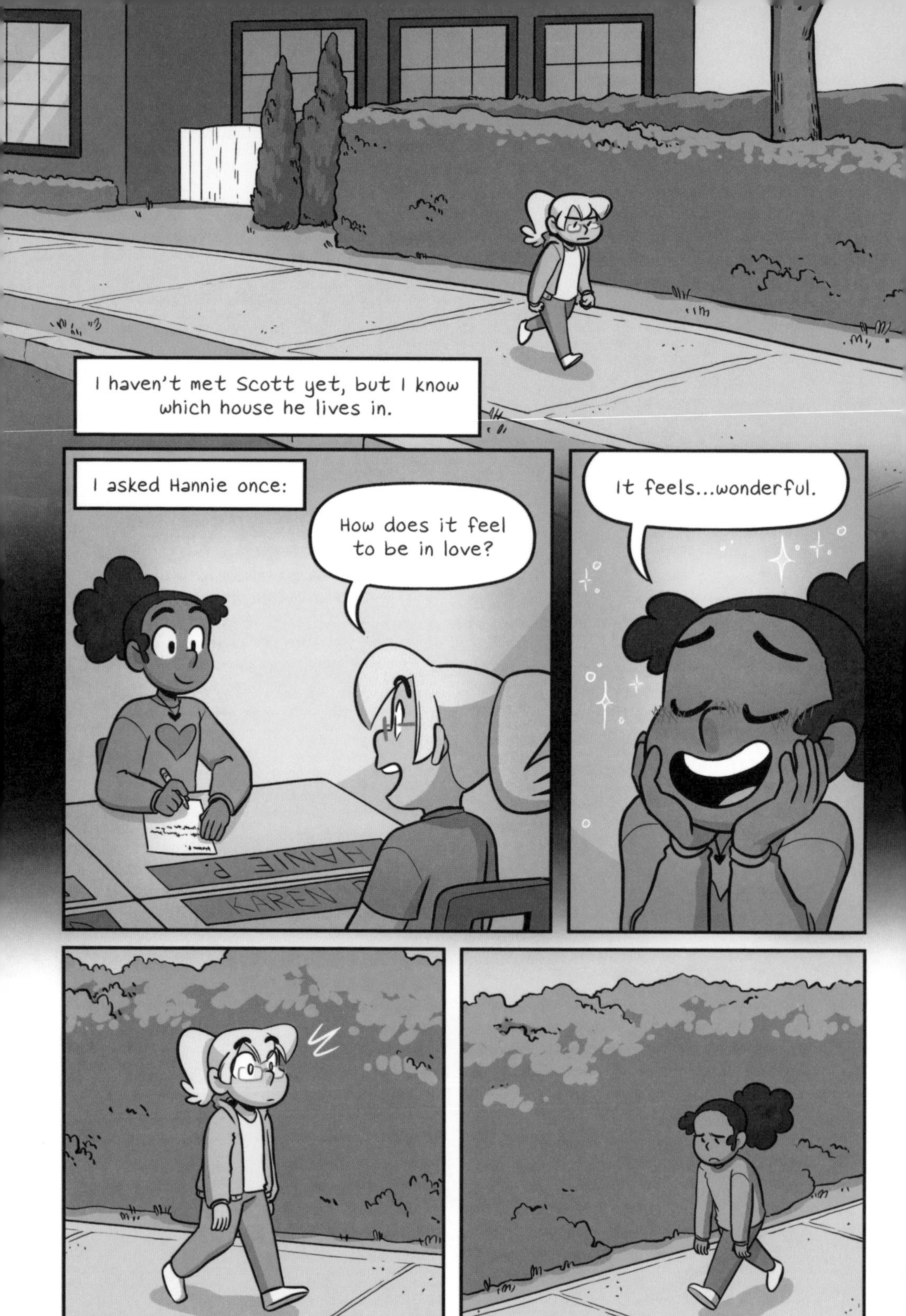
I haven't met Scott yet, but I know which house he lives in.
I asked Hannie once:
How does it feel to be in love?
HANIE P.
KAREN
It feels...wonderful.

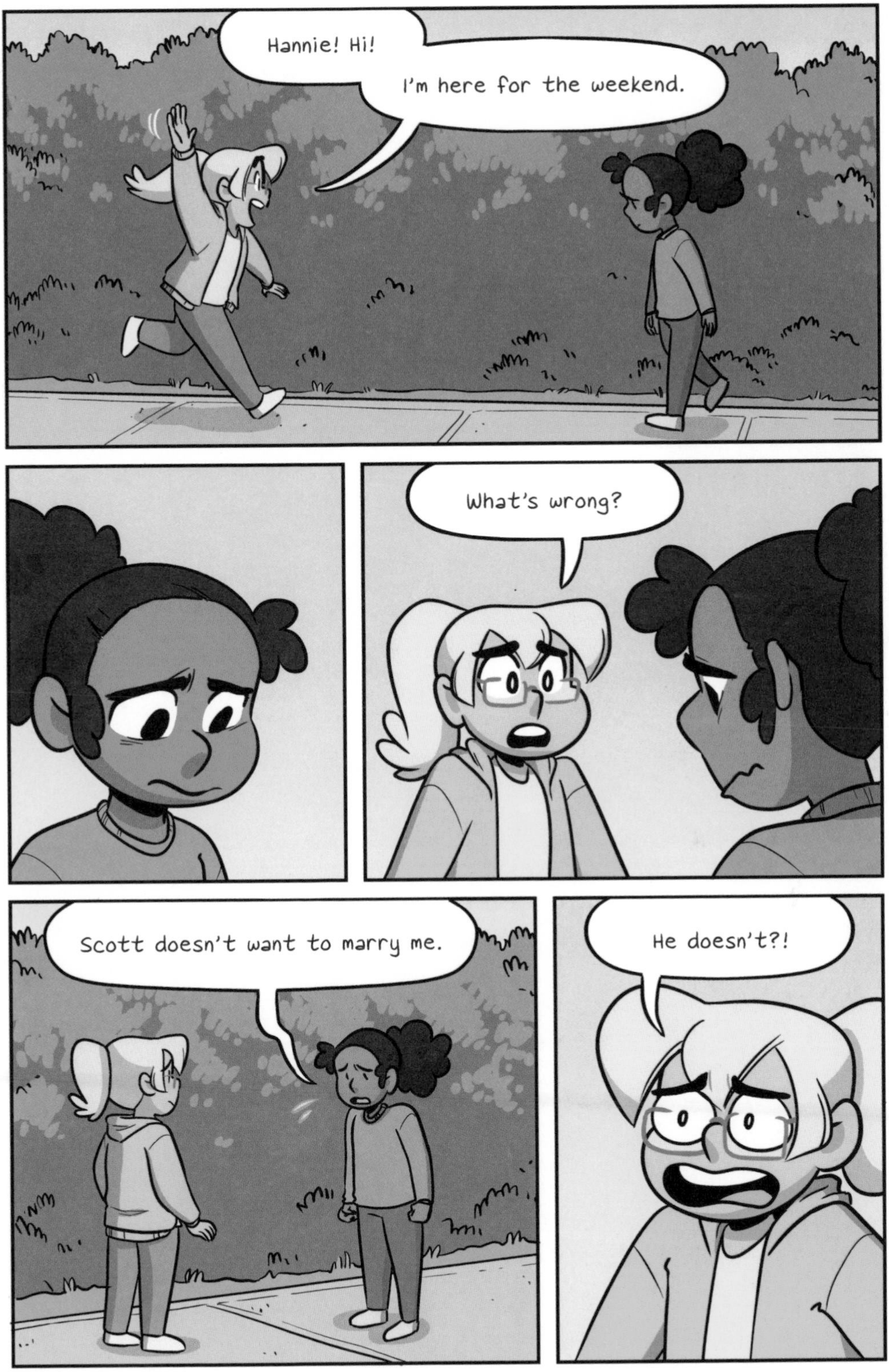
Hannie! Hi!
I'm here for the weekend.
What's wrong?
Scott doesn't want to marry me.
He doesn't?!

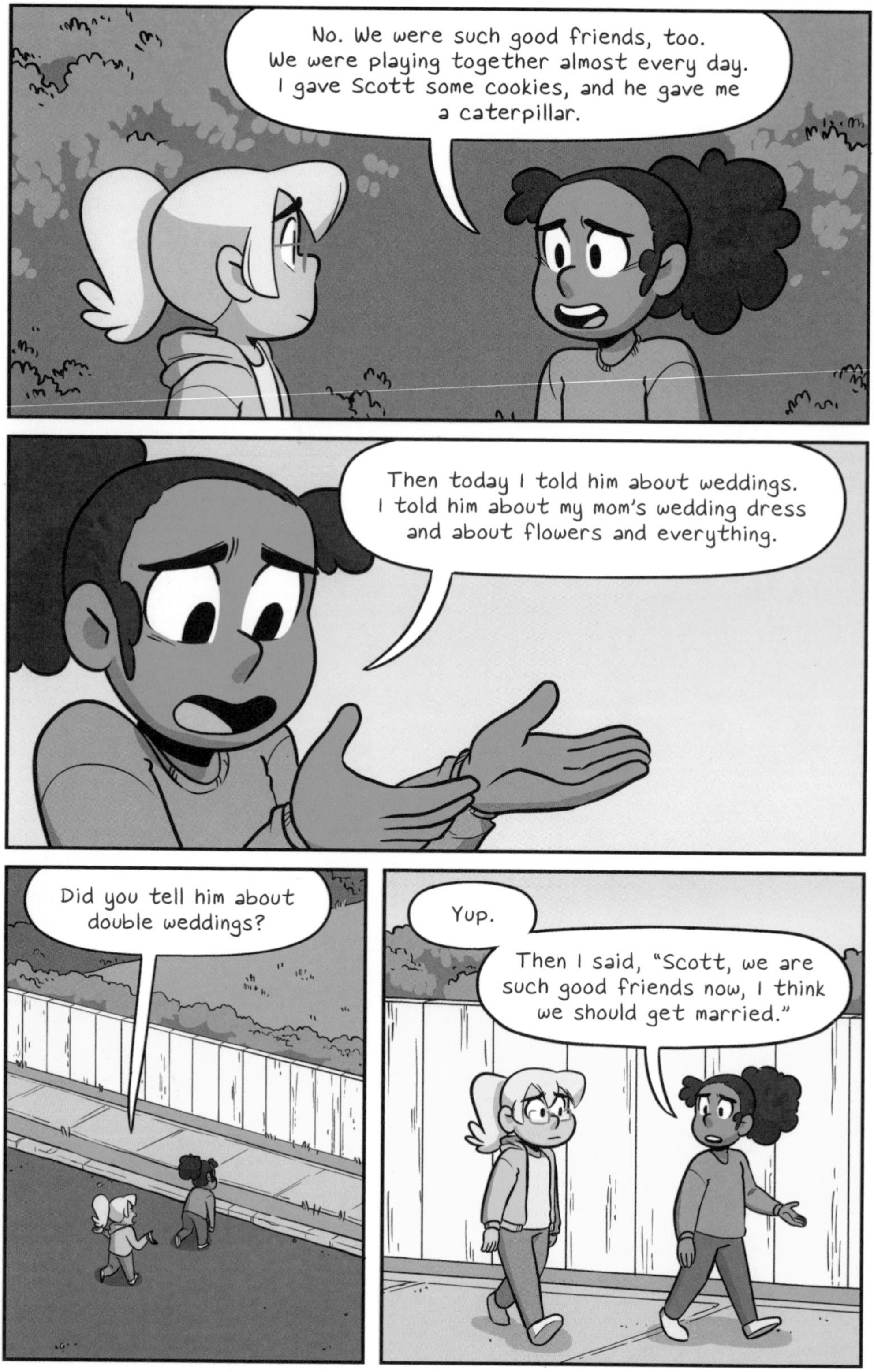
No. We were such good friends, too. We were playing together almost every day. I gave Scott some cookies, and he gave me a caterpillar.
Then today I told him about weddings. I told him about my mom's wedding dress and about flowers and everything.
Did you tell him about double weddings?
Yup.
Then I said, "Scott, we are such good friends now, I think we should get married."

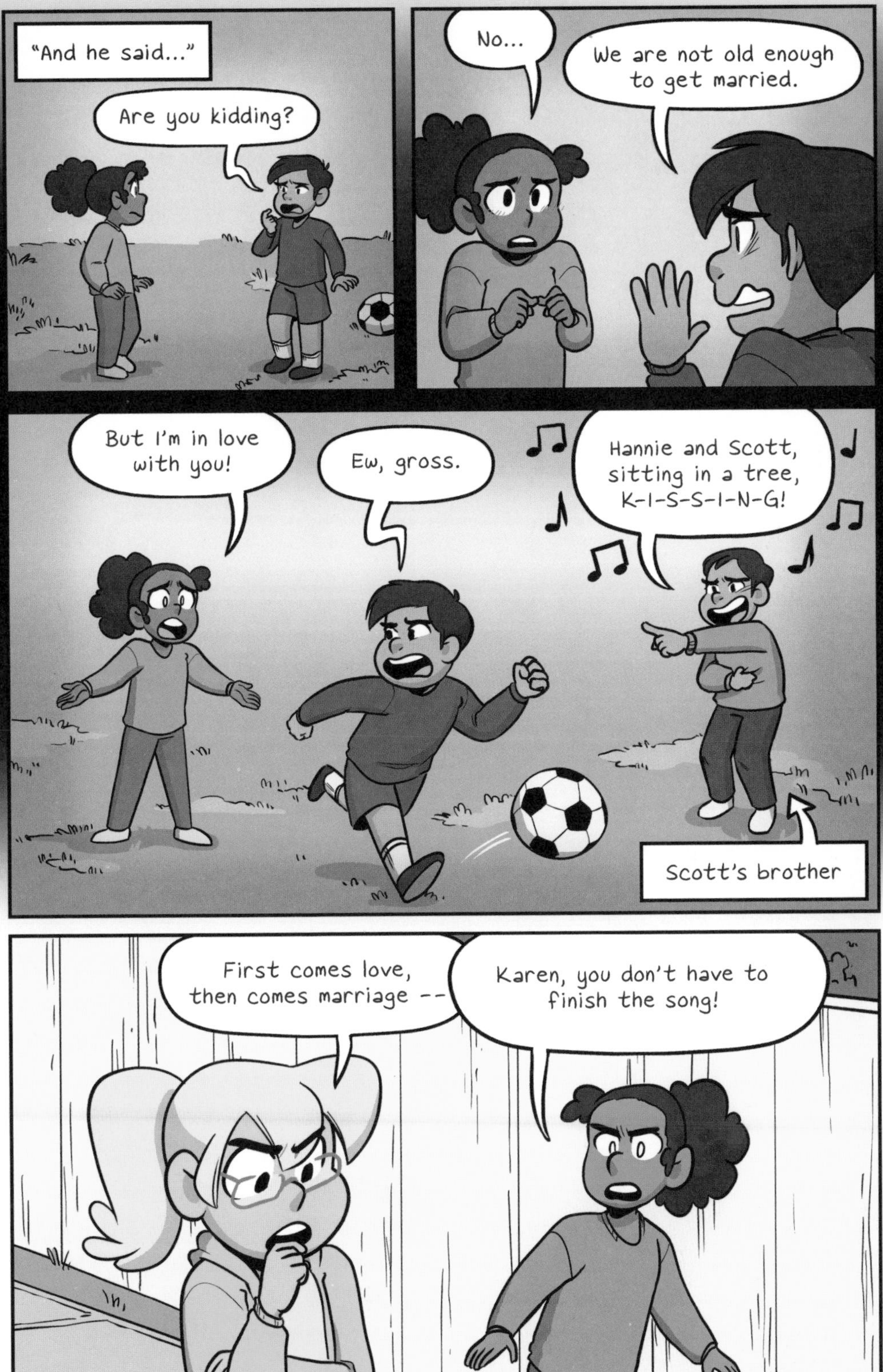

"And he said..."
Are you kidding?
No...
We are not old enough to get married.
But I'm in love with you!
Ew, gross.
Hannie and Scott, sitting in a tree, K-I-S-S-I-N-G!
Scott's brother
First comes love, then comes marriage --
Karen, you don't have to finish the song!

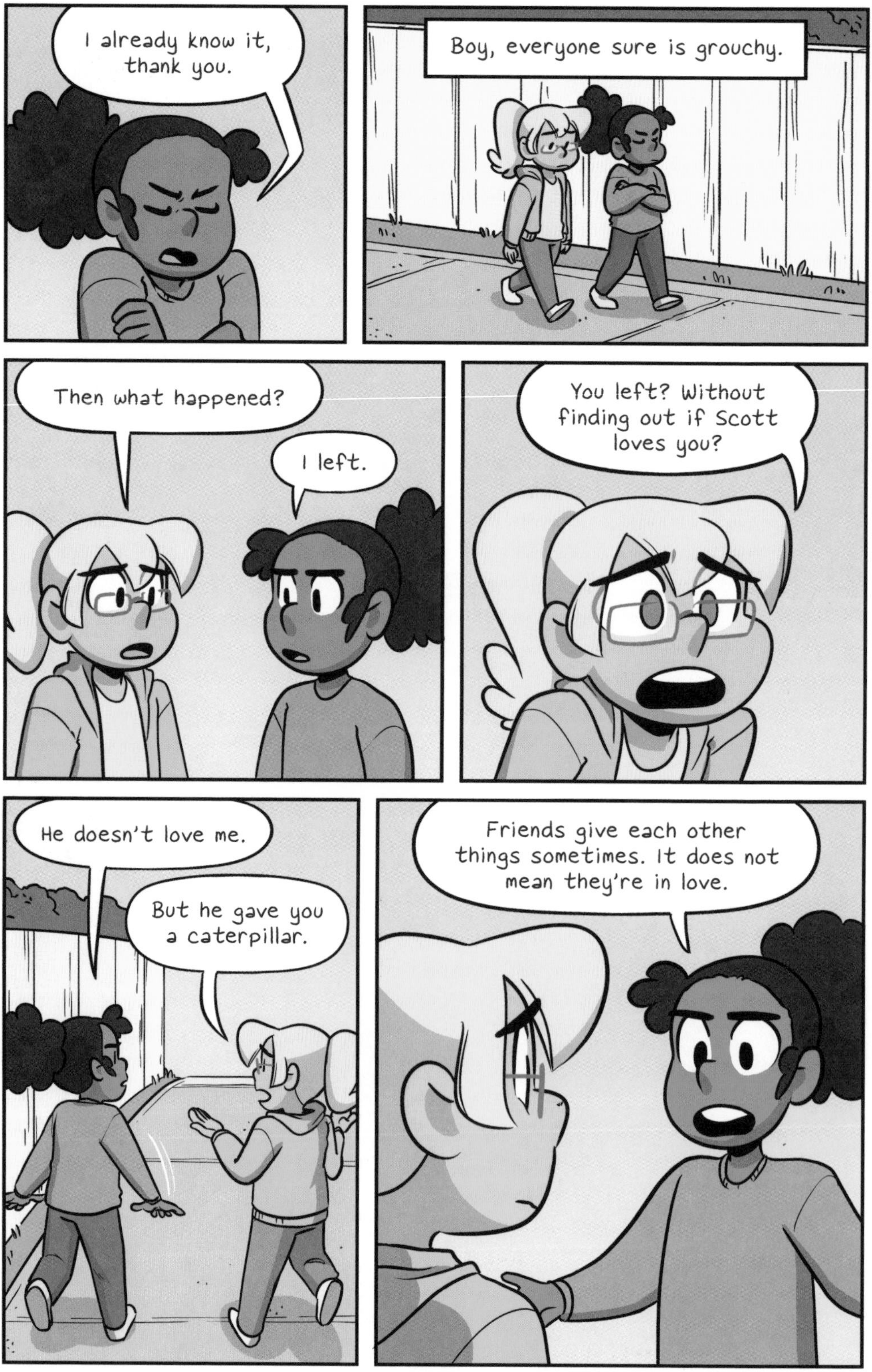
I already know it, thank you.
Boy, everyone sure is grouchy.
Then what happened?
I left.
You left? Without finding out if Scott loves you?
He doesn't love me.
But he gave you a caterpillar.
Friends give each other things sometimes. It does not mean they're in love.

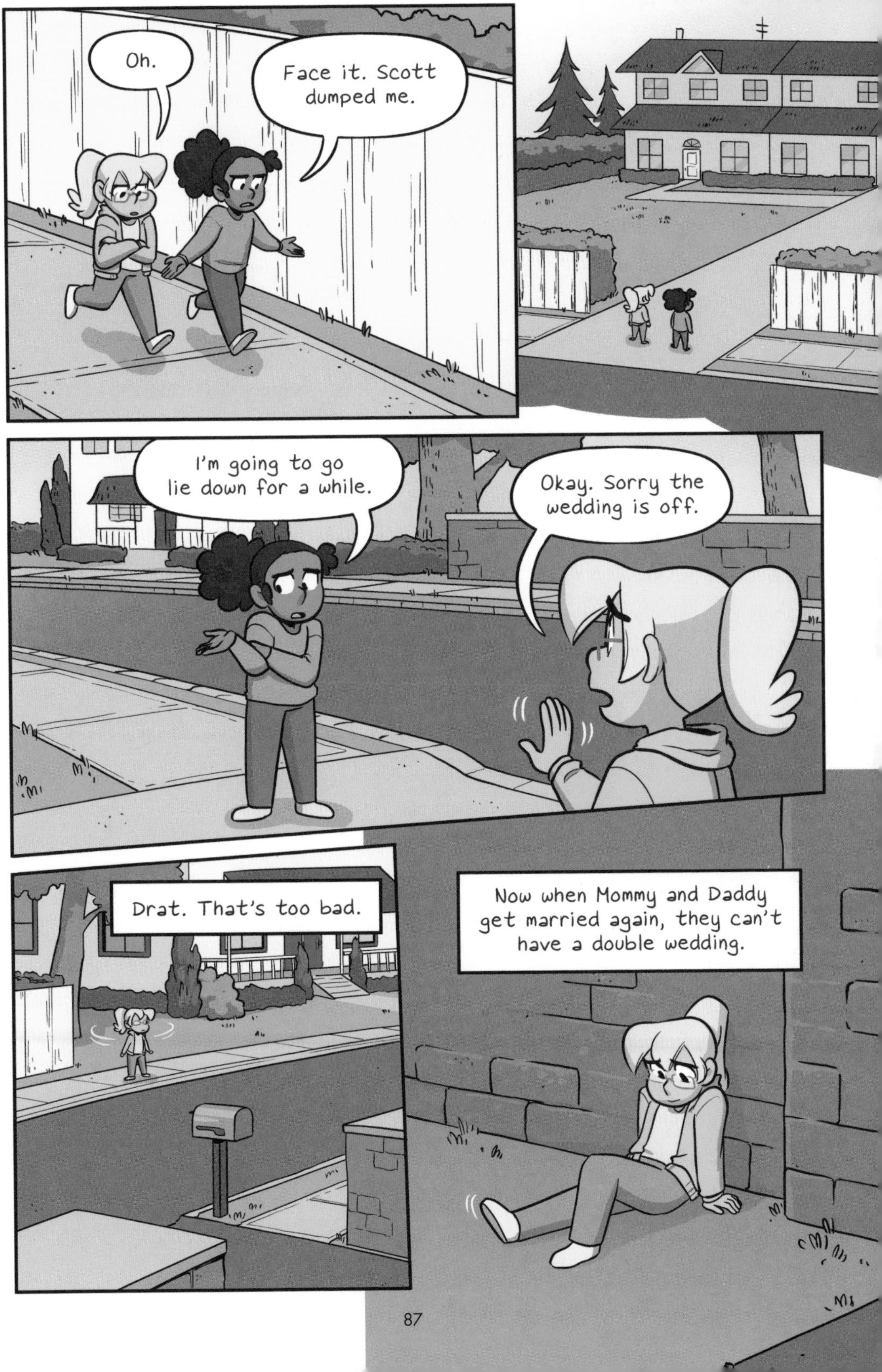
Oh.
Face it. Scott dumped me.
I'm going to go lie down for a while.
Okay. Sorry the wedding is off.
Drat. That's too bad.
Now when Mommy and Daddy get married again, they can't have a double wedding.

CHAPTER 7

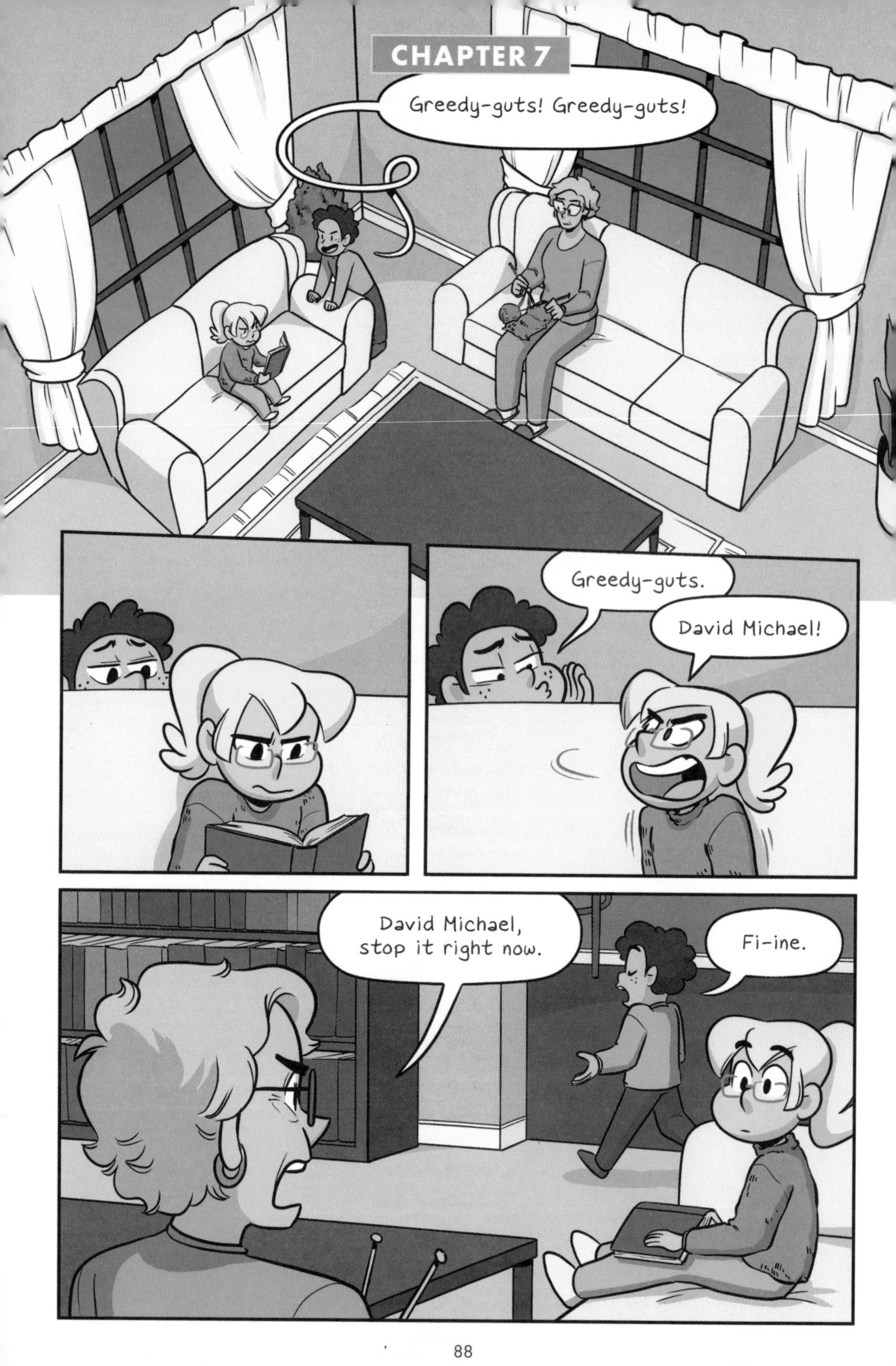
Greedy-guts! Greedy-guts!
Greedy-guts.
David Michael!
David Michael,
stop it right now.
Fi-ine.

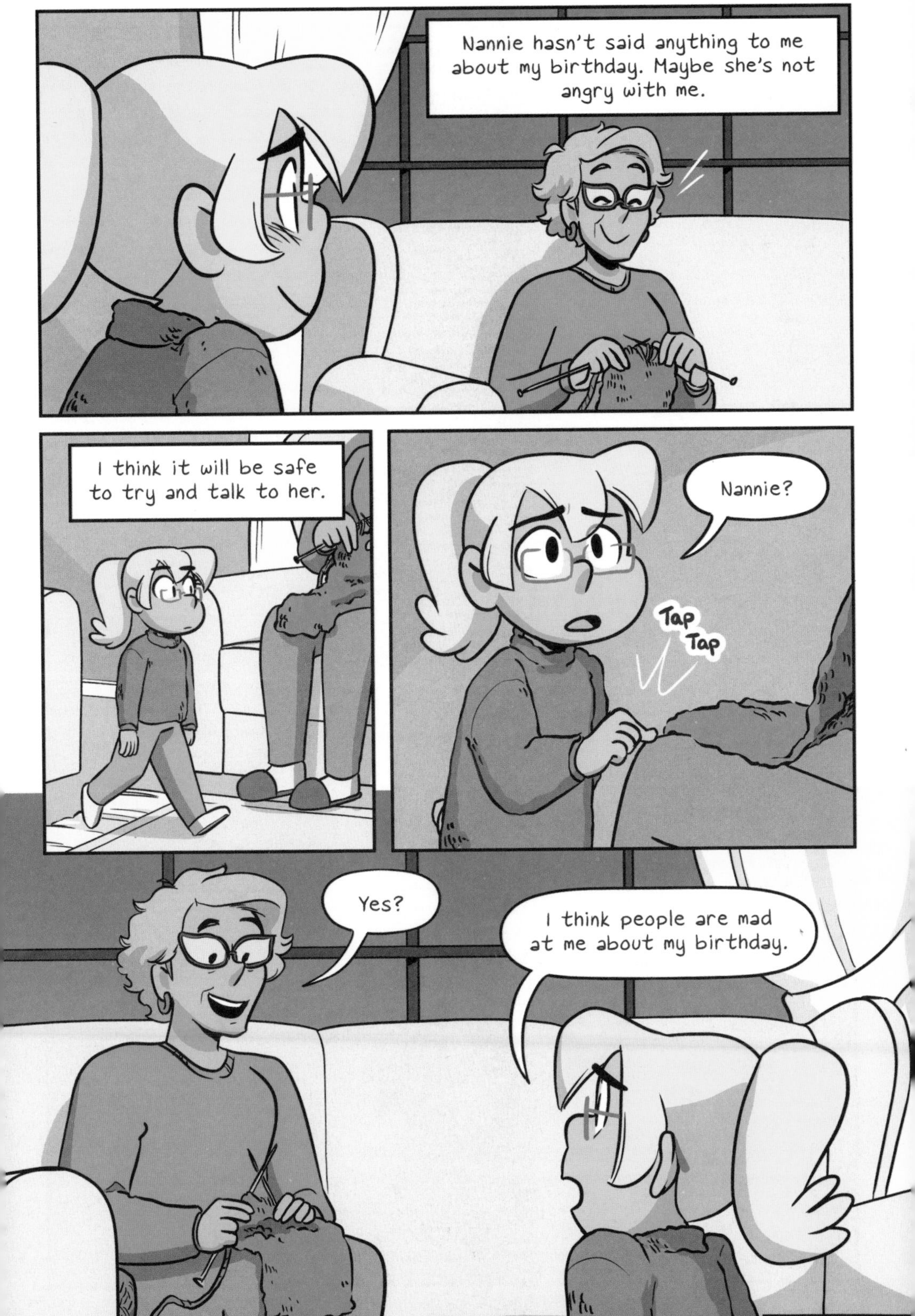
Nannie hasn't said anything to me about my birthday. Maybe she's not angry with me.
I think it will be safe to try and talk to her.
Nannie?
Tap
Tap
Yes?
I think people are mad at me about my birthday.

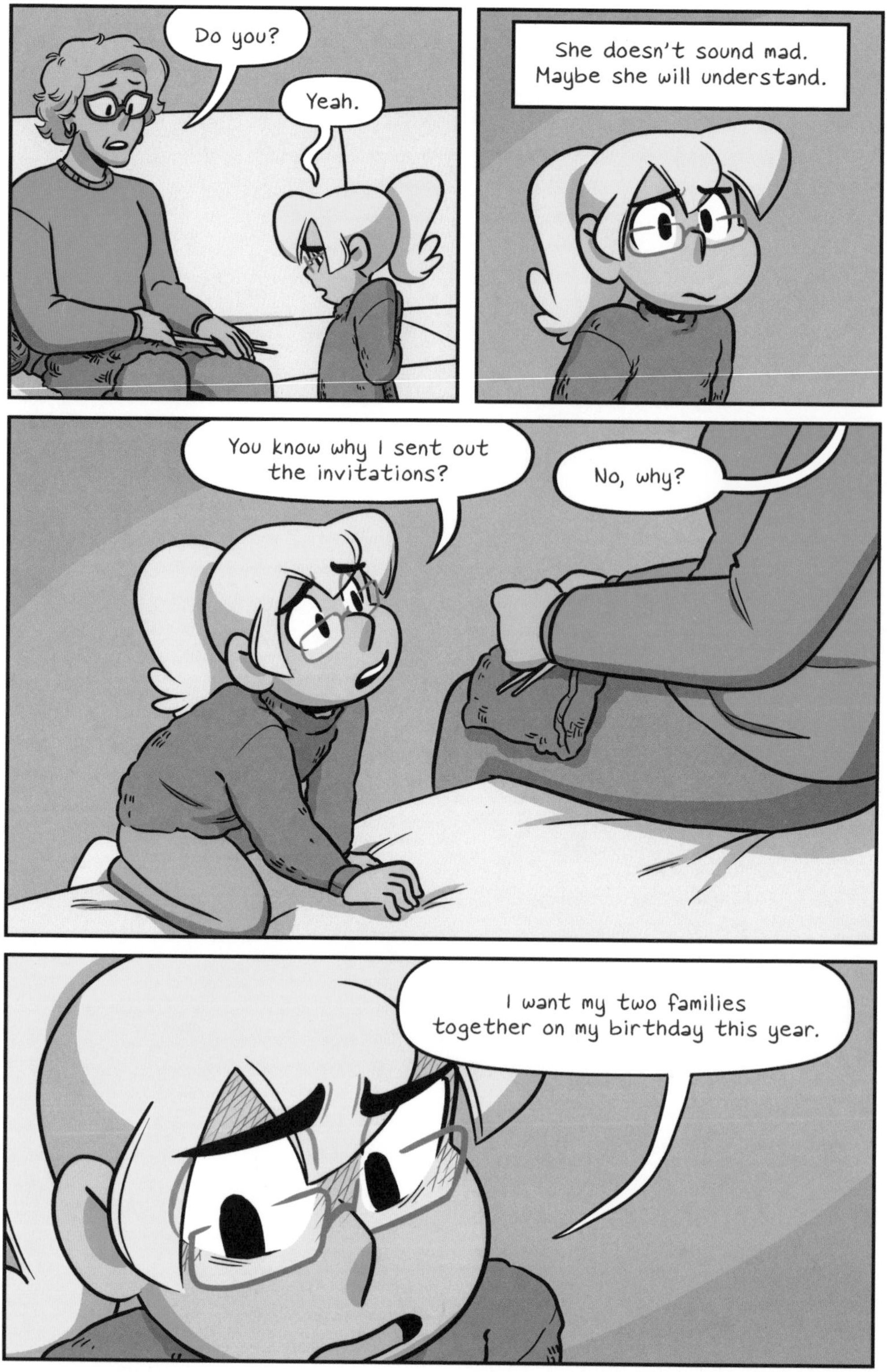
Do you?
Yeah.
She doesn't sound mad. Maybe she will understand.
You know why I sent out the invitations?
No, why?
I want my two families together on my birthday this year.

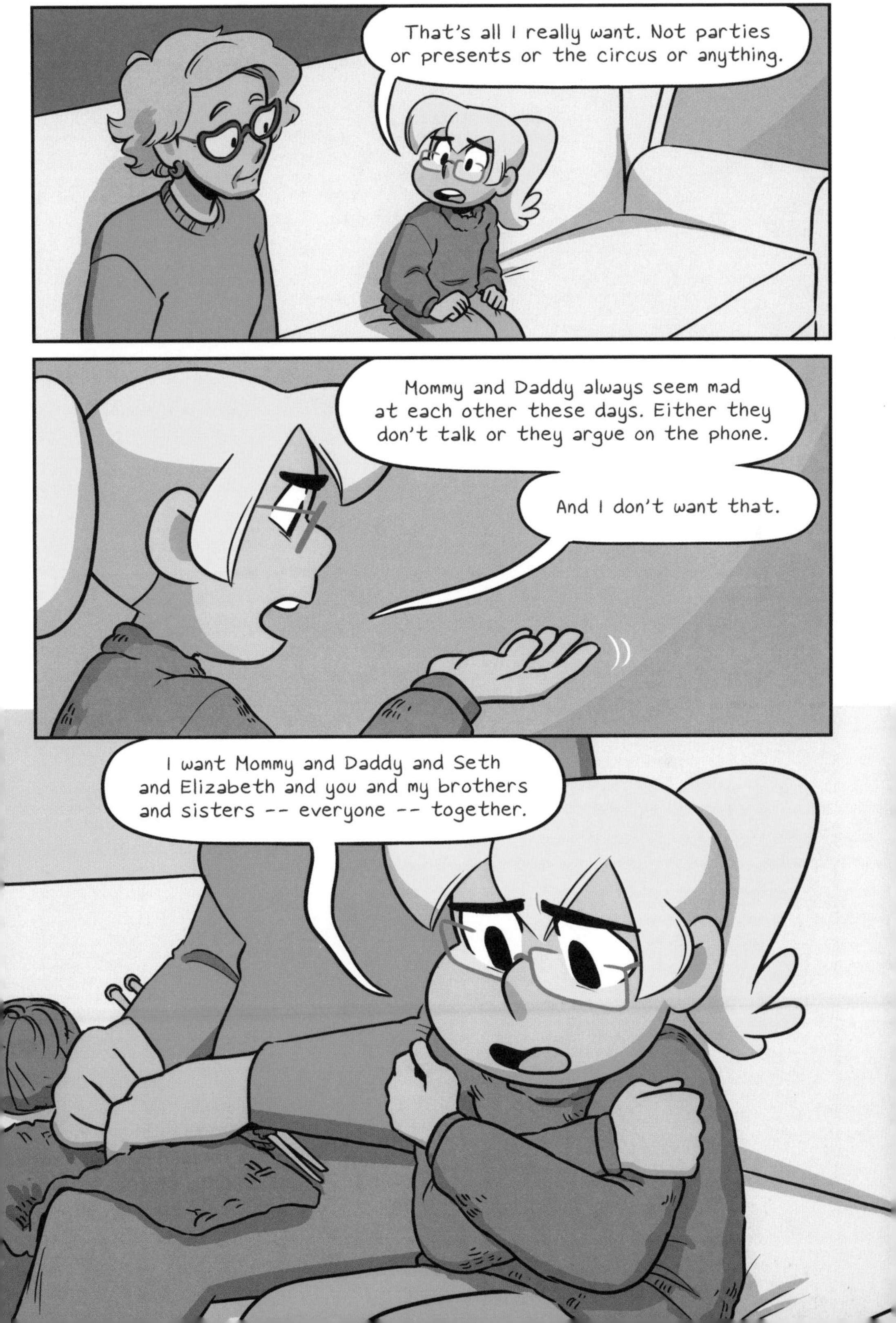
That's all I really want. Not parties or presents or the circus or anything.
Mommy and Daddy always seem mad at each other these days. Either they don't talk or they argue on the phone.
And I don't want that.
I want Mommy and Daddy and Seth and Elizabeth and you and my brothers and sisters -- everyone -- together.

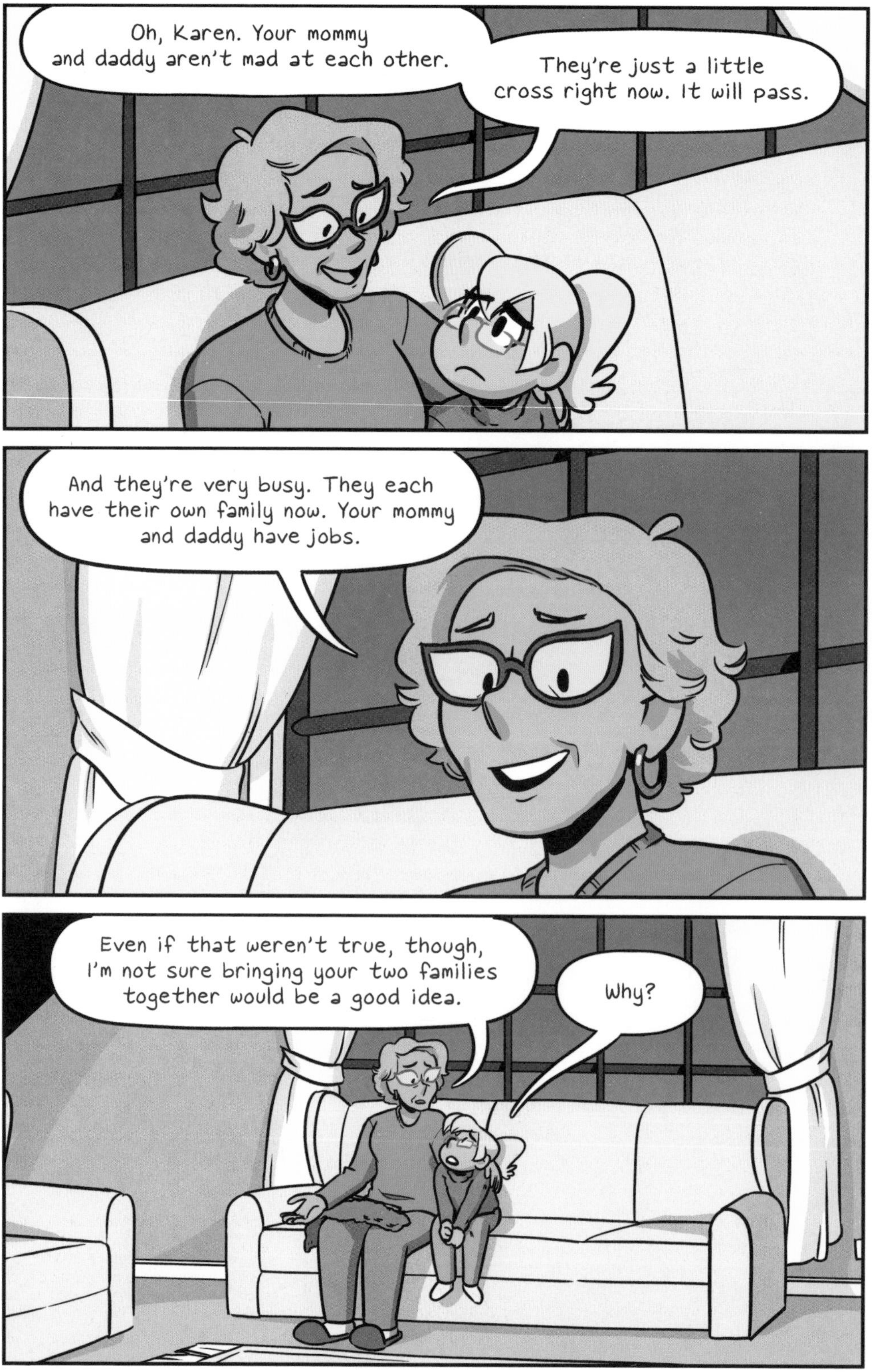
Oh, Karen. Your mommy and daddy aren't mad at each other.
They're just a little cross right now. It will pass.
And they're very busy. They each have their own family now. Your mommy and daddy have jobs.
Even if that weren't true, though, I'm not sure bringing your two families together would be a good idea.
Why?

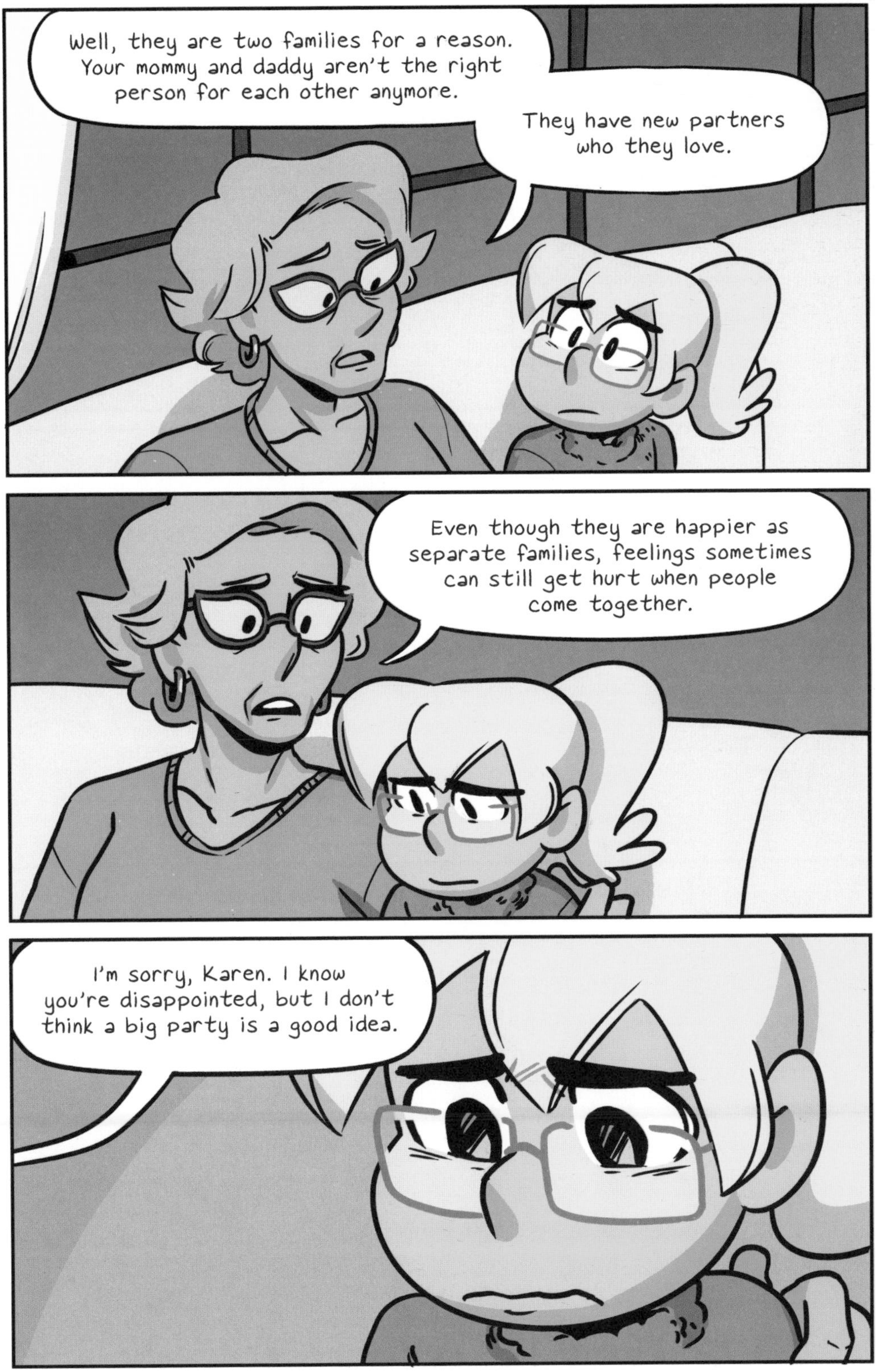
Well, they are two families for a reason. Your mommy and daddy aren't the right person for each other anymore.
They have new partners who they love.
Even though they are happier as separate families, feelings sometimes can still get hurt when people come together.
I'm sorry, Karen. I know you're disappointed, but I don't think a big party is a good idea.

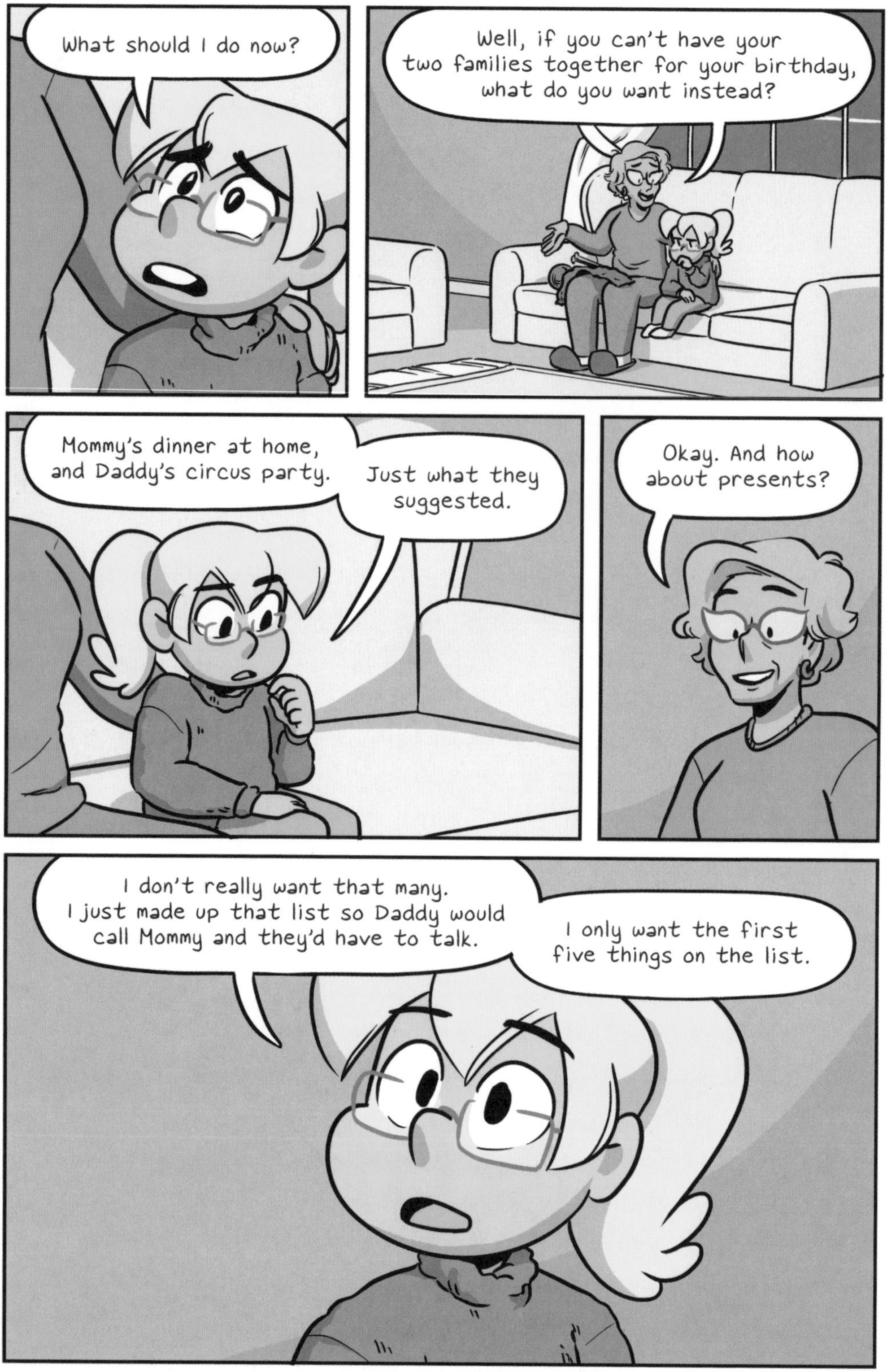
What should I do now?
Well, if you can't have your two families together for your birthday, what do you want instead?
Mommy's dinner at home, and Daddy's circus party.
Just what they suggested.
Okay. And how about presents?
I don't really want that many. I just made up that list so Daddy would call Mommy and they'd have to talk.
I only want the first five things on the list.

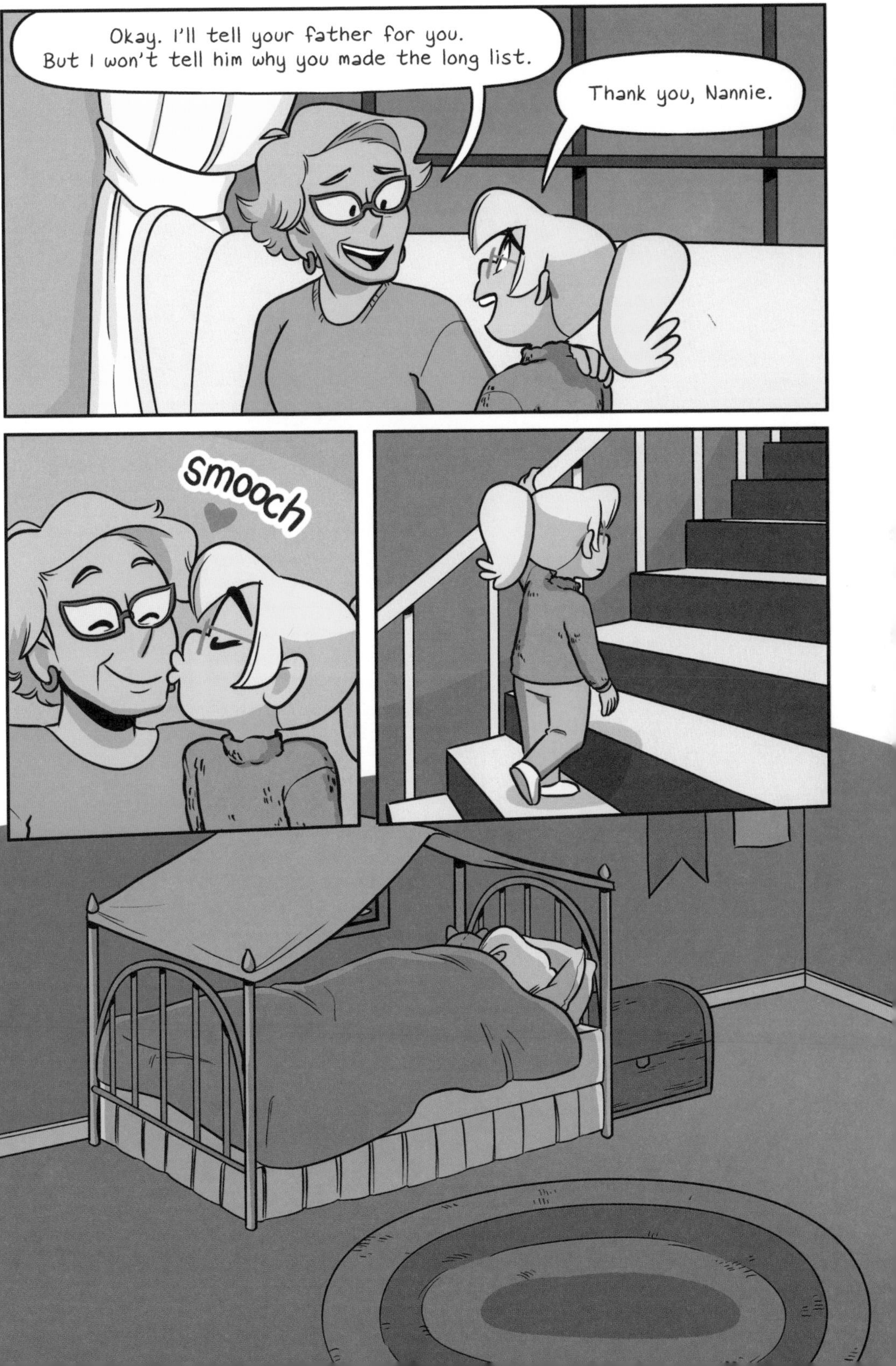
Okay. I'll tell your father for you. But I won't tell him why you made the long list.
Thank you, Nannie.
smooch

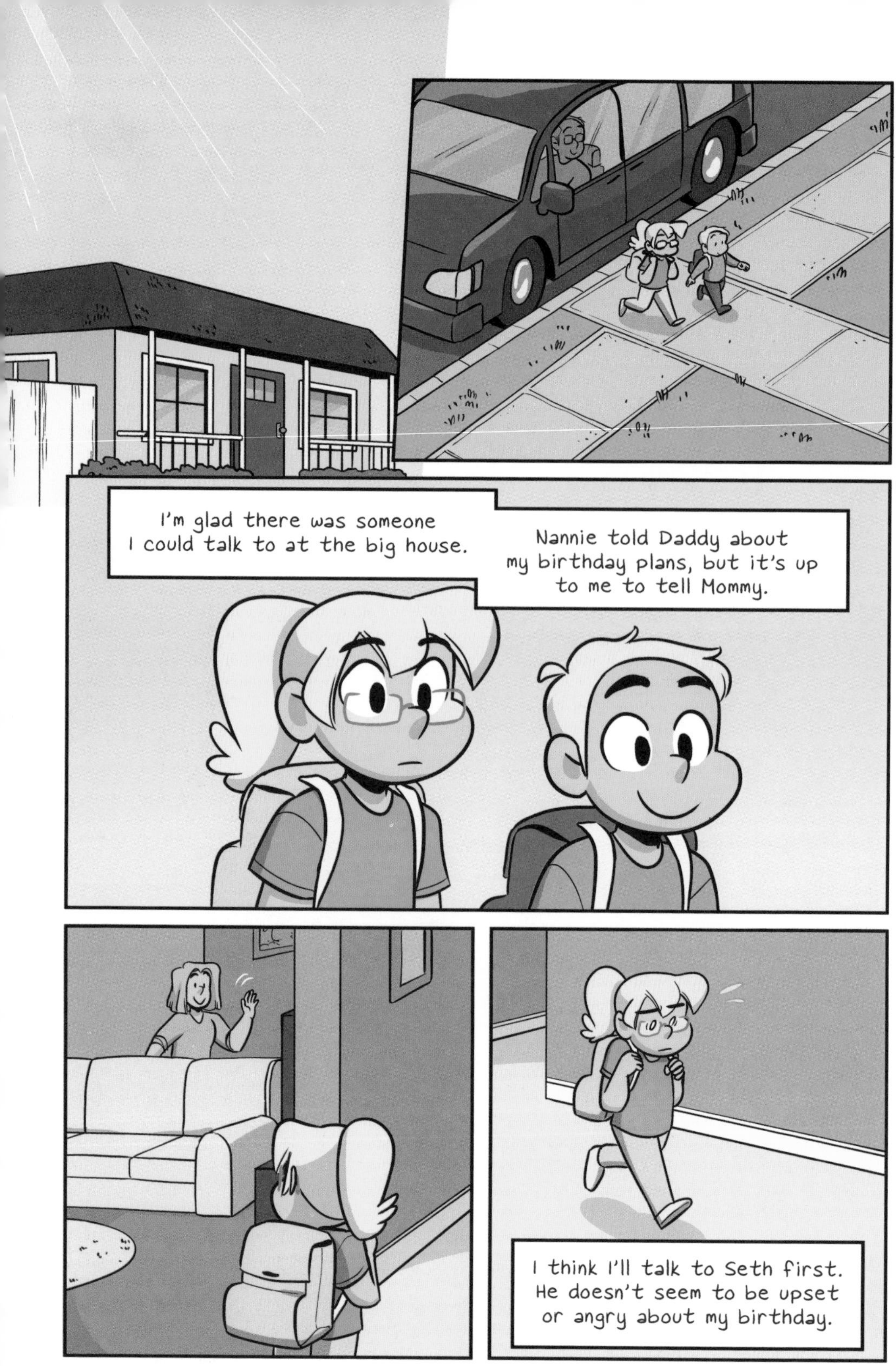
I'm glad there was someone I could talk to at the big house.
Nannie told Daddy about my birthday plans, but it's up to me to tell Mommy.
I think I'll talk to Seth first. He doesn't seem to be upset or angry about my birthday.

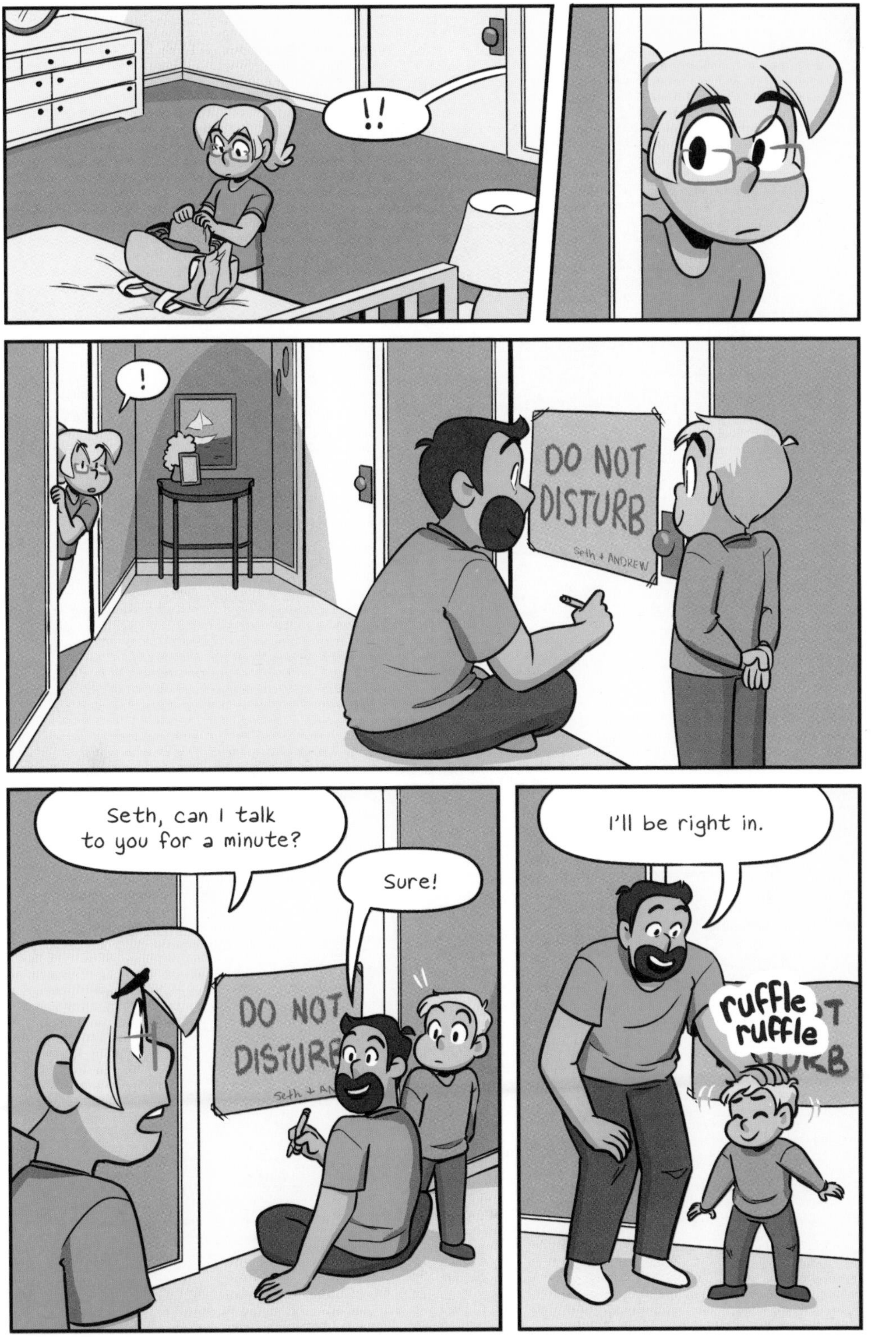
!!
!
DO NOT DISTURB
Seth + ANDREW
Seth, can I talk to you for a minute?
Sure!
DO NOT DISTURB
I'll be right in.
ruffle ruffle

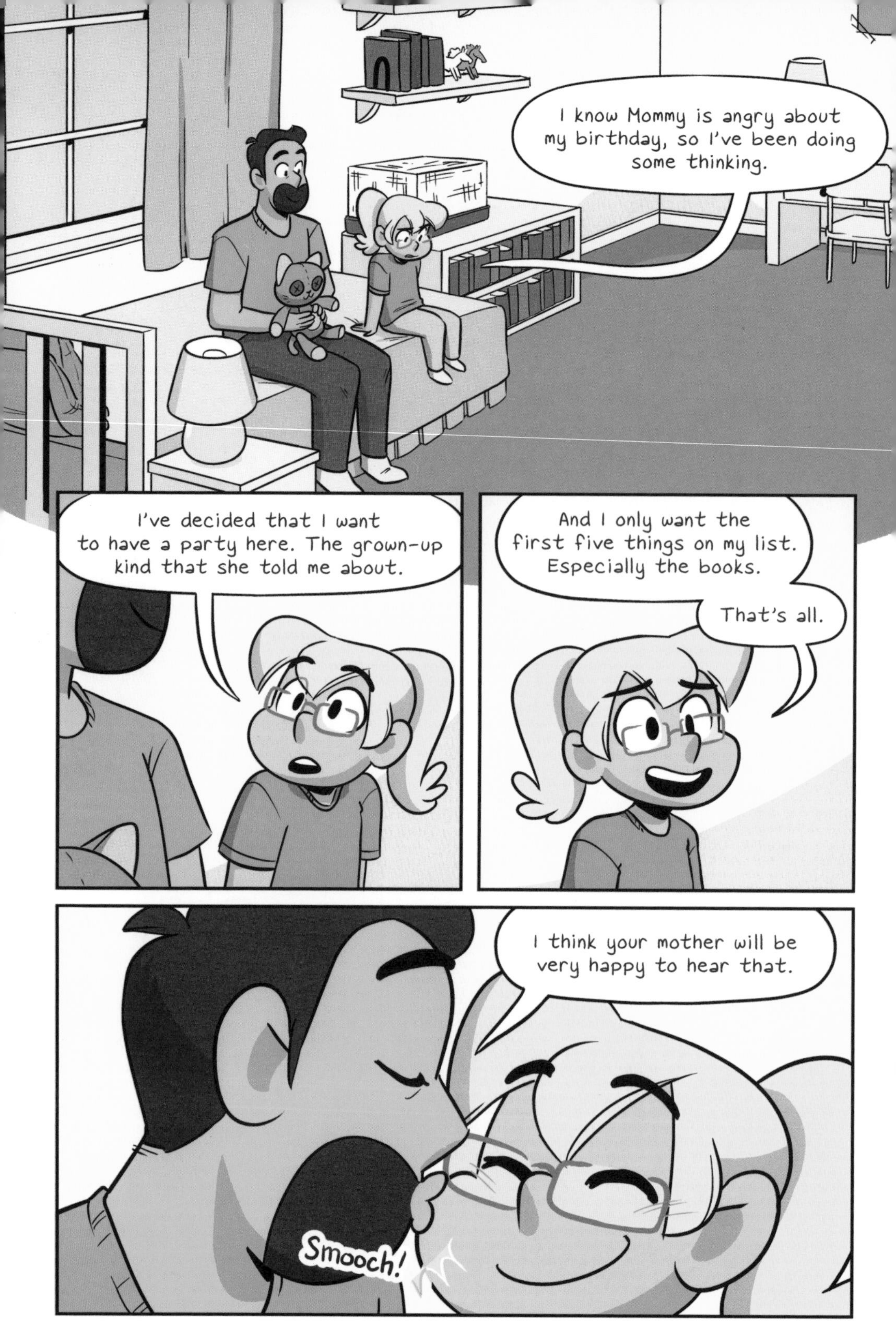
I know Mommy is angry about my birthday, so I've been doing some thinking.
I've decided that I want to have a party here. The grown-up kind that she told me about.
And I only want the first five things on my list. Especially the books.
That's all.
I think your mother will be very happy to hear that.
Smooch!

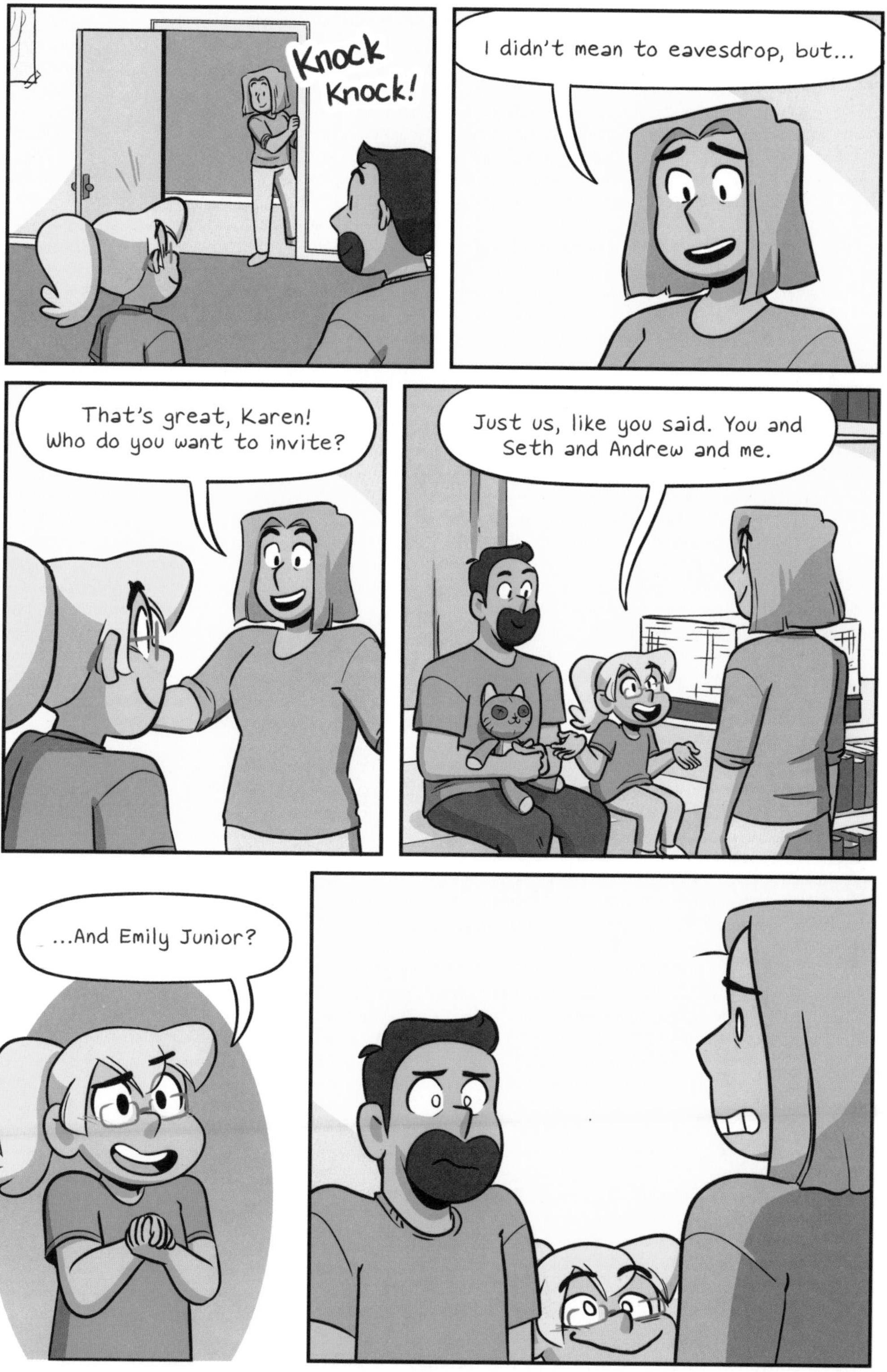
Knock Knock!
I didn't mean to eavesdrop, but...
That's great, Karen! Who do you want to invite?
Just us, like you said. You and Seth and Andrew and me.
...And Emily Junior?

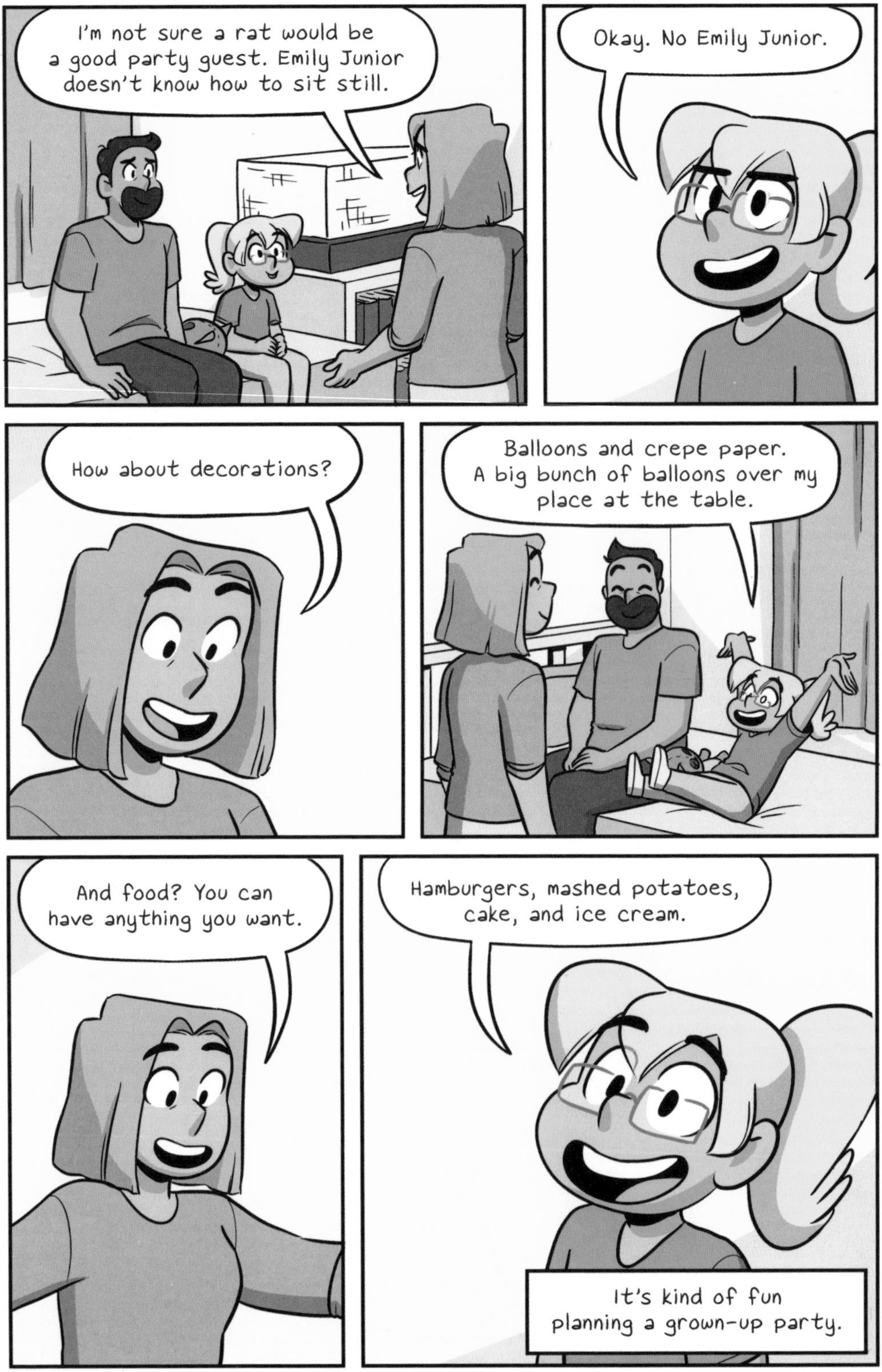
I'm not sure a rat would be a good party guest. Emily Junior doesn't know how to sit still.
Okay. No Emily Junior.
How about decorations?
Balloons and crepe paper. A big bunch of balloons over my place at the table.
And food? You can have anything you want.
Hamburgers, mashed potatoes, cake, and ice cream.
It's kind of fun planning a grown-up party.

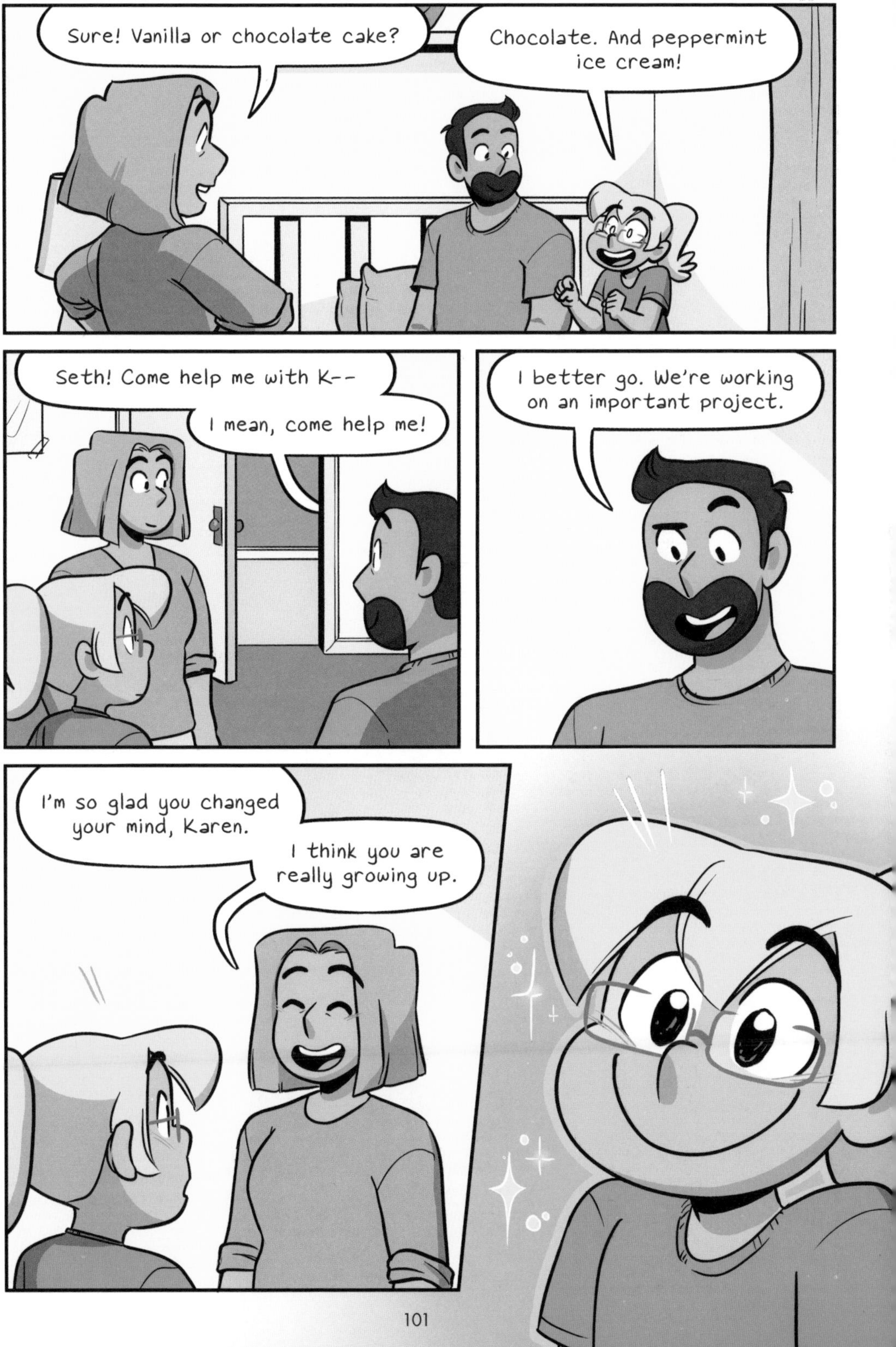
Sure! Vanilla or chocolate cake?
Chocolate. And peppermint ice cream!
Seth! Come help me with K--
I mean, come help me!
I better go. We're working on an important project.
I'm so glad you changed your mind, Karen.
I think you are really growing up.

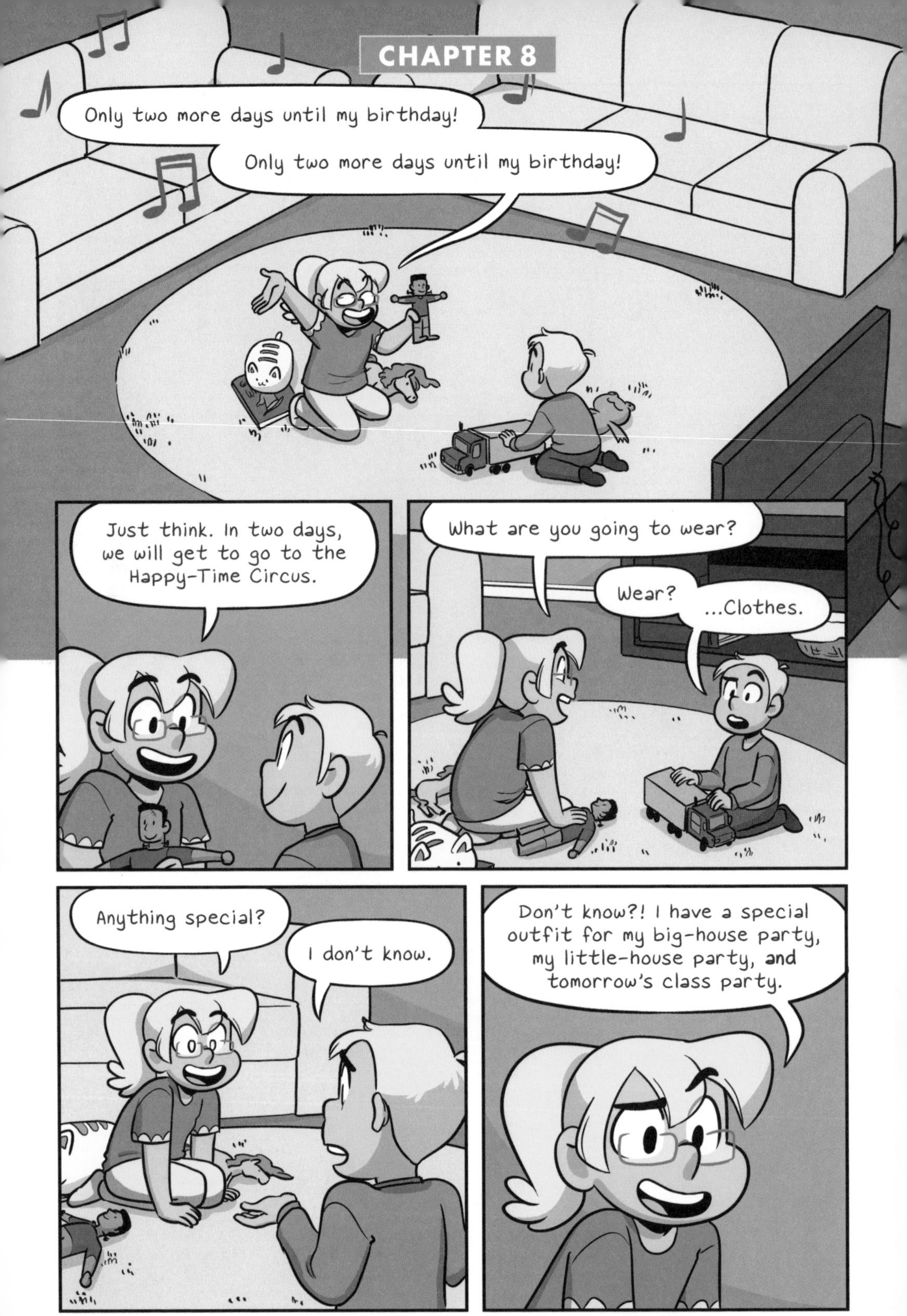
CHAPTER 8
Only two more days until my birthday!
Only two more days until my birthday!
Just think. In two days, we will get to go to the Happy-Time Circus.
What are you going to wear?
Wear?
...Clothes.
Anything special?
I don't know.
Don't know?! I have a special outfit for my big-house party, my little-house party, and tomorrow's class party.

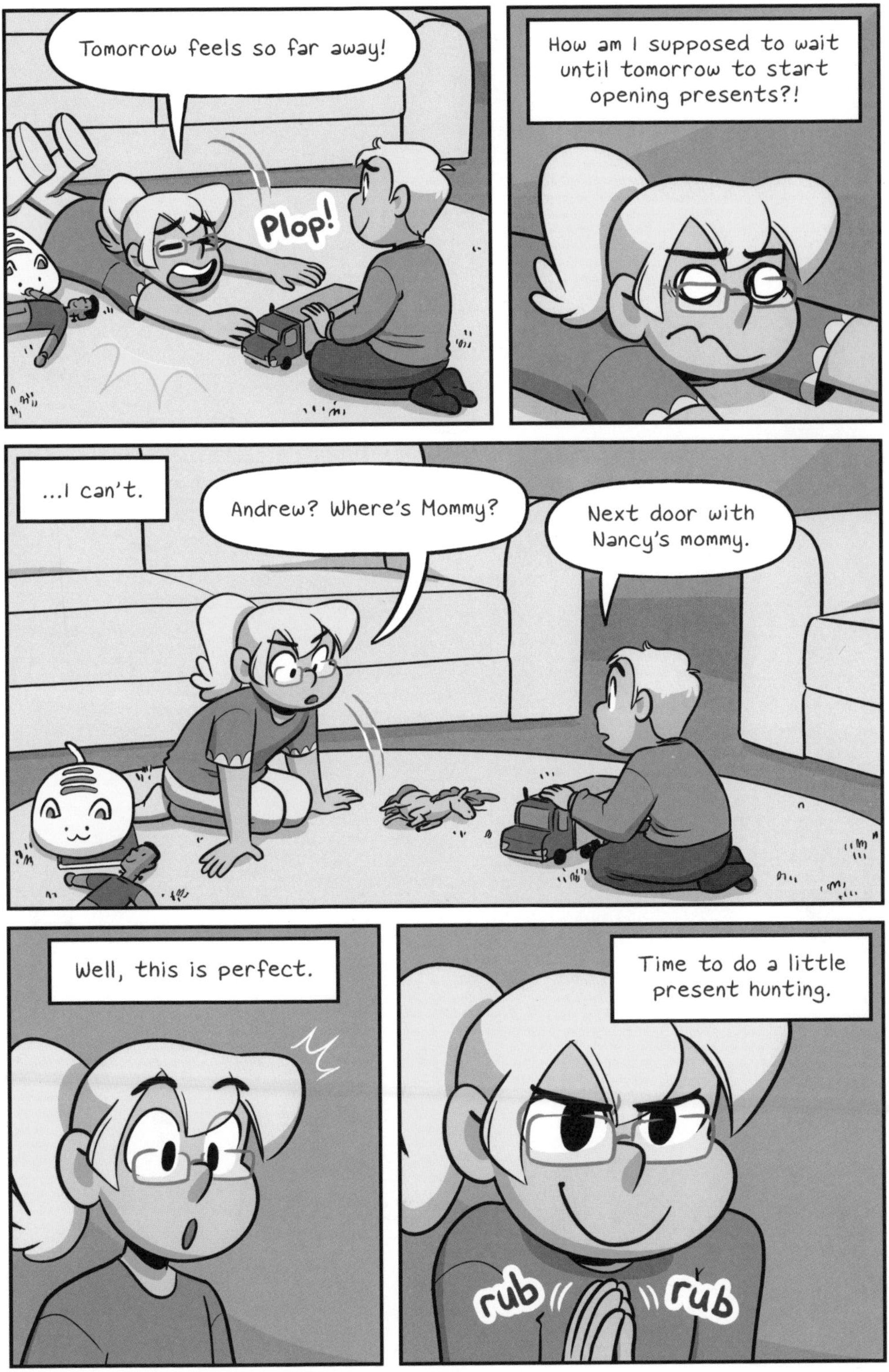
Tomorrow feels so far away!
Plop!
How am I supposed to wait until tomorrow to start opening presents?!
...I can't.
Andrew? Where's Mommy?
Next door with Nancy's mommy.
Well, this is perfect.
Time to do a little present hunting.
rub rub

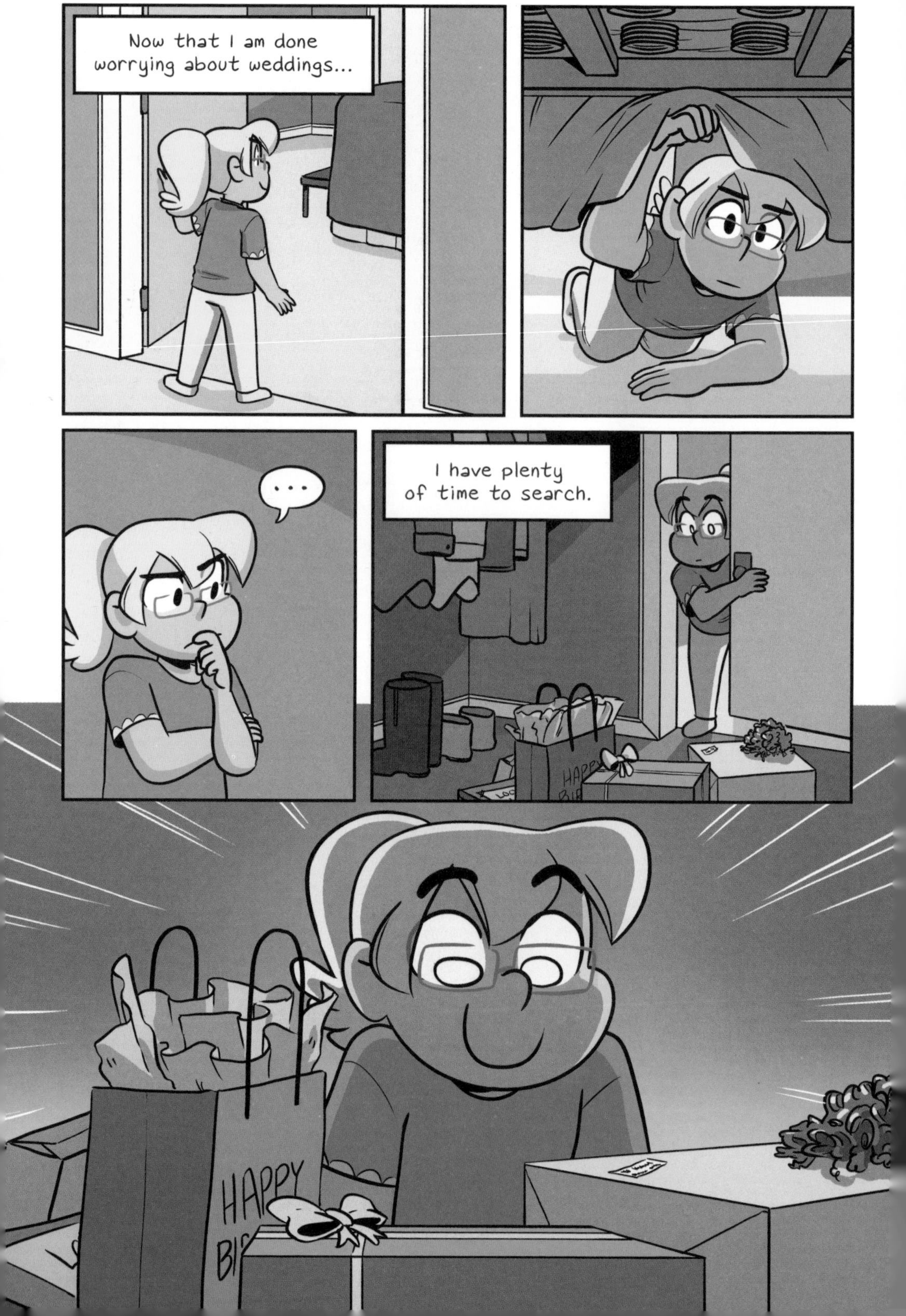

Now that I am done worrying about weddings...
. . .
I have plenty of time to search.
HAPPY

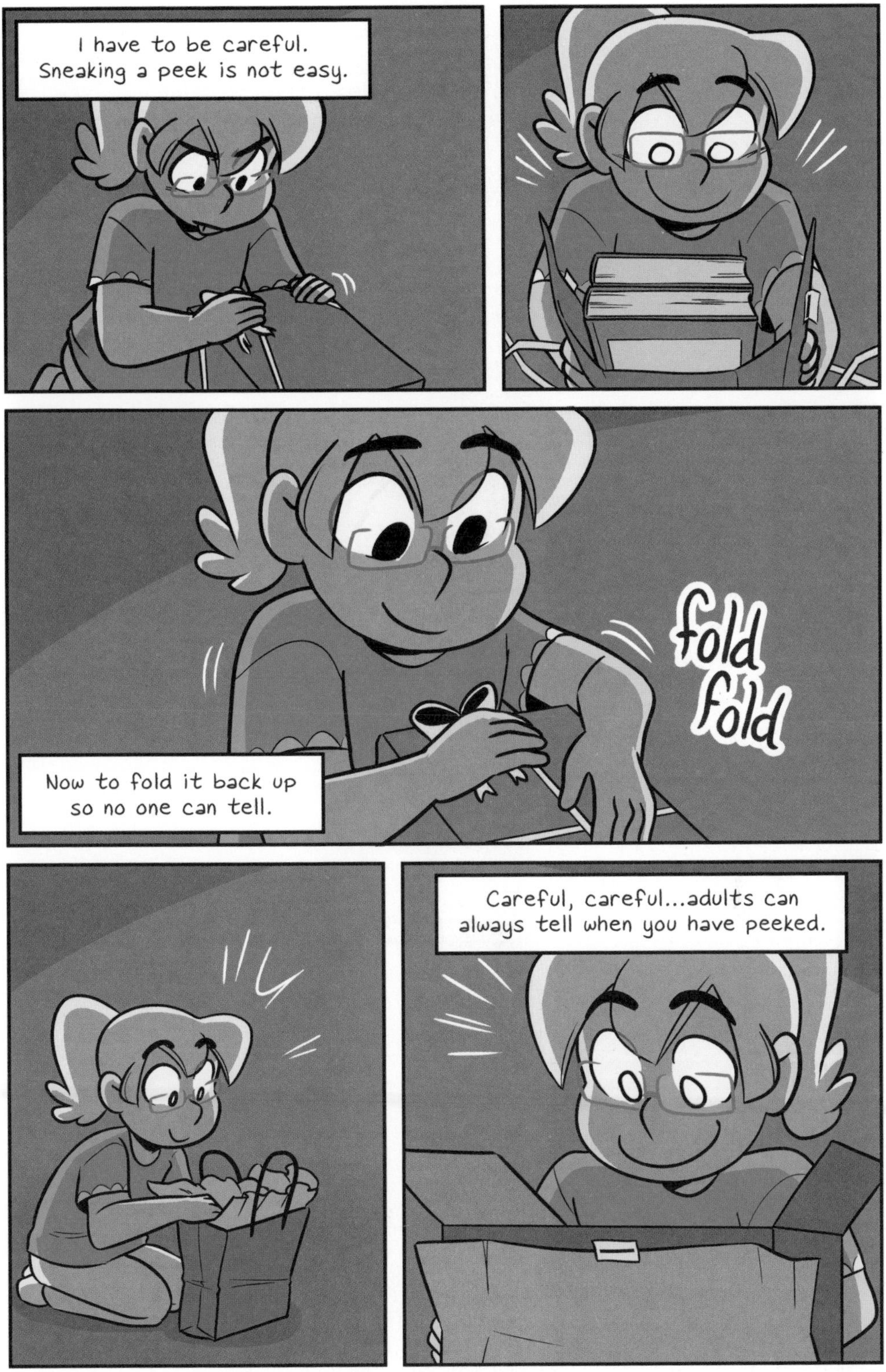
I have to be careful.
Sneaking a peek is not easy.
fold
fold
Now to fold it back up so no one can tell.
Careful, careful...adults can always tell when you have peeked.

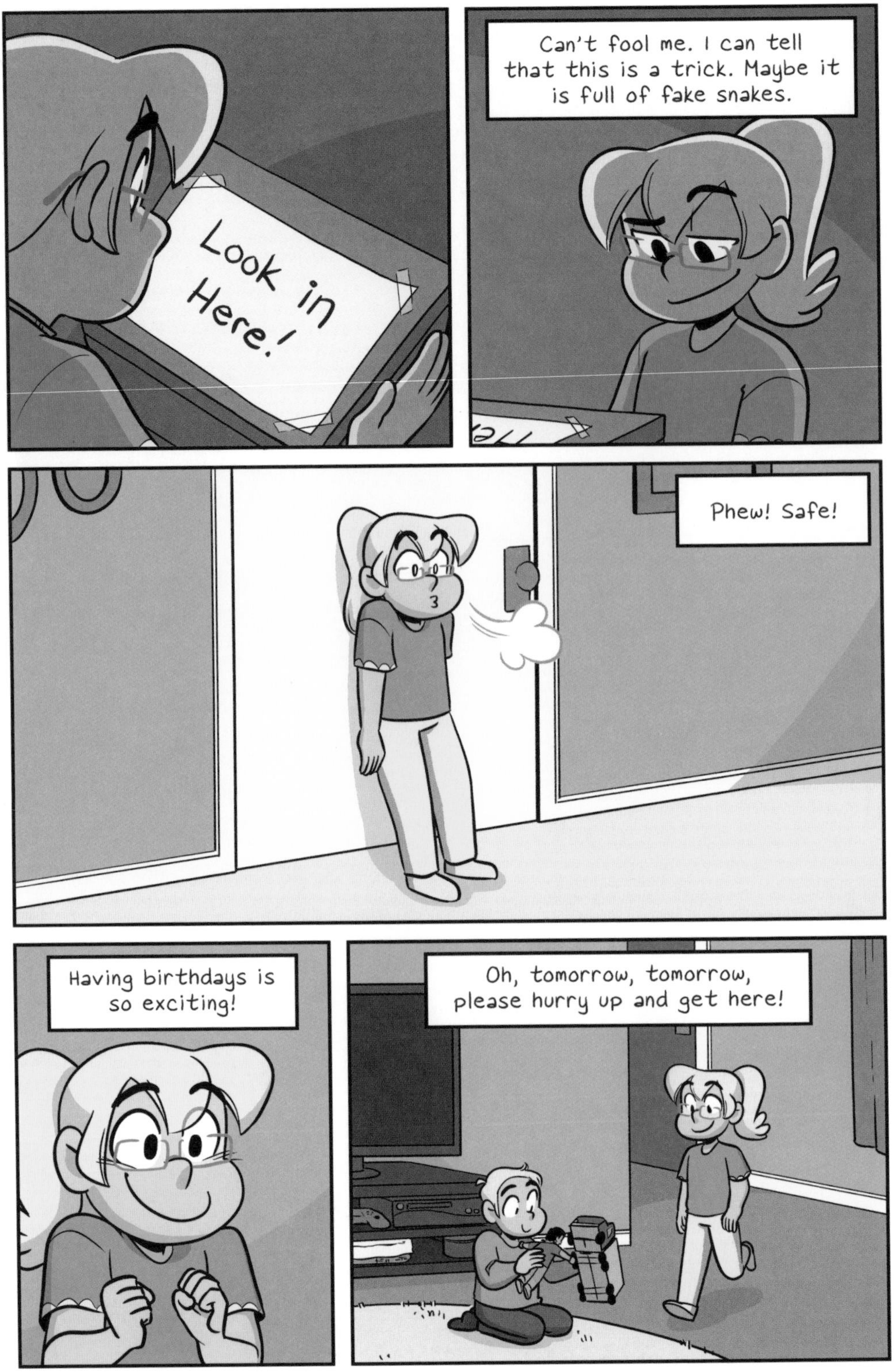
Look in Here!
Can't fool me. I can tell that this is a trick. Maybe it is full of fake snakes.
Phew! Safe!
Having birthdays is so exciting!
Oh, tomorrow, tomorrow, please hurry up and get here!

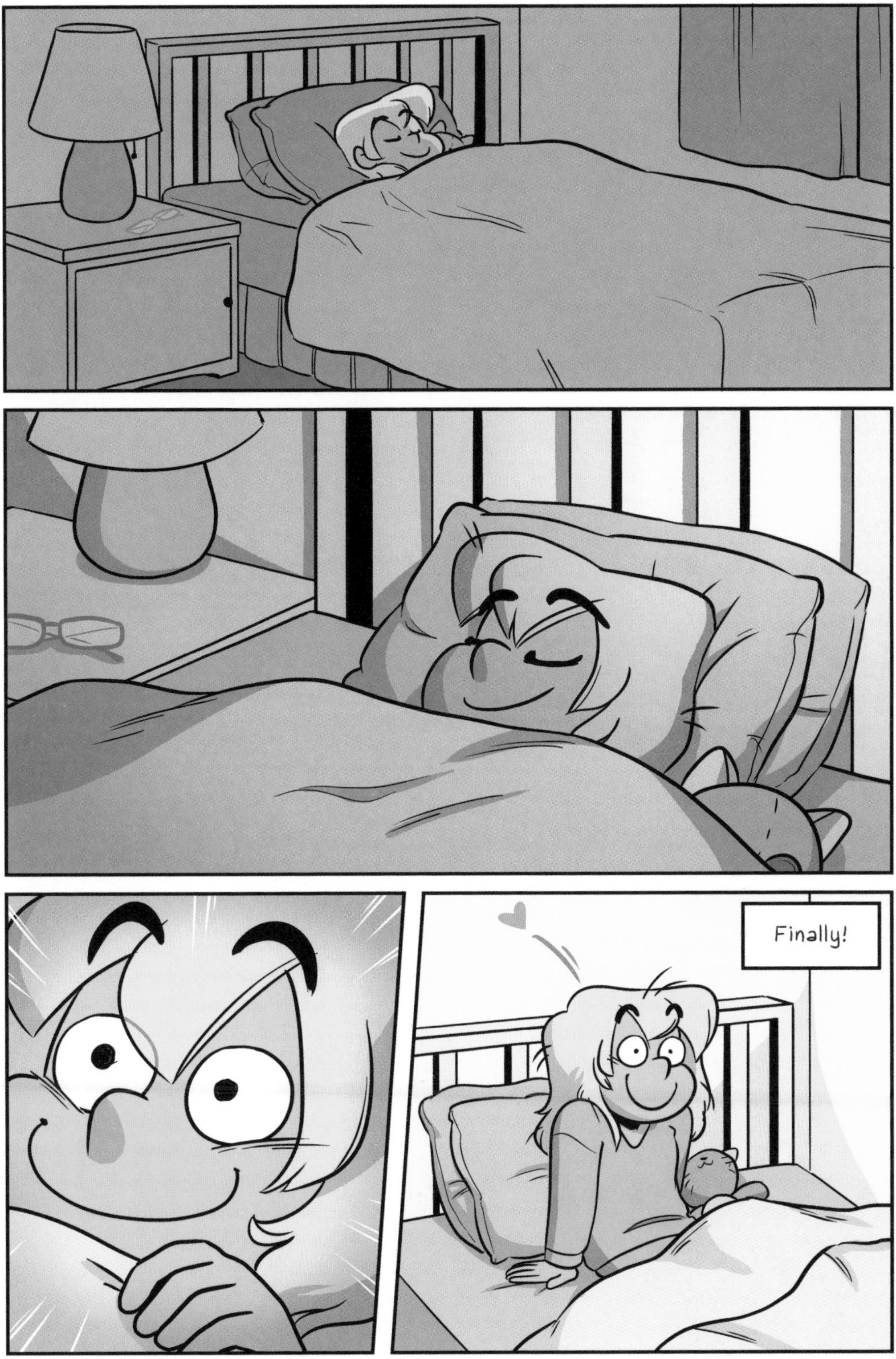
Finally!

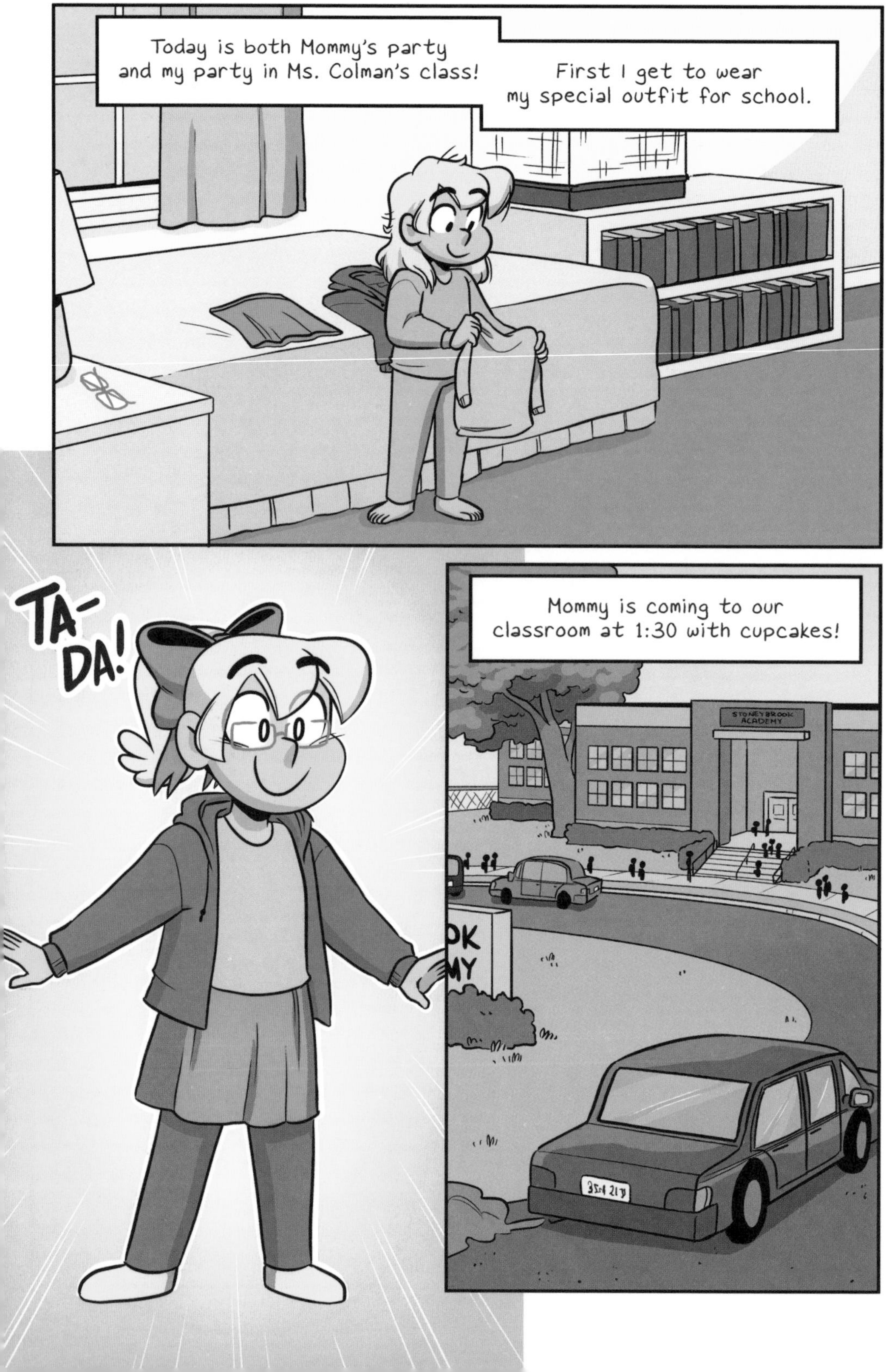
Today is both Mommy's party and my party in Ms. Colman's class!
First I get to wear my special outfit for school.
TA-DA!
Mommy is coming to our classroom at 1:30 with cupcakes!
STONEYBROOK ACADEMY

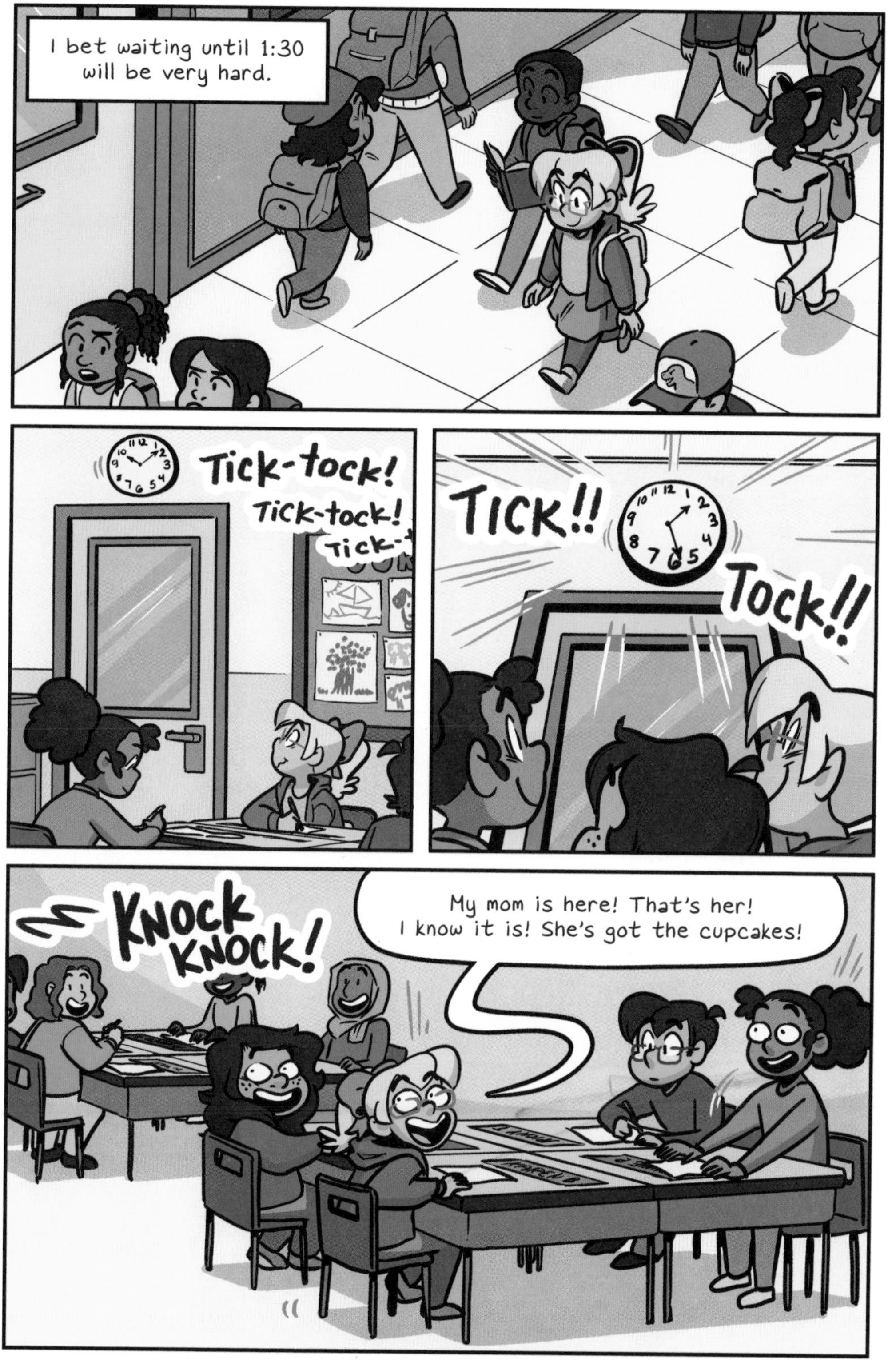

I bet waiting until 1:30 will be very hard.
Tick-tock!
Tick-tock!
TICK!!
Tock!!
KNOCK KNOCK!
My mom is here! That's her! I know it is! She's got the cupcakes!

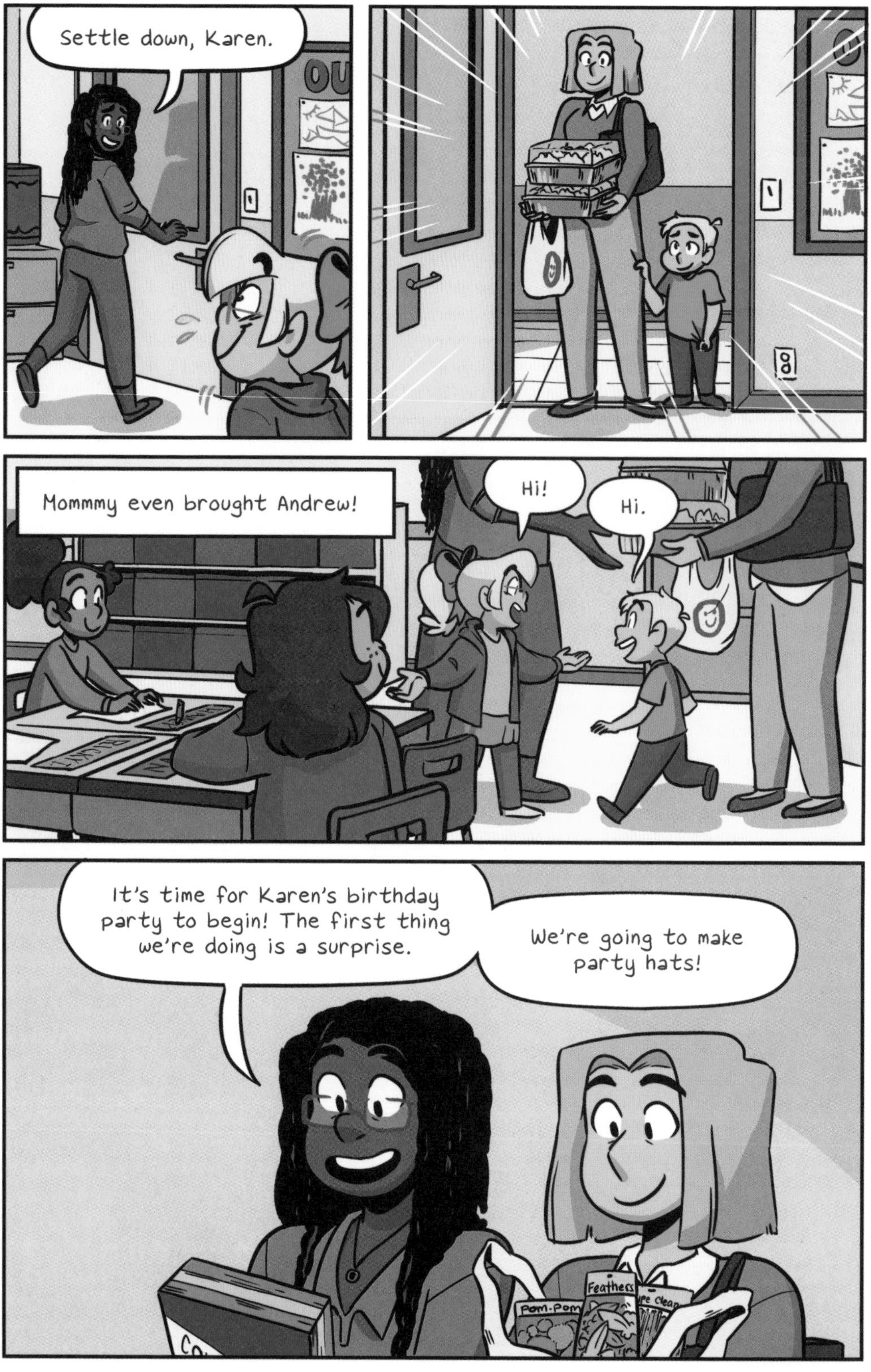
Settle down, Karen.
Mommmy even brought Andrew!
Hi!
Hi.
It's time for Karen's birthday party to begin! The first thing we're doing is a surprise.
We're going to make party hats!
Feathers
Pom-Pom

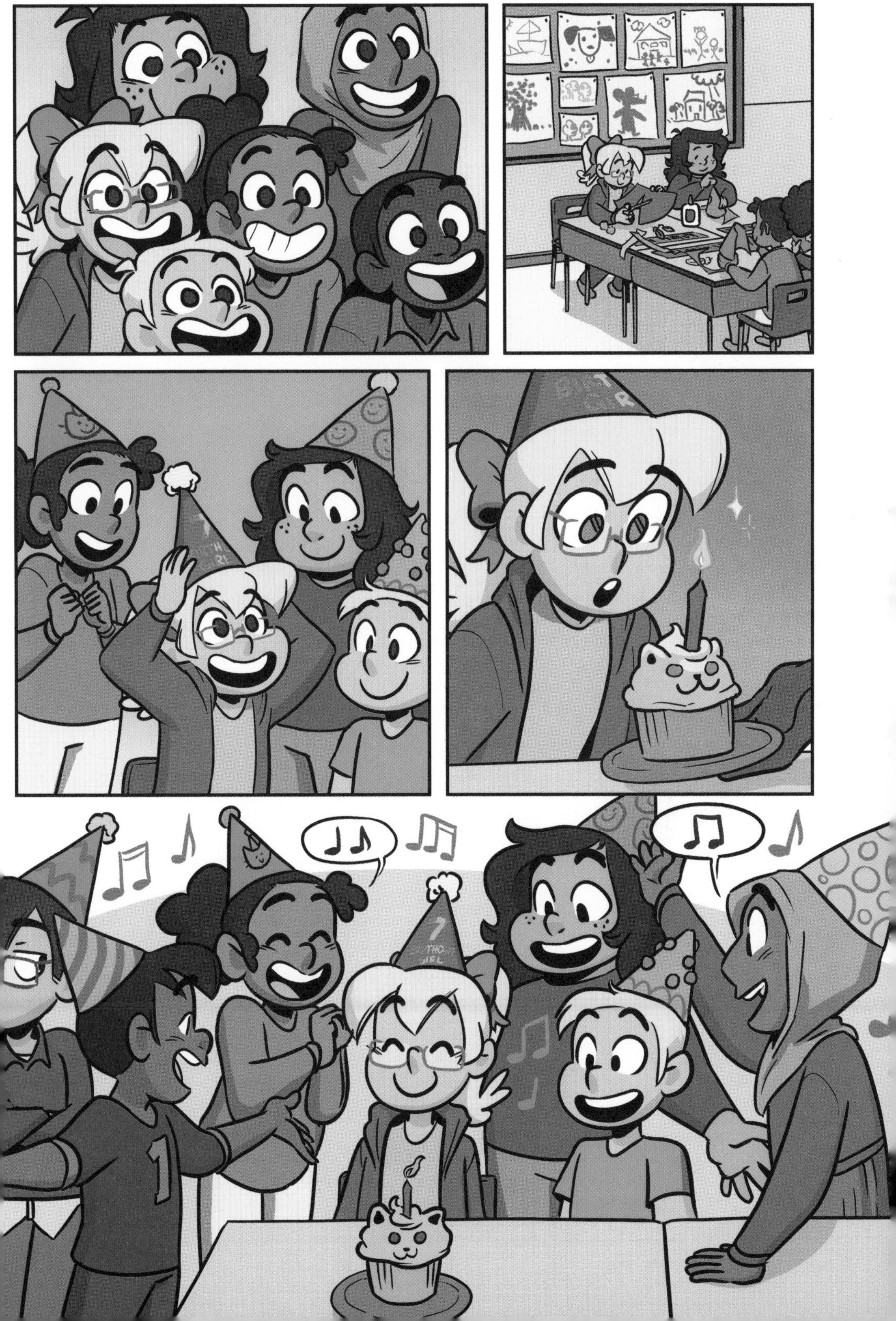

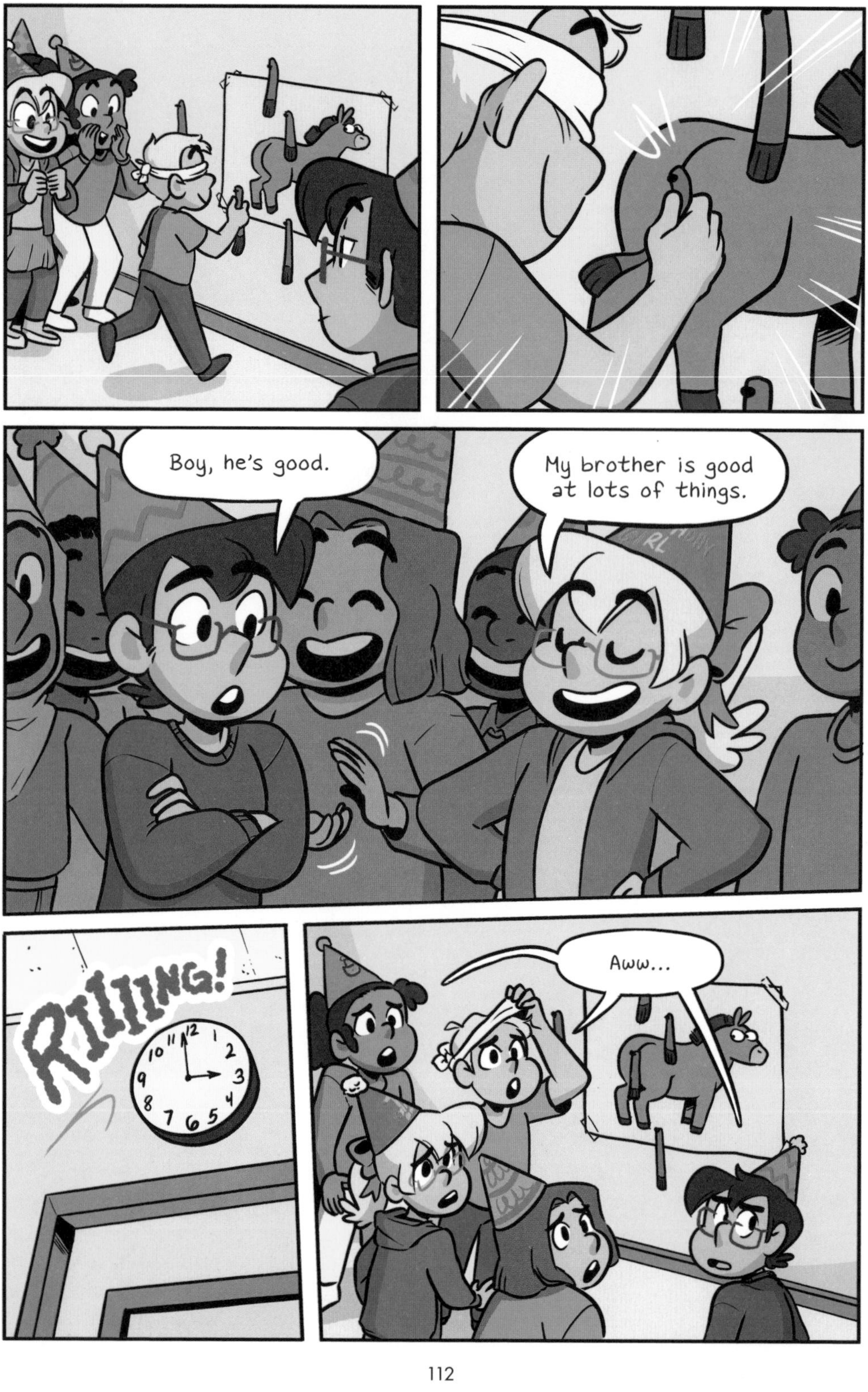
Boy, he's good.
My brother is good at lots of things.
RIIIING!
Aww...

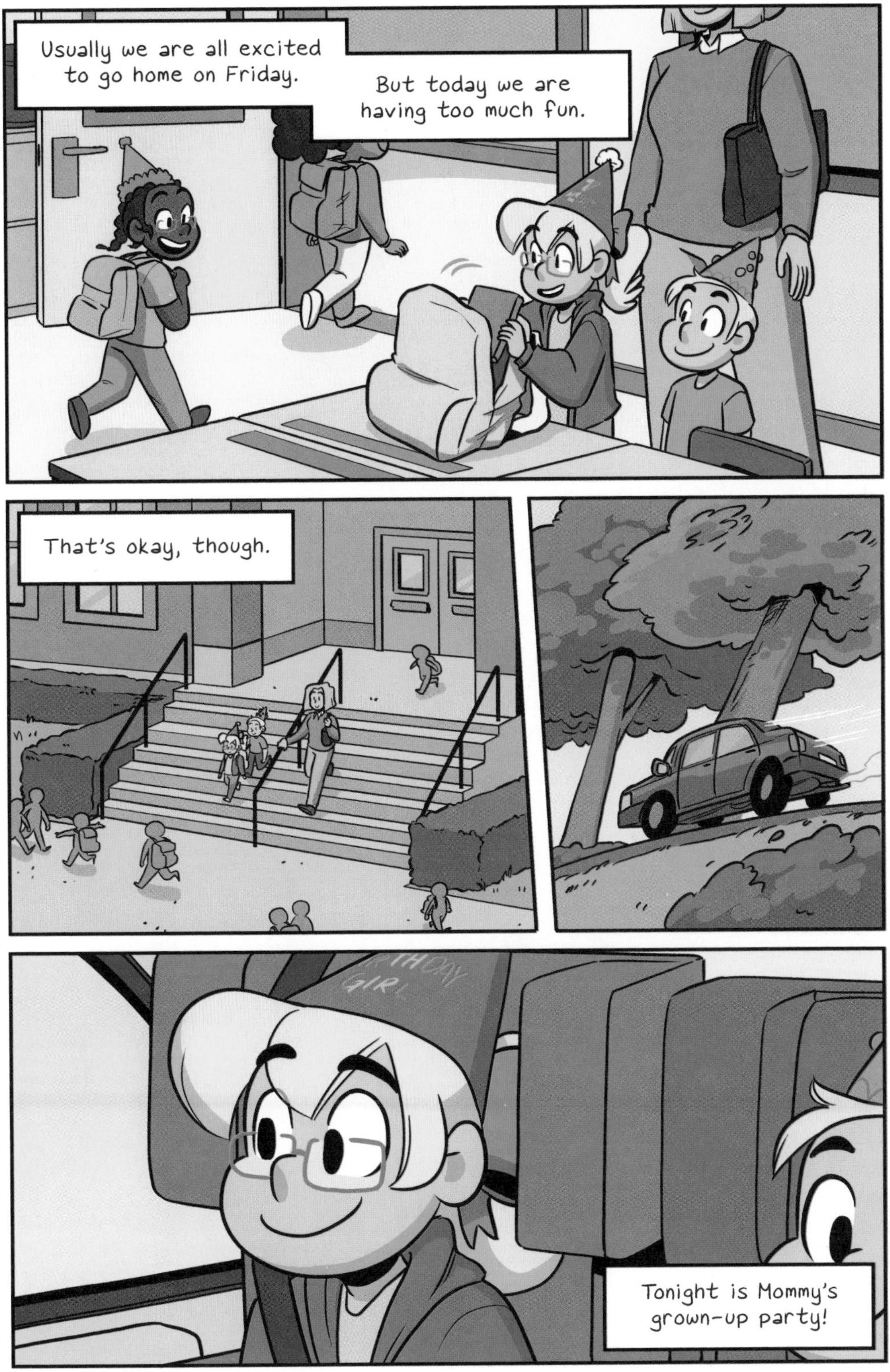
Usually we are all excited to go home on Friday.
But today we are having too much fun.
That's okay, though.
Tonight is Mommy's grown-up party!

CHAPTER 9

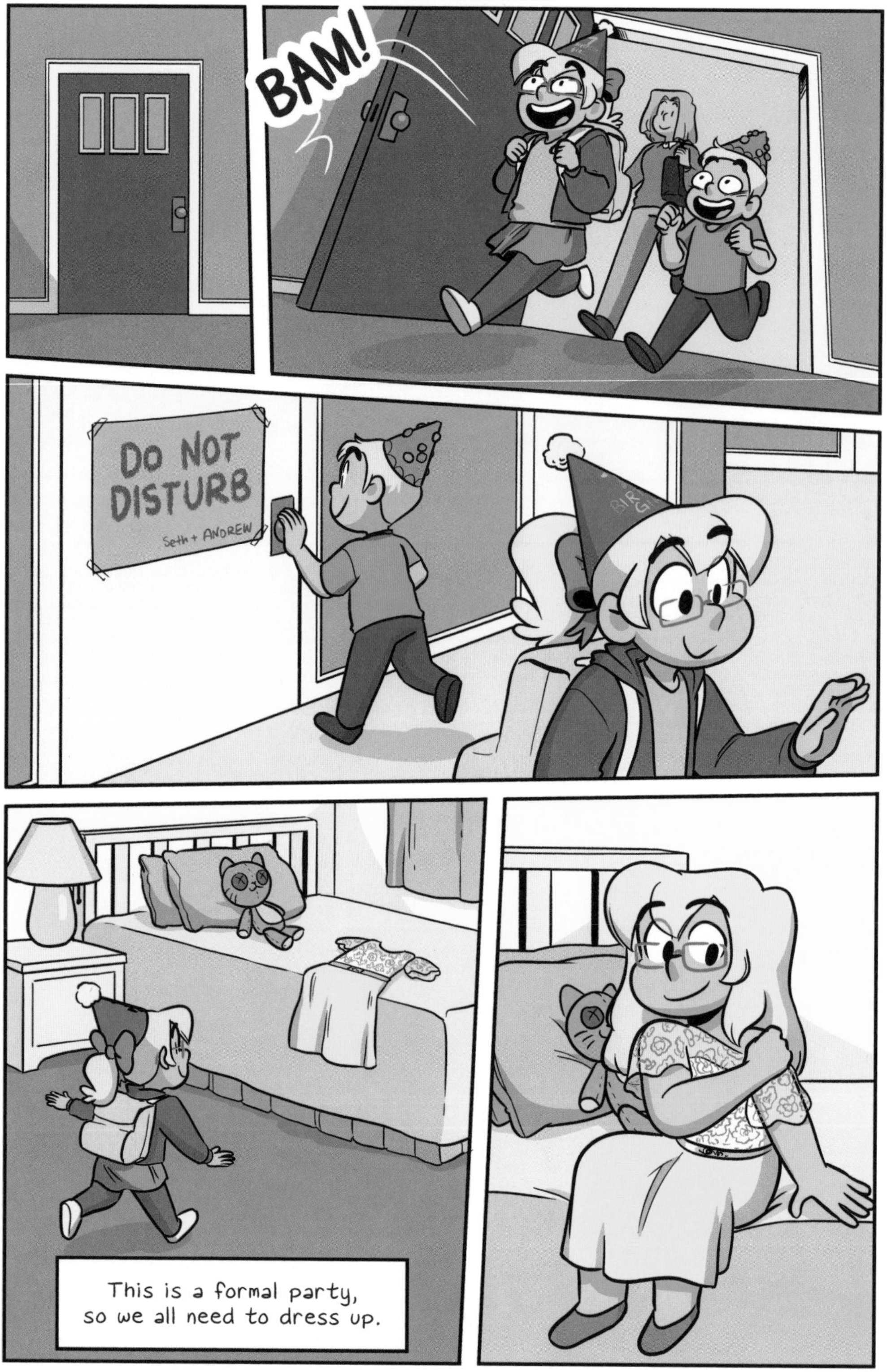
BAM!
DO NOT DISTURB
Seth + ANDREW
This is a formal party, so we all need to dress up.

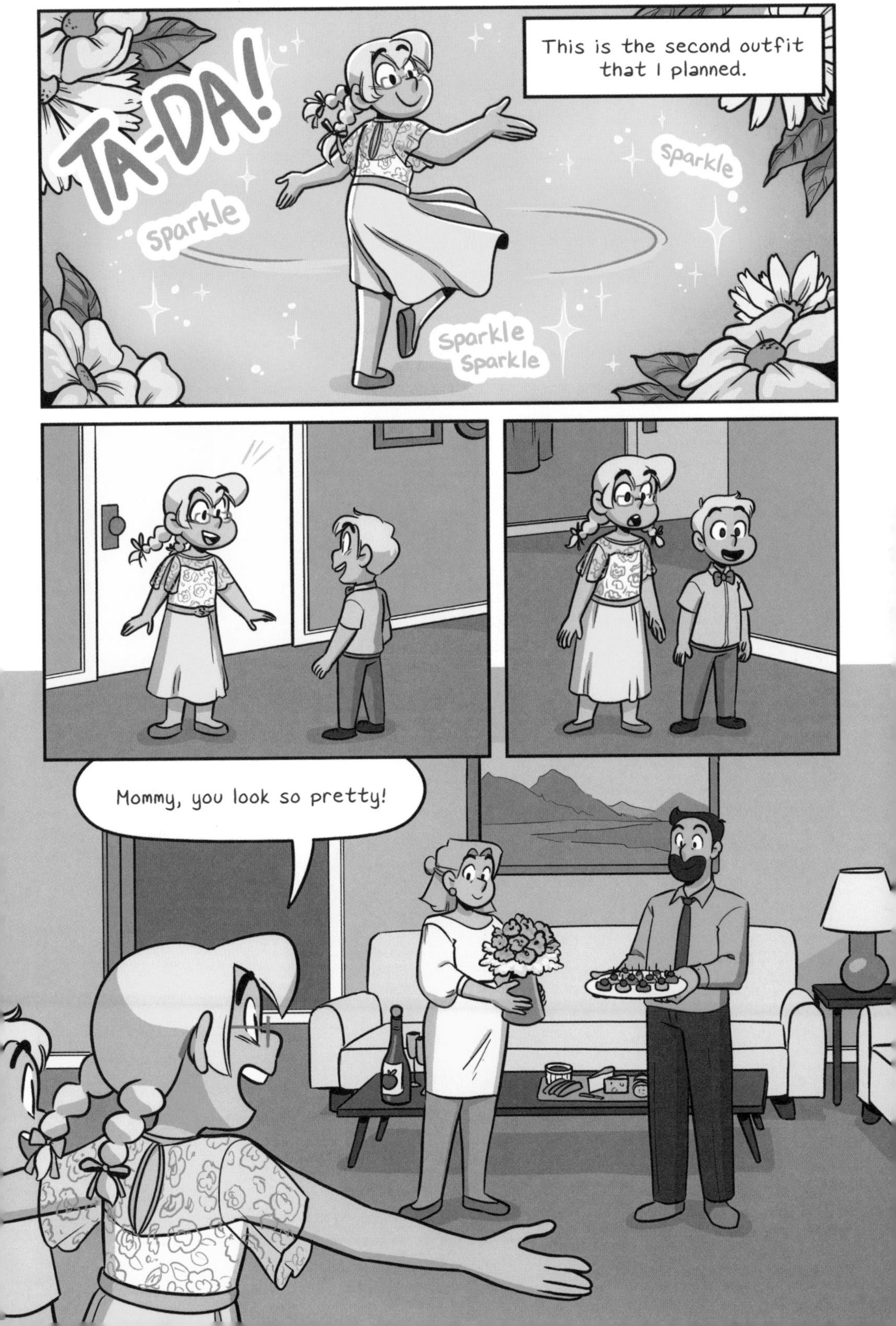
TA-DA!
This is the second outfit that I planned.
Sparkle
Sparkle
Sparkle
Sparkle
Sparkle
Mommy, you look so pretty!

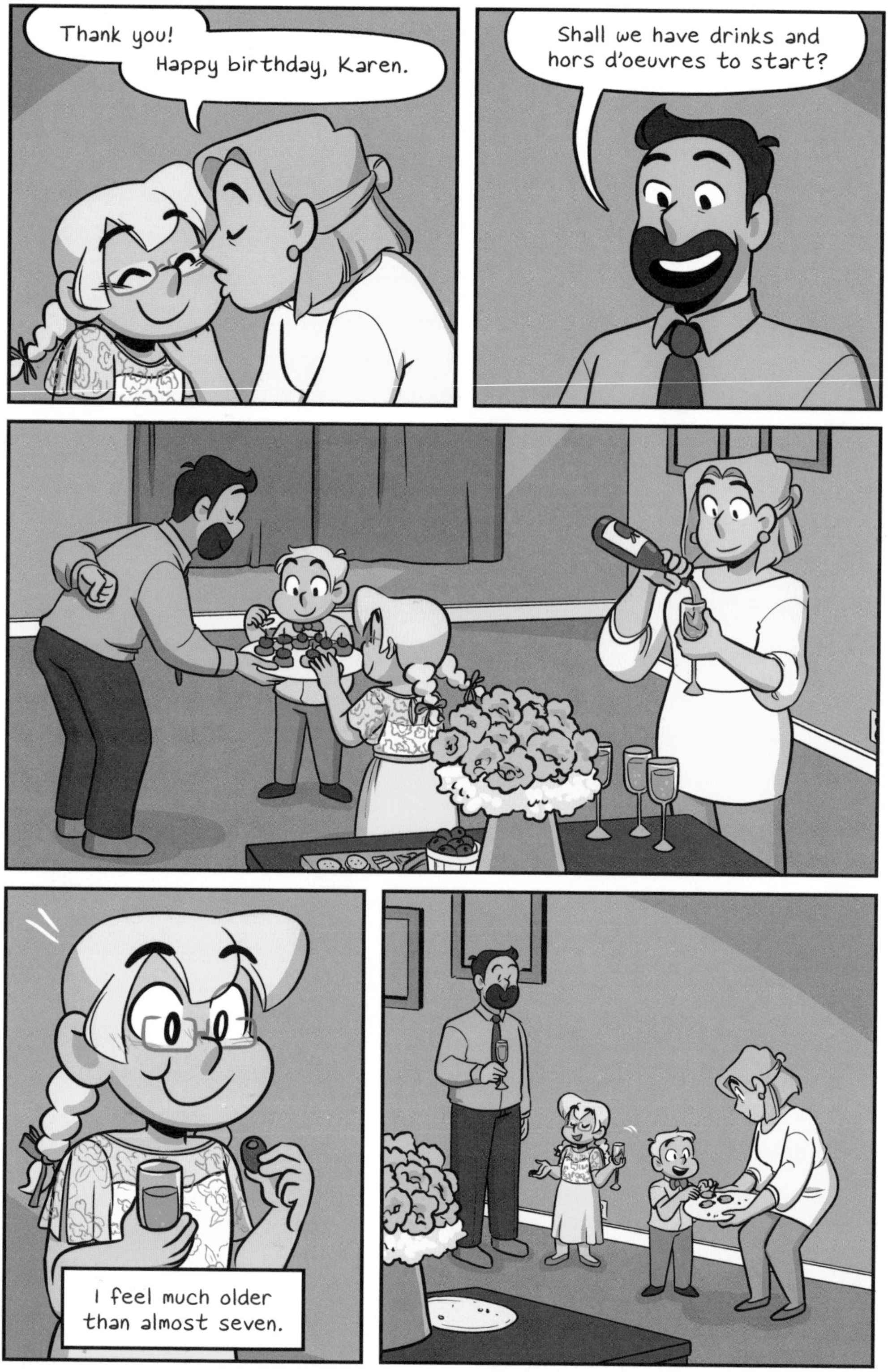
Thank you!
Happy birthday, Karen.
Shall we have drinks and hors d'oeuvres to start?
I feel much older than almost seven.

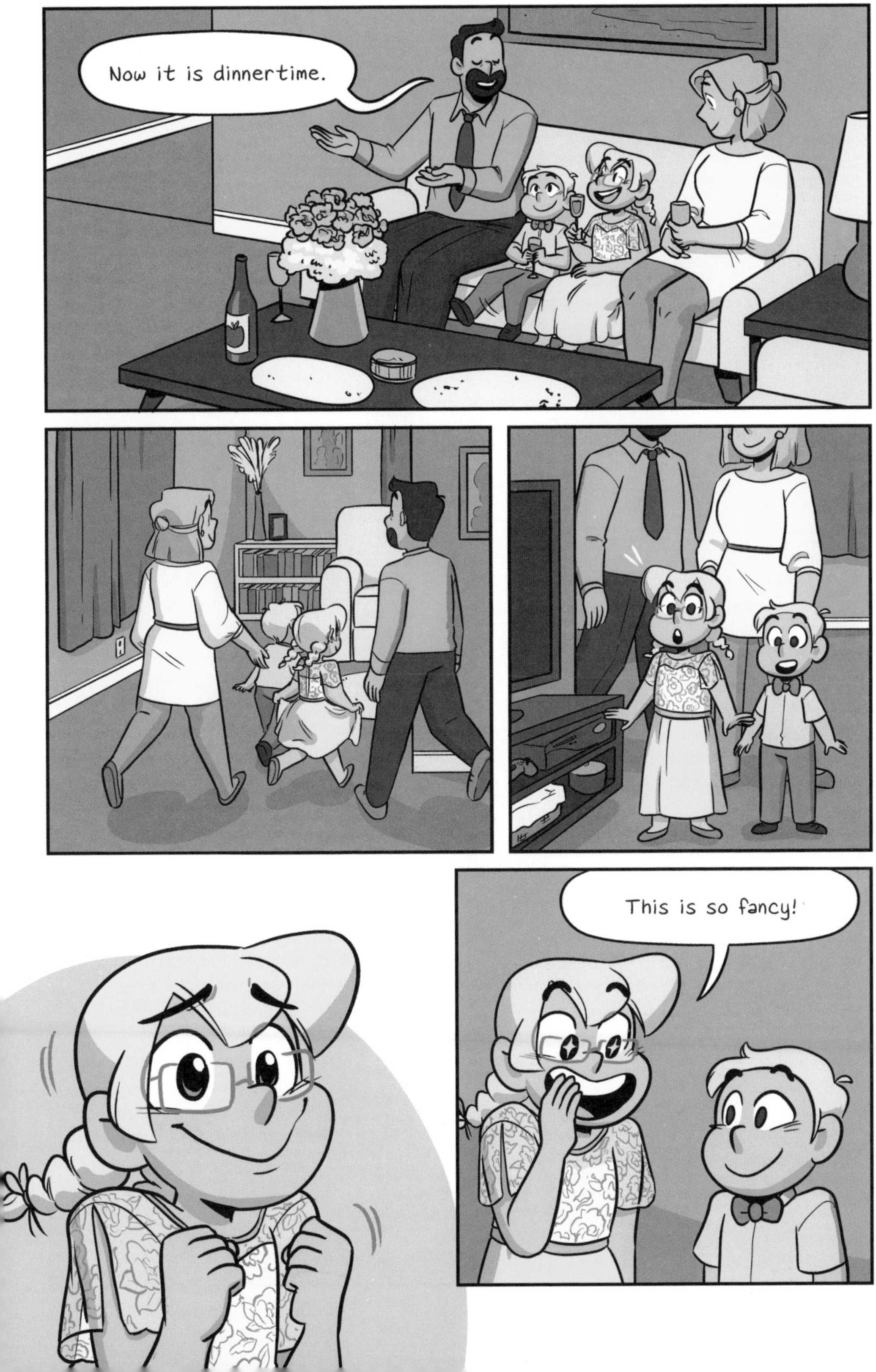
Now it is dinnertime.
This is so fancy!

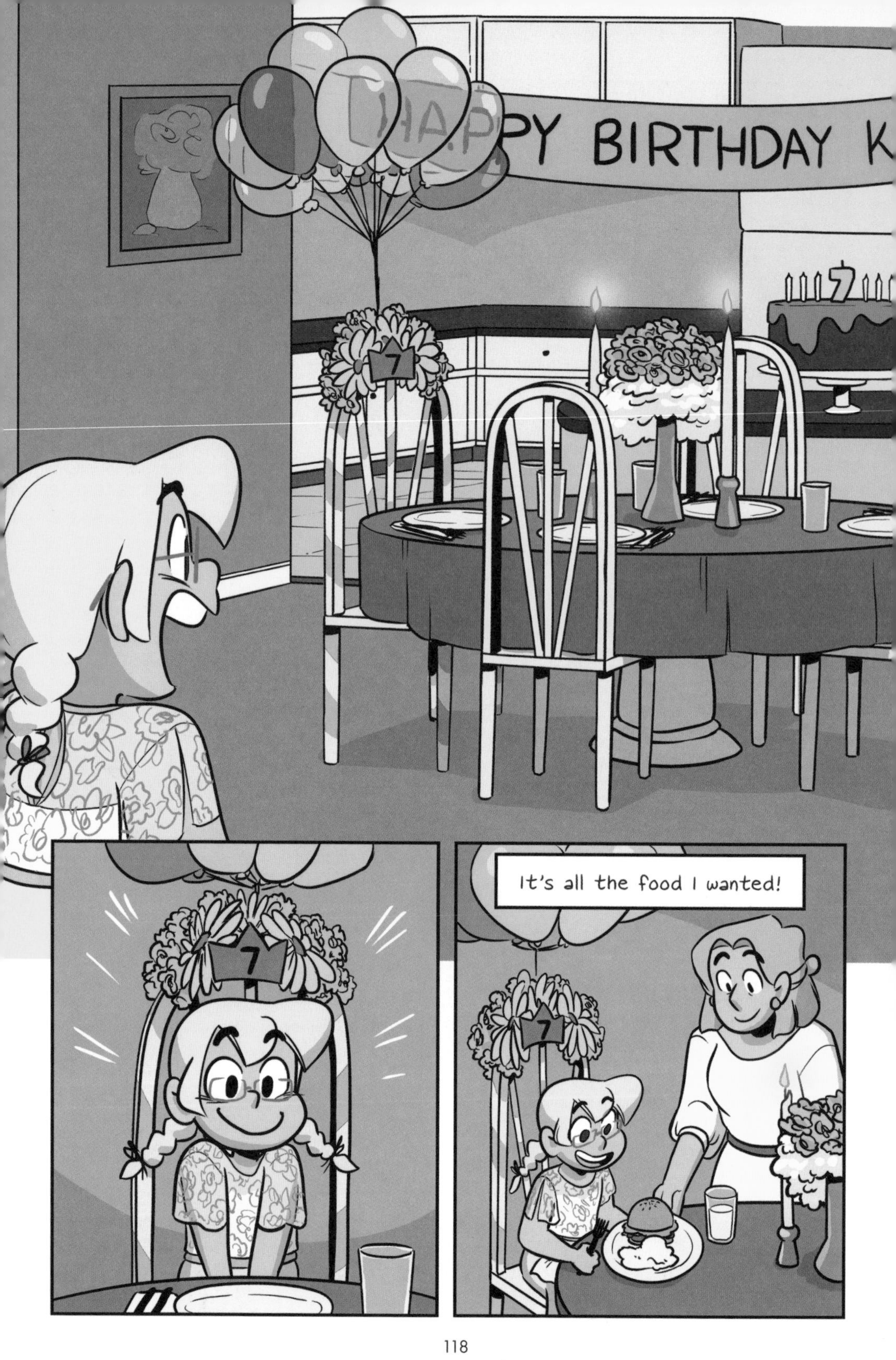
HA.P
PY BIRTHDAY K
7
7
7
It's all the food I wanted!

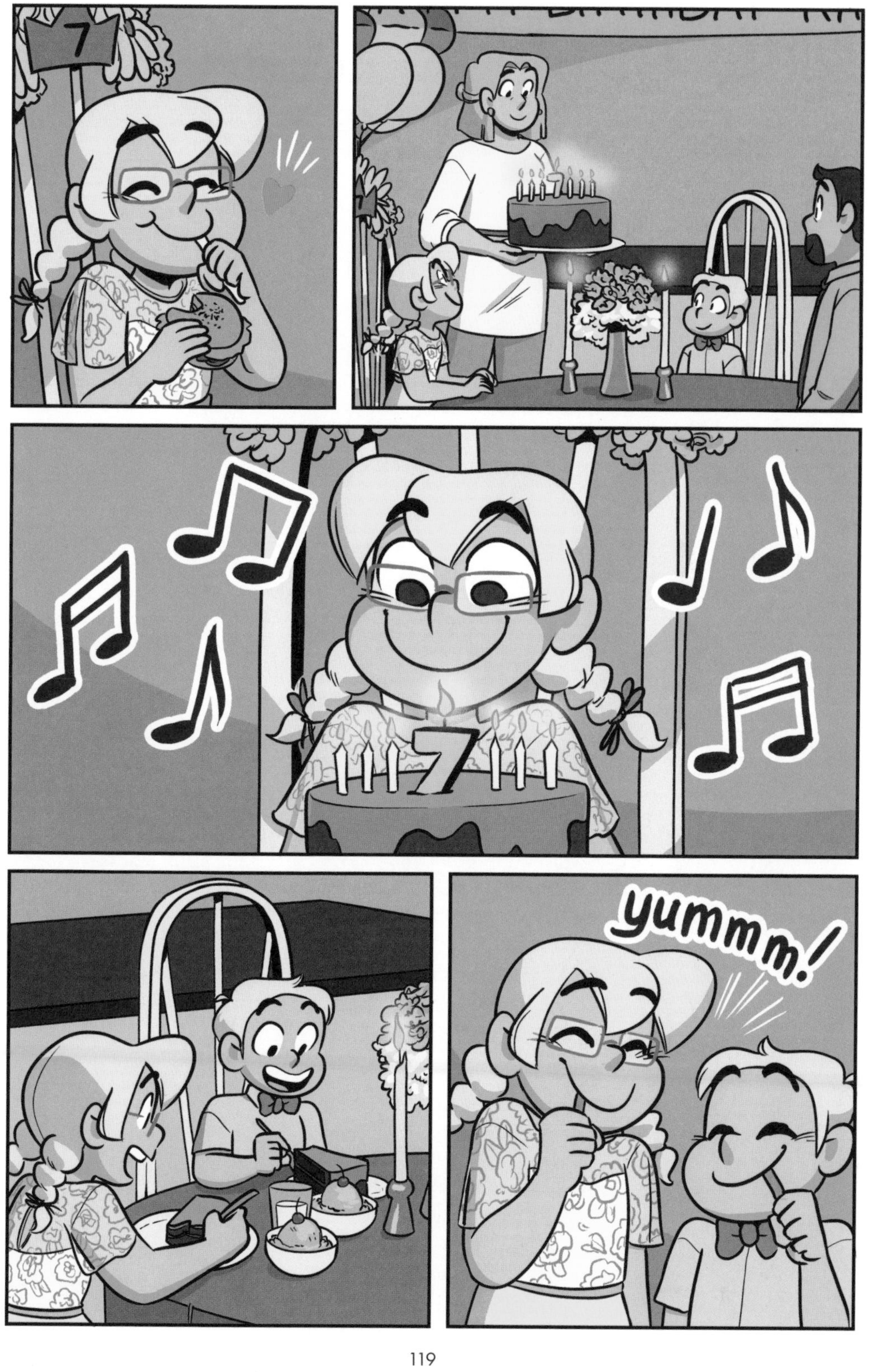
yummm!

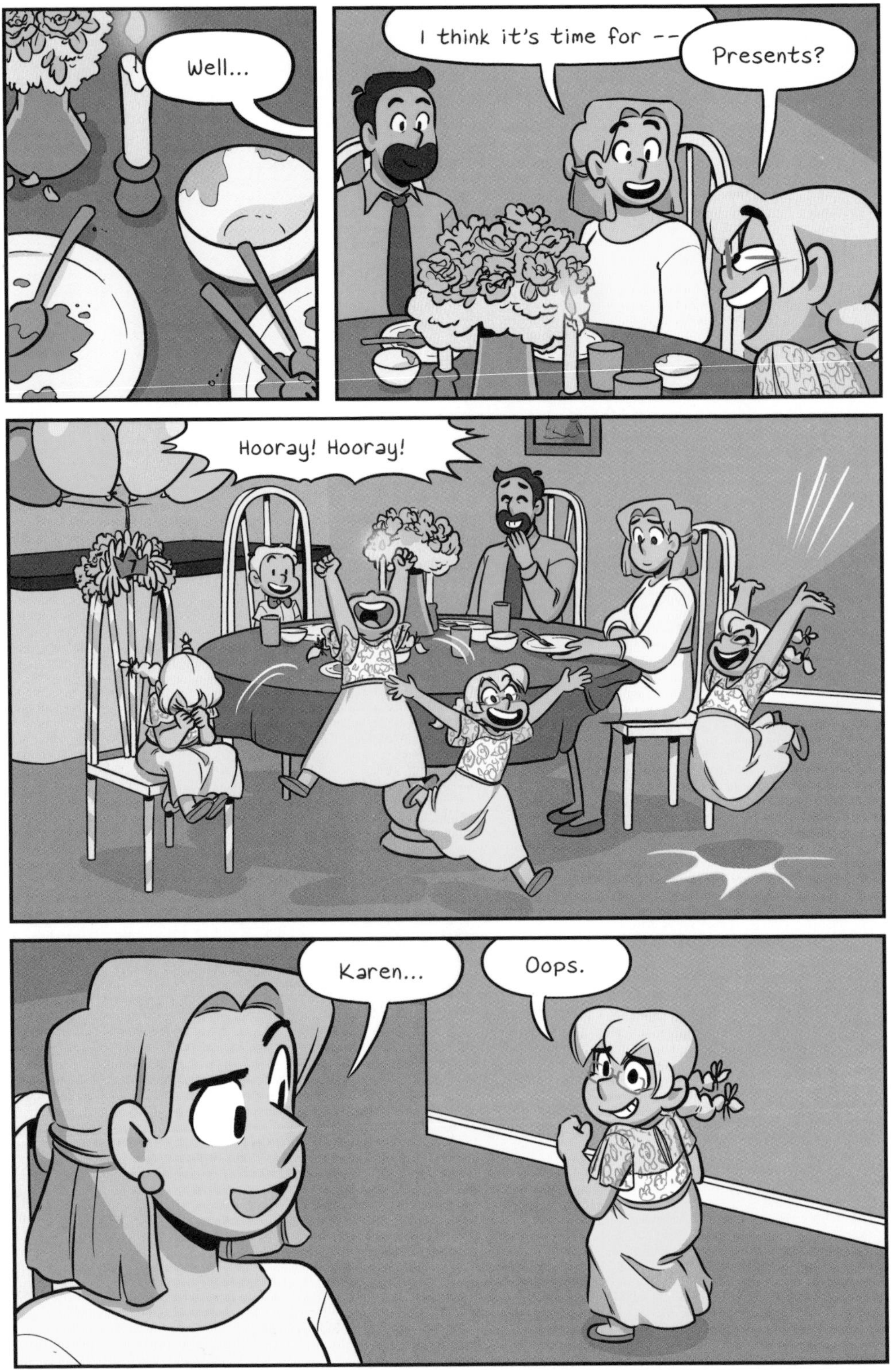
Well...
I think it's time for --
Presents?
Hooray! Hooray!
Karen...
Oops.

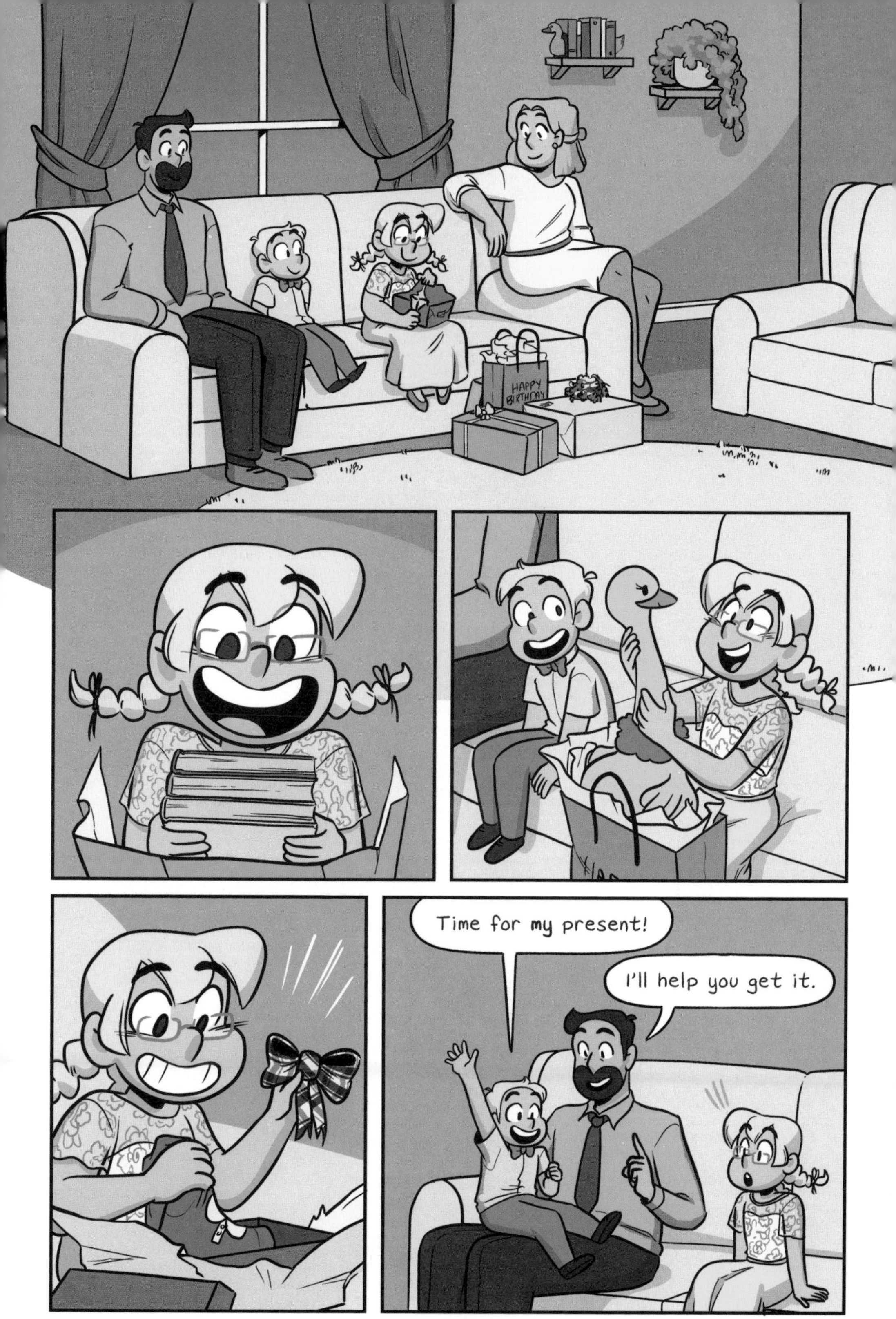
HAPPY BIRTHDAY
Time for my present!
I'll help you get it.

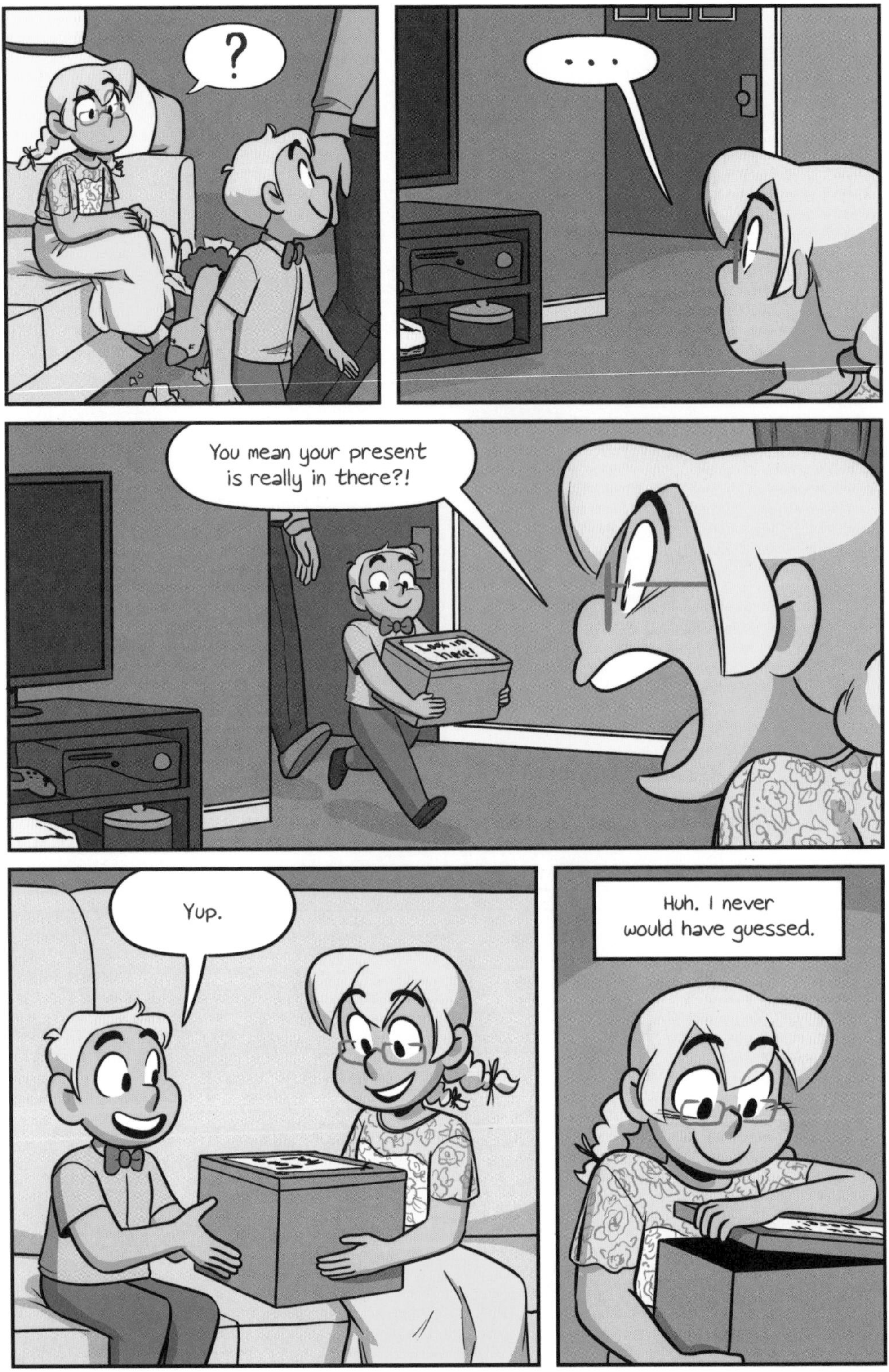
?
. . .
You mean your present is really in there?!
Look in here!
Yup.
Huh. I never would have guessed.

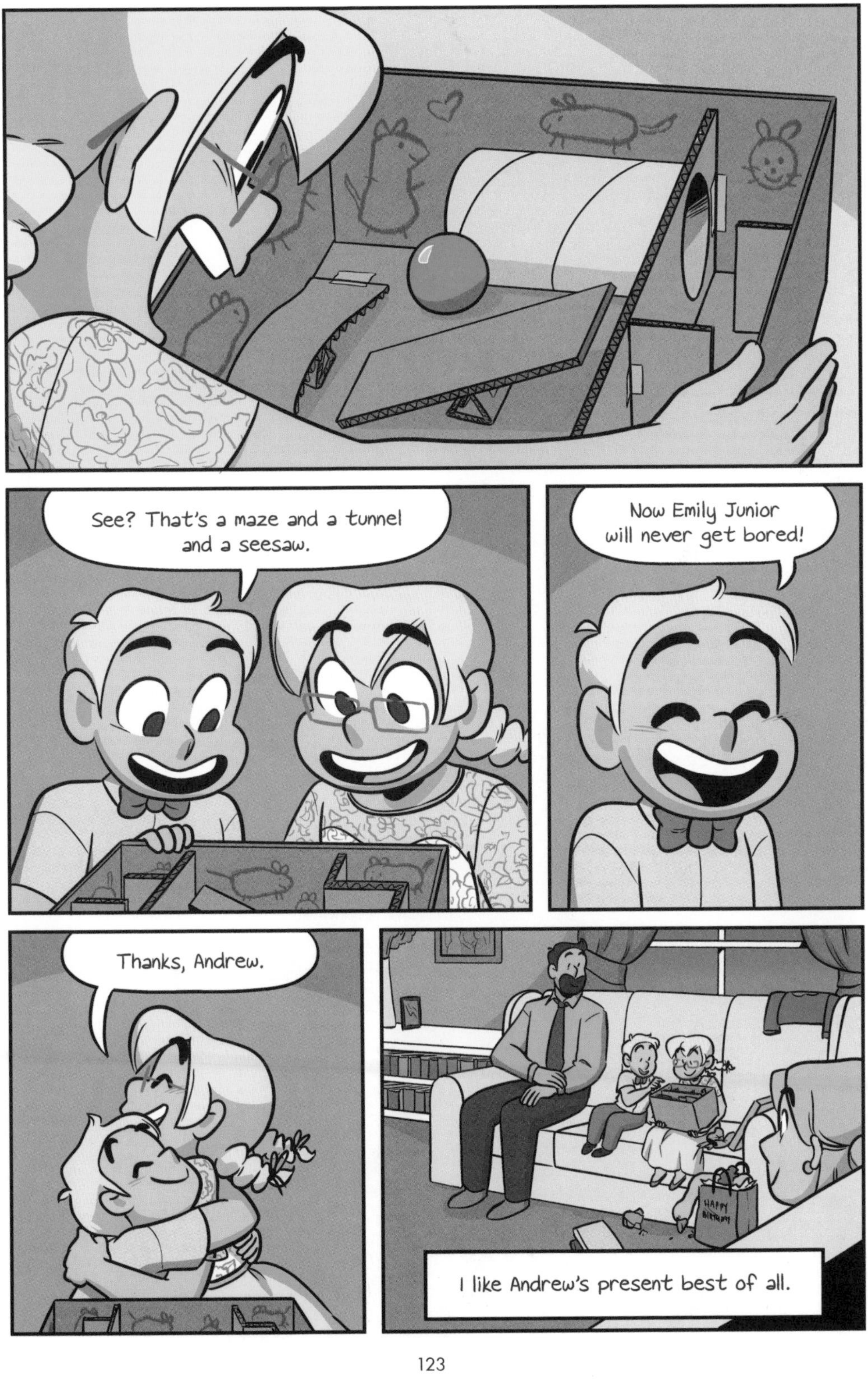
See? That's a maze and a tunnel and a seesaw.
Now Emily Junior will never get bored!
Thanks, Andrew.
HAPPY BIRTHDAY
I like Andrew's present best of all.

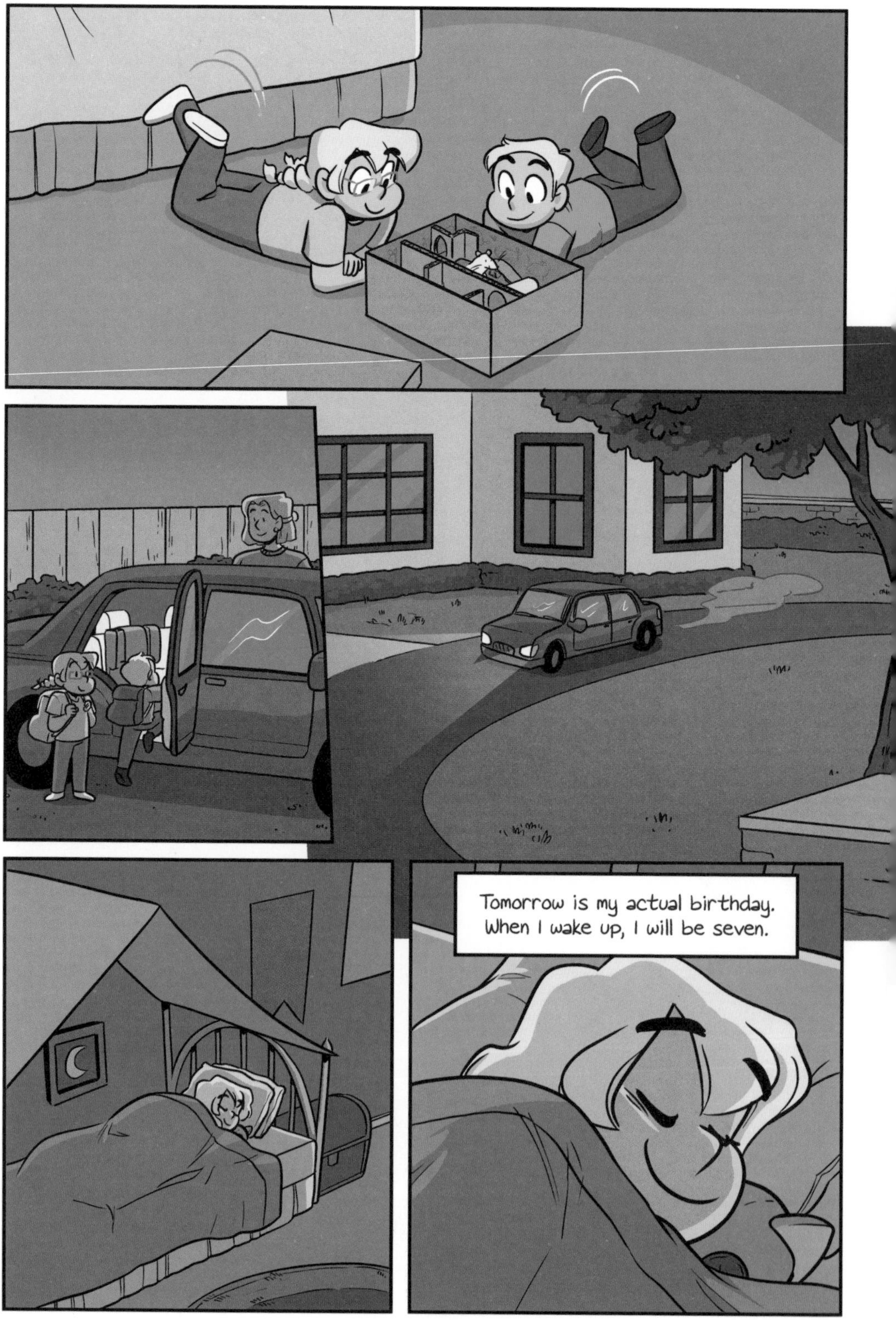
Tomorrow is my actual birthday.
When I wake up, I will be seven.

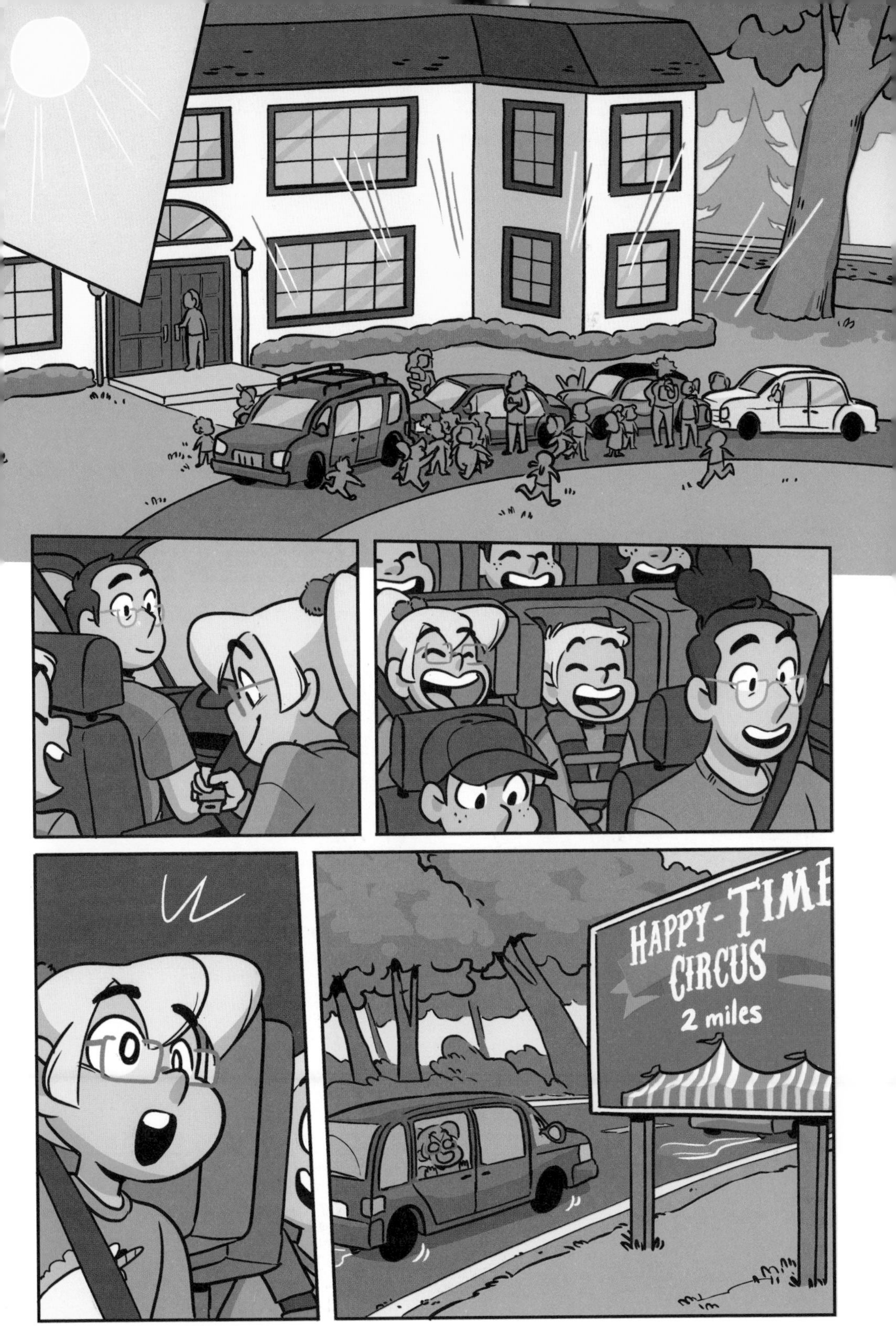
HAPPY-TIME
CIRCUS
2 miles

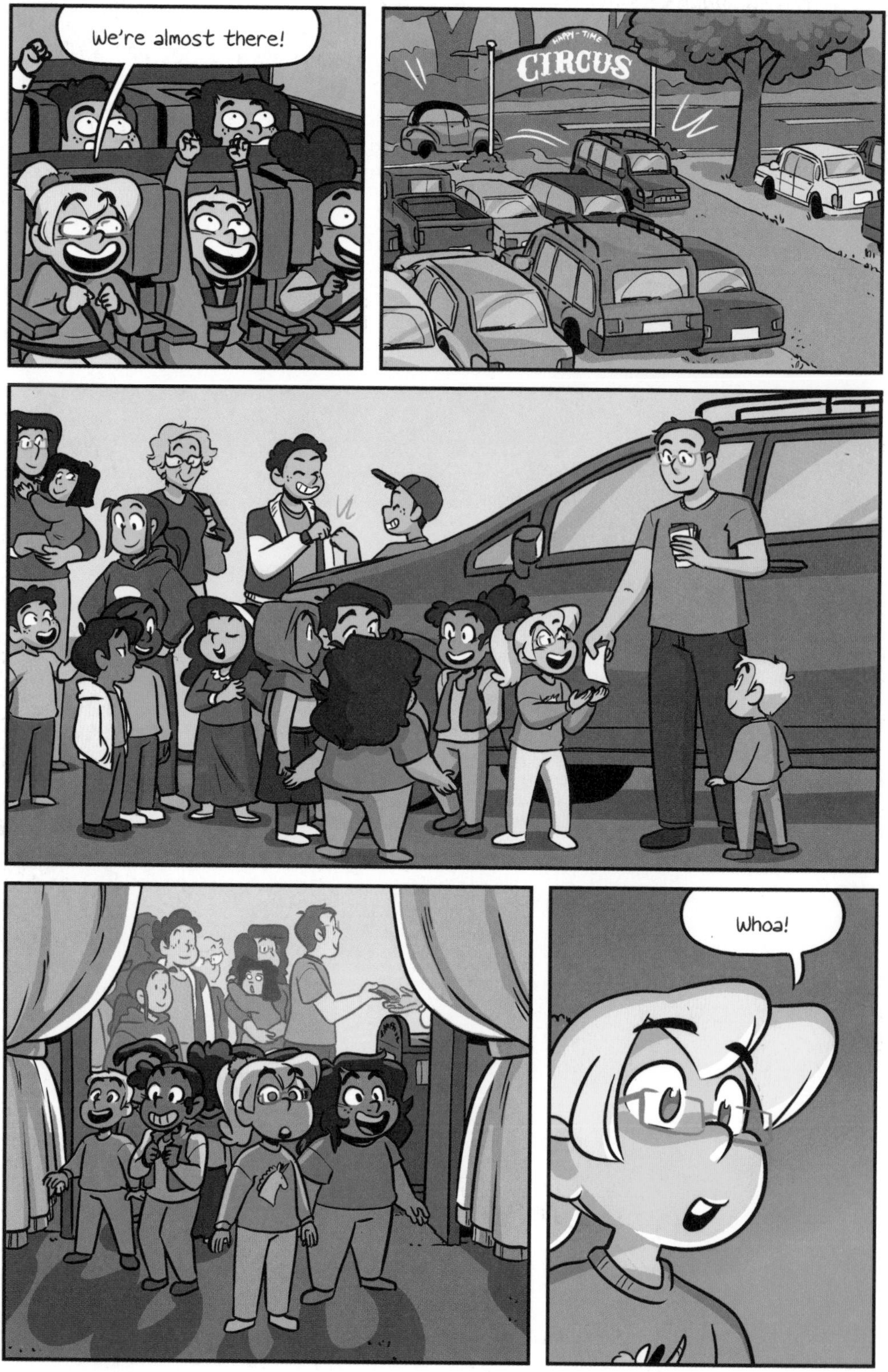
We're almost there!
HAPPY-TIME
CIRCUS
Whoa!

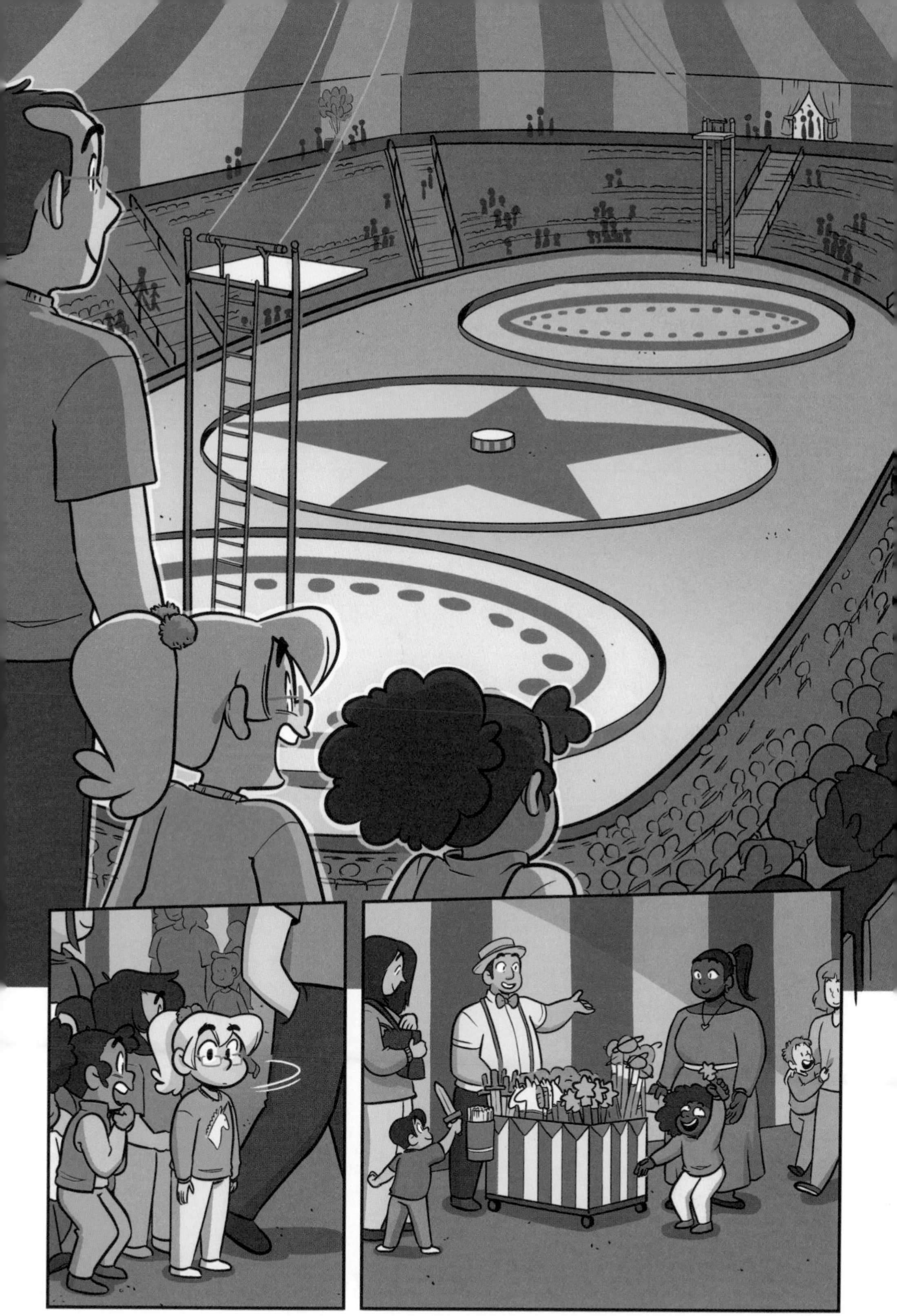

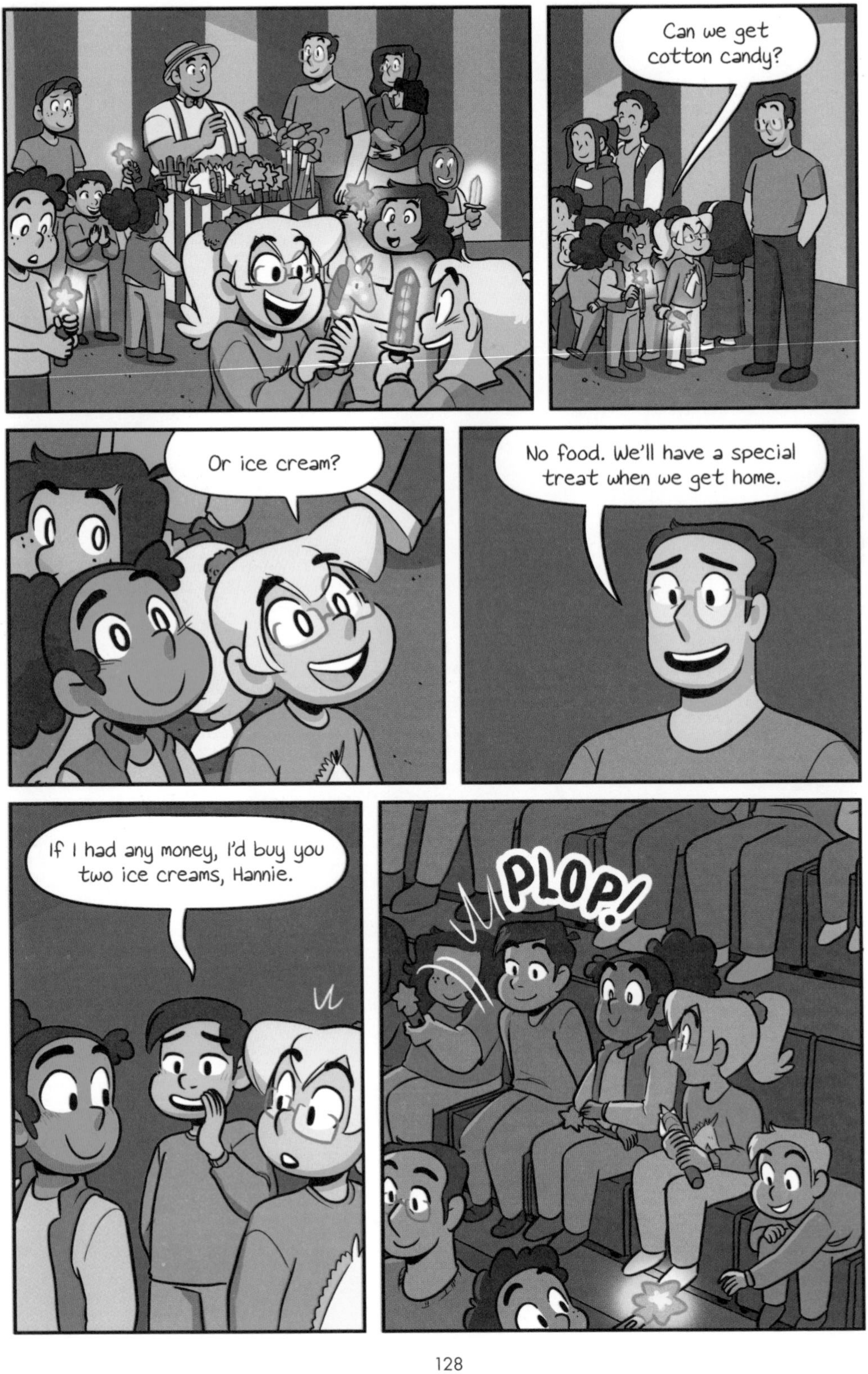
Can we get cotton candy?
Or ice cream?
No food. We'll have a special treat when we get home.
If I had any money, I'd buy you two ice creams, Hannie.
PLOP!

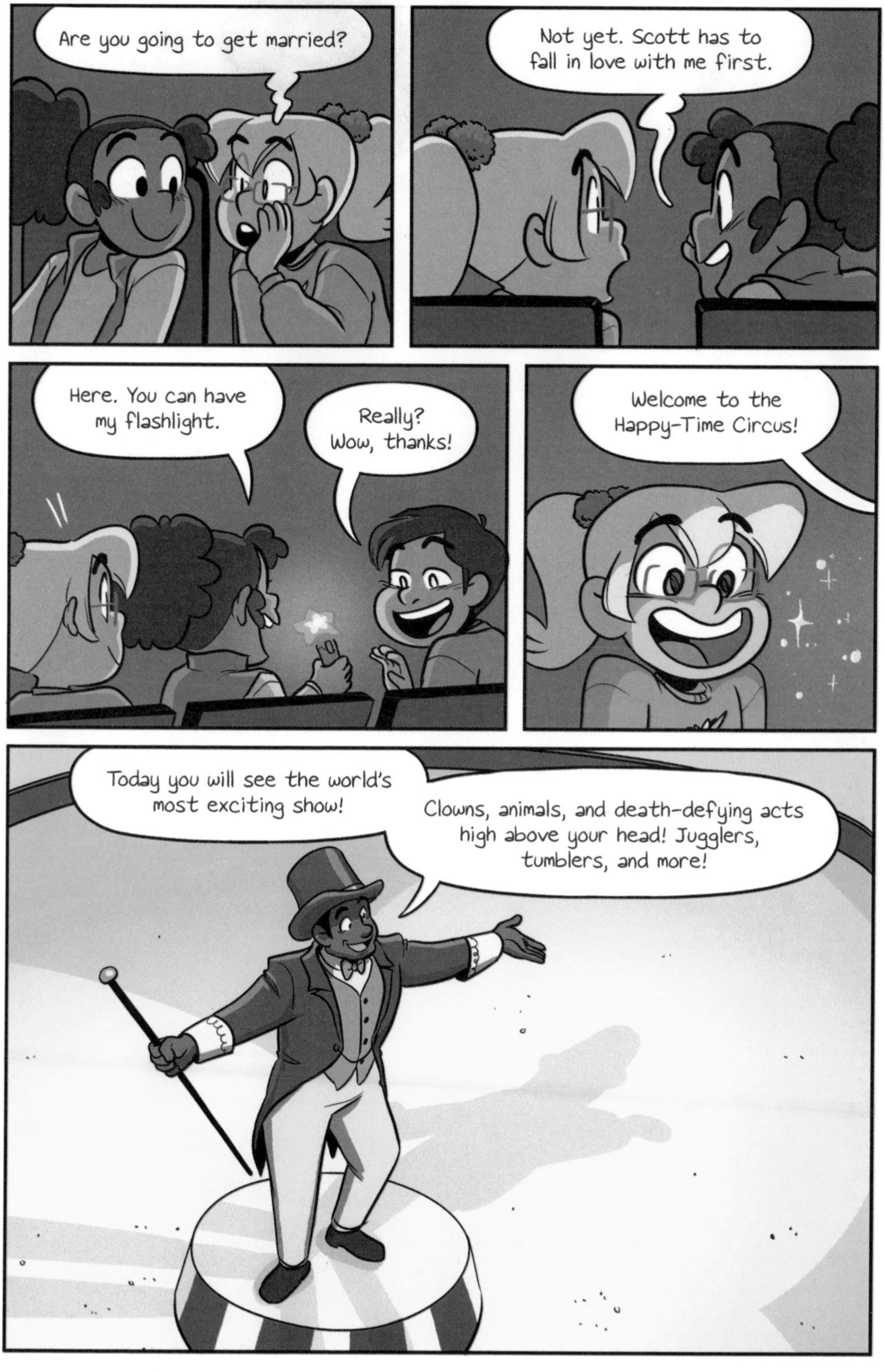
Are you going to get married?
Not yet. Scott has to fall in love with me first.
Here. You can have my flashlight.
Really? Wow, thanks!
Welcome to the Happy-Time Circus!
Today you will see the world's most exciting show!
Clowns, animals, and death-defying acts high above your head! Jugglers, tumblers, and more!

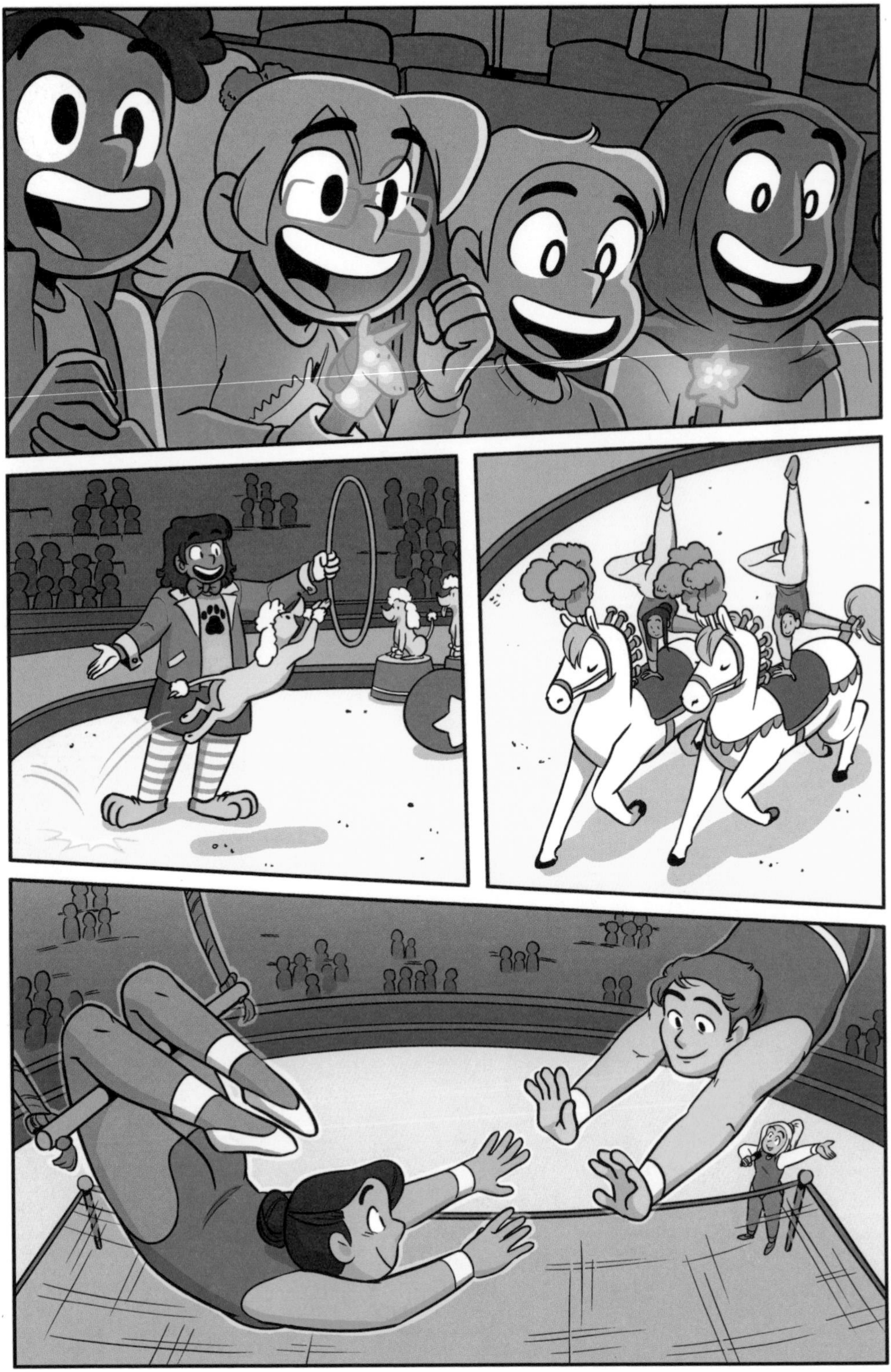

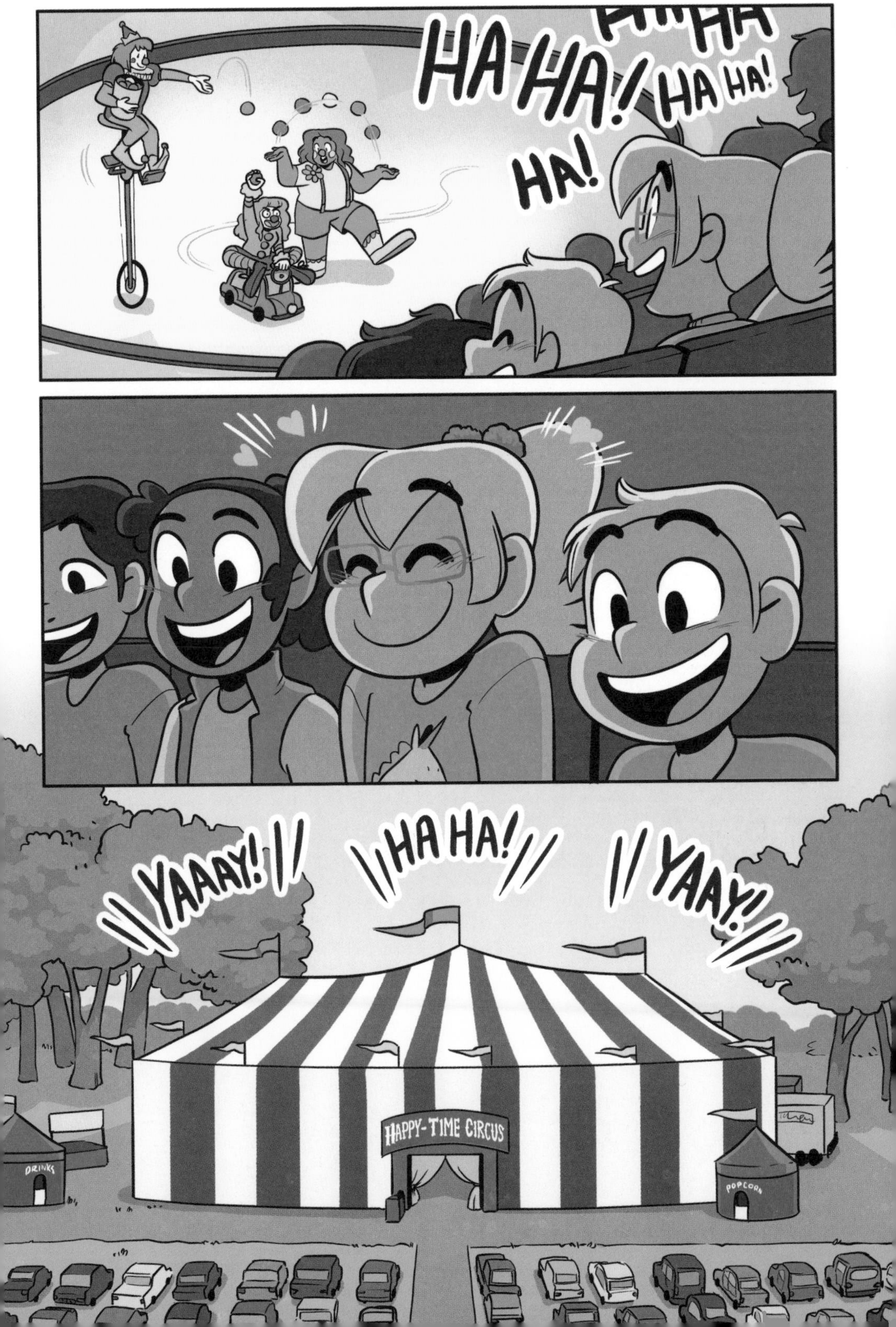
HA
HA HA!
HA HA!
HA!
YAAAY!
HA HA!
YAAY!
HAPPY-TIME CIRCUS
DRINKS
POPCORN

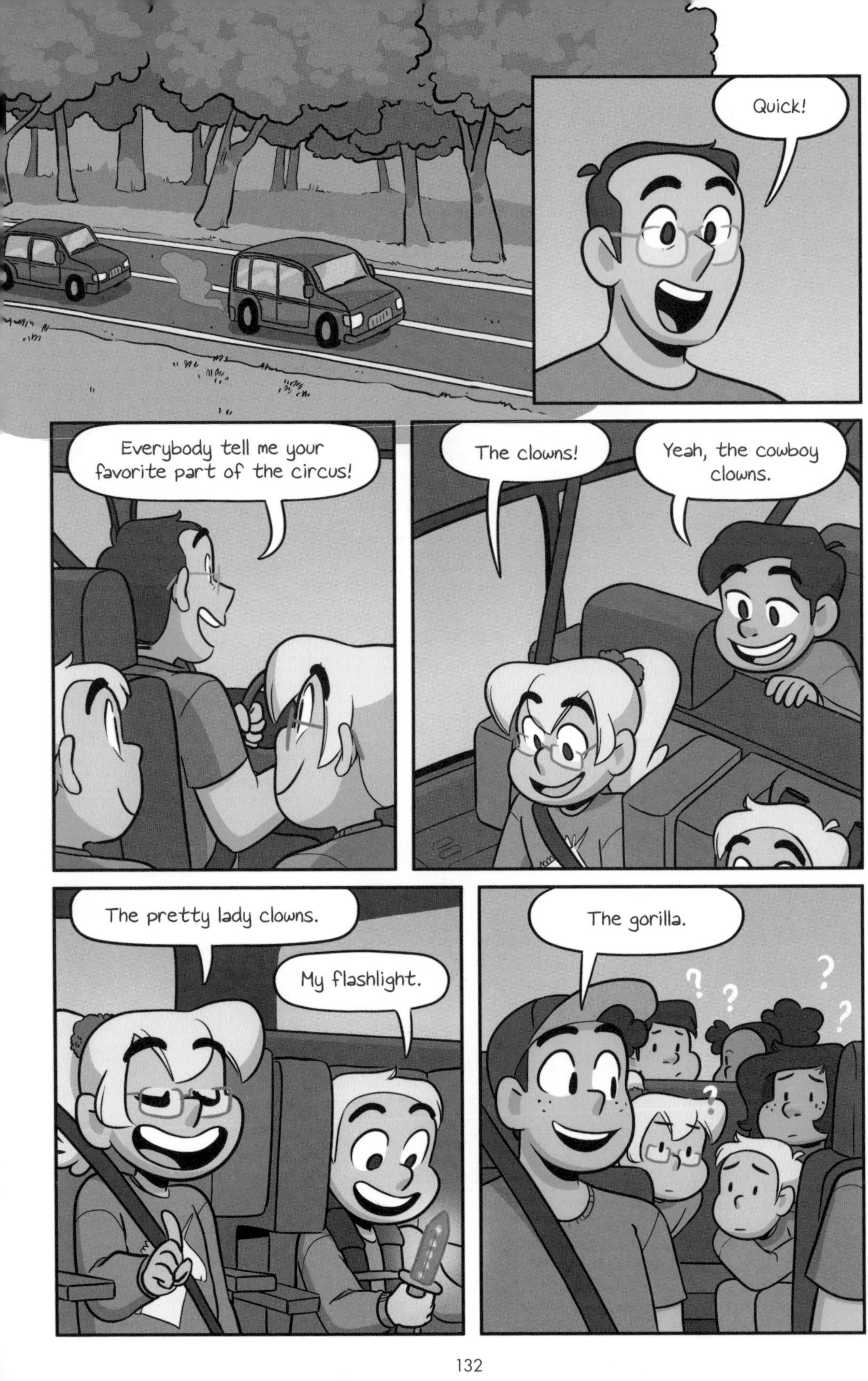
Quick!
Everybody tell me your favorite part of the circus!
The clowns!
Yeah, the cowboy clowns.
The pretty lady clowns.
My flashlight.
The gorilla.
? ? ? ? ?

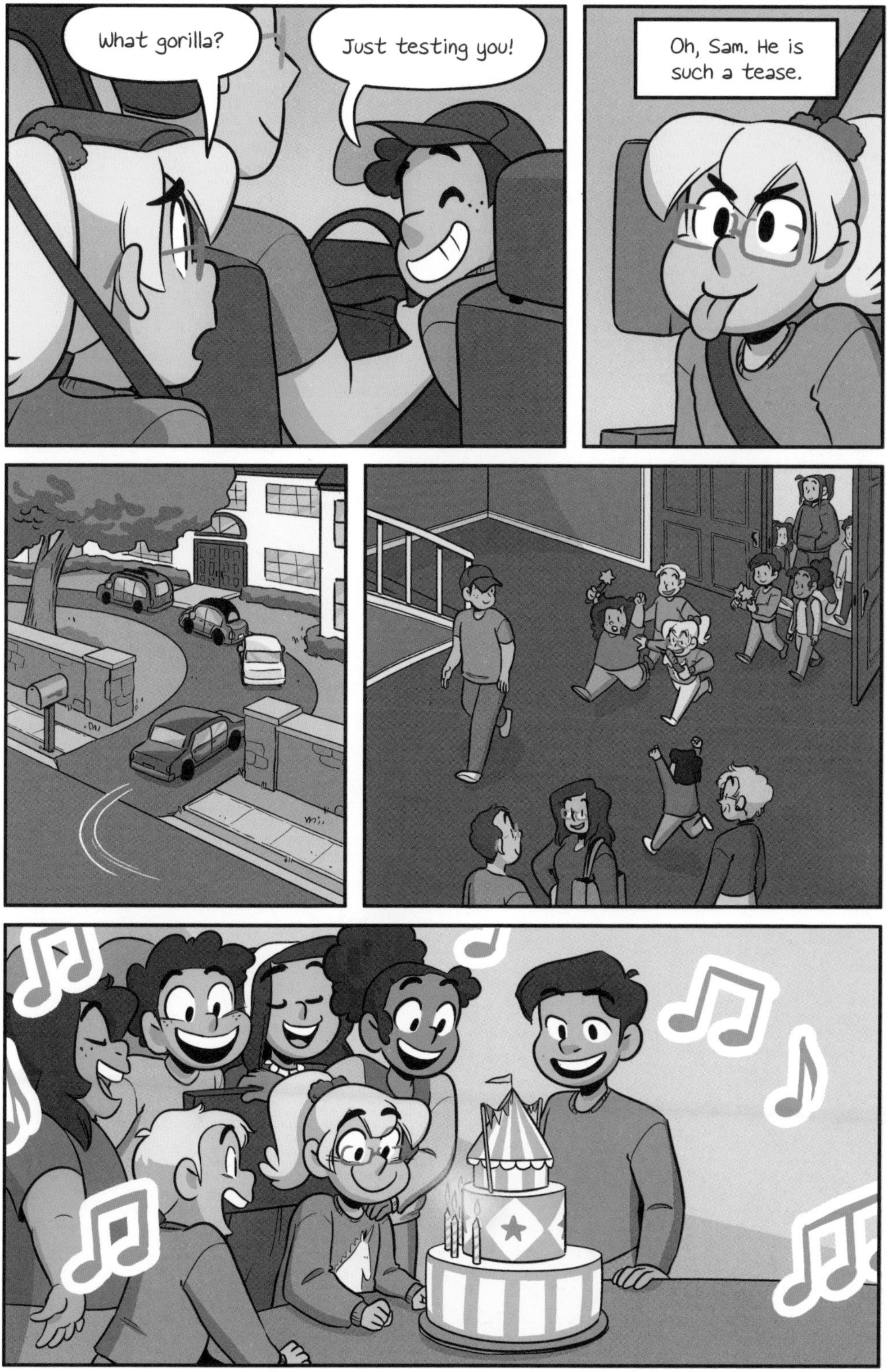
What gorilla?
Just testing you!
Oh, Sam. He is such a tease.

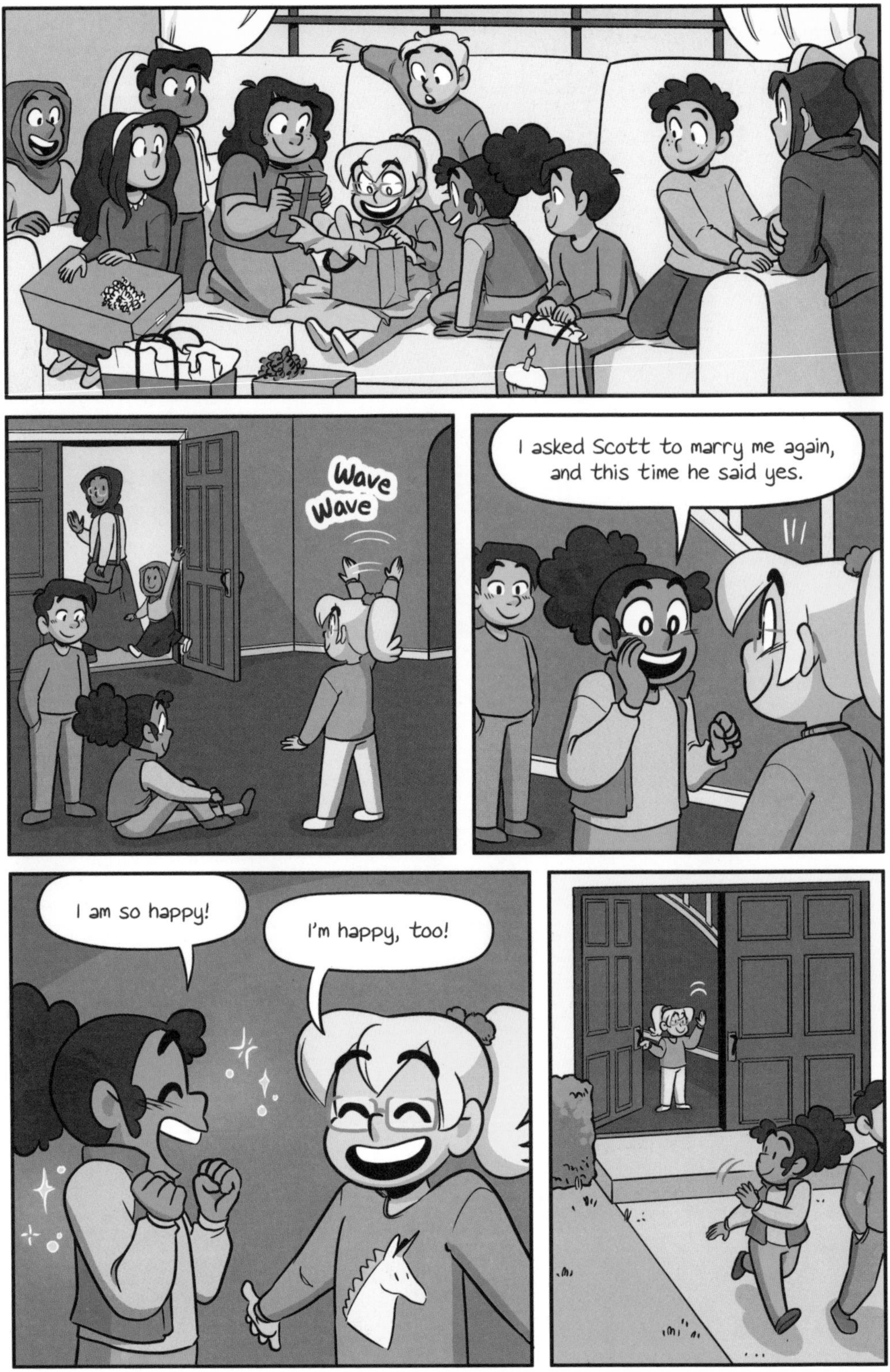
Wave
Wave
I asked Scott to marry me again, and this time he said yes.
I am so happy!
I'm happy, too!

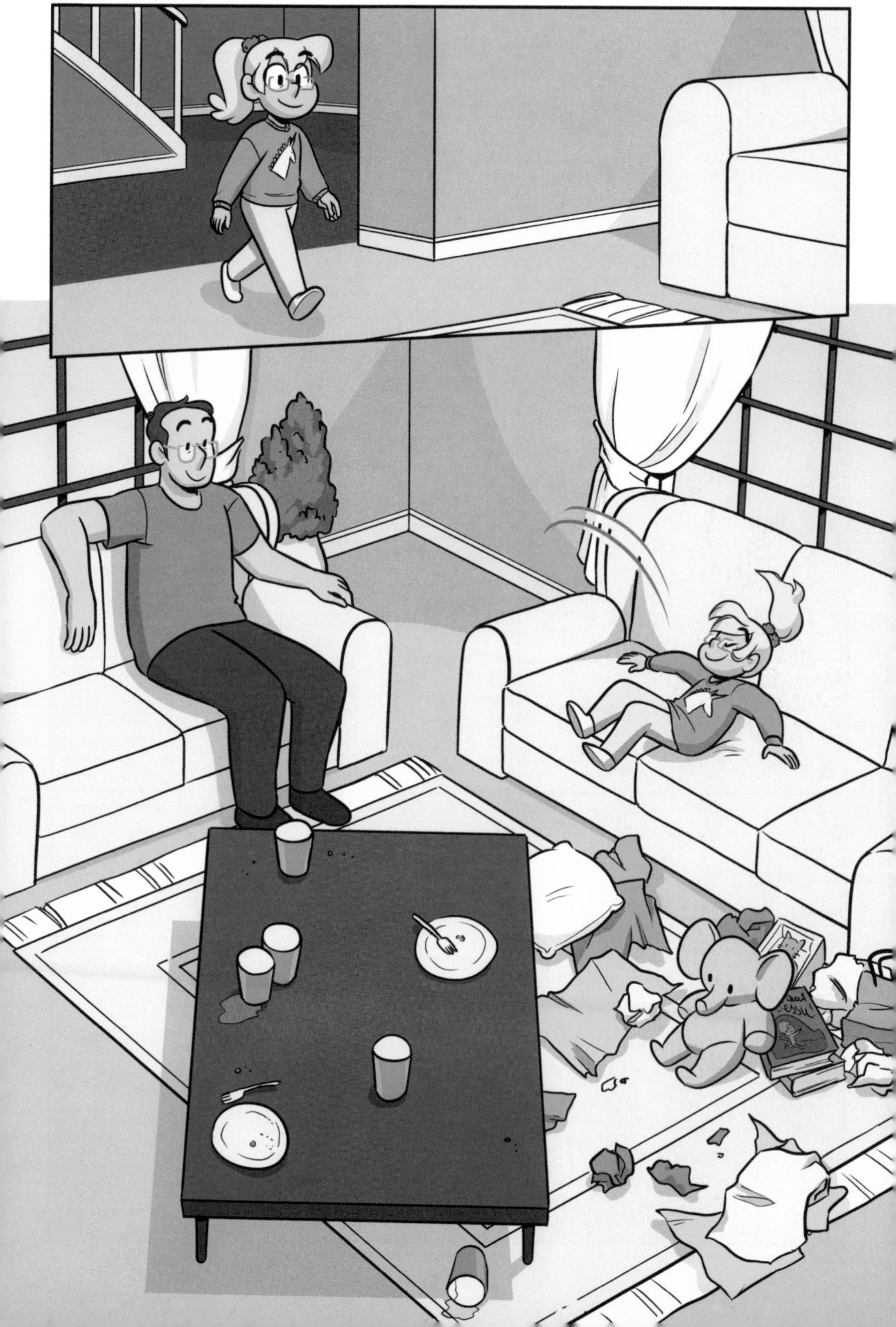

CHAPTER 10

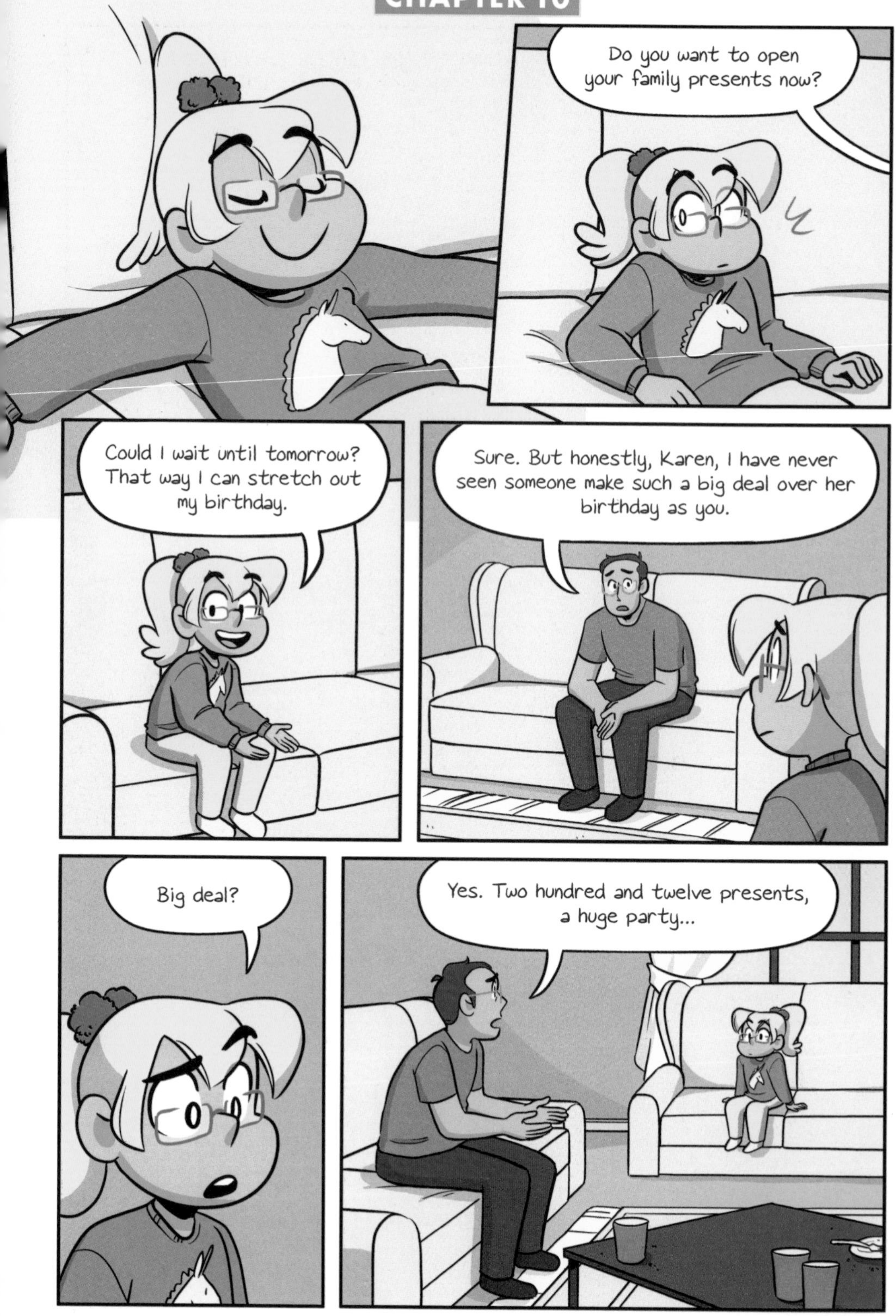

Do you want to open your family presents now?
Could I wait until tomorrow? That way I can stretch out my birthday.
Sure. But honestly, Karen, I have never seen someone make such a big deal over her birthday as you.
Big deal?
Yes. Two hundred and twelve presents, a huge party...

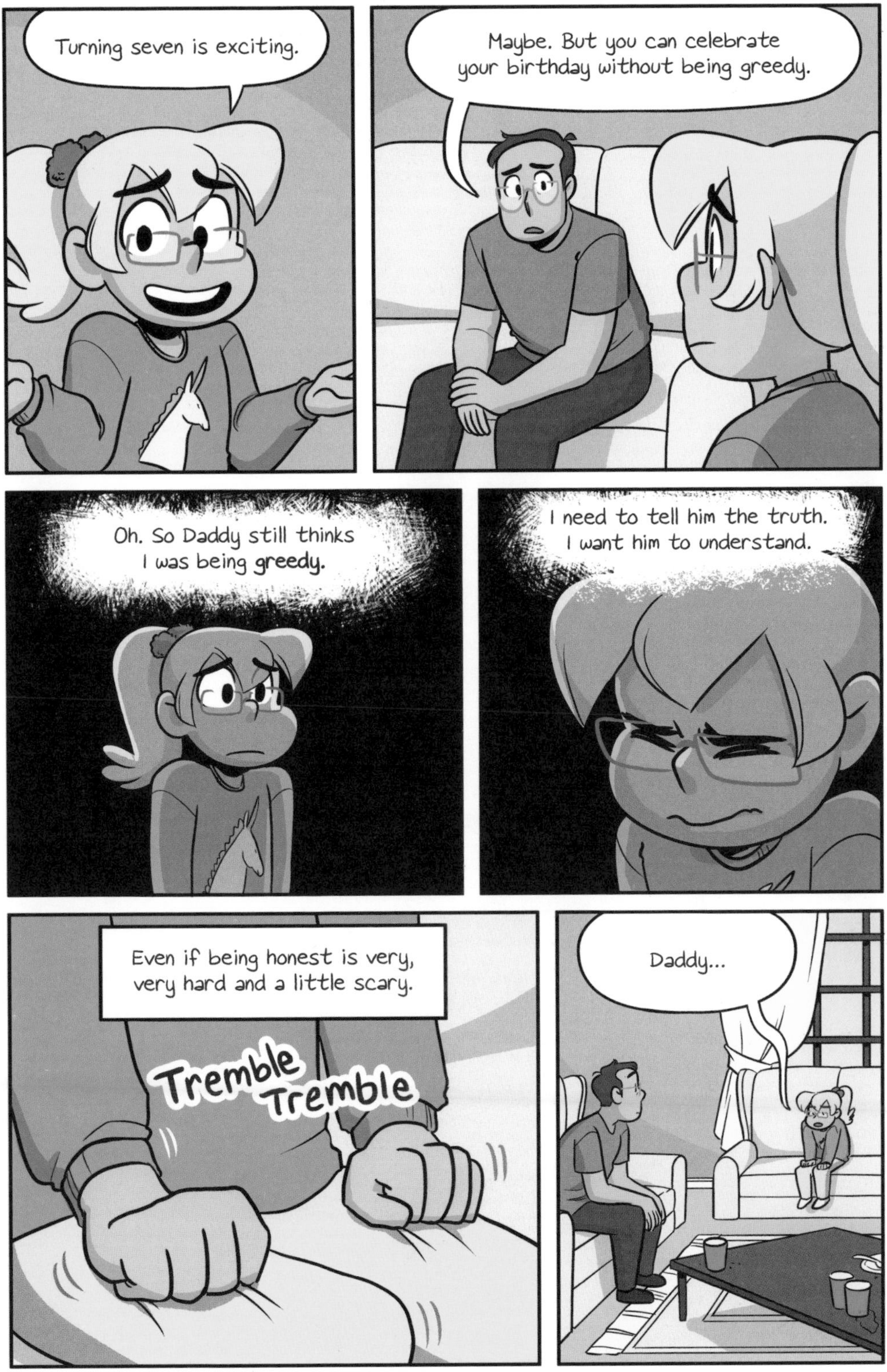
Turning seven is exciting.
Maybe. But you can celebrate your birthday without being greedy.
Oh. So Daddy still thinks I was being greedy.
I need to tell him the truth. I want him to understand.
Even if being honest is very, very hard and a little scary.
Tremble Tremble
Daddy...

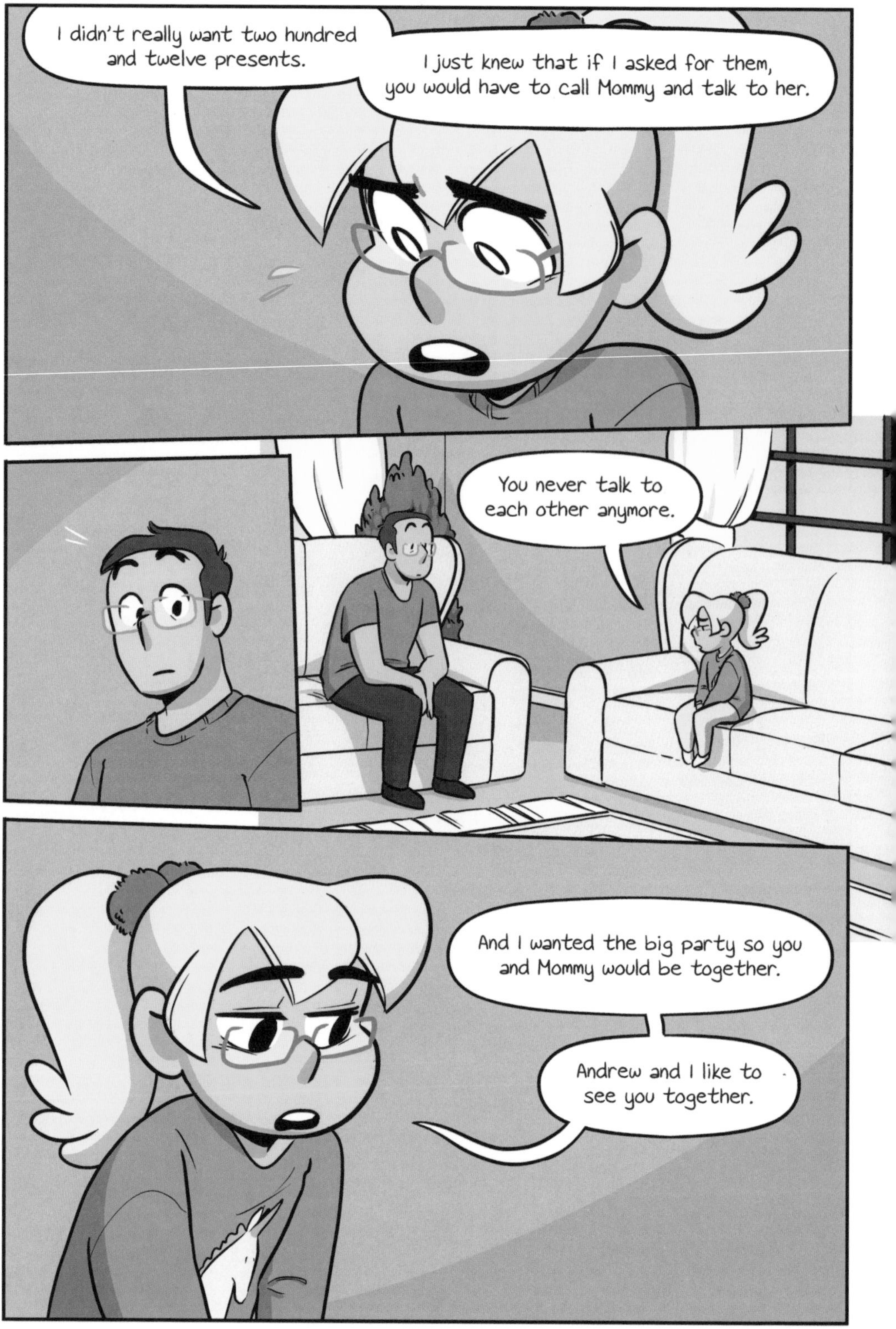
I didn't really want two hundred and twelve presents.
I just knew that if I asked for them, you would have to call Mommy and talk to her.
You never talk to each other anymore.
And I wanted the big party so you and Mommy would be together.
Andrew and I like to see you together.

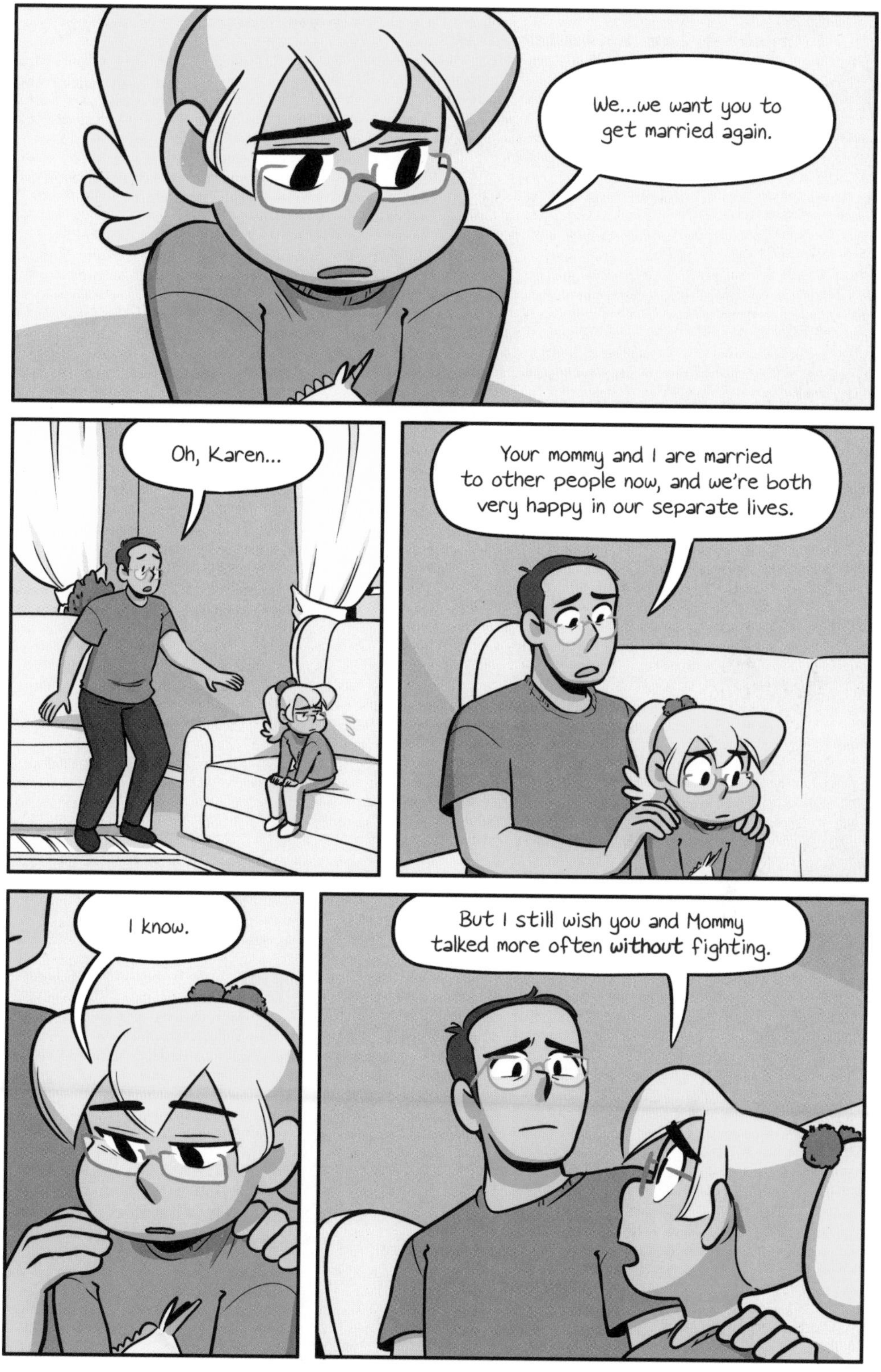
We...we want you to get married again.
Oh, Karen...
Your mommy and I are married to other people now, and we're both very happy in our separate lives.
I know.
But I still wish you and Mommy talked more often **without** fighting.

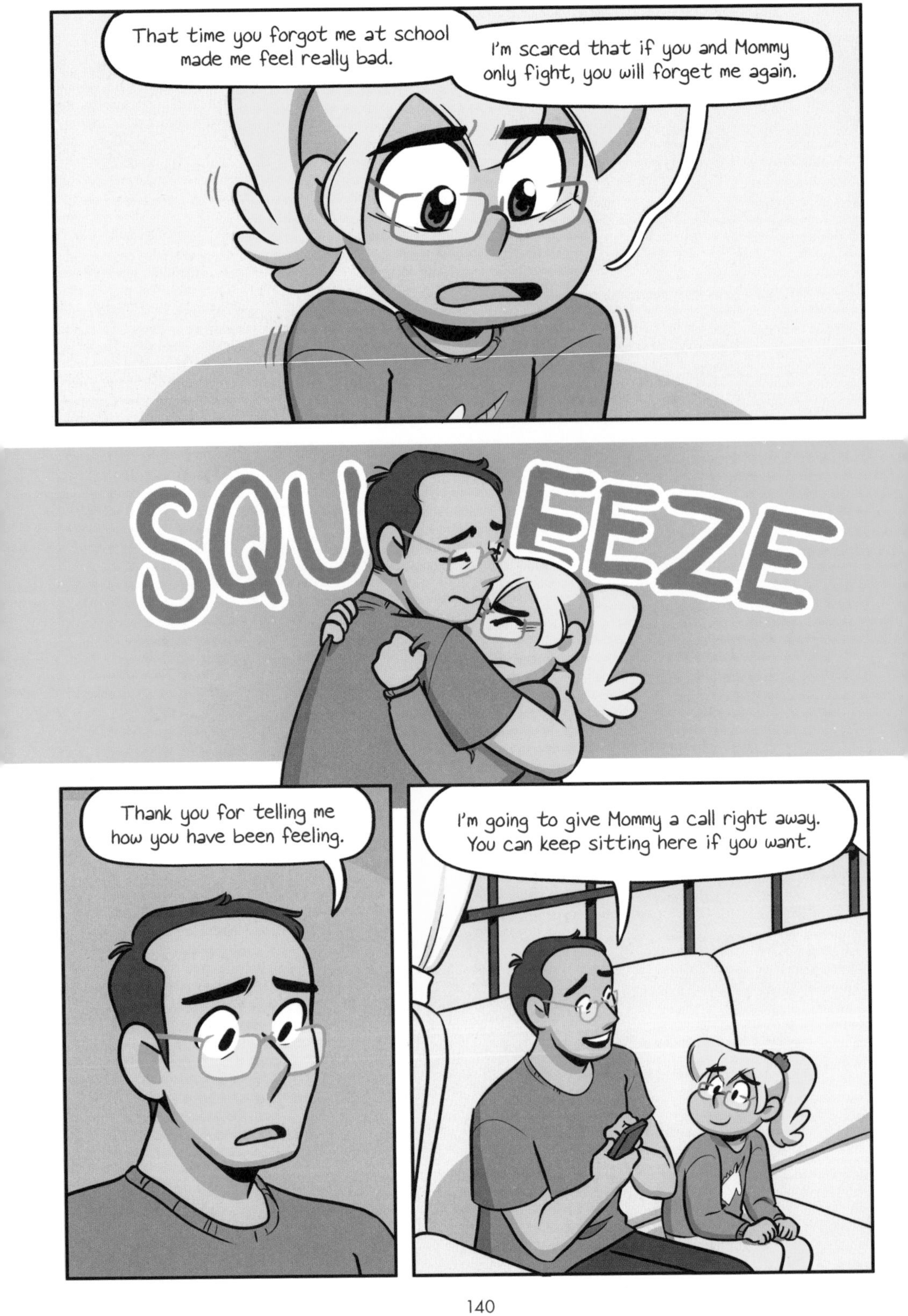
That time you forgot me at school made me feel really bad.
I'm scared that if you and Mommy only fight, you will forget me again.
SQUEEZE
Thank you for telling me how you have been feeling.
I'm going to give Mommy a call right away. You can keep sitting here if you want.

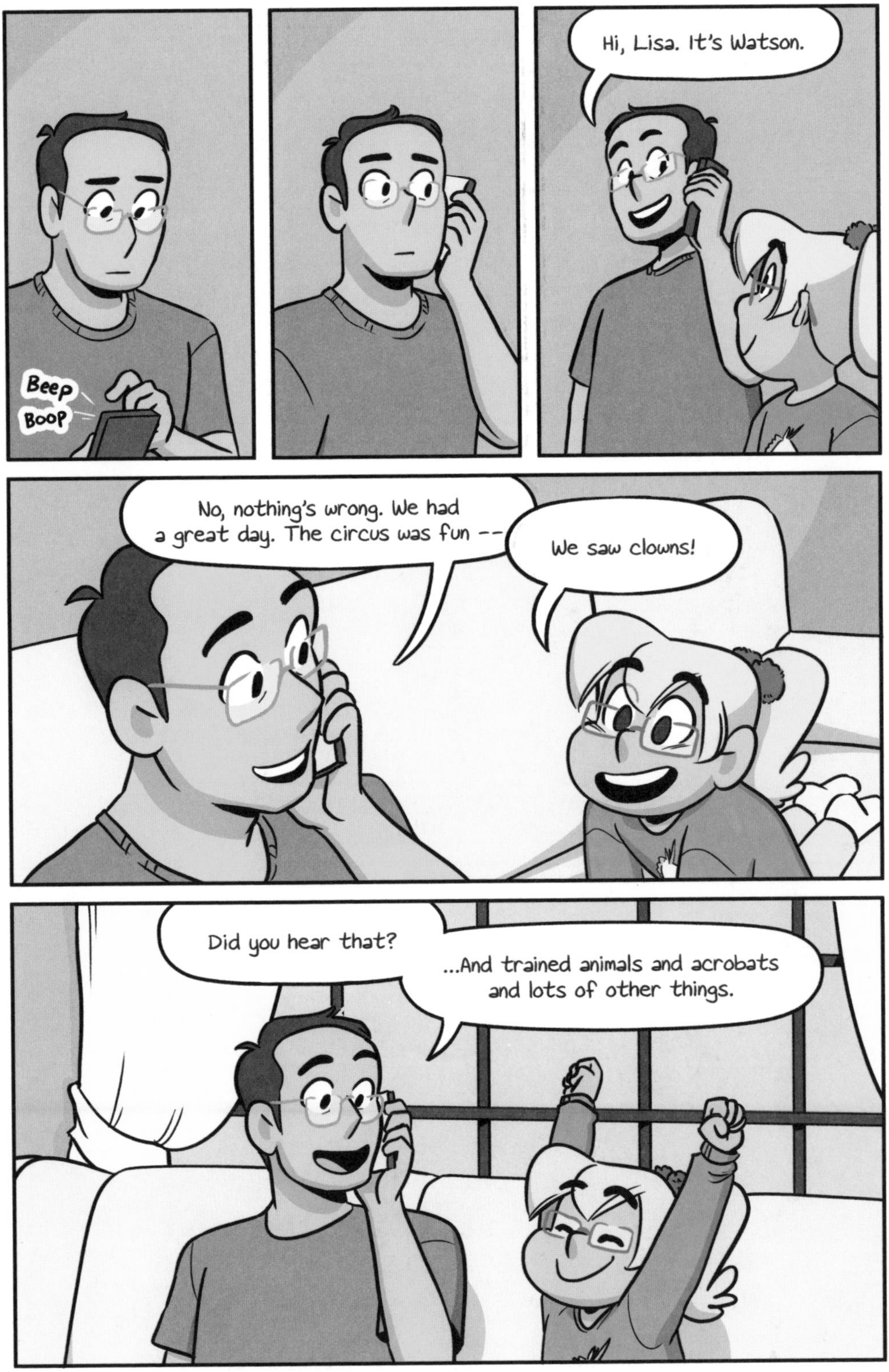
Beep
Boop
Hi, Lisa. It's Watson.
No, nothing's wrong. We had a great day. The circus was fun --
We saw clowns!
Did you hear that?
...And trained animals and acrobats and lots of other things.

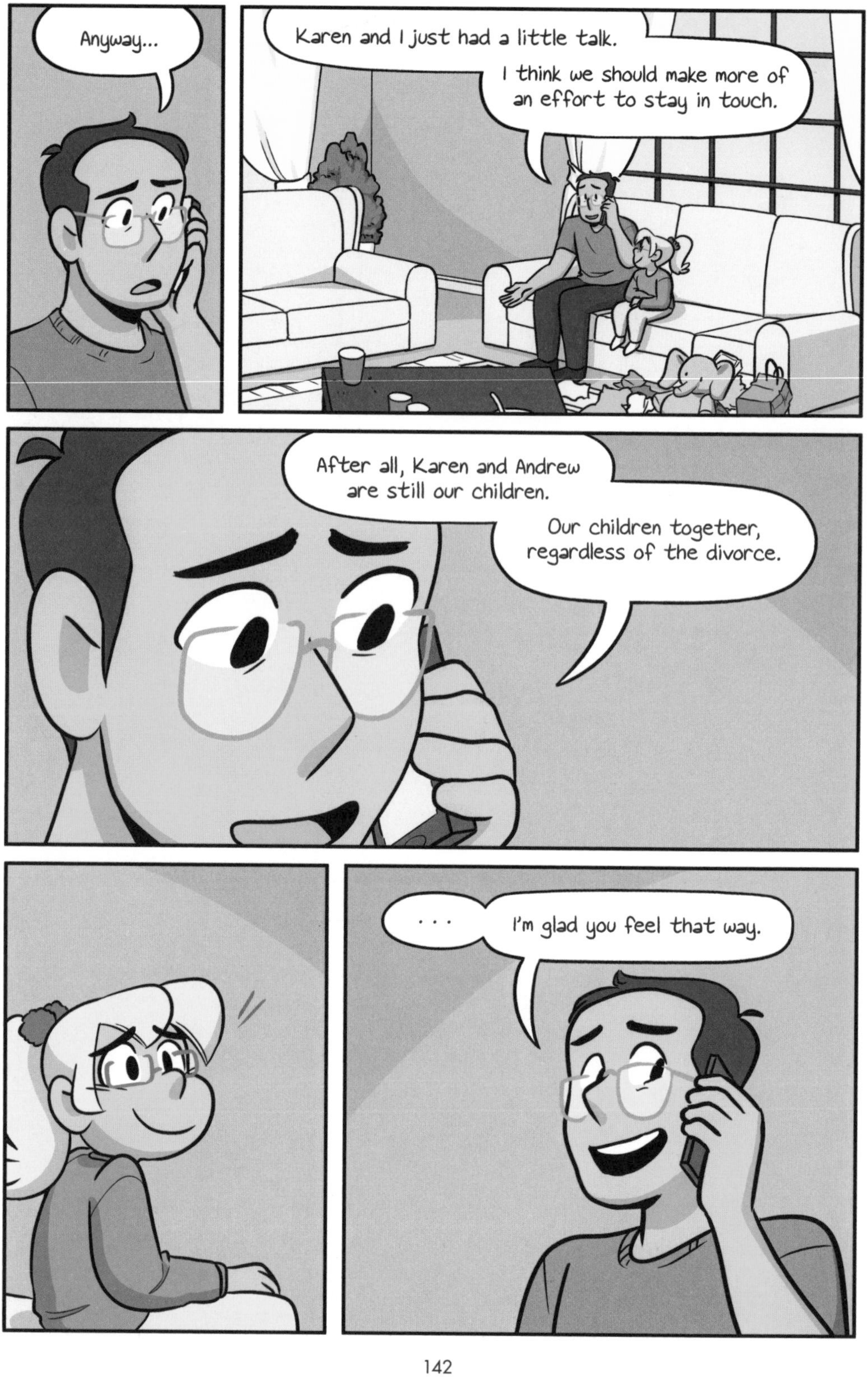
Anyway...
Karen and I just had a little talk.
I think we should make more of an effort to stay in touch.
After all, Karen and Andrew are still our children.
Our children together, regardless of the divorce.
. . .
I'm glad you feel that way.

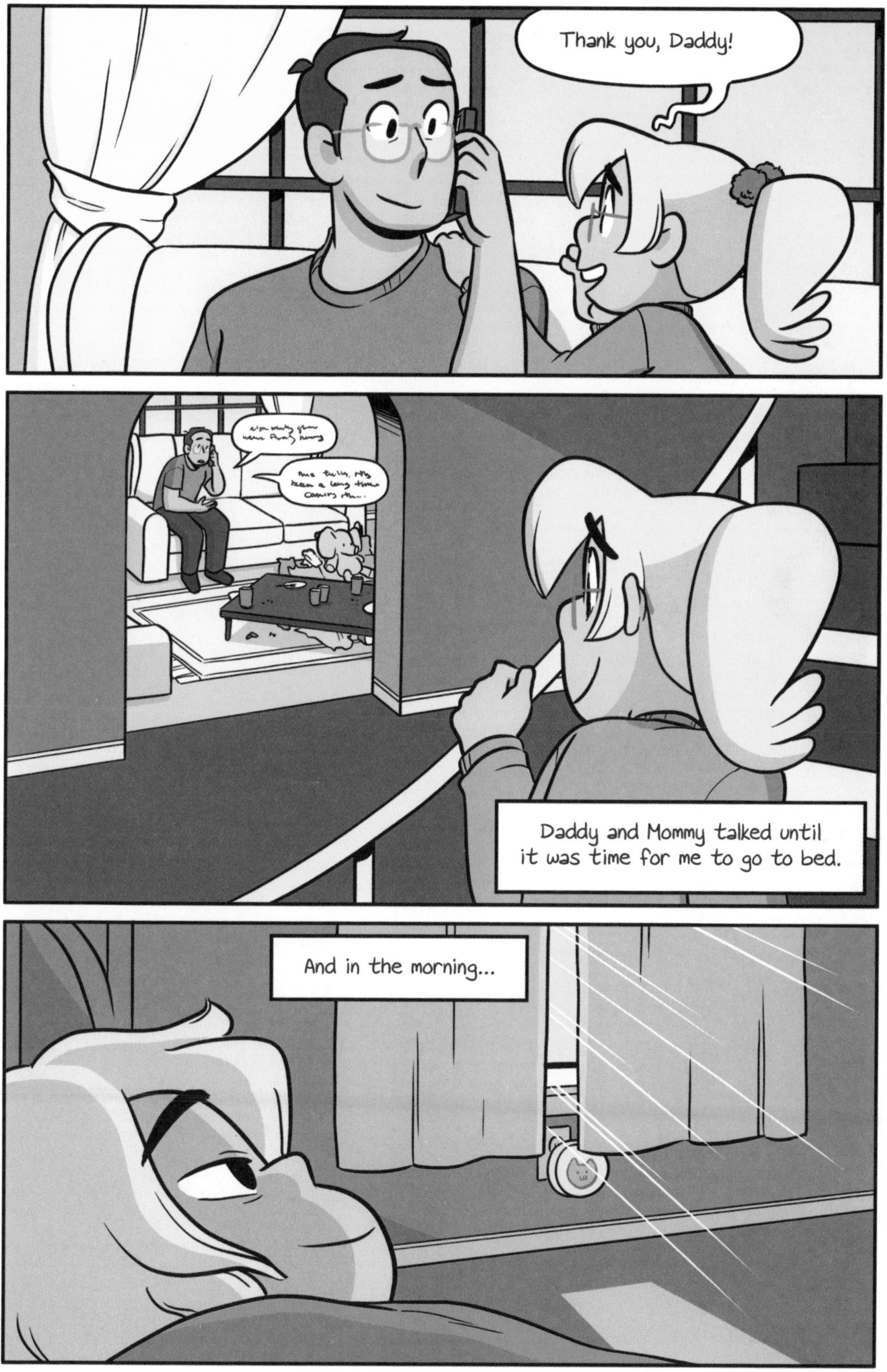
Thank you, Daddy!
Daddy and Mommy talked until it was time for me to go to bed.
And in the morning...

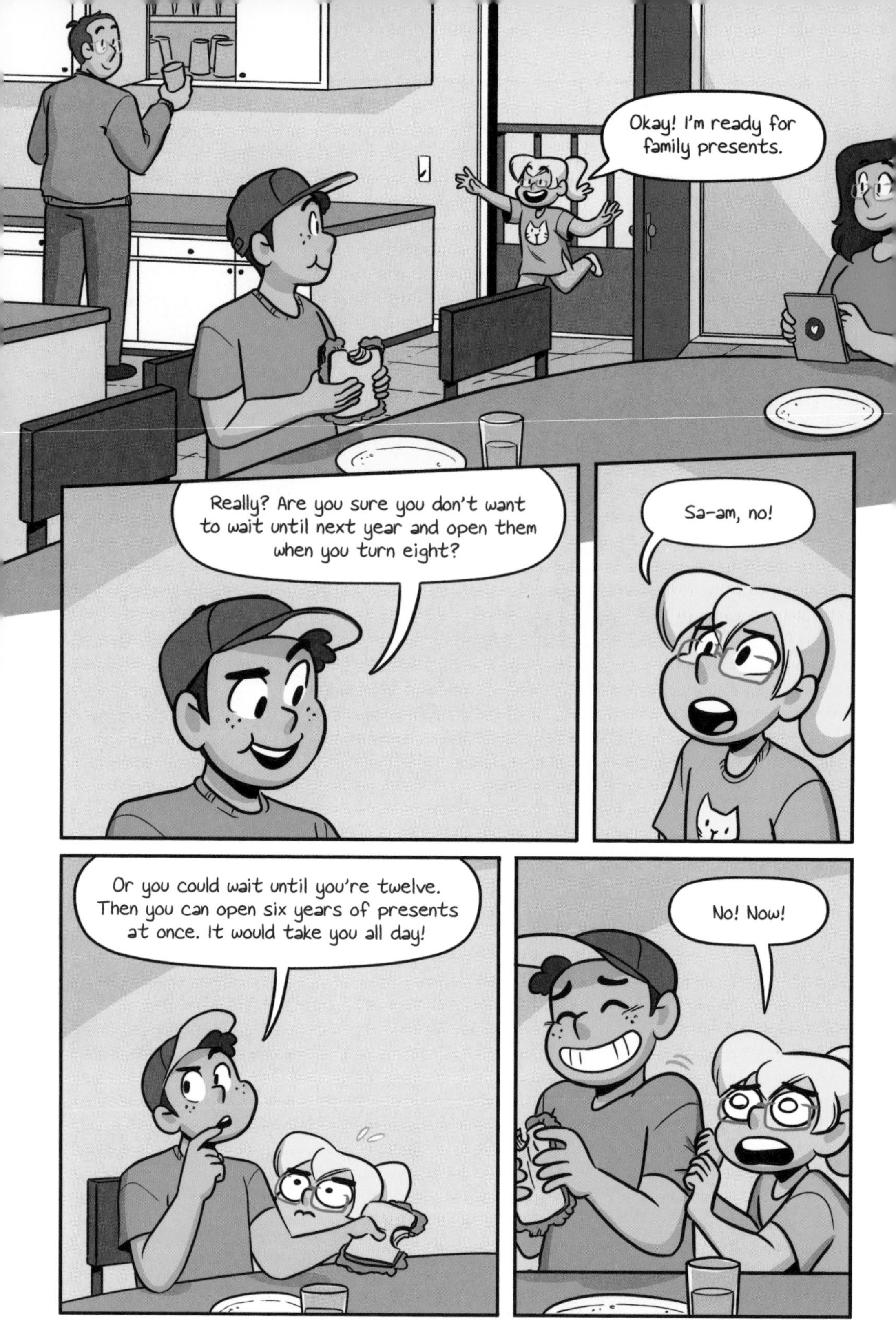
Okay! I'm ready for family presents.
Really? Are you sure you don't want to wait until next year and open them when you turn eight?
Sa-am, no!
Or you could wait until you're twelve. Then you can open six years of presents at once. It would take you all day!
No! Now!

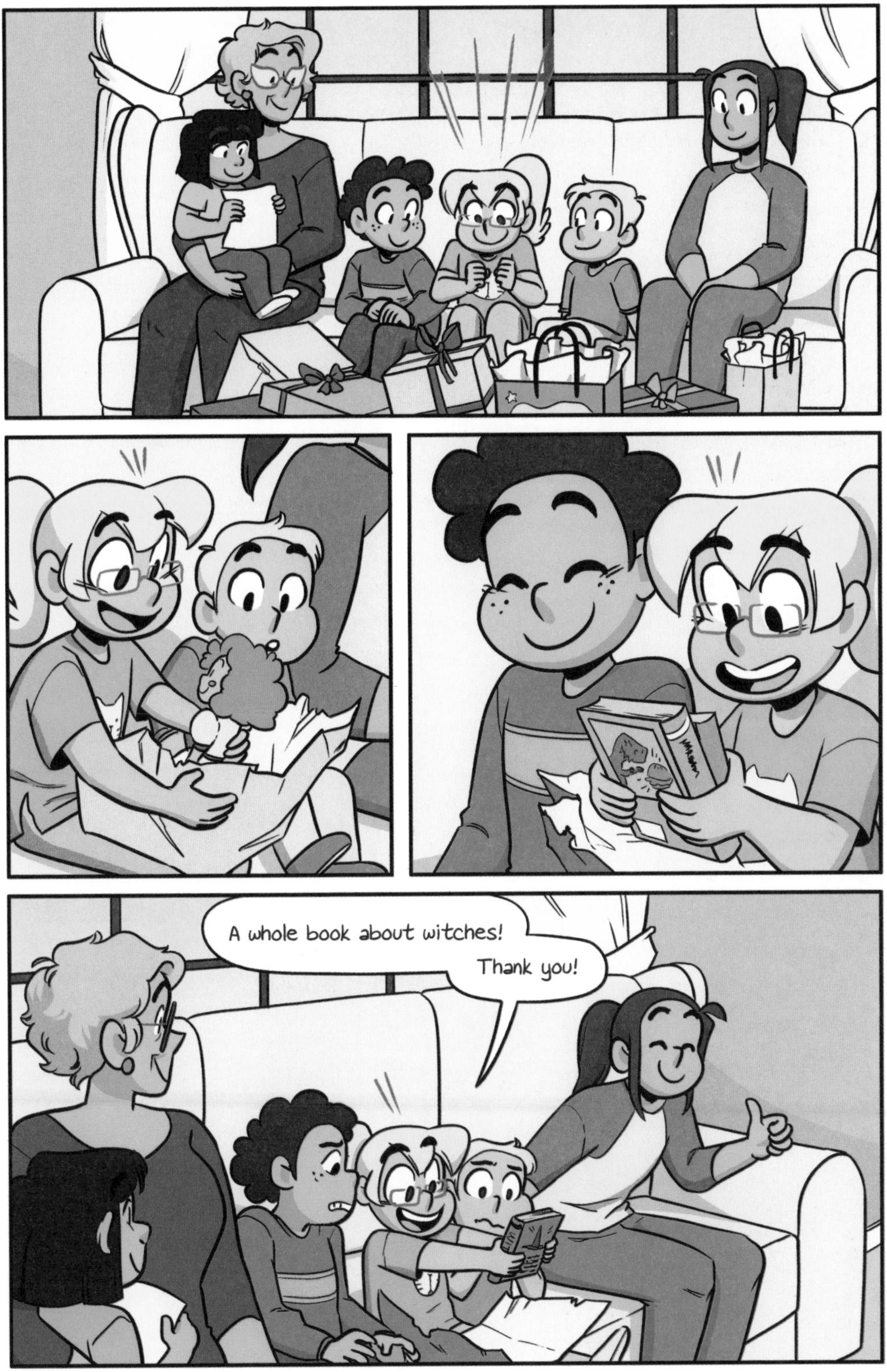
A whole book about witches!
Thank you!

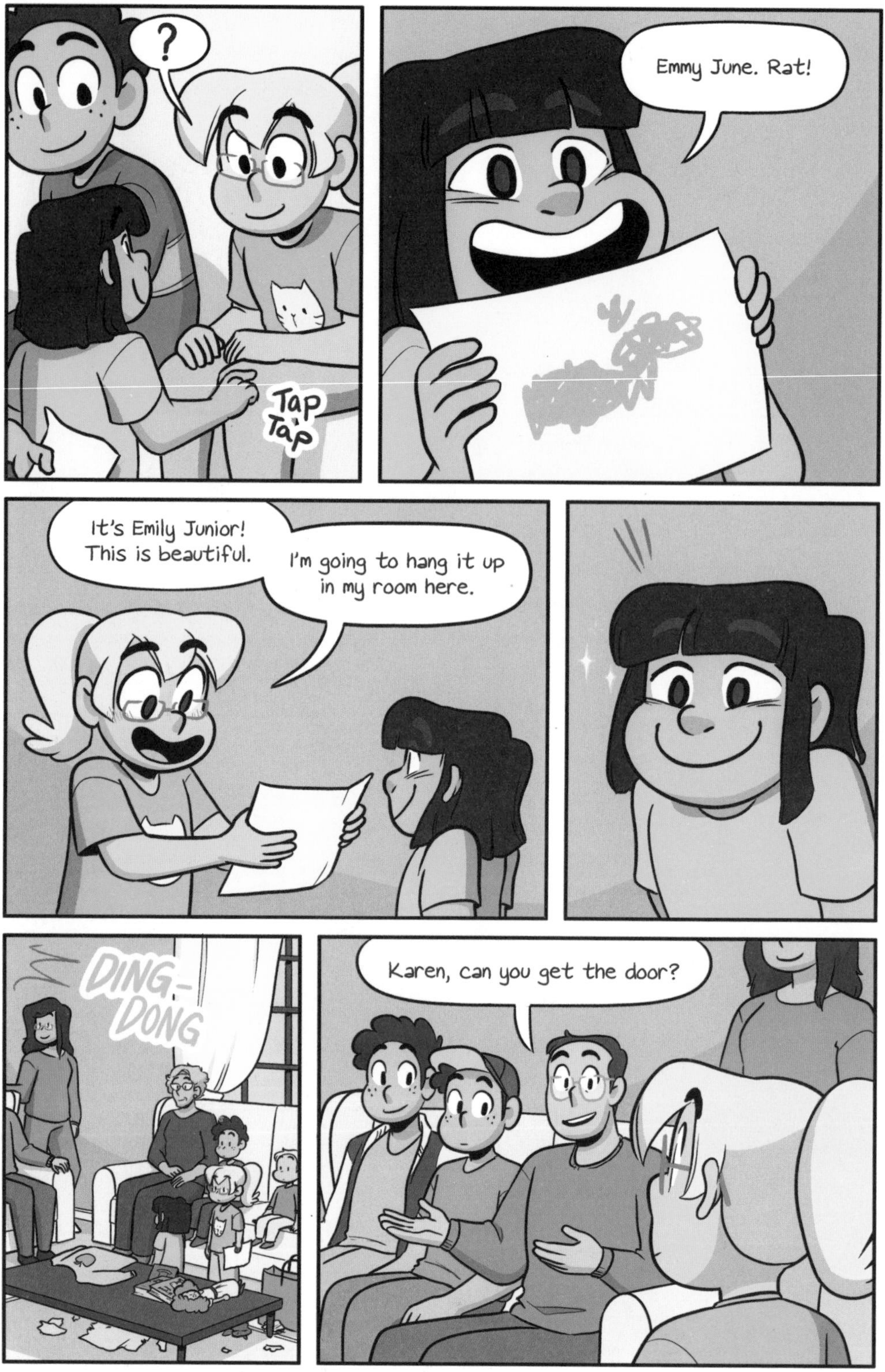
?
Tap Tap
Emmy June. Rat!
It's Emily Junior! This is beautiful.
I'm going to hang it up in my room here.
DING-DONG
Karen, can you get the door?

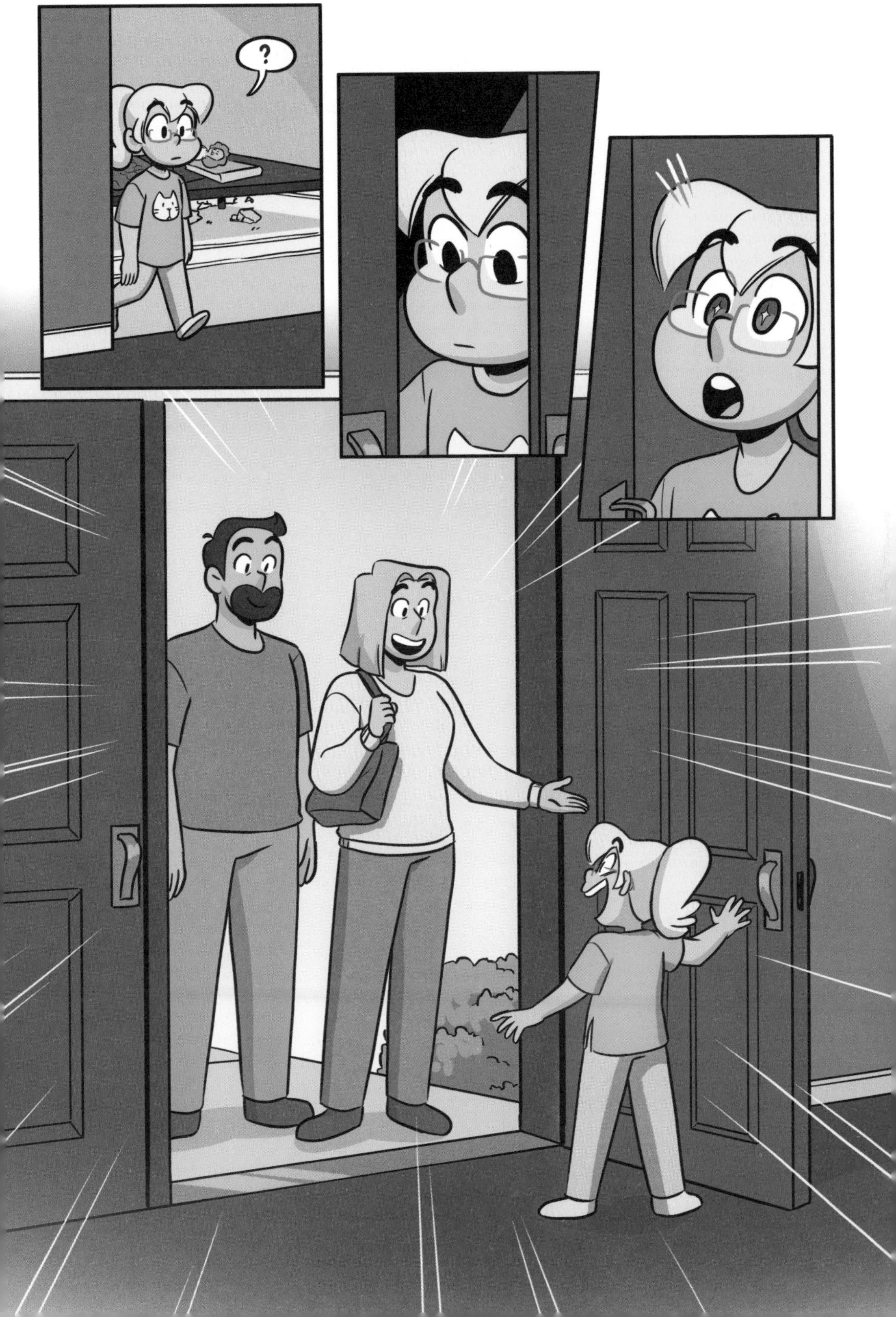
?

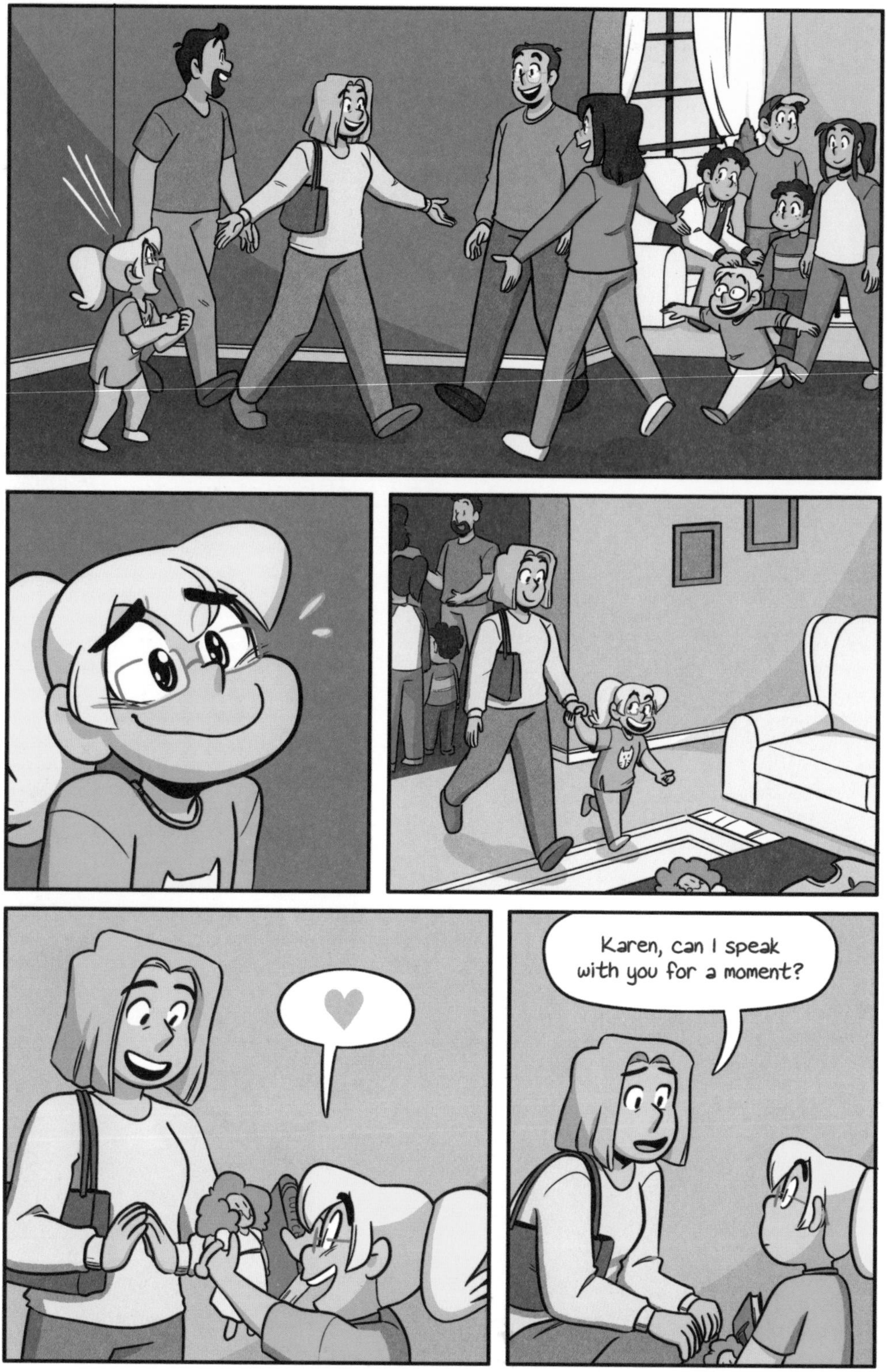
Karen, can I speak
with you for a moment?

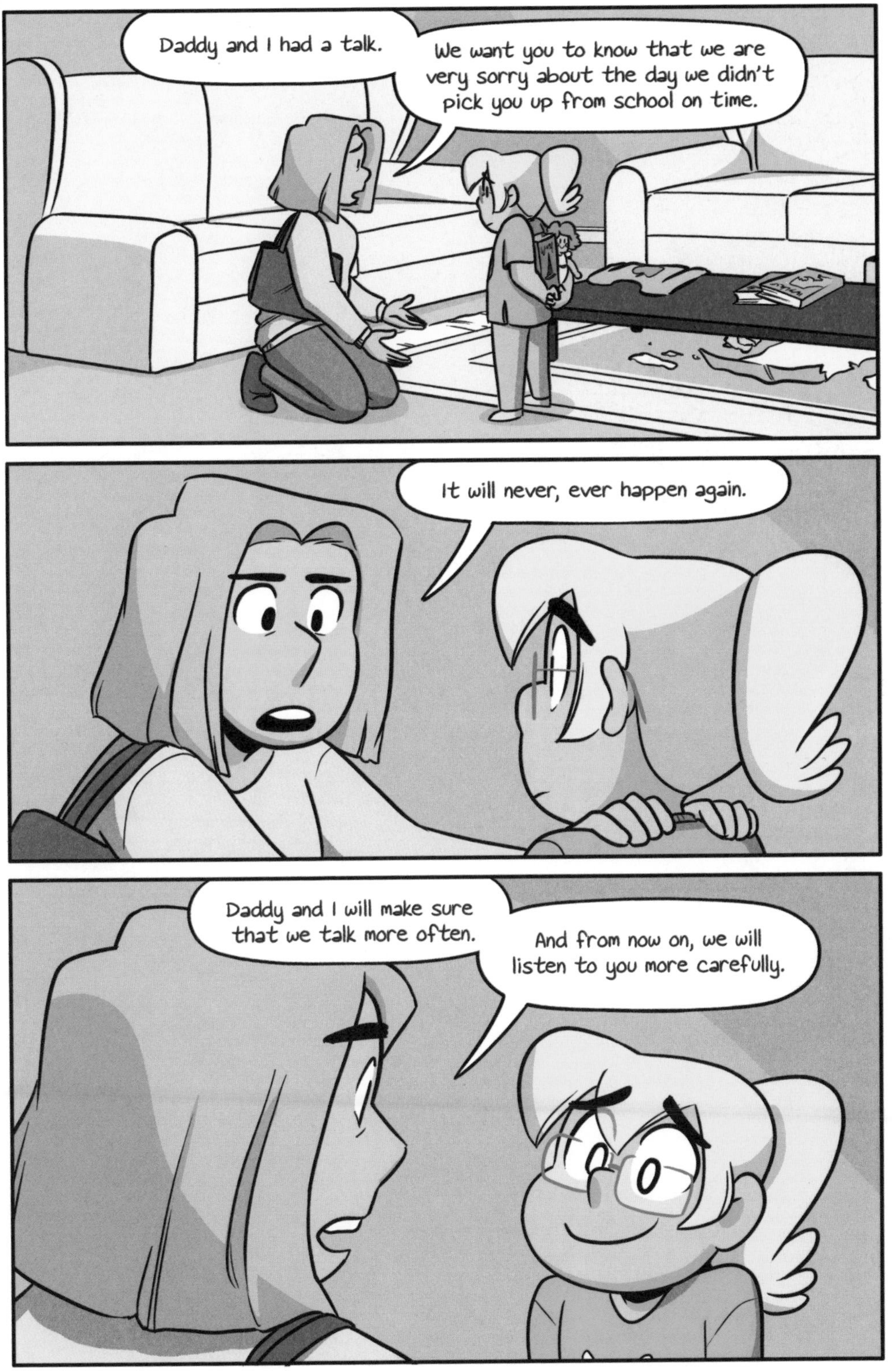
Daddy and I had a talk.
We want you to know that we are very sorry about the day we didn't pick you up from school on time.
It will never, ever happen again.
Daddy and I will make sure that we talk more often.
And from now on, we will listen to you more carefully.

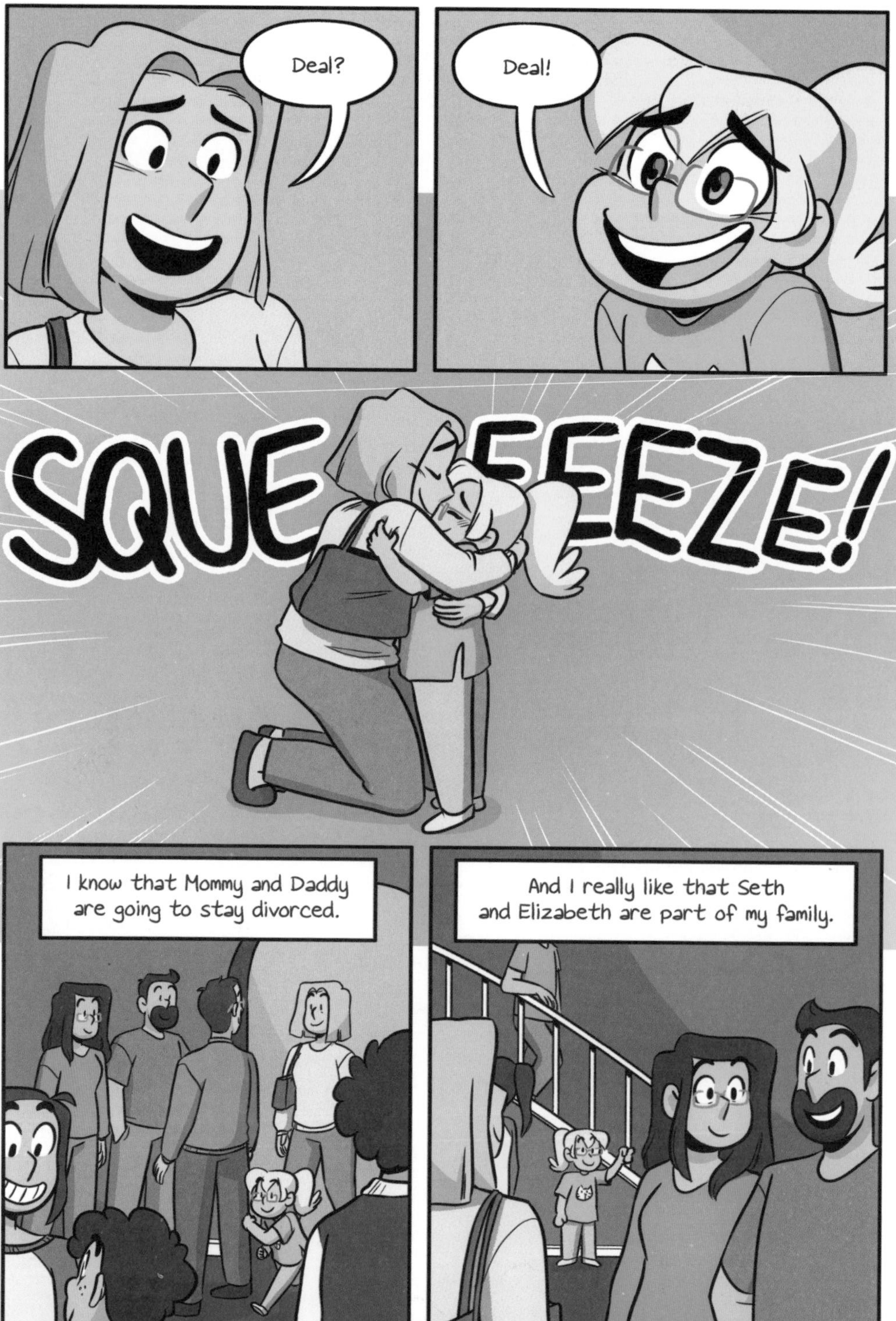
Deal?
Deal!
SQUEEEEZE!
I know that Mommy and Daddy are going to stay divorced.
And I really like that Seth and Elizabeth are part of my family.

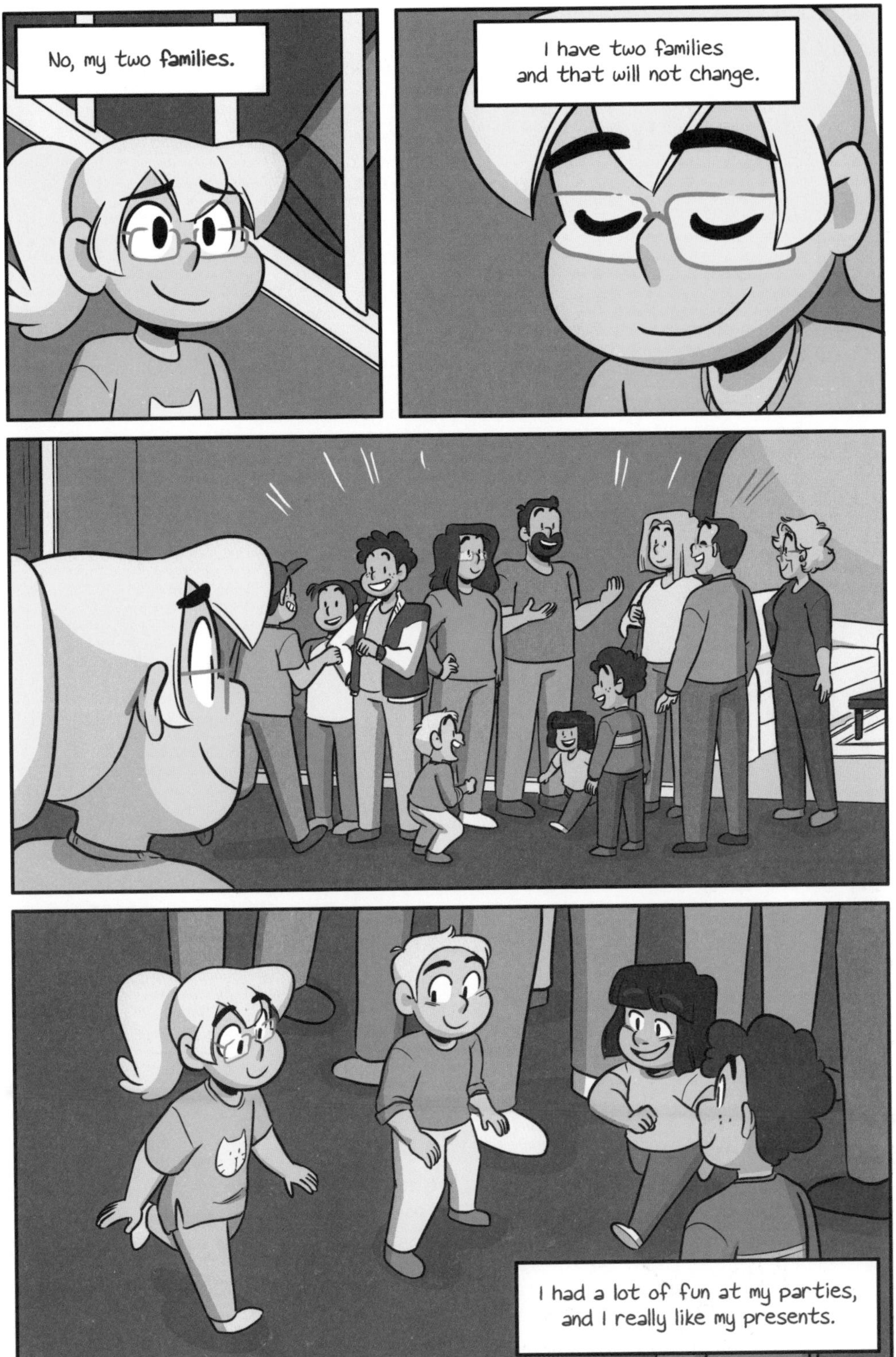
No, my two families.
I have two families and that will not change.
I had a lot of fun at my parties, and I really like my presents.

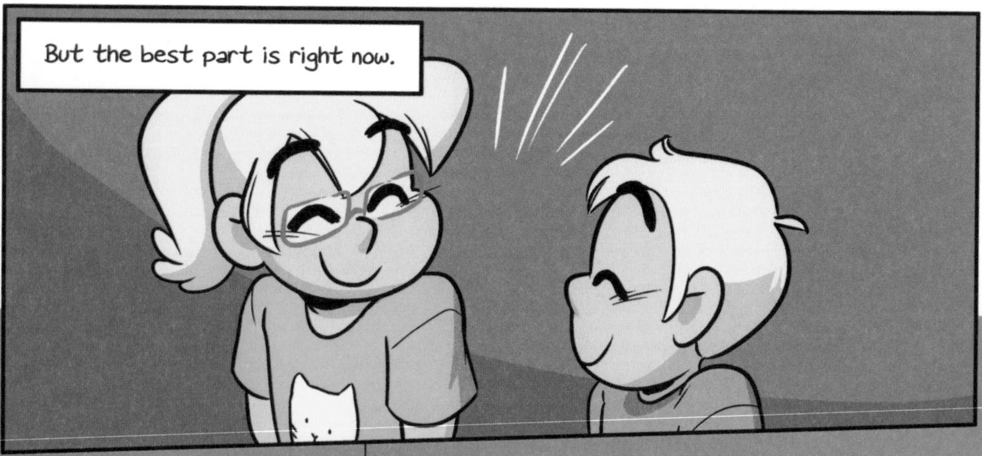
But the best part is right now.

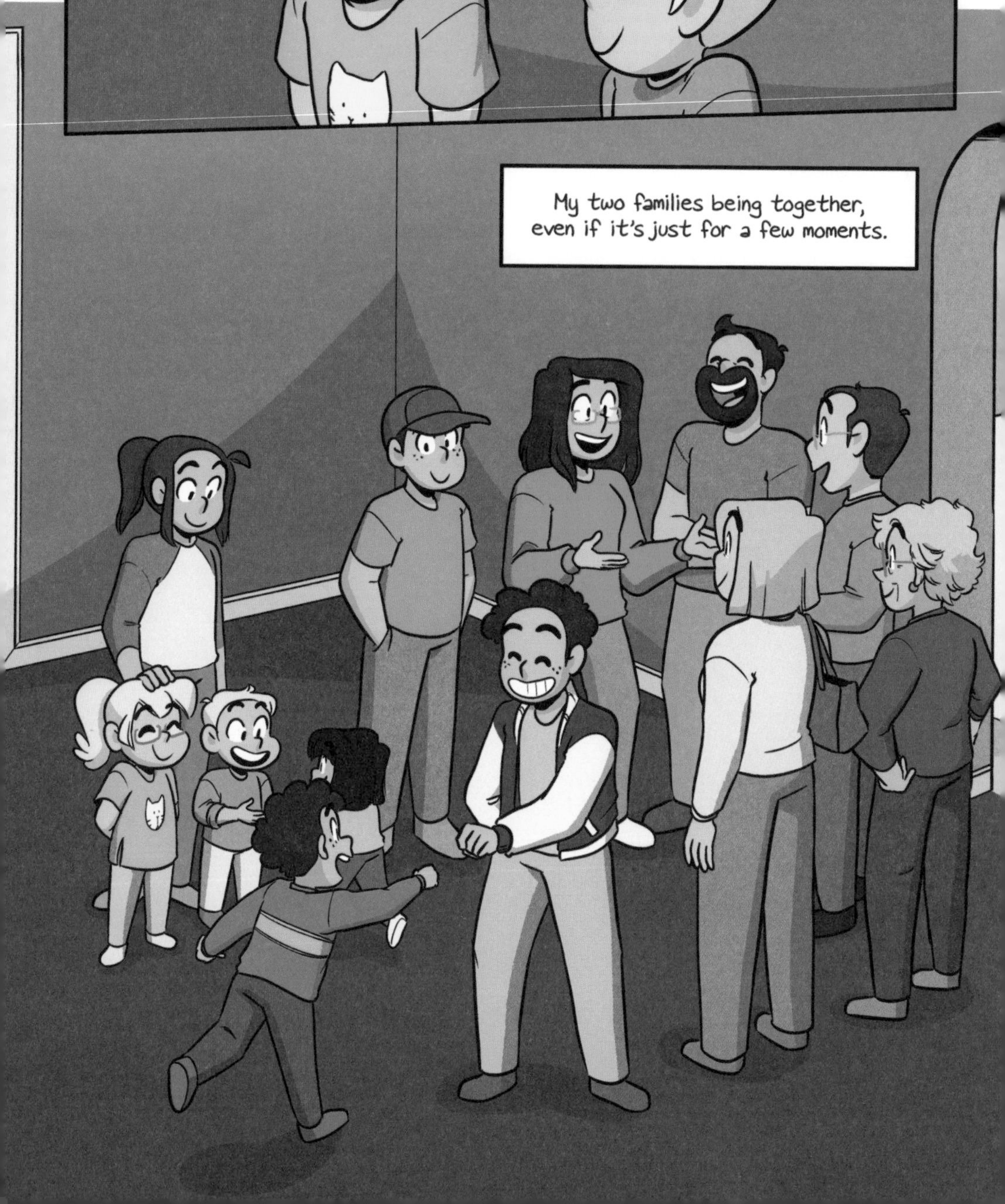
My two families being together, even if it's just for a few moments.

ANN M. MARTIN'S The Baby-sitters Club is one of the most popular series in the history of publishing — with more than 190 million books in print worldwide — and inspired a generation of young readers. Her novels include *Belle Teal, A Corner of the Universe* (a Newbery Honor book), *Here Today, A Dog's Life,* and *On Christmas Eve,* as well as the much-loved collaborations, *P.S. Longer Letter Later* and *Snail Mail No More,* with Paula Danziger, and *The Doll People* and *The Meanest Doll in the World,* written with Laura Godwin and illustrated by Brian Selznick. Ann lives in upstate New York.

KATY FARINA is the creator of the *New York Times* bestselling graphic novel adaptations of the Baby-sitters Little Sister series by Ann M. Martin, and of an original graphic novel for young readers, *Song of the Court*. Previously, she painted backgrounds for *She-Ra and the Princesses of Power* at DreamWorks TV. Katy lives in Los Angeles with her husband and two rambunctious cats. Visit her online at katyfarina.com.

DON'T MISS THE OTHER BABY-SITTERS LITTLE SISTER GRAPHIC NOVELS!

A GRAPHIC NOVEL BY
KATY FARINA
BABY-SITTERS LITTLE SISTER
KAREN'S WITCH
BASED ON THE NOVEL BY
ANN M. MARTIN

A GRAPHIC NOVEL BY
KATY FARINA
BABY-SITTERS LITTLE SISTER
KAREN'S ROLLER SKATES
BASED ON THE NOVEL BY
ANN M. MARTIN

A GRAPHIC NOVEL BY
KATY FARINA
BABY-SITTERS LITTLE SISTER
KAREN'S WORST DAY
BASED ON THE NOVEL BY
ANN M. MARTIN

A GRAPHIC NOVEL BY
KATY FARINA
BABY-SITTERS LITTLE SISTER
KAREN'S KITTYCAT CLUB
BASED ON THE NOVEL BY
ANN M. MARTIN

A GRAPHIC NOVEL BY
KATY FARINA
BABY-SITTERS LITTLE SISTER
KAREN'S SCHOOL PICTURE
BASED ON THE NOVEL BY
ANN M. MARTIN

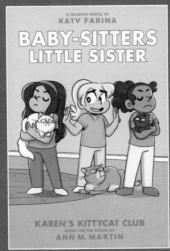